IN THE WAKE OF CAPTAIN LORD

A TONY FLANER MYSTERY
BOOK 3

JOHNNY WORTHEN

In the Wake of Captain Lord
Paperback Edition

Rough Edges Press
An Imprint of Wolfpack Publishing
9850 S. Maryland Parkway, Suite A-5 #323
Las Vegas, Nevada 89183

roughedgespress.com

Paperback ISBN 978-1-68549-323-3
eBook ISBN 978-1-68549-322-6

For Laurence Sterne

IN THE WAKE OF CAPTAIN LORD

1

"YOU'RE BLAMING THE WRONG PERSON," I said into my phone.

"Who is to blame, then?" said Allie on the other side.

That was a trap. It was not as obvious as the "Does this dress make me look fat?" question, and not as devious as the "What are you thinking about?" one that I keep forgetting to censor, but make no mistake; when you're fighting with your girlfriend, even over the phone, and she challenges you to place blame somewhere, you damn well better watch yourself. I was stuck. I'd walked right into it. I'd set the snare myself, brought the bait and now, with a mouthful of goat, I had to think quick to get myself out.

"Uhm…the gubment?" I said.

I heard on a radio that the gubment is behind most bad things and that lizards could be behind them. I don't listen to that station much.

"How do you figure that, Tony?"

"Eh? Taxes are too high?"

"So get a real job and pay them."

So much for extricating myself out of the trap. I'd jumped out of the snare and into a deadfall.

"Look, Allie, honey, gorgeous girl, love of my life, I can't talk right now. I'm on the plane and everyone's giving me looks."

"Are the looks scabby, accusing, and unflinchingly judgmental?"

"Some of them, yeah. There's the big guy who bought two seats. He's looking at me like he wants to either kill me or eat me. Wait, he heard that. It's definitely kill."

"Good," Allie said. "I'm glad you're getting crusties because that's what I'm giving you right now."

"I can sense that."

"I'm pretty pissed at you right now, Tony."

"Because I didn't move to Moab?"

"Dammit. Keep up. Because you didn't even tell me about this thing, let alone invite me."

"Uhm…it kinda just…I needed some…oh look, here's the stewardess with a stun gun. I gotta go."

I turned off the phone.

"We'll be taking off soon," the stewardess said to me through a lifeless smile. "In the meantime, please refrain from using any personal electronic devices."

"Okay," I said.

"We're sitting on the fucking tarmac," said Dara from the seat behind mine. "We've been sitting here for forty-five fucking minutes. Nothing is happening. Tell me again why I can't tweet?"

"Federal regulations," she said.

"They don't like real-time Twitter complaints about the airline service," Garrett said. He was not in a good mood, either. None of us was, but his was particularly sour because they'd made him stow Critter in his checked baggage after the altercation with the TSA agent. Critter was a felt-fanged googly-eyed puppet. He was the other half of Garrett's stand-up act, and unless you followed Garrett's arm up into Critter's body, you wouldn't know they were the same guy. I often forgot they were. I had to figure that Garrett had a split personality and Critter was the physical and hilarious manifestation of that psychosis. Critter had called a TSA agent a "minimum-wage fascist, jack-booted thug who'd failed out of idiot school and so had to smell people's shoes for a living." This was in retaliation to being called a "stupid sock puppet." Don't mess with Critter. He'd made the man cry and got shipped in Garrett's luggage. Garrett was moody and morose. I didn't look forward to a long flight with only him to talk to. Critter would have been fun.

The stewardess took her strained smile and sweaty brow away, not wanting to dignify Garrett's rather accurate Twitter assessment with a response.

"What a bunch of complainers," said Standard Flox across the aisle.

"Who? Me or Dara?" said Garrett.

"All of you," Standard said. "Garrett the pouty, Dara the bitchy, and Tony the whipped. What a way to travel."

Just then a baby in the seat behind Standard emptied its bowels in a loud slosh that silenced the plane.

It was hot—sweltering in the cabin. The weak air conditioning couldn't begin to keep up with the sun beating down on us from a cloudless sky. The realization that the plane was about to be a fetid poop-stink oven was, to say the least, disheartening. A couple, newlyweds by the sound of their earlier happy chatter, broke down together in sobs. The baby then screamed like it was covered in ants, adding an audio component to its olfactory assault. The mother tried to get out of her seat with the baby but was told to go back.

"The plane will be leaving any moment now," the stewardess called from eight rows away. "Remain seated."

"For the love of God," said Standard.

"What a complainer," I said.

"Shut up, Flaner, or I'll box your ears," he said. The first vapors reached me then.

"I'm not whipped," I said.

Garrett had his face under his t-shirt. I scratched at the oxygen mask release panel above me, my eyes watering.

It wasn't the best start to a vacation, but I can't say it was unusual. I'd worked in the airline industry for a while, and I learned first-hand what travelers are taught every day: air travel sucks. It sucks balls. It's the worst thing in the world. I'd rather eat a live rodent than travel by commercial aircraft in America. In fact, if I'd been able to get to Seattle to meet Perry by eating a hamster, I'd have done it. But the Hobson's choice I had, offered no rodentia and only stand-by on a dubious twenty-five-year-old oven box with a sick baby.

It was all Perry's fault. I should have told Allie to blame Perry. Wish I'd thought of that. Perry had called me the day before from Seattle.

"What's wrong?" I said immediately. Perry is "crisis-prone," a sad side effect of his mental illness and paranoia. He's the funniest of all us and is actually making a career of stand-up comedy, not an unenviable position to be in. So we—meaning Dara Sutter, Standard Flox, Garrett Corta, Critter, and I—envied him. But we liked him. We could have hated him for it, we can be that shallow. We often are. Usually, actually, but we loved Perry and lived vicariously through his show business success. He deserved it even though he was often insane. As crazy as he was sometimes, spewing conspiracies and wearing tinfoil hats—actual tinfoil hats—he was funny. He was also a real nice guy who tossed us bones when he could and allowed us to ride on his coattails, if only for free drinks at the clubs he played.

Perry had had a very successful run at The Lucky Arrow Casino in Arizona and got picked up by the Royal Danish Cruise Line for a season aboard the *Success*. I'd gotten a quick email about the gig and then nothing for a month until Perry called me yesterday.

"Nothing's wrong, Tony," he said. "Don't be paranoid."

"Seriously, Perry? You're calling me paranoid?"

"Don't change the subject."

"We have a subject?"

"I'm on this cruise ship, you know," he said.

"Yes…"

"Well, this week's cruise has a charter from some corporation that bought out a slew of rooms and couldn't fill them. If you can come out, I can get you onboard for like a fifth of what it usually costs."

"What does it usually cost?"

"I think eighteen hundred."

"Ouch," I said. "Sounds great, but I'm tight on money right now. I have these two houses and taxes and no job."

Just then the backhoe roared to life and rattled off its trailer in front of my house. It'd been there for days. I'd seen them setting up for a week. It was starting. Salt Lake City has two seasons: winter and road construction. Sugarhouse, a suburb of Salt Lake, is not immune to the majestic seasons, and my street was slated for some ungodly re-work that would cause me to park three blocks away and was guaranteed to interfere with my ten am wakeup call.

"What was that, Tony?" Perry said. "There's some noise on your side."

"How much for the rooms?"

That's how I work. Push and pull. Push—road work in front of my house; pull—ten-day Alaskan cruise. I didn't have to be a genius to see that fate again was looking out for me. I was philosophically compelled to jump at the opportunity. Not being a genius, however, meant that I jumped at the opportunity without contacting my girlfriend, Allison Braise. Allie.

There were several levels of inconsideration at work, not the least of which is my not asking her to come along. It's doubtful Allie could have gotten away. She has a bustling livery operation down in Moab, but I'm sure it would have been a good idea to invite her anyway. Then there's the fact that I was supposed to go down there and help her with said livery. Moab is a tourist town, and May is prime time. There was a rodeo next week that could make or break her season in three days. Since I didn't have a job, I promised Allie I'd help with it, but now I would be in Alaska. Yeah, I'd stepped in it this time.

After talking to Perry and before thinking of Allie, I gathered the comic troops, and miraculously, the whole bunch of us could get the time off and had the money to go. I was feeling pretty good about the whole thing, thinking fate was laying out happiness on a silver platter. Using what connections I still had in the god-awful, thrice-damned airline industry, I'd gotten us on a waitlist for Seattle in time for the cruise departure. And will wonders never cease, we'd gotten on the first plane out. I was just thinking how wonderfully everything was working out when everything went to shit. Figuratively at first, then literally with baby protein-shake behind Standard.

For reasons not important enough to share with the passengers, the plane sat on the tarmac for an hour. I suspect it was all part of a government experiment to measure the tolerances levels for frustration and inconvenience on a broad cross-section of Utah travelers—or, as it's referred to in the industry, air travel.

I was wedged between Garrett and a comb-over with a briefcase between his feet. He was thin and suited and stared at the back of the seat in front of him like his neck was fused. For all I knew, the left side of his face was tattooed and had been ritually sacrificed by a Polynesian shaman. But at least he minded his own business and let me have the armrest.

I was about to start a petition demanding that the mother with the baby be allowed to change her child's diaper, if not for the benefit of the passengers, then for the security of the nation, mentioning the presence of biological nerve agents, and suggesting the involvement of the TSA if not Homeland Security, when the plane finally lunged forward and moved toward the runway. After only another fifteen minutes, we finally took off.

"About fucking time," said Dara.

"Excuse me, miss. Do you have to swear so much?" It was the big guy in the seats across the aisle from me, the one who'd bought two seats. I'd been making fun of him for buying two seats, but I was in fact envious. My fat ass barely fit in the middle seat I had, airline seats having been designed for stick-figured starving dwarves sometime in the last century before McDonald's became its own food group. I'd put on a little weight recently and was a little self-conscious of it. By recently, I mean since college, and by self-conscious, I mean I loathed myself.

"I don't have to swear so much," Dara said to the man. "But I'm fucking going to."

Dara was a petite girl, an inch short of five feet tall. Her pig-tailed hair, elfish grin, rolled-up socks, and skirt made her look like a fifties throw-back to the girl next door. She was the girl next door if you lived on a wharf and sold fish to mongers, whatever the hell a monger is. She'd made her stand-up act around blowing up her virtuous cute appearance with language that went beyond blue, to levels of profanity so dark it made people question their faith when their God did not smite her on the spot. She could control her tongue when she wanted to, but when she was riled up, tired, and cranky, she could offer more curses than an Egyptian tomb Christmas catalog.

"There are children present," the man said. "You don't want to injure their ears."

"What about my fucking nose?" she said.

"You have to forgive my friend," I said. "She has Tourette's."

He gave me a look that told me he hadn't forgotten my description of him to Allie.

"I don't fucking have Tourette's," she said.

I raised an eyebrow, and he nodded in understanding.

"Whatever," she said.

Comics are an insecure bunch by nature. You'd think it would be the opposite. You'd think that anyone who would willingly put themselves on a stage in front of people had to be safe in their own skin. You'd be wrong to think that. Boy, would you be wrong. Most comics get into the business so they can control how people laugh at them. We realize early that we're going to be laughed at, that our insecurities will be an easy target, and that we are going to be ridiculed. We then take control of the laughter and learn to steer it and use it. It's a kind of pathology that someone will one day earn a prize for studying. Dara may be the exception to the rule. She may have become a stand-up to find a venue to vent her verbal wrath. If I hadn't headed off the big guy across the aisle, I have little doubt that Dara would have unleashed her fury upon him until he was a bawling gibbering pile of dead hopes and crushed self-image. We already had one bawling baby on the plane. An additional three hundred fifty pound one wouldn't have shortened the flight any. Not for me, anyway.

"What's the deal with the rooms again?" said Garrett.

"We have two rooms," I said. "There are four of us—"

"I'm not staying with Dara," he said.

"Fuck you," came the response.

"Me neither," said Standard. "I'll room with Garrett and Critter or Tony."

"Fuck you too," Dara said. "I'll bunk with Tony. Sounds like he's single now, anyway."

"Don't say that," I said. "I'm not single."

"Don't flatter yourself. I don't like fatties."

"Ouch," said Garrett.

"I can't room with Dara. Allie will kill me."

Dara said, "Last I heard, you two were broken up."

"No," I said. "Just a misunderstanding."

"Sorry, Tony," said Standard. "I can't room with Dara. I just can't take it."

"Fuck you."

"Neither can I," said Garrett. "You two go well together."

"What the hell does that mean?" she said.

"Yeah, what does that mean?" I said.

"So it's settled," said Standard. "Garrett, Critter, and me in one room. You and Dara in the other."

Dara said, "Fine with me, you fucks."

"No," I said.

"Too late."

The words echoed, but not about the room. "Too late" might well describe my position with Allie. I let my ears pop in the foul-aired cabin and thought about my idiocy. I'd pulled the biggest boner of my life with the girl of my dreams, and I didn't even know why I'd done it.

2

WHEN I SAY that Allie was the girl of my dreams, it's not hyperbole. I never exaggerate. Never. At least not about this. Much.

I met Allie when I was ten years old. She was my first kiss. Though I moved away and didn't run into her again for nearly thirty years, I'd never forgotten her. She inhabited my fantasies and dreams as only an idealized first love can. When I met her again, I was in a weird place and doing weird things. So yeah, the usual me. We hit it off and became something of a couple. We'd have been more than something of a couple if we didn't live two hundred thirty-three miles apart: she in Moab, Utah, and I in Salt Lake City, Utah. We're in the same state but not really. Moab's in the middle of a beautiful nowhere, and Salt Lake is just nowhere, well at least to people who don't live there.

I have a home in Sugarhouse, an upscale neighborhood of Salt Lake City, full of old, small but pricey homes the gentry renovated to create a little cultural enclave of expensive little houses. My ex-wife, Nancy, bought the house for me as a parting gift when we divorced. She kept the other house, the equity, and our son, Randy. I got a new start in an old neighborhood with neighbors who didn't like me.

If I had to guess why they didn't like me, I might say that they frowned on my yard care, which I'd characterize as "rustic," "organic," and "natural," but which they called "a fire hazard," "non-existent," and "not in keeping with a level of civilization attained by a Neanderthal slacker, which Mr. Flaner most resembles." I've also had a few break-ins, a fire or two, a couple of shootings, and more cops at my house than a Krusty Kreme premier. I have single-handedly dropped the property value of the entire neighborhood by twenty-five percent, according to court documents, and have skewed the county crime reports to the point that I'm "actively attracting gangsters, pimps, and prostitutes." This last accusation came after Dara got into a fight with my neighbors. I'm not sure which one they thought she was. My neighbors have guaranteed me a good price for the house if I move out. They started a fund at a local bank branch for the earnest money and have each pledged their yuppie credit ratings toward the mortgage. If they think they can chase me away and flip my home for a profit, they're crazy—who'd buy a house in that declining neighborhood?

Allie thinks I should take them up on the offer. If I did, it would solve several problems in my life, like all the yard-related hate mail I get. It would go a long way to solving my financial problems, and it's not as if I don't have another house to live in. I have a very nice two-story brick house in Moab just a little ways from Allie that I own free and clear. That's part of the reason I'm in financial trouble. I was gifted the money to buy the Moab house and the ignorant government said that's income of some kind and expect me to pay taxes on it. Plus, the Moab house is in a good neighborhood and is appreciating wildly. The property taxes on the house are staggering and as yet unpaid.

Nancy, my ex-wife, is rich. She's a million-dollar realtor who actually made a million dollars. Her face has been on bus benches for years, and she's still going gangbusters. As part of the divorce, she provided me with a little stipend or, as I like to think of it, an allowance. It's buried behind layers of trusts, lawyers, and annuity companies so I can't get at it and do something stupid like buy a collection of original Spanish doubloons I've had my eye on. It's enough to live on, provided I don't buy Spanish coins or a second house in a tourist town. She protected me from the coins, but not the house, so I blame Nancy for my current problems.

So why don't I sell the Salt Lake house and move to Moab? I have a bunch of reasons. Some of them, the minority I grant you, are actually reasonable, but the real reason is that I don't want to. Moab is an eensy-weensy, itty-bitty, teeny-tiny little berg on the Green River with nothing to do and crap internet. It's a paradise for some people, the kind of folks with tans and muscles and an appreciation for the outdoors, things I generally don't have. It's a lively place during the tourist season—packed roads and overflowing hotels, some live music, lots of loud throaty motors, but in the off season, it's just cold and sad. I like to visit Moab. I have generally good memories there, and I really like Allie. I think I love her actually, and that's another reason I don't want to move down there.

I am by nature a slacker, and slackers are not fans of change. I mentioned that my life is a series of pulls and pushes. One day I'll get the pull/push thing and decide what to do with Allie, but it hasn't happened yet. Neither has the house thing coalesced. Until it does, I will dig my heels into the ground and resist any and all attempts at change. It's what I do. It's what I'm good at.

Another thing I'm good at is being a private detective. I have a history of skipping from job to job like an itinerant table repairman, and who doesn't love itinerant table repairmen? I finally found my calling as a private eye when I had to become one to save my own skin. After that, I hung a shingle up and got some jobs, and then I did a little personal work down in Moab. I got results, but the results sometimes got mad at me, thus the shootings, break-ins and a couple of the fires at the Sugarhouse home.

Contrary to the popular pulp fiction depiction, most private eye work centers around cheating spouses. Once in a while, you get a fat dog-napping case, but they're rare. Although I gave up sleazy divorce investigations a while ago, several of my erstwhile employers are just now getting around to demanding child custody, the timeshare, and the retirement accounts. I know this because I've started receiving new hateful phone calls, letters, and bullet holes in my constantly smashed mailbox. The renewed aggression against my house, and my porch light in particular, was doubtlessly one of the factors pushing me onto the cruise ship with my friends.

Another thing slackers are good at is denial. The truly gifted, like myself, will so wholly ignore a problem that they'll forget it even exists. That's the best excuse I came up with on the plane out of Salt Lake to Seattle for why I hadn't invited—or even told—Allie about the sudden Alaskan cruise.

"I'm a jerk for not calling Allie," I bemoaned at thirty thousand feet.

"Yes. You're a jerk. What have I been telling you all these years?" said Dara.

"You're whipped," Standard said.

"It's your subconscious, Tony, trying to tell you something," Garrett offered.

"It's telling you you're whipped."

"Say that sexist word one more time and I'll tear your tongue out of your fat head and cram it up your ass," said Dara.

"You needed some time apart," Garrett went on. "You're spontaneous. It's a good thing."

"I feel like a heel," I said.

"Dude," said Standard, taking a safer approach to helping me. "You got distracted. You had to put all this together like overnight."

"Or literally overnight, if you want to be accurate, but why start now?" said Dara. Her mood had improved thanks to a beer and the fact that she alone among us actually fit in the airline seat.

"Talk to her. You two can work it out," said Garrett.

"God, Tony, are you going to be like this all week?" said Dara. "Lighten up. We're on vacation."

"Yeah, Tony, relax, man. There'll be plenty of chicks on the ship. Bikinis and rum, baby!"

"Standard," I said. I always called him Standard because he liked to be called Stan. It's the little things that make life worth living. "You do know that we're going to Alaska, right?"

"So? It's a cruise. Am single, will mingle."

"Is it that kind of cruise?" asked Garrett. "I thought it was some kind of marketing meeting."

"That's part of it," I said. "There'll be seminars, dinners, and such. We're signed up automatically by taking the rooms. They were part of the block."

"What is it?"

"Hell if I know."

"I can sit through a PowerPoint presentation for a cheap ten-day cruise to Alaska," said Dara.

"I thought Perry got the rooms," said Garrett.

"He applied an employee discount to the already reduced room rate."

"Why were they reduced?"

"The company bought a block and got a deal and then couldn't fill them all. They were desperate to pack them."

"So we're doing them a favor," said Dara. "Screw the slide show."

"I'll be up on deck with the ladies."

"Do you know how inane you sound?" Dara said.

"Yeah, Standard, when did you become a lustful frat boy?"

"It's a cruise, guys. Spring break. Hot bodies and suntans."

"It's May," said Garrett.

"It's Alaska," said Dara.

"It's a cruise," he said.

I listened to my friends fall into their usual meaningless bickering. I tried not to think of Allie or my houses or my money problems or my street repair or the divorcees out to get me and instead found something I could really stew about: my weight. I'd told Allie that I was going to lose a few pounds. Sweet as she was, she said she didn't care, and as insecure as I am, I didn't believe her. I wanted to show her that I was capable of doing something to better myself, and that I wasn't a complete waste of time and effort. I wanted to surprise her with a new sexier me. I'd filled my house with celery, carrots, kale, and cucumbers and had intended to eat it all raw, without melted Velveeta cheese, brown sugar, or fudge sprinkles in a meaningful start to the new me.

Once I got off the phone with Perry, it was like all that no longer existed. I'd opened my last box of Pop-Tarts and ate two packages calling the gang together. I'd finished the box stuffing a suitcase full of dirty clothes to take on the ten-day, buffet-style-dining, Klondike getaway without a thought for anything other than how I was going to make the short deadline to get all of us on the ship the next day. I'd like to think I'd laser-beamed my mind onto the singular goal, having been so occupied with the immediate mission that I'd forced all the extraneous thoughts like health and happiness out of my mind. But I know myself better than that. My mind jumped, leaped, and danced at the chance to ignore these heavy issues and use my precious remaining bank funds to escape for a while.

As my flight circled for a landing in Washington State, my better nature came forward and accused the baser me of crimes against responsibility. The jury didn't have to leave the room. Guilty as charged. I am a selfish immature slacker.

My only chance at clemency, I saw, was to come back to Allie a better man. I needed to show her some change, something good in me to justify my selfish and thoughtless act, which, not surprisingly, I was still planning on going ahead with. I needed some progress somewhere. Something to show a different, maturing me. I lit on a plan, or rather the continuation of a previous plan: I would diet. I was relieved to feel the familiar patterns, two forces directing me to the same thing. And it'd be easy. I mean, how hard could it be to lose weight on a ten-day, all-you-can-eat, buffet-style dining, luxury cruise vacation? Allie was going to be so proud of me.

3

THE ROYAL DANISH Cruise Line ship, *Success,* was one of the older ships in their fleet, six years old, which meant stone age in the luxury cruise business. By modern standards, it was tiny, 965 feet long with a maximum beam of 105 feet, so we had to get in close to use the phasers. It had twenty-seven feet of draft, which I assumed was on the upper decks, where it was most windy. It ran on diesel-electric engines that could go up to 22.5 knots, which I converted into 57.8 snarls or 76.9 tangles, all of which conferred to me the same amount of useful information. It could hold 2,394 passengers—double occupancy—and had 1,099 crew members to serve them. The gross register tonnage was 93,530. I don't know if that was with or without the passengers and crew. It had fifteen decks, some of which were off-limits to passengers. I knew all this, memorized it in fact, because I had two goddamn hours to study the ship brochure while standing in line to get on board.

If you thought the security at airports was rough, try a cruise ship. Not only are they looking for the vacationing Al-Qaeda splinter cells and Grade-A Anasazi Red Rope marijuana smugglers, but I learned that prohibition has come to the high seas. When they finally, and I mean finally, separated me from my luggage, they opened it and searched everything. They confiscated three bottles of Seattle micro-brew I bought on the way from the airport.

"What gives?"

"You can't bring alcohol on board," said the Temperance League representative.

"You've got to be kidding me," I said. "No booze on the boat? I thought this ship was Danish, not Baptist."

"Oh, there's plenty of alcohol on board. You just can't bring any."

"What if I wash my hands first?"

"You can buy drinks on board."

"I thought the cruise was all-inclusive."

"Food and basic beverages are, but not alcohol."

"I take it the drinks are expensive," I said.

The woman looked me over, noted my torn tie-dye shirt, faded jeans, extra flab, and micro-brew breath, then said, "It's charged to your room."

"Do I need to fill out a credit app?"

She opened my shampoo bottle and smelled it with a smirk. She thumbed through the pages of a book to see if I'd hollowed out a space for tequila mini bottles. She studied the alcohol content of my mouthwash and put it with my beers.

"Have a nice cruise," she said, handing me a paper ticket. I watched as she slid a plastic tub of my bottles one way and my suitcase another.

"But…"

"They'll be waiting for you when you get back."

"What if I want fresh breath?"

"Have a nice cruise, sir," she said firmly. I was holding up the line.

After a body scan, pat-down, and passport check, we were issued personal room key IDs that we could use to charge drinks and open doors, the same function, really.

"There it is," said Standard, pointing to a banner over the hallway.

Welcome Nutri-Pods®! it read.

"What the hell's a Nutri-Pod?" said Dara.

"You don't know Nutri-Pods?" said a middle-aged housewife in bulging slacks, sunglasses and big hair. "Why, everyone's heard of them. They're the innovative nutritional dietary supplement everyone is talking about."

"Really?" I said.

"Oh yes, now with ginseng and aloe root."

We shook our heads.

"Here's a strawberry pod," she said, digging in her purse.

"This is the marketing group that bought up the rooms?" said Garrett.

"Yes," she said. "It'll be a wonderful seminar." She placed a small object in my palm and folded my fingers around it like it was a precious treasure. Then she winked at me.

I opened my hand. It was a small plastic bottle with a conical lid, about the size of a grape. It was translucent and with red liquid splashing inside. I suddenly recognized the shape and size of the bottle.

"Is this food coloring?"

"No," she said. "It's a strawberry Nutri-Pod, now with flavor enhancers."

"You talk like a commercial," said Dara.

"I'm enthusiastic."

"This is the same bottle," I said, popping off the cap. "Are you sure it isn't food coloring?"

"To keep prices down, Nutri-Pods International has acquired a plant in Mexico. We're using their bottle design to keep prices down. Drink it," she said.

"What's in it?"

"Vitamins and minerals, enrichment flavoring, eel oil, garlic and cloves—"

"Eel oil? Did you say eel oil?"

"Very nutritional, full of pro-antioxidants," she said. "Try it."

I tilted the bottle into my mouth and squeezed. Three oozing drops trickled onto my tongue. It tasted like greasy strawberries and aspirin.

"Is this how you're supposed to eat these?" I said.

"You can do that, or cook with them, or mix with ice cream and milk for a super energy power drink that will keep you sharp all day."

"Or you could put it on a snow cone," said Garrett.

"Yes, that would be good too," she said.

I handed the bottle to Standard who smelled it and squirted some in his mouth and flinched.

"Wow," he said.

"You can really taste the eel oil, can't you?" I said.

"Yeah." He offered it to Dara who shook her head.

Garrett took it and said, "When in Rome."

"It's made in Necio, Mexico, by skilled and happy workers. See? Here's the brochure."

"Eel oil," said Garrett, retching a little.

"Thanks for the sample," I said. "Now we know what it's about."

"Ten dollars," she said.

"They retail for that much?" I said, impressed. "Wow."

"I'll take a check."

I was standing alone with the big-haired woman, my friends absorbed into the cheapskate ether. I handed over a couple of fives and put the cap back on the bottle. It looked like a teardrop, not a pod. Maybe the name was a reference to slimy sludge in the *Matrix* battery baths.

I caught up with my friends and followed the line up a flight of stairs until we found ourselves stopped in front of a canvas backdrop depicting rugged snow-bound peaks and a technicolor blue sky.

My legs were swollen to sausages from the hours of shuffling, and my carry-on bag had eaten through my shoulder and was gnawing on my clavicle.

"Smile!" said an eager tan photographer behind a flash umbrella.

"No," I said.

"Come on, it'll be a great souvenir," said Garrett. He pulled me into Standard and Dara, and the flash went off.

I was not smiling.

"You can pick up your picture on the Parrot deck tomorrow."

"You don't have to buy it if you don't want to, Tony," said Garrett. "Don't look so crestfallen."

"It's not the picture that's caused me to look this way," I said.

"Constipated?" suggested Dara.

"Heart attack?" said Standard.

"Forgot to pay your electric bill?" said Garrett.

"No," I said. "Well, yes, actually. I am behind on my electric bill. It'll be turned off before I get home, but look over there." I gestured up the gangplank. "See that guy in the pink shirt, white coat, and slacks?"

"The Las Vegas reject?"

"Yeah. His name is Mr. Bailey Peigne, pronounced 'pain' and in 'R-O-Y-A-L Pain.'"

"He looks like an asshole. How do you know him?"

"I caught him cheating with a soccer mom from West Valley last year," I said.

"Is that her?"

"No. She's new."

"Water under the bridge," said Garrett. "He probably doesn't remember you."

Just then, he saw me. I read on his lips a series of four-letter words followed by a one-finger salute.

"Or maybe he does."

"His divorce just went final," I said. "I know this because he called me up drunk to read me the settlement agreement which included a now not-so-secret off-shore account that the IRS is interested in."

"You found it?"

"Yep. It was the only reason I took the job. His wife suspected he was embezzling."

"Divorce, embezzlement, and the IRS? Man, he's had a bad year."

"And what better way to relax than on a ten-day cruise with the very guy who made it all happen?"

"Thanks, Standard," I said. "Remind me to push you overboard."

"He's gone," said Garrett. "Let's move up."

We shuffled along the inclined gangway, edging ever closer to the actual ship. The line left the concrete security bunker, and we were outside. We caught glimpses of sky and the shapes of distant horizons the map said were across Puget Sound. We could smell the sea.

Still shuffling forward, I glanced to my right and saw another gangway extending from the building onto the ship. That one was straight, with no Disneyland maze architecture there. It connected to an upper deck where an officer in a blue jacket, pressed pants, and sharp cap shook the hands of the arriving passengers. Judging from his gray beard, gold sleeves, and regal stance, it had to be the captain.

I did a double take when a slumped man and a tall woman appeared on the ramp and approached the captain.

"There's a familiar face," said Standard.

"You know her, too?" I said.

"What? Who? No. Look there. It's Perry."

Our line tottered forward and then suddenly we were on the ship and the crowds dispersed. It was a miracle. We were free. After the hot sweaty crowds and queues, I wanted to kiss the deck for joy, but the line was too long.

Instead of a captain shaking hands, we had porters directing traffic and handing out water bottles to the line-weary guests. Perry stood down the deck and waved us over.

"You made it," he said. "Did you get the tickets alright?"

"That was a terrible experience," Dara said. "Fucking terrible."

Perry nodded. "There's a sign in the employee cafeteria that reads 'Make the cruise so great they forget coming on board.'"

"Does it work?"

"I think so. It'll all be a bad memory by tomorrow and forgotten the day after that unless you write it down or something."

Who'd do that?

"What's with that other gangway?" I asked.

"That's for the VIPs," said Perry. "There are three classes on board: VIPs, passengers, and crew, in that order."

"You look good, Perry. Sea life agrees with you," said Garrett. He was being polite. Perry was pale and hunched over. He stole furtive glances from under his blond bangs and kept his hands in his pockets.

"I have good days and bad days," he said.

"How's the work?"

"Repetitive, but easy enough. I do a ninety-minute stage show, a lounge show, and a dinner routine."

"What the hell is that about?" said Dara.

We all turned to follow her gaze. Moored next to our big white cruise ship was another big white cruise ship. But unlike ours, it did not have exhausted but excited vacationers prancing on its decks. Instead it had blue-robed spacemen with portable oxygen tanks and garden sprayers.

"That's the Circus *Trapeze*," said Perry.

"Looks like a ship to me."

"Circus is another cruise line. The *Trapeze* is the name of that ship. The health department shut it down. Mold or something."

On the top deck, a dark man in a white uniform stared at us. Even at this distance I sensed his hateful glare.

"'Scuze me." An old woman with an aluminum walker appeared behind us.

"Hi, Mrs. Hunter," said Perry. "How are you?"

"Fine, fine. I got my pills." She shook her purse and it sounded like a maraca. She pushed past us and into a side corridor.

"How do you know her?" said Standard.

"She's a Gray," said Perry. "She lives here."

Before we could follow up on that, the deck erupted in the noise of a scream-out argument. We turned to see a camera crew orbiting two beefy, rugged men yelling at each other.

"I can out-fish you with my eyes shut!" said one.

"That's the only way you know how to fish!" said the other.

They looked strangely familiar.

"I can't wait until I get my own boat so I can fire your sorry ass!"

"Dream on! The day you get a boat is the day they're handing them out at an AA raffle!"

The last insult hurt and the insulted man's lip quivered as the camera zoomed in to see it.

"Wait, I'm sorry, Dwayne…" said the insulter. But it was too late. The first guy turned and stormed away, disappearing into the crowd of passengers.

"Oh, I heard about that," said Perry. "There's some crab fishing show that'll be filming on the ship this week."

"That's where I know them from," I said. "That reality show about Alaskan crab fishing."

"This is the off-season. They're trying to make a spin-off show."

"Crab fishers on vacation?"

"Something like that."

"I'd watch it," said Standard.

"You've just described yourself better than I ever could," said Dara. "I want to get to my room and drop this damn bag off."

"Yeah, you guys settle in," said Perry. "We can talk later."

He'd backed away and set himself against a wall between two round portholes. I could see one of his episodes in the making. He continued to scan the faces of the people slogging their way onto the ship and sweat appeared on his forehead. The deck was crowded. It wasn't a deck as much as a hallway with a metal wall on one side and a railing over the dock on the other, but they called it a deck. I figured Perry's fragile mental state was reacting to the throng of pushing sweaty, pissed-off humanity coming aboard. I'd been in a crowded, claustrophobic fit since I got up this morning—airports, planes, lines. I could relate.

"Let's go get a drink, Perry," I said. "I'm sick of these losers."

"Yeah, okay," he said.

"Catcha later," said Standard. "Time to mingle."

"Knock before you open the door, Tony," said Dara. "Always."

"You two sharing a room?" said Perry.

"It's okay. I owe penance for a life ill-spent."

"Couldn't you just have flagellated yourself?"

"Next time."

Inside the ship, we found barstools overlooking an open space of shops. Nothing was open. We couldn't get a drink at any price, but the menu told me I'd have passed on them anyway. I was just happy to find a chair. We were practically alone. The passengers were all settling in or standing outside, waving to people they didn't know like the movies said they were supposed to do. Our privacy was only interrupted by an occasional crew member buzzing by with an obvious destination and an even more obvious hurry.

Perry's mood hadn't improved. He kept looking around as if expecting to see the fabled Men in Black talking into their sleeves, observing him from the shadows. I'd seen him this way before, spooked so badly it nearly cost him his career.

"What's eating at you, Perry?" I finally asked him. "You sounded fine yesterday on the phone."

"*Absit omen*," he said.

"Absinthe? Amen," I said. "Sounds good. I'll join you. I could use a drink. How'd you get liquor onboard?"

"No, it's Latin."

"I thought it was French."

"Not absinthe amen, you alcy. Absit omen. It's a Latin proverb. It means, 'may it not be an omen,'" he said. "Kind of a prayer that what you're seeing isn't a portent of bad things to come. Kind of like 'God Forbid.'"

I'd heard the phrase before, studied it actually, but Perry wasn't making any sense, per usual.

"What the hell are you talking about?" I said.

"Since I called you, things have gotten weird around here."

"Like what?"

"The ship's not filling up," he said.

"Looks plenty packed to me."

"No, it's not. It's like a fourth empty. It's the first cruise since the ship was made that it's been so deserted. The officers are in a tizzy."

"Okay, I'll bite. Why do you think it's so deserted?"

"It's the stupid pod people."

"Nutri-Pods? The folks I have to thank for the cheap room?"

"The sailing schedule was changed three weeks ago when the *Trapeze* got pulled. With discounts and ship changes, the line managed to keep most of the reservations. But then news got out about Nutri-Pods."

"The innovative nutritional dietary supplement everyone is talking about?"

"That's the one. The pod people had pre-bought a block of rooms and had a hard time filling them even at a reduced rate, but worse, they advertised the living hell out of it. They tweeted and emailed and ran ads and everything."

"And that didn't help?"

"It helped scare away the other passengers. Most of the empty rooms were cancellations after they found out the pod people would be here. They're pushy. Very pushy. They're famous for it. It's a multi-level marketing thing."

"Oh," I said. "Yeah, I can see that. But is that all that's bugging you? Can't you retreat to the secret decks the passengers aren't allowed to see?"

"That's another thing. This morning I heard that the onboard security system is shot and can't be fixed before we leave."

"Is that a big deal?"

"I don't know, but the security officer is freaked."

"So what I'm getting here is that your bosses are in a bad mood. That's how jobs are. It's not an omen; it's a workday."

"I got a feeling about this, Tony. Everything's off. The juggler isn't here."

"We don't have a juggler? Shit, you're right. We're boned."

Perry tore a napkin into bits and scowled. "The juggler is my opening act," he said. "And there's no caviar."

"That's it. I'm going to sue."

"Tony, it's unheard of. The VIPs expect it. It's a scandal."

"Maybe it's all a good thing," I said. "Caviar is rank. Nobody needs that. Let them eat Cheese Whiz like real people."

"It is nasty," he agreed.

"If you need an opening act, Perry, any one of us Cellar Dwellers would give their eyeteeth to have a set. It's not often we get to perform for a captive audience."

"People can still walk out on you," he said.

"But only so far," I reasoned. "It's an opportunity. Maybe there're some talent scouts, movie producers or desperate underage comic groupies here."

"I know some Grays who'd do a comic."

"Aliens from Area 51?"

"Retirees who live on board. Like Mrs. Hunter," he said. "Still, it's not a bad idea. Do you think the gang would be up for a set?"

"We're insecure comics desperate for attention. Of course we will," I said. "Do you think you can arrange it?"

"I'll see," he said, cheering up slightly. "Dara, though…not a chance."

"How about an after-hours show? Twenty-one and over?"

"Maybe," he said. "Okay. I'll pitch it. But it's still weird, all the things going wrong."

"Coincidence," I said.

"But—"

"It's not always about you, Perry," I said. "Maybe the company bounced a check and so didn't get the caviar. You've already explained the empty ship and the pod people. Relax. Shit happens. It doesn't mean it's about you."

"Is that what you think? That I think this is all about me?"

"Yes."

"Well, I don't," he said.

"Not even a little?"

"People on ships are superstitious, you know. Half the crew threatened to quit because we're setting sail today."

"What? Why?"

"It's a Friday."

"I see," I said. "Wait. No the other thing. What the hell does Friday have to do with anything?"

"It's unlucky to set sail on a Friday. Everyone knows that."

"I don't. These people getting on board today don't. I bet you didn't a week ago."

"So?"

"Wait a minute. Aren't these cruises all scheduled months in advance?"

"This one's all messed up. It's ten days instead of seven. Circus Cruises lost a dock spot or two, and the Danish line has swooped in to grab them. They're bringing another ship up through the Panama Canal to take a spot. In the meantime, everyone is being juggled around a day or two to keep the dock space. First come, first consideration."

"You still haven't told me how any of this affects you."

"The crew's jumpy."

"And now that you're part of the crew, you feel you have to join in?"

"I can tell. Bad things are going to happen."

"God, Perry, really? Usually your mania has some basis in reality. Sailing on a Friday? Get it together, dude. You're our host. Put on a happy face."

"You sound like Sandra, the cruise director."

"Perry, I'm sure running a big boat like this and fifty more just like it is a pain in the ass, but it's not your pain in the ass. It's not your ass, you ass. Don't borrow trouble. Your bosses, the company and all that have problems. Not you. It's going to be a fun cruise."

He confettied another napkin and nodded.

That's when the first alarm went off.

4

IT WAS nothing like you'd expect. It was not a big gong or a ringing bell or a booming klaxon. It was a soothing female voice coming over the PA. "Oscar. Code Oscar, port side. Oscar." It could have been a birthday announcement. But it wasn't. Perry's eyes went wide and then a door to the outside opened and we heard urgent shouts. Oscar's party was heating up.

We went outside, following the noise. The walkway was packed with excited people pressed to the railing, craning to look overboard.

"'Code Oscar' means 'man overboard,'" said Perry.

We worked our way along the deck until we could scoot into the railing ourselves and see over it. In the bay, far below us, we saw a figure splashing in the dark water, churning up a white, salty foam. Ring life-preservers rained down from the boat like rocks on a sieging army. Oscar was a woman with a severely short hairstyle. Though there were at least twenty floats already in the water, and more still flying down, none was remotely near Oscar. Best intentions, plus panic, plus quirky foam ring aerodynamics equals one drowned vacationer, or at least it might have had, not the Coast Guard appeared.

A motorized rubber raft straight from a SEAL's training video or a Jacques Cousteau special sped around the front of the ship and zipped between the rings like a skier on a slalom course. It circled once and then spun up next to the woman without splashing water on her. Two men pulled her onto the little boat in one deft practiced lunge. Once she was secure and prone, one of them leaned in and tried to give her mouth-to-mouth but was then promptly ejected from the boat like a flipped coin. Head over heels, all flailing arms and surprise, he went into the water. Oscar had gotten her legs up and wasn't in the mood for a smooch.

After an awkward moment we could feel all the way on the top deck, Oscar and the other rescuers pulled the rejected resuscitator out of the bay. Once all were aboard, they offered Oscar a blanket at arm's length, which she took and wrapped around her shoulders. They all settled in and then the boat sped back the way it came.

The whole thing lasted only a minute or two. After the sound of the motor disappeared around the ship and all was quiet and calm. The threatening sea was now a serene black reflecting plate festooned with red and white floating wreaths bearing the ship's name, *Success*.

"That ever happened before?" I asked Perry without thinking.

"Not since I've been here."

"Well, it's reassuring to see how quickly they pulled her out."

"That's dock security. There's nothing like that once we're out of the bay."

"Good to know."

Perry looked less pleased.

"I'm going to go explore," I said. "Catch up with you later."

"Okay."

Perry skulked through a "crew only" door and disappeared.

Meanwhile, the damp passenger had not dampened the excitement of the other passengers. The ship whistle blew, and the crew applauded to encourage everyone to do the same.

Two rockets flew up in celebration. Lines were released, anchors pulled up, rats stowed away, and the Royal Danish Cruise Line ship, *Success*, moved impossibly sideways from the dock, pushed by perpendicular thrusters the Romulans had yet to master. And then all at once, we were free of land and sailing north out of Elliott Bay.

It was one of the rare nice days in Seattle. I felt privileged because I know they were rationed; Seattle only gets three or four of them a year. The water was calm, the sun shining, the mood excited. The Olympic mountains watched us go from behind a picturesque skyline of The City of Flowers, The Emerald City, The Queen City, or Gateway to Alaska, depending upon which Seattle visitor's guide you had. I joined the others in waving goodbye as if I'd left someone on the dock clutching a bounced check for dental work.

I did a circuit around the main deck, then again on the one above and below and then went in search of my stateroom.

Waiting for an elevator, I met a tall muscular Jamaican man who introduced himself as Xavier Polatés, "well-being expert" and personal trainer. He gave me a flier for the "Sweat Out the Dawn" exercise group, which met every day at sunup on the basketball court, rain or shine. He gave me an appraising look, taking in my chubby tummy and said, "See you 'dere man?"

I gave him an appraising look right back, taking in his fat-free face, defined biceps, and rippling six-pack abs under his shirt—okay I imagined that part, but I knew they were there—and I said, "Probably not."

"Enjoy your cruise."

The elevator door opened.

Ships are basically floating skyscrapers. Much is made of vertical space. I guess that's the difference between a cruise ship and cruise barge: decks. The elevators were packed with people exploring as I was, so I took the stairs, which were also crowded. Our discounted rooms were very far down on the ship. We had an inside berth, which didn't matter because if we'd been on the outside and had a porthole, it would have been beneath the waterline. Our room promised to have a goldfish aquarium, so the effect would be the same.

When I got to the room, I saw a note taped to the door from Dara. *I am not staying in this goddamn room. I upgraded us. You can pay me when you see me.*

I slid my key into the slot and the door opened. I went inside. It was about as I expected; two beds, a bathroom, a closet, a writing desk like a raven, a television, and a big mirror to make the room look large. Including the reflection, it was about the size of the back seat of my Prius. I closed the door behind me and felt suffocated, the air still and heavy. I heard the sound of engines beneath me. Maybe heard isn't the right word. Felt, yeah. I felt the motors through the floor, walls, and ceiling. It was a vibration, low and steady. The room was like a shipping container, and it was, really, come to think of it. It would serve for a place to keep your stuff and sleep, but I wouldn't want to spend much time in there. I'd tried the sensory deprivation tank therapy thing once and didn't like it. I'd snuck in a Sharpie and doodled an epic scene of dinosaurs running from meteor showers. I thought it was really good, but I had to pay to have the tank repainted before they kicked me out. Wish I'd have at least taken a picture of it.

A key and a note on the bed told me where Dara had moved us.

The new room was much nicer. It was basically the same room, same dimensions and layout, but it was on a higher deck and had a patio. Dara had staked out the big bed with her luggage, leaving the little pull-out for me. That didn't seem fair. Considering our size difference, and since she wasn't there at the time, I moved all her stuff onto the smaller bed and piled my luggage onto the big one. To drive home the point, I knotted the sheets around my suitcase and dropped a pair of underwear on the pillow.

In the bathroom I found towel monkeys. They were adorable works of art; towels folded into the shape of monkeys. I took a picture of them. My first photo of the trip.

I don't know what the upgrade cost was, but it was money well spent. The added light from the glass door alone justified it but being able to go outside in private and watch the majestic blue ocean and serene purple mountains without pants on, my junk caressed by nautical winds, was priceless.

I fished a fresh pair of shorts out of my bag and put them on to go explore some more. I put my pants back on too, just so you know.

They advertise cruise ships as floating cities, and it's as accurate a description as any. There're restaurants and nightclubs, chapels, libraries, cafes, bars, pools, movie theaters, bowling allies, spas, massage parlors, gyms, putting greens, driving ranges, skeet ranges, helipads, basketball and tennis, and of course, shuffleboard courts. The colors were lively and the lighting bright and warm.

The decorating was a little schizophrenic. There was a general Nordic theme—Vikings and pictures of Danish royalty decorating the halls alongside pictures of the other, bigger, newer ships in the growing fleet. There was also an overly decorated Italian restaurant with leaning towers and gondolas spilling out of the walls in front. There was a whole Mexican deck with cactus paintings and sombreros on the walls. I found a cartoon palace with Hanna-Barbera characters made out of Styrofoam, luring children into unknown crevices beyond. All this was seasoned with a generous helping of piracy, or rather, "pirate-themed" restaurants and decorations—Jolly Rogers, peg legs, and such. I supposed I'd get used to it all, but it was an assault on the senses that first day.

The elevator promised passage between decks four through fifteen, but I noticed that neither deck fourteen nor fifteen would light for me. There was a key card reader like the one on my door in the elevator panel that I assumed permitted entrance to the super cool upper decks where the VIPs were housed away from the unwashed new underwear wearers. I contented myself with the thirteenth floor. I made my way forward to the Eye Patch Lounge and thought I'd investigate drink prices.

The bartender greeted me with a napkin. "Where you from?" he said.

"You first."

"Philippines."

"And him?"

"Philippines."

"Those guys?"

"Philippines."

"The cook?"

"Philippines."

"Cleaning team on deck ten?"

"Philippines."

"How about—"

"Philippines."

"I'm sensing a theme here."

"Philippines."

"So, Philippines?" I said. "Any Danes on board?"

"Captain Finn Olsen and some of the officers," he said. "What'll you have?"

"Give me a beer."

He popped the cap off an orange bottle and poured it into a glass for me.

"Red Horse?" I said. "Is that from Washington?"

"Philippines."

"Of course." I slid over my room card. The cost of the cruise just increased by ten dollars. Still, I had to admit, it was a good beer.

A woman appeared at my side. Good beer sometimes has that effect. She was an executive in a beige pantsuit. She had a people-person smile and a clipboard. "Getting settled in?" she said to me.

"Had to change my shorts," I said.

She pretended like that was a normal response. "What deck are you on?"

"I'm in room 9578."

"That's deck nine." She looked at her clipboard. "I'm showing that as a vacant room."

"My friend upgraded us."

"Smart move. It's practically free at this point."

"Who are you?"

"I'm sorry," she said. "I'm Sandra. I'm the cruise director. If you need anything, just talk to me."

She flashed her people-person smile again and I smiled back.

"You got something in your teeth there," she said. "Just there. No, there. There. You got it."

"I'm Perry's friend," I said, wondering what could have been in my teeth and for how long.

"Perry Whitehouse? He's so funny. Who are you?"

"Tony Flaner."

"Oh, Perry told me about you. You're the detective."

"Among other things."

She glanced at her watch. "I've got to go," she said, whisking herself out the door. "Enjoy your cruise."

The Eye Patch Lounge was in the front of the ship and had a wall of curved windows from side to side. Comfortable couches and conversation nooks skirted the glass walls and a sunken stage with seating for over a hundred. It reminded me of the Comedy Cellar and other nightclubs I've visited, except there were more parrots and cutlasses than I was used to. The crowds were against the windows watching the ship move through Puget Sound and into the Salish Sea. A handy map behind the bar helped me navigate. The Salish Sea—you can't make that shit up.

A group left their sofas in search of food, and I slipped onto a vacated couch and put my feet up. The beer was good, I was tired, and the view was nice. I was on vacation. I allowed myself another sip before I remembered that I was also on a diet. The beer was too good to be healthy—nothing can be so good and be good for you. I'd have to limit myself to only a few. This would help my finances as well. It would be a win-win. I was in control. To celebrate, I ordered another Red Horse. I toasted myself and wiped the foam from my lip before I realized the irony.

This was going to be a hard cruise.

"Do you know about Nutri-Pods?" It was a tawny-haired twenty-something weightlifter dude who'd seen me sitting alone and must have figured I needed some eel in my diet. "It's the innovative nutritional dietary supplement everyone is talking about."

"Now with ginseng and aloe root?" I said.

"And flavor enhancers."

"Never heard of it."

"Well, let me tell you how you can be a part of the fastest-growing multi-level marketing sensation in the country."

"Multi-level marketing?"

"Marketing sensation."

"I'm here for the seminar," I said.

"What? But you said…oh. Okay. You got me." He clicked his tongue and left, doubtlessly hunting for new targets.

A few minutes later, Bailey Peigne and escort came into the bar. I hadn't taken a close look at the adulterer's new squeeze beyond noting she was not one of the ones I'd caught him with before. She was the same brand though, just a newer model. She was thin and bulbous and wore jeans she'd had to be poured into and cut out of. Her open-toed heels were three inches off the ground, which might explain why she clutched Bailey's arm the way she did. The ship was moving, and based on her failing sweater, her center of gravity was about five inches in front of her. She was made up well, everything done, but not overdone. She was a thirty-five-year-old blonde trying hard to look twenty-five, and for the most part, succeeding.

Bailey looked the same as I remembered him. His appearance hit you in waves. The first thing you noticed was his big, square-toothed grin, which he offered over-eagerly. Then you noticed the citrus-tinged tan skin, blue eyes, and pencil mustache ending before the corners of his mouth. Stepping back, you took in his dark dyed hair, Botoxed crow's feet, tight sports jacket, white Nikes, and lounge lizard swagger. If you were still looking at him at that point, you might ask yourself why a girl with such obvious physical charms would be on his arm. The answer was, of course, money.

Bailey Peigne made his stack as a stockbroker. His pedigree went back to the infamous Salt Lake penny-stock houses of the 1980s where he started out. The SEC swooped down and put some order into the system eventually, doing the very thing that so many reformers wish would happen on Wall Street today. Bailey survived and moved to a reputable house. He eventually married the owner's daughter, Amber, and lived happily ever after for five years—cheating on her and embezzling money. I found forty thousand in the Caymans, and I suspected he had more hidden away. Last I heard, he was in serious negotiations with a potpourri of federal agencies trying to keep himself out of jail. Oh, and he's divorced now.

He beamed his bleached grin around the bar like a lighthouse warning of rocks and fell on me and my beer. I twiddled my fingers and watched the veins in his neck pulsate and swell. He grabbed his girl by the arm and led her out of the bar. A moment later, he returned, collected his room card from the bar where he'd left it, and stormed out again, this time staring murder at me.

"Absit omen," I muttered.

"What did you say?" said a woman by the window.

"Nothing."

The bar was crowded with excited, happy pod people. If I didn't want to talk about garlic and cloves, eel oil, and flavor enhancers, I had to make myself more aloof.

"Tony? Tony Flaner?"

I turned to see a tall woman with short brown hair, hazel eyes and narrow glasses. I recognized her first as the woman I'd seen boarding the ship on the VIP gangway, the one I thought I knew. I was pleased to see I was right, I did know her, as proved by the fact that she knew me. I was less pleased with not remembering how I knew her or who the hell she was.

"Hi," I said. "How have you been?"

"Good, good, and you?"

"Fine, fine," I said. "The family?"

"I got married."

"Did you?" I said, buying time for my underpaid cerebral interns to locate the missing data about this woman. "Who'd you marry?"

"Vincent Bror," she said.

"Congratulations," I said. "Did you keep your maiden name?"

"No," she said.

"Oh. Is this your honeymoon?"

"No. We've been married eighteen months."

I nodded agreeably, turning this information into actionable intelligence as to the whereabouts of a name. She was about my age, maybe a little older. The glasses may be new. I tried to visualize her without them. Maybe with lighter hair, fatter, thinner, as a man.

"Oh, what a surprise to see you here," she said. "I read about you in the paper."

"Which paper?" I said.

"You know, the *Trib*."

"Ah, the *Salt Lake Tribune*," I said, eliciting a nod from her. Okay. She was from Utah. "That's a good paper."

"Didn't you do something in Moab too?"

"Yes, that was me," I said. She was well informed. People went to pains to bury that entire story and my name with it. "So are you still working at the, ah—"

"I'm not working anymore," she said. "I married Vincent Bror."

Vincent. A man. So she was probably not a lesbian. She could be bisexual. How many bisexuals did I know? And what kind of name is Bror? Wasn't there a war in Africa with that name? Was that the one with spears? I loved that movie. Michael Caine was great in it.

My interns sucked.

"Well, isn't that something," I said. "You look great. Can I buy you a drink? These are pretty good."

"Thanks."

"Who's Vincent Bror?" I said, reaching for threads.

"He's my husband. He's rich."

"Oh? How rich?"

"Millions."

"Then you should buy the drinks," I said.

She laughed and sat down. "I should."

"So money, huh? Uhm, so you don't, eh…anymore?"

"Teach? No. Not for a long time."

Teach. A teacher. Stop the presses. Recall the ships. We have liftoff. Buy bonds and tip your waitress.

"Latin! Kristen Michaels," I said. "You're Kristen Michaels. I remember you."

"Right," she said. "You didn't before?"

"Oh, I did, of course. I just couldn't remember which classes we had together. Do you still spell your name with a 'K?'"

"I do, believe it or not."

"Cool," I said. Is there anything worse than running into an old friend and not remembering their name? Yes, I can think of one thing: say it's a woman, and you'd forgotten her name, and you'd slept with her.

Absit omen.

5

I LOVED COLLEGE. I spent seven years there getting a four-year degree. I know how that sounds, but my grades were great. I just couldn't decide what I wanted to be when I grew up. I kept changing majors. I spent my time and money in classes that never fit into an actual degree but were offered to round out a general education—those "other" classes the university was always talking about. I took classes like "Horseback Riding" and "Hiking," "Prehistoric Feminism," "Pi as a Concept," "Common Medicines," "Herb Lore," "Film History," "Thermodynamics of Plasma Waves in Quantum Space"—I dropped that one)—and "Communications." All interesting, and occasionally handy things to know, but not likely to get you out into the workforce anytime soon. If there'd been an actual underwater basket weaving class, which was the joke at the time, I'd have taken it. I was disappointed when I saw it didn't exist and made do with scuba and pottery instead. Combining the two got me kicked out of the pool for a semester and got the intramural freestyles moved to Ogden.

I'd met Kristen Michaels during college. I'd decided that I had been sorely lacking in classical languages, and since Greek looked like math, and I didn't like math much, I went to Latin. Kristen was a teacher's assistant, a graduate student doing all the heavy lifting for a mumbling Texan instructor who was thick on character and accent, but thin on record keeping and office hours. Kristen taught the class two days a week and the instructor two more, leaving that hour open on Friday for "Advanced Lawn Care."

I took Latin for a year and some change with the intent of going on to teach at Harvard when I was done, little realizing, or rather repressing the fact, that some kids are taught Latin in elementary school, or English boarding schools, or are Catholic, or actually have the ambition to teach at Harvard.

Kristen and I had hit it off. There'd been one final ugly incident when I'd turned an essay in late and she'd failed me, but before that, we'd been friends. I'd even taken her on a date or two before my life was forever altered by Nancy, my now ex-wife. She said she didn't date people younger than herself, and I had won her over by showing her my driver's license and explaining my interminable undergraduate status.

She'd changed since college. Big surprise. She was older, for one. Yeah, I know. She must have worn contacts then because she told me she'd always needed glasses. She looked good. Unlike some people, she hadn't let herself go in adulthood. I sucked in my gut.

"There was only so far you can go in the classics," she explained. "Like the humanities in general, there are always more applicants than jobs. After I got my PhD, I tried some tutoring and then fell into odd jobs. I was manager at a Sizzler for five years until a man wanted the job."

"Any kids?"

"No," she said. "Vincent doesn't want any."

"Where'd you meet your millionaire husband? Are there women there too?"

"You might have met him at the university. Did you ever take any electrical engineering courses?"

"I missed those. Don't know how."

"He ran the labs as a graduate student. It's where he developed his chip."

"Cool Ranch?"

She laughed, which surprised me. It was a lame joke. Either I was funnier than my friends, agents, club owners, and audiences were letting on, or she was an easy sell.

"He developed a microchip for power regulation. He's tried to explain it to me, but I don't get it. Something about shared electrons and amperage. He got the patent back in the '90s. Two years ago, Apple licensed it, then Samsung, and now Microsoft and the Pentagon. Suddenly we're rich. It's really weird."

"I feel for you."

She laughed again. "Vincent was born dirt poor. A real hard-luck case. I actually first dated him because I felt sorry for him. His parents died when he was a kid, his brother when he was in college. He had to work his way through school and never had a pot to piss in. But he has a really good attitude about it, you know? Really positive about things. He figured he'd work hard, take his chances when he got them, and eventually he'd make it. And he did."

"I remember you being a positive person."

"It was easy for me. I used my parents' money to study Cicero. I'd never had it as rough as Vincent had it growing up. It was easy to be perky when you knew where your next meal was coming from."

"But you said you've only been married a few months," I said.

"Eighteen. Nineteen, maybe. But we lived together for years. We've been a couple forever. We only made it legal when the money came."

"Why'd you wait?"

"It wasn't me," she said. "It was him. Personal pride." She wistfully looked out the window behind me and I sipped my beer. "You have to meet him. You have to have dinner with us," she said.

"I'd love to. I'm here all week. I'm in room 9578. That's on the ninth floor."

"We're in 14500," she said. "That's on deck fourteen."

"Right, they're called 'decks' here, aren't they?" I said. "Do you have a nice room?"

"Our room has two floors and a garden."

"Millionaires, huh?"

"Millionaires," she said lifelessly. "Are you traveling alone?"

"With some friends," I said. "A gang I hang out with. One's working on the ship. So, five of us."

"Are you married?"

"I'm divorced," I said. Allie flashed into my mind, but I numbed it with another drink. I'm an ass, I know.

"You look good," she said.

"How many beers did you have?"

She laughed. "You seem comfortable in your skin, Tony. That's what I meant."

"I should be comfortable in it. There's plenty of room."

She laughed again.

"I'm on a diet," I told her.

"On a cruise ship vacation? Good luck."

"Thanks," I said. "Where there's a will, there's a way."

"A will," she sneered. "That's funny. I mean, it's impossible."

"I know what you meant. I can read you like a menu."

"Well, I should go." She got up.

I stood up too, ever the gentleman impersonator. "Good to see you, Kristen."

She kissed me on the cheek. It was a nice gesture, but her lips lingered a little long, and her aim was remarkably close to my mouth.

I sat down and watched her go.

A great and wise person, maybe Robin Williams or Marc Maron, once said that there is not enough blood in a man's body to fuel both his head and his penis. Add to this a cruise ship vacation, a couple of beers, a spat with the girl at home, and you might just see the sleazier side of a man. When the subject of relationships come up, you might hear "divorced." With a period.

Full stop. Where it should have been 'comma-ed:' "I was married, I got divorced, now I'm in a relationship with really nice woman I've treated poorly and don't know why." When offered an opportunity to make a metaphor, the blood-drained, horny man might say, "I can read you like a menu," conveying sensual excitement of a meal, sweet dessert, coffee maybe. A thinking man in said relationship would have been better served in the long run saying something like nothing, skipping the innuendo, and not filling his head with guilt eggs to hatch later.

When Kristen left me, my blood was gone from my head and my pants were too tight. In the space where rational thinking used to be were images of one-night stands and the memory of the one awkward night I'd had with Kristen way back when.

I got up to follow her after a minute, though I had no idea what I'd do if I caught her, probably just rub against her leg or something. I felt faint from suddenly standing. I sat down hard and decided to look out the window for a while longer until the strong beer left me and circulation returned. An ice water appeared on the table, and the bottles were gone. Thoughts of Allie slipped into my head from the sidelines and sat on the eggs. Visions of nice men not needing their wives distracted completed the setting as pitchforks-wielding cartoon devils danced in anticipation of my damning.

"You look like you need a Nutri-Pod."

I looked up, expecting to see another stranger pushing vitamin-enriched food coloring, but it was Standard Flox. "God, not you too?" I said.

"I was joking." He flopped on the couch beside me.

"I couldn't tell."

"I tell you what, there're going to be some dead bodies on this ship if those pod people don't lay off. Look at this." He reached in his pocket and took out a half dozen teardrop-shaped bottles of varying colors.

"How much you pay for those?"

"Free samples. I was hitting on this girl and all she could talk about was these stupid Nutri-Pods. 'It's going to revolutionize the dietary industry,' 'two chimpanzees have kicked cancer by eating nothing but pods and undergoing chemotherapy.'"

"Really?"

"Yeah."

"I had to pay for mine."

He shrugged. "Anyway, turned out she was with someone. She could have mentioned that before poisoning my Mai Tai with a eucalyptus pod. Then three other people pushed me about it. It's like I'm surrounded by brainwashed cultists. 'Join us. Join us.'"

"Don't fall asleep," I said.

"Amen."

"I'm hungry. Let's eat."

We took the stairs down to the Freestyle Eatery, the all-you-can-overeat buffet always open. The smell of melted cheeses, pork chops, and fresh breads added a pound to my ass before I got to the door.

"Washy-washy!"

Our way in was barred by a petite Filipina woman with a smile that could soften steel.

"Washy-washy!" she said, pushing a bottle of hand sanitizer toward us.

Before I could take offense at being singled out for disease prevention, I noticed her twin squirting gobs of disinfectant into the palms of others. Standard was already working the alcohol into his fingers, so I offered up mine.

"Seems I have a paper cut," I said. "Thanks for bringing it to my attention."

"It's for the Hantavirus," Standard said. "There's a sanitizer dispenser every ten feet. Look."

He was right about the dispensers. They were everywhere. He was wrong, however, about the virus.

"Norovirus, dipshit," said Dara, coming up behind us.

"What's the difference?" Standard said.

"Oh. Can I take this one?" I asked, taking a tray. "It's the difference between a ship full of sick people and a city full of dead ones."

"That," said Dara.

"Where's Garrett?"

"Saving us a seat," said Dara.

I surveyed the tables of buffet food and despaired about my diet.

"Salad?" I said.

"Get real." Dara pushed past me to the prime rib.

I didn't want to be rude, so I joined her. On the way to the vegetables, I stumbled into the pasta bar. Before I could find fruit, I found the fresh-baked bread. By the time I'd hit the dessert table, I had no more room on my plate and put chocolate cake in the horseradish. I'd have to make another trip for flan and pie. And maybe those sugar cookies. The soft-serve ice cream bar had banana. That's a good flavor.

"Our room is like a box," said Garrett.

"Dara upgraded us to a balcony. It's cool."

"We should do that, Stan."

"Why? We're only going to sleep there."

"I'd like a window."

"By the way, you owe me two hundred," Dara said. "I'll take the cash now if you have it."

"You paid cash?"

"No, I charged it, but I could use the cash."

"Why? Everything's included," said Garrett.

"So I know I have it," she said.

"I resemble your implication. Contact my accountant when we're back," I said. "I'm not giving up my cash."

"You have an accountant?" said Garrett.

"I used to. I forgot to pay him."

I was on my third plate—broiled chicken and potatoes, still no salad, when the buffet feeding frenzy ratcheted up to a real frenzy. A woman squealed and men whooped. We looked up and saw throngs thronging a mild-mannered balding man in a nice suit.

"Who the hell is that?"

"That would be Paul Vinalez, creator of Nutri-Pods," said Standard, tossing out a brochure.

There he was on the back of it; a confident forty-year-old in the same suit. He looked like a banker except for a little something in his eyes. They stared off the page and into me like he was reading my mind. Looking up at the buffet line, I saw a modest man carrying his food through a crowd of admirers, accompanied by a white-coated kitchen officer pointing out the delicacies of the Sterno-heated buffet line and making recommendations.

"Pods have changed my life," cried one woman.

"I couldn't have kids before I discovered Nutri-Pods," said a man.

"I bought my second house thanks to you," said a teenager.

He was a regular guy carrying a tray of food through a buffet court surrounded by admirers.

"See you at the seminar tomorrow," he said to them and walked by.

I almost would have bought the "everyman" schtick had it not been for one guy with a briefcase a step behind him and one bodyguard with an earpiece surveying the crowd for threats two steps behind the briefcase. A trophy wife, second cousin to the eye candy Bailey Peigne carried around, was also present, but she had an assistant to carry her tray.

"He looks like my uncle," said Garrett.

"Sleaze," said Standard. "Another Utah pyramid scheme."

"He's from Utah?" I said.

"Yes. Haven't you heard about this?"

"Only this trip."

"You've spent too much time in Moab," Standard said. I'd been thinking the opposite since Kristen's kiss. "Nutri-Pods was born in Nephi. Utah. It's less than a year old and already is looking to get on NASDAQ."

"How do you know all this?"

"Pod people," he said.

"I heard of them before the trip," said Garrett. "A neighbor told me. She wasn't as bad as this group, though."

Vinalez and his retinue found a table and sat down. He had a timed rhythm, I observed. Every few minutes, he glanced at his watch and squeezed a Nutri-Pod into his mouth. He'd smile broadly afterward in case any cameras were watching and tilt his neck as if he could feel the vitamins mending bones.

They ate like casual folks while people around them snapped photos and gawked. He made a big deal out of taking a pod or two from his pocket and squeezing it out on his salad before forking a mouthful into his mouth with a grin and a wink. He had all the moves. His wife was less enthusiastic and only put a couple of drops into her coffee before adding a half liter of cream. The bodyguard and the manager held back, careful to stay out of camera range.

"I get the big bed," I said to Dara.

"The hell you do."

"I outweigh you by twenty pounds—"

"Eighty," she said.

"—so I get it."

"We'll see about that."

"Don't you have two identical beds?" asked Garrett.

"One big one and a pull-out," I said.

"It's all they had. Deal with it."

"Oh, I've dealt with it."

She looked at me suspiciously.

I showed her a mouthful of Jell-O. She wasn't impressed, but it was the healthiest thing I'd eaten that meal, and I felt the need to share. She wanted to share her fingernail varnish, one long nail in particular.

6

THE NEXT MORNING I woke up duct-taped to the bed. But at least it was the big bed.

I'd gotten to the room before Dara. We'd all sat through an orientation presentation in the main theater that showcased the ship's facilities, talked about the ports of call, and advertised the onshore excursions available to each, with particular emphasis on the fantastic shopping opportunities we were sure to enjoy. Every port we stopped at had between eight and thirty-eight gem and jewelry stores where we could stock up on precious stones and metals. In case we didn't get to shore, there were two jewelry stores on board that specialized in tanzanite and larimar, which should quadruple in value before we get back to Seattle and be worth more than the Louvre by Christmas. The presenters could not think of a better investment and told us so.

The gang had gone drinking, but I'd turned in early, driven to bed by a Red Horse hangover and guilt about talking to Kristen while ignoring Allie.

I gnawed through the tape while Dara slept. The sun was shining outside though I could see low puffy clouds through the window. I flossed the tape out of my teeth and showered. When I got out, there were papers on the floor by the door.

It was a ship's itinerary showing all the fun things happening on board that day, leading off with the "Sweat Out the Dawn" exercise extravaganza which I'd blissfully already missed by a couple hours. We'd be at sea all day, sailing to Juneau via the Inside Passage. There was a special section "for our special guests" outlining the Nutri-Pods seminar itinerary.

Alongside the papers was an envelope with a note from Kristen inviting me and my friends to the Wild Angus Steakhouse that night for dinner. It included five coupons so we wouldn't have to pay for the meal. A prouder man would have torn up the coupons, manned up, and bought dinner himself. I clutched them like the 'One Ring' and considered keeping all the 'Preciouses' to myself.

I dressed and left Dara sleeping. I considered doing something devious to her, perhaps with an ice bucket and a can of shaving cream, maybe even a rat. Aren't there always rats on ships? I left her alone, though. I knew that whatever I did to Dara would be looked upon me tenfold.

I slipped out the door and nearly tripped over a rat in the hall. It scurried a few paces away, stopped and looked at me. I stared back. It was white as a snowball and about the same size. Its eyes were red and its twitchy nose held high, perhaps sniffing for shaving cream, looking for a way to be useful.

"Look, Mommy, a kitty," said a gangly tyke, seven or eight years old in a Buckeyes sweatshirt. He stood in a cabin doorway, pointing at the rat. The animal turned and threw him a sniff before running down the hall and around a corner.

"Did you see the kitty, Mister?"

"I did," I said.

In the elevator, I saw another one.

At breakfast, it was the main subject of conversation that I couldn't help but overhear. They were all over the ship.

A crew member tried to explain. "Everything's all right," he said. "They're pets."

Pets were allowed on the cruise. That much I remembered. Garrett was worried they wouldn't allow Critter and had made a big deal of it in the cab ride from the airport.

I filled my plate up with fruit and yogurt with a side of bacon or two. After a cup of okay coffee and a view to die for, I was ready to start the day.

I looked around hoping and dreading that I'd see Kristen, but she wasn't there. I doubt the VIPs took many meals in the eatery with the steerage passengers and a plague of white rats. There were restaurants on board that were not part of the all-inclusive ticket and charged enough to keep anyone who had to look at the prices away. The Wild Angus Steakhouse was one of them. There was also a sushi place and a French restaurant where you could get over-buttery sauces ladled onto tiny portions of snails for a small fortune. These were the places Kristen and Vincent Bror would be taking their meals if and when they ever left their suite on the fourteenth floor —*deck*, I corrected myself. I suspect Paul Vinalez and the other Nutri-Pods royalty would be doing the same now that the cafeteria photo-op was fulfilled.

The eatery had not a fraction of the crowds I'd fought through the day before. Yesterday everyone was tired and hungry from traveling, anxious to see what the all-inclusive food was like and had packed the tables like weary eighth graders after a three-hour honor roll assembly. Today, people were relaxing and settling in, coming in for food in smaller groups or alone. Plus, I knew many of the passengers from yesterday had already eaten and were now in the Nutri-Pods seminar.

I found my way to the "Captain Finn Conference Room" to check out the Nutri-Pods seminar because, why not? I was late by several hours and didn't want a demerit, so I slipped quietly in the door and hugged the back wall, taking it all in.

It was a wide-open room with a low ceiling. There was a small stage at the end. Captain Finn, having enough sea views from the bridge, had put his conference room mid-ship and the curtained windows looked out onto hallways and cabin doors. There were ample chairs and several hundred people sat in them. Some had laptops open, while others took notes the old-fashioned way with pen and paper—savages! Everyone had a blue binder and a striped paper packet with goodies. A table by the door had binders and packets and bottles of "Nutri-Pod-enriched Power Beverages!"

I noticed the woman who'd fallen overboard the day before in the crowd, her severe haircut making her easy to spot. The woman who'd charged me for a sample in line was also there, sitting up front, practically frothing at the mouth for the wisdom Paul Vinalez was imparting from the stage. I saw many of the faces I remembered adoring their leader in the buffet line. All eyes were wide and willing, eager and charged.

To my surprise, I saw Garrett and Standard in the crowd. When Vinalez went to PowerPoint slides and the room darkened, I worked my way up to them.

"Combining ancient nutritional wisdom with modern marketing, Nutri-Pods will revolutionize the way the world 'nutriates,'" Vinalez said. He glanced at his watch, smiled and squirted a Nutri-Pod onto his tongue with relish, throwing it a little half-orgasm shudder when he swallowed.

"Hey guys," I said. "What the hell are you doing here?"

"Garrett pulled me in," said Standard.

"Shhh," said Garrett.

"Oh god," I said. "Where's Critter?"

"Back in the room."

"The old style of marketing is corporate and impersonal, but Nutri-Pods will use the face-to-face connections we all naturally have in our lives. Using your enthusiasm and these patented, tested tools, you should be able to assimilate four or five 'pods' beneath you. These 'pods' will, in turn, assimilate four or five more, and the income stream will be secure with saturated Nutri-Pod distribution."

Applause.

"Classic pyramid scheme," Standard said.

"But with a robust Rod Serling flavor."

"Quiet. I'm interested in this," said Garrett.

"No, you're not," I said.

"I'm not?"

"No. If Critter found out what you were doing here, he'd have your head."

Garrett considered this gravely for a moment. My friends are not well. I admit that.

"Perry's doing it," he said, pointing.

It took me a minute to find him, but Garrett was right. Perry Whitehouse, paranoid conspiracy buff, Alex Jones without the anger, was in a corner taking down notes. I hadn't recognized him because he had on a heavy coat, glasses, and a wig. It was a woman's wig. He made it work, though. It was the twenty-first century after all.

"Oh no," I said and scooted toward him.

"You are the first hatchlings, the first wave, the ground floor seedlings," Vinalez said, struggling to mix his metaphors into a smooth eel-oiled message. "We're limiting Nutri-Pod's organic marketing campaign to only ninety-nine levels, and you are in the first crop, the stalks in the garden."

English butchery aside, Paul Vinalez was a dynamic and charismatic presence. He had to be. He was selling slime wrapped up in a Ponzi scheme based on a fad that had yet to materialize. But he was doing it. He'd brought a couple hundred adherents onto a boat for some hardcore indoctrination Amway and Scientology could appreciate.

I wasn't remotely surprised to learn that Nutri-Pods had been hatched in Utah. There's something about the believing nature of the Utah-born and the capitalist entrepreneurial spirit—i.e., greed—in that cultural landscape that spawns multi-level empires and causes Utah to be known as "America's scam capital." There's a joke about "The Great Pyramids of Utah" with a certain not-to-be-named overly litigious company shining at its peak. That certain company has done pretty well and now uses its deep pockets to fight off the Federal Trade Commission while inspiring a plague of imitators.

Multi-level marketed Nutri-Pods combined the pyramid pay structure of a chain letter with a gimmicky plastic bottle and dubious dietary claims of ginseng and clove, and God help us all, eel oil. "Product-based" multi-level marketing schemes are legal in Utah after the targeted castration of the former "Utah Pyramid Scheme Act" in 2006. Once that pesky consumer protection law was nixed, people were free to make neighbors into salesmen and family into customers. Some say it made churches into moneychangers, but I can't speak to that. I will, however, mention it because it sounds cool.

I figure Nutri-Pods had a better-than-average chance for success, and by success, I mean of making its creators rich. Vinalez's followers, however, I didn't have as much hope for. Time would tell.

Before I got to Perry, Paul Vinalez began leading a chant. "I see the future and I am well and strong!"

"I see the future and I am well and strong!" the crowd repeated.

"Nutri-Pods, its leaders and partners will make me stronger if I do my best."

"Nutri-Pods, its leaders and partners will make me stronger if I do my best."

"Perry, what are you doing here?"

"Tony, you're not buying into this, are you?"

"Hell no, but why are you here?"

"I'm doing surveillance," he whispered. "It's not often you can see actual brainwashing in action."

He had a point.

"Here." I gave him a ticket Kristen had left for me. "Come to this dinner tonight."

"Where'd you get this? Who sent you?"

"Calm down. An old friend. Kristen Bror."

"Vincent Bror's wife?"

"You know them?"

"Sub-micro power regulator," he said as if I hadn't done my homework.

"Yeah, those guys," I said. "They're on the ship. I know Kristen from before, and she invited us. You should come."

"I will," he said. "I'd like to ask Bror if he understands the implications of his invention. It can be used for evil purposes."

"So can duct tape."

"Don't I know it. Oh. Right. Sorry about that. Dara made me get it for her."

"No worries," I said. "Listen, I'm leaving before I become a Manchurian Candidate."

"I don't know how much of this I can take either," Perry said, adjusting his wig.

"Don't drink the Kool-Aid."

The steroid poster boy I'd seen the day before shadowing Vinalez was on his feet pulling Standard and Garrett by their shirt collars toward the door.

"What's all this then?" I said.

"You're not on the list either," said the man. "This is a private function. You have to leave."

It wasn't hard to figure out what the bruiser's previous occupation had been.

"You got something to hide?" I said.

He gave me the steely look bouncers all over the world give to people right before something unpleasant and painful happens.

"Okay, we're leaving. We're not part of the flock."

"Garden," he corrected me.

At the door, I looked back and saw no sign of Perry. He'd either changed wigs and seats or left through another door.

"Look what I got." I passed out the dinner coupons.

"Where'd you get these?" asked Garrett.

"A millionaire gave them to me and invited us to dinner."

"Why not just pick up the check at the restaurant? Why the tickets?"

It was a good question. "Maybe we need a ticket to get in?"

Standard took one but explained he'd seen a South American beauty the night before and excused himself to stalk her. Perry had arranged with Sandra, the cruise director, for Garrett to do a kids' show, and he had to collect Critter from the room.

"You can't go blue, you know," I reminded him.

"It's Critter, not Dara," said Garret.

"Right."

I tried to call Allie, but my cell phone didn't have any bars. I found an internet cafe without coffee and read the connection charges. I figured my money would be better spent buying Allie a new ranch when I got back than apologizing to her now at those costs.

I had lunch and made peace with Dara. We caught the end of Garrett's show. One of the kids made to pull Critter off Garrett's arm. Critter ducked and then turned to face the kid. He'd been singing a song about tolerance of 'turkeys for ducks, and Volkswagens for trucks' but fell silent and stared with his googly, unblinking eyes at the misbehaved child.

"Listen, kid," Critter said. "How would you like someone to grab you by the neck and twist your head off? How'd you like that? What do you think that would feel like?" Critter didn't say it as much as he hissed it, a low menacing sibilation that made the boy's lip quiver for just a minute before he broke down crying and ran from the rumpus room.

"And that's why we're nice to each other," said Garrett to the other children.

It was one of those awkward moments that could have moved into either screams or cheers—you couldn't tell which, but you knew it was going somewhere. Dara and I clapped our hands and whistled to end the act in the right direction. Eventually the kids joined in, and I think we avoided a lawsuit.

I hadn't brought anything formal on the cruise, believing the "freestyle" description of the ship meant anything from nude to shorts. I'd thought my jeans would be overdressed, but passing by the Wild Angus, I saw nothing but ties and dresses for their lunch diners. I hadn't a tie, but maybe I could borrow one of Dara's dresses.

She wouldn't share, so I did the best I could with a clean shirt and pants that hadn't been stone-washed, acid-washed, or brainwashed and hoped they'd let me in.

We arrived as a group like beggars at the wrong door. After a "washy-washy" attack by two giggling hand-sanitizing gnomes, we were let in. The maître d' reluctantly led us to a table in a dark corner that would have been the prime spot to sit if we were corporate spies sent there to bribe an official. As it was, it hid our uncouthness from the VIPs onboard.

Kristen saw me across the room and waved me over.

"Your millionairess calls," said Standard.

"I was afraid of this," Kristen said, getting up to meet me. "We're sitting with the captain."

"Sounds like fun," I said excitedly. "I'll get the gang."

"No," she said. "*We.* Vince and I. Sorry, you're not invited. A mix-up."

"But I bathed and everything."

"I can at least introduce you," she said. She took my arm and marched me across the room to a broad table where Captain Finn Olsen himself sat at the head, looking regal. Though he tried to look salty and wise, confident that he wouldn't steer us into an iceberg—which was a real threat, come to think of it, in this setting at least—with a grand captain's table, with place settings and name cards, Captain Finn Olsen was a caricature—a sailing mascot, primed for photos and full of trivia about knots and tonnages, bilge water and timetables. He glanced at me when I approached, his eyes full of judgment about my sneakers.

"Vince, this is Tony," Kristen said to the man sitting next to the captain.

Vincent Bror looked like me. That was the first thing I thought when I met the microchip patent millionaire. He was about my height, had a similar build, and nearly the same coloring—brown hair and chocolate eyes. His complexion was ruddier than mine, but I put that off on the champagne I smelled on his breath. He had more hair than me with less gray in it. Maybe I was a fraction taller, perhaps, and wider of course, but from a distance and in raincoats, say, we'd be identical. His grip was firm and his hands weren't exactly rough, but they weren't the soft squishy things I usually got from a person who made their living off the interest. He wore his tailored suit, not like he was born into it, but like he'd gotten used to it.

"Glad to meet you, Tony," he said. "I hear we were at the university at the same time, which isn't saying much. I was there a long time. Sorry I don't remember you."

"Yeah, what's up with that?" I said to test his sarcasm tolerance. He measured a seven on the Flaner scale, so I knew I was alight. "Actually I was there a long time too."

"You're not a scientist, I take it?"

"More of a jack-of-all-trades," I said. "A Renaissance Man."

"Unemployed?"

"Oh, yeah."

"How can you afford to eat here?" he said.

I sensed Kristen flinch.

"I'm going to dine and dash," I told him. "What's the worst that can happen?"

"I've done that before," he said. "Well, enjoy your meal."

Kristen said, "And this is Captain Finn Olsen."

The captain said, "Hi."

I responded, "Hi."

It was over. I was dismissed. Vincent Bror sat down. I should have just left, but I lingered a little. The captain's table had a commanding view of the restaurant, and just then Paul and Ashley Vinalez, his wife whose name I'd learned through osmosis, both dressed for the Oscars, got escorted from the door to the other side of Captain Finn. I was finally shooed away by a bald man with a fine waxed mustache and cook's clothes who, after I left, personally put menus into the hands of the captain's guests.

"I wish I was so cool that I didn't have to pick up a menu," I muttered.

I saw pod people from the morning's seminar trying to pretend the prices didn't affect them but most of the diners were the kind of people who ordered without menus, calling for steaks or lobsters or "chef's choice" or "surprise me and my accountant" while making a big deal of turning a champagne bottle upside down in a bucket.

Back in the murky shadows of our "they really shouldn't be in this crowd" table, Garrett asked, "So how is it to mix with the big shots?"

"Kind of weird," I said. "Part show and pomp, part class cold warfare."

"The tickets don't cover drinks," complained Dara.

"And there's no mention of gratuity."

"No tipping on board," said Garrett. "Remember from orientation? There's a tip surcharge we'll get dinged for, like two hundred bucks."

"Typical," said Dara.

The dark of the room became bright and filled with loud voices at the door.

"You'll get a captain's seat when you prove you can handle it!"

"I've been ready for years. You're just hogging it. You said five years. It's been six!"

"Show me you're ready."

"At least I'm sober."

"What does that mean?"

The two crab fishermen were up in each other's faces with their film crew. The maître d' stepped in and put his hand over the camera lens.

"Gentlemen," he said menacingly.

The camera pulled back, turned its bright spotlight around the restaurant and then went off.

"Pick this up later?" said one of the fishermen.

"Okay," said the other, calm as could be. "Juneau? At the glacier?"

"Good backdrop," said the director. The cameraman nodded.

With that, the four of them found a table and ordered a meal.

I looked at the captain's table to see what ol' Finn thought of the show, if he'd be embarrassed or upset he'd not been in the shot. That's when I saw the color drain from Vincent Bror's face. He was looking out into the crowd with a hand on his brow shadowing his eyes. I couldn't see where he was looking, but I'm sure it wasn't my table. The expression on his face was difficult to identify. It could have been surprise, dread, or even fear. It could have been all three.

He dropped his hand into his lap and for a moment, he just sat there like he was about to be sick. Kristen said something to him, but he ignored her, and she turned her attention to the other guests.

A minute later, Vincent Bror emptied his champagne flute down his throat, caught a burp in his fist and stood up. He looked ill. He looked upset. He looked angry. After excusing himself to the captain and kissing Kristen curtly on the cheek, he turned, and keeping his eyes downcast, left the restaurant through a back door.

7

THE VOICE WAS surreal and soothing, and it spoke gibberish. It was easy to incorporate into my dream. "Code Bright Star," it said. "Bright Star. Sierra Team, Code Bright Star." My dreams turned into a Disney fantasy cartoon with commandos rescuing princesses from castles with night-vision goggles and helicopters. After the goblins were sent to Gitmo, my subconscious returned to its usual scheduled programming.

I absorbed the sound of someone knocking on the door into the dream I was having. Donald Sutherland was pointing at me in a city square, a terrible howl issuing out of his mouth—an accusation straight from hell. It stuttered and broke, changed into chirps that changed into raps, not unlike knuckles on a cabin door. This all made as much sense as my fifth-grade homeroom teacher hovering over the Great Salt Lake in my Prius' passenger seat, which I also had to deal with. Plus I had a trig final in an hour and hadn't even cracked the textbook.

"Get the goddamn door, Flaner," said Dara. "You're closer."

"Okay, Mom. I have a test today." I rolled out of bed and rubbed my eyes. Getting my bearings, I staggered to the door and opened it. "What?"

"Tony Flaner?"

"I'll get him," I said.

"Aren't you Tony Flaner?"

"I know my rights, man."

"Mr. Flaner, get dressed and come with me."

"Who are you?"

"I'm Ola Peterson, security head."

"Dammit, Flaner—make him go away."

"Hold on there, chief. Give me a minute," I said and closed the door. "Dara. Dara, did I do something stupid last night?"

"Fuck off, Flaner. I'm sleeping."

"Did I?"

"Probably."

It was dark outside. The clock said 2:35.

I tried to remember what had happened the night before to get me arrested. I couldn't think of anything. We'd seen a musical stage show, an abbreviated montage review of *Cats!* and *A Chorus Line*—"Rum Tum Tugger's One Singular Jellicle Sensation"—which sounded to me like a hairball but was more line-dancey. Afterward, we cruised the bars for an expensive hour before I returned to my room to watch the ocean from the balcony and then going to bed. I'd kept my pants on, so I couldn't figure out why I was being arrested now.

I threw on some clothes and opened the door. "So you're Security Head?" I said.

"Yes, Ola Peterson. Come with me."

"Better than 'blackhead,' I suppose, or 'dick.'"

Stone-faced, he led me down the hallway. A white rat poked its nose around a corner and Peterson tried to step on it, but it was too fast.

The elevator door opened, and we stepped inside.

"Ola!" I said.

"Yes?"

"Nothing, I'm just happy I don't have a trig test today. Your name is a celebration. Ola!"

"You're a smart-ass, aren't you?" he said. His accent was foreign, but probably not to him. I figured it for Danish.

"I am," I said. "Ola!" I snapped my fingers over my head and stamped my feet for effect.

He stared at the closing door.

"Do I get a phone call, or do I have to use semaphores?"

He took his name badge out of his pocket and went to slide it into the elevator panel slot but paused before he did.

I leaned over and saw that the brass plate around the slot was scratched up, and bent open a bit.

"Something not shipshape?" I asked.

Without inserting his badge, he pushed fourteen. He flinched when the button lit up and the elevator moved.

"Fourteen?" I said.

He pushed fifteen, and it too lit up. He sighed.

"Uhm, you want to tell me what's going on?" I said.

"Mrs. Bror asked to see you."

"Moonlighting as a butler?"

"Don't talk," he said.

I was sarcastic and half groggy. The quiet ride up in the elevator gave me time to de-grog.

Ola Peterson's uniform had more lines on his arms than a zebra in pinstripes. He dressed like a sailor, smelled like a cop, and looked like Lief Erickson. He was a tall Nordic man with sea-blue eyes and straight yellow hair. I could see him a thousand years earlier with a braided beard and an iron ax plundering England in longboats, if he could be bothered to get up. He carried himself like he was used to getting things done but no longer cared if they happened.

The door opened not onto a hallway but onto an indoor garden, complete with fountain and songbirds. Oh, and a white rat that Ola picked up by the tail.

One of the crab fishermen I'd seen arguing stubbed out a cigarette and came at Ola. "I've got a right to have my camera crew up here," he said. "This is good television."

"Go back to your room, Mr. Lewis, or I'll throw you in the brig."

"You can't."

"I think he can," I said.

"I can."

Unhappy, Mr. Lewis disappeared into one of the nicer, but not the nicest, room on the ship. The nicest room was the one I was led to. 14500—the Brors' suite.

When Peterson opened the door, I smelled it. Blood. Whatever excitement I might have been cooking up for a midnight millionaire party, sipping Kristal from a supermodel's naval, dissolved with one sniff of that sticky, metallic smell. Plus, there was no music.

After a large entranceway, I was brought to a huge living space. There was a grand piano and a bank of windows overlooking the half-frozen pool mid-deck. I'd wondered what was behind those windows from below when I'd been out there before. Now I knew. A dead guy. No, not just a guy, but Vincent Bror himself lay on the floor, a steak knife in his neck. He was still dressed in his suit, tie, and cuff links. The pool of blood beneath him was expansive and dark, a terrible contrast to the loud Caribbean-themed carpet of the room. Hibiscus leaves never go out of style. Until they do.

Casino carpet aside, I had a hard time looking at the body. It's never easy to come face to face with death. It's as if seeing death reminds one of their own mortalities. No, actually, it's exactly like that. This was particularly terrible for me because except for the suit and gold rings, the dead guy looked like me.

"She's in the bedroom." The man talking to me looked like all the other Filipino petty-officers I'd seen onboard, white uniform and black leather shoes, trimmed hair, and attentive dutiful posture, except this one had a big black gun in a big black gun holster on his hip.

Ola led me by the arm past a conference room to a glass-walled garden patio that opened up to the sky outside. He took me down another hallway and through a little art gallery, past a series of guest rooms, an amphitheater and pool. Finally, I was brought to the master's bedroom, which was twice as big as my stateroom, including the balcony. Kristen sat on the edge of the bed, her eyes wide and searching, but surprisingly dry.

No one gets used to seeing a dead body, and seeing someone you knew dead is even worse—trust me. I could only imagine what level of shock Kristen was in with her husband murdered in the next room.

"Tony," she said. "Thanks for coming. Vincent is dead."

She lifted up her hands and showed them to me. They were covered in blood to the elbows.

I looked at Ola.

"She wanted to see you," he said.

"What can I do?"

"I have no one here, Tony," she said. "They think I killed Vince."

"Why?"

"We had a fight," she said carefully. "I went to bed. I thought I heard a noise and got up to see what it was. That's when I found Vincent."

I looked at the Security Head. The head looked back.

"She will be turned over to the police in Juneau," he said.

"But she said she didn't do it, and she's rich. Don't you have to believe her and do as she says?"

He shook his head. I could never figure out why laws worked on rich people sometimes and not others.

"Why do you think she did it?"

"Look at her."

"Why are you covered in blood?" I asked.

"He had a knife in his neck," she said. "I pulled it out. Blood squirted everywhere. I didn't know what I was doing."

"She admits to stabbing him," Ola said.

"I tried to stop the bleeding by putting the knife back."

"Seriously?"

"I thought it was like a cork," she said, and the first tear rolled down her cheek.

I couldn't help myself. I laughed. The tension and horror was too great, and the cork bit too unsettling.

She laughed too, first a giggle, then a laugh, then a cry, then she broke down completely and the doctor came in.

"Mrs. Bror said you were a family friend," said Ola while the doctor made her drink a glass of water and offered her a fistful of sedatives. I never got offered drugs when I was under suspicion for murder, and I'd had several chances.

"I killed him! I killed him!" Kristen cried.

I sat on the bed and held her.

"I didn't mean to," she said. "I was trying to help."

"Kristen," I said. "I know you're upset right now, but I think you should stop talking. Do you have a lawyer?"

"I've already called Salt Lake City," said Peterson. "Mr. Kline will be waiting for her in Juneau."

"I didn't do it," she said. "No, I did. I did do it."

Kristen broke down sobbing. Shaking, she clung to me for a long time, long enough for my shoulder to be wet with her tears, and my shirt rusty with Vincent Bror's drying blood.

The guy who'd given her pills slipped a blood pressure cuff on her arm and pumped away.

"Isn't there something more important for you to do?" I asked him.

"Nothing I can do in the other room, if that's what you're asking."

His English was perfect, familiar.

"Who are you?"

"I'm PMO Felix Reyes," he said. "Principal Medical Officer."

"Are you a doctor?"

"Yes."

"Then why not just call you Doctor?"

"I don't know," he said.

"Where'd you study?"

"University of Utah Medical School."

"No shit?"

"No shit," he said.

After a while Kristen calmed down and swayed unsurely on the bed like she was about to pass out.

"I'm so tired," she said. "I want to sleep."

"She'll sleep," said Reyes.

"She can't sleep here," said Ola. "I'll take her down."

"Down where?" I said.

"The brig."

"You really have one of those?"

"With six cells."

The armed guard accompanied Ola, Kristen, and me to the deep innards of the ship. There's a separate set of elevators for crew, and we took one of those down to deck three.

There were no floral-patterned carpets on the lower decks. The corridors were wide, painted metal, and labyrinthine. Even at that late hour, they were crowded with busy people pushing carts of laundry into cubbies and frozen bread dough into secret elevators.

Once out of the elevator and two steps around the first corner, I was completely lost and couldn't have told you if I was close to the front or back of the ship, port, or sherry. There were painted arrows on the walls, but they said unuseful things like "storage locker 307-320" and "Culinary A."

Kristen's eyes were closed as we led her into the security office. Ola looked at her skeptically.

"She's no good for more questioning," he said. "Let's put her in number one."

"Don't question her without her lawyer," I said. "She has a right to remain silent."

"We are at sea," he said.

"Aren't there laws at sea?"

"No Miranda rights here," he said, helping me put her on the bed. "But I can wait until tomorrow."

The cell was small but nicer than most I'd been in, if only for the fact that she had it to herself. There was a bed built right into the wall with a mattress and blankets. There were stainless steel bathroom fixtures within arm's reach of the bed, in case she woke up and wanted to brush her teeth without getting out from under the covers. There were no windows. The light bulb was behind a steel grate, and the door had a sliding peephole. And of course, it smelled like vomit. It was a jail cell after all.

"I'd like to clean her up," I said, looking at the blood.

"I'll get one of the nurses down here to do that," said Ola.

She was passed out and drooling before I could put a blanket over her.

"Felix gave her some strong shit."

"She has no body weight," said Ola, noticing I had plenty to spare.

The Security Head pulled the door shut and it clicked with that final metallic sound that all jail doors seem to possess. I followed him out of the cellblock and into his office.

He looked surprised that I'd come in.

"I'll have someone show you back to your room," he said with a sigh. "The Royal Danish Cruise Line respectfully requests you not spread rumors among the passengers about anything that happened here tonight."

"Oh?"

"Actually, we'd like you to put that in writing. I have a form here." He reached into his top right-hand drawer and pulled out a pad of printed documents, peeled one off, and started filling in boxes.

"So what's going to happen now?"

"Police in Juneau will take Mrs. Bror off the ship tomorrow at two. Mr. Bror's body will be taken too, and we'll sail at ten for Skagway."

I pulled over a chair and sat down. He slid the form in front of me with a pen. I looked at it but didn't really see it.

"What happened up there?" I asked.

"I don't know."

"Are you going to find out?"

He shrugged.

"Where are you from originally?"

"Aarhus. It's in Denmark."

"You start out as a sailor?"

"No. I was a policeman."

"How'd you get here?"

He shrugged again.

"Must be great working on a cruise ship," I said. "Always on vacation."

"It gets old after a month. Very tiring."

"You look tired," I said.

He lit a cigarette and looked tired.

"How long you been Security Head on the *Success*?"

"Only a year. Before this I was on a bigger ship, the *Westwind*, for three years."

"So the *Success* was a demotion?"

He didn't answer.

"And before all this naval stuff, you were a policeman in Aarhus. Is that a big place?"

"Pretty big."

"Nice?"

"Yes."

"Can I see the videotape of deck fourteen tonight?" I asked, hoping our new bond of familiar friendship would make him agreeable.

"No," he said.

"Why?"

"Two reasons. First, you aren't authorized. And second, the closed-circuit system is broken."

"Oh right. Perry said you had some kind of security breach before the ship sailed."

"Who's Perry?"

"Perry Whitehouse. The comedian you have here. He's a friend of mine."

"Yes, the comedian."

"What happened to your security system?"

"Sign the paper, Mr. Flaner, and go back to your room. This no longer concerns you. I don't have any more time for you."

"I'm not convinced Kristen killed her husband."

"It's not your problem."

"Is it yours?"

He shrugged.

"She asked for my help," I said.

"Mrs. Bror is not without resources," Security Head Ola Peterson said. "I wouldn't worry about it."

"Not worry about a murder charge?"

"Have you signed the form yet?"

"I'm looking at it."

"You seem like a smart fellow," he said. "I'll let you in on a secret. Crimes on cruise ships are notoriously hard to prosecute. Jurisdiction is hell to figure out. Add to that the fact that cruise companies hate bad publicity and will do everything in their power to avoid it. Passengers are dispersed after the ship docks. Crews turn over every eight months and live all over the world. Collecting witnesses back for a trial is all but impossible. If you want to commit a crime, even a big one like a murder, a cruise is the place to do it. Even if you're caught red-handed like Mrs. Bror was, it's difficult to press charges. It's a bad situation, but even if she didn't have millions of dollars, I'll be surprised if she doesn't get away with it."

"You say that like you think she did it."

"Yes," he said. "I think she did it. She wouldn't be the first."

"Boy, are you cynical," I said. "Maybe you really are a cop."

"Sign the paper, please."

"What if I don't?"

"Nothing," he said. "My superiors just like to have it."

"So they can threaten me if I make trouble?"

"Are you going to make trouble?" he said, lighting another cigarette.

"I like to keep my options open."

8

"WHAT THE FUCK HAPPENED TO YOU?"

I opened my eyes and saw Dara holding up my blood-smeared shirt.

"Oh, damn," I moaned. "It wasn't a dream."

"What the hell, Flaner?"

"It's not my problem."

"No," she said. "Looks like someone else had a problem, a big fucking problem on your shirt."

I rolled over and pulled a pillow over my head. I didn't know what time it was, but it was too early to start this day.

"Later," I said.

Dara went into the bathroom and I fell asleep. When I woke up again, I was alone, and the sun was up, though I couldn't see it through the gray clouds. I regretted not showering the night before. The maids would think something dreadful had happened in my bed. They'd probably seen worse and would file away the bloodstained sheets with the duct tape from the day before and come to their own conclusions.

I caught up with the gang at the ass-end of the boat having breakfast. They were all wrapped up warmly against the gray day, poking at scrambled eggs and sausages.

"Who died?" said Standard. Witty as always.

"I'm not supposed to say," said I. "Vincent Bror was killed last night in his suite. They arrested Kristen, his wife, for the murder."

"Judging from your clothes, they got the wrong person," said Dara.

"I met Ola Peterson," I said to Perry. "What a burn-out."

"Most are," he said. "Life on a cruise ship is crap. I'm getting sick of it myself, and I just got here, relatively speaking."

"Doesn't seem that bad," said Garrett.

"It's a dead end," Perry explained. "It's a place to end a career, not build one."

"So what happened to Bror?" asked Dara.

I told them what little I knew. Kristen and Bror had an argument, she went to bed, and she found him stabbed and then stabbed him again trying to help. "That's her story anyway," I said.

"You don't believe her?"

"I honestly don't know. I don't know Kristen, not really. Ola was pretty sure she did it. She looked like she'd done it. She confessed a little too."

"'She confessed a little?' Is that like being a little pregnant?" said Dara.

"Yeah, I guess so. But it's not my problem. She's being put off the boat in Juneau. Him too. His body anyway. People will meet her there, lawyers and cops and such."

"I bet they told you not to talk about it," said Perry.

"Yeah."

"They're going to hush this up? Wow," said Garrett. "What about public safety? There could be a serial killer on board."

"It really doesn't concern anyone but the people it concerns," said Dara.

"Well put," said I.

She gave me the finger.

"I had to sign something before they hired me," Perry said in a low voice. "I will be fired and possibly sued if I say anything derogatory about the cruise ship line or spread rumors or truths about what happens here that may hurt the company."

"And you signed it?" said Dara.

"I signed Tony's name. Not mine," he said.

"What?"

"I'd never sign anything like that," he said. "I forged your name. They saw a signature and took the form. I got the job. They didn't read whose name I put down."

"I don't think that'll stand up in court," Garrett said.

"It will," said Dara. "For fraud."

Perry's face darkened.

"I didn't sign it either," I said. "But if I get the chance again, I'll sign your name, Perry."

"You wouldn't dare."

"So you're messed up in this now?" said Garrett. "Can you leave the ship? Are you under suspicion?"

"No," I said. "I'm not involved. Kristen just wanted a shoulder to cry on."

"And a hand towel," added Dara.

"She'll be all right," I said. "She has resources, and I'm not sure she did it."

What I didn't say is that I wasn't sure she didn't do it either. I'm not above flattery, and I could be making more out of the kiss on the cheek than was there, but if I wasn't, that had been a serious pass. Kristen had been wistful in describing her marriage and she kept secrets from her husband, like the dinner coupons she sent us. Plus she'd had a fight with Vincent. I've done enough marriage work to know that nothing brings out the knives in people quite like a messed-up marriage. A family argument is the most dangerous place in the world. Cops would rather kick in the door of an Aryan Brotherhood crack house than go into an apartment with a domestic dispute.

But it wasn't my problem. Damn straight. I had my own problems, like why I'd let my imagination run away with Kristen when I loved Allie.

"What's the plan today?" I said.

"Juneau," said Perry. "Ten hours."

"I got us on some tours," Garrett said. "We're going to see a glacier, and there's some tram thing we can go up."

"Cell phone service?"

"Roaming charges, but yeah," said Perry.

"Sounds like a full day."

Americans as a group don't know shit about geography. Ask them where Ecuador is and half of them will turn a globe upside down and point to South Africa. Ask them which side the French were on in every single American conflict and you'll despair for the country. So, unless you ask a ninth grader fresh off his AP Geography test, you're unlikely to find many people outside of our 49th state what the capital of said state is. Alaska is the 49th state, by the way. Its capital is Juneau.

If you'd said Sitka is the capital of Alaska, you'd have been right about a hundred years ago, but really, you'd be wrong. Sitka was the capital until 1906 when it was moved to Juneau because Juneau has a long history of shady politics and excessive drinking. Sitka just couldn't keep up.

The story of Juneau's founding is characteristic. As Rome had Romulus and Remus, and Lewiston and Clarkston across the river had Lewis and Clark, Juneau was founded by two explorers, Joseph Juneau, called Joe, because he didn't have a sparkly coat, and Richard Harris who would later go on to play King Arthur in the 1968 Academy Award-winning adaptation of *Camelot*. I think it was the same guy. Maybe not. But that doesn't matter.

The story goes that in 1880 a German mining engineer called George Pilz, working out of Sitka, ran into a Tlingit Indian called Chief Kowee who said there was gold up in them thar hills, or something like that. Gold was on everyone's mind because if you were going to go all the way up to godforsaken Alaska, you'd better have a good reason and come back with something to show for it. Stories of gold were rampant, helped along no doubt by the local Indians' use of the metal to make bullets—lead being hard to find.

Pilz grubstaked the two explorers and sent them on their way with Kowee to explore up around the Gastineau Channel. When they got there, they found people there, Tlingit Indians: specifically, the Auke and Taku tribes.

Most people call Tlingits Eskimos, and most people are wrong. Not the same folk. Not at all. Tlingit means "people of the tides," which gives you some idea where they lived and the state of their footwear. Since they were among the last people messed with by white men, their numbers weren't decimated by smallpox and other European diseases until the late 19th century. If you've ever seen a totem pole, chances are it's Tlingit. That's what they are most famous for today, but back then, they had something even better to the white travelers: alcohol.

Harris and Juneau famously traded away their entire grub steak—blankets, kettles, food, rifles, girlie magazines, and playing cards for "hoochinoo," or homebrew. If you think this sounds like "hooch," meaning "home brew," you're on your way to being a licensed linguistic historian.

After a couple of sloppy months where they fell down a lot, threw up more and traded their boots for another round, they went back to Pliz empty-handed. "Nope. No gold up there," they said. "Do you have any aspirin?"

Chief Kowee, not wanting to look like a liar, insisted there was gold. He suggested they look at Gold Creek. They'd spent plenty of time at the bottom of it with the brewskies and party animals among the Auke and Taku but hadn't gone upriver.

It was a tight job market, so Pliz sent Joe and Rich back to look harder.

They followed Kowee up the river to Silver Bow Basin, and lo and behold, gold. Lots of it. Lots and lots of it.

Though they would later go back to Sitka with a thousand pounds of gold, the first order of business after finding it in the middle of frozen nowhere was to make up laws to benefit them, "legalizing" their claim in a lawless place. The day after the discovery, the two noble drunken founders of Alaska's one-day capital drafted "A Code of Local Laws." This established a 160-acre town on the beach which included just about all the available land that didn't require Sherpas to visit, Juneau being basically a delta between mountains that Sauron would find homey and a sea so nasty just dragging the bottom for crabs gets you the title of having "the most dangerous job in the world." What the Tlingits thought of the new laws and redistricting is unknown.

Joe Juneau couldn't write English, so Richard Harris, while wondering what the simple folk do, wrote up the document. That might explain why the town was originally called Harrisburg.

Hearing news of the find a month later, Lieutenant Commander Charles

Rockwell took his US naval vessel up the channel with the first gold stampeders. Now, maybe he was ordered up there or maybe he just went, but the fact remains that he got there and had a big boat with big guns. He made a lot of money, and the town was miraculously renamed Rockwell.

Thus began the Alaskan gold rush.

Rockwell, formerly Harrisburg, became Juneau in December 1881 when seventy-two town inhabitants voted to change the name. Juneau received forty-seven votes, Harrisburg twenty-one, and Rockwell four. Rockwell may have had guns, Harris the pen, but Juneau had booze and bought drinks for all the attendees and won. With lobbying like that, the town was destined to be the seat of government.

Awash in booze and questionable administration, Juneau was born and on its way to be a state capital. The oldest buildings still standing in Juneau today are, of course, bars.

Though the town was named after him, Joe Juneau moved to Dawson and opened a restaurant before dying there in 1899. He drank his money as fast as he got it, and a thousand pounds of gold just didn't go as far as you'd think.

A year after Joe died, in 1900, Congress dictated that the capital of the District of Alaska be changed from Sitka to Juneau, because Sitka was so last century. The real reasoning for the change is lost in backroom deals, politics, and absinthe binges, but six years later, in 1906, Juneau was the capital and Sitka became a footnote on a Juneau travel brochure.

Not much more happened to Juneau or Alaska until 1959 when the United States needed a forward missile base against the Ruskies and made it the 49th state of the Union. For the next half-century Alaska was the destination for military maneuvers and cruise ships tours, nature show hosts, and crab fishermen, outdoor adventurers destined to starve in abandoned school buses and the occasional drunk sea captain piloting single-hull oil tankers into ecologically fragile bays. Then in 2008, Juneau was again in the national news when Alaska's bubble-headed, scandal-ridden, half-term governor was named the Republican vice-presidential candidate ushering in the country's first black president. A Democrat.

Today Juneau is a big city if you just look at the many square miles the township claims. It's the second biggest city in the United States, the biggest not being listed in the guidebook I had access to. Juneau is bigger than Delaware and Rhode Island separately and nearly so combined. Its entire population, however, could each invite two friends and still not buy out the Rose Bowl.

Right on time and in a light drizzle, the Royal Danish Cruise Line ship *Success* sailed into Gastineau Channel and parallel parked on the dock between two other cruise ships. Already tied up and disgorging passengers were the Circus Cruise Line ship *Clown Car* and the Merriment Cruise Line's newest behemoth, the *Mirth*, which probably had an airfield on the top deck and its own gravity.

We couldn't see the town from where the boat tied off, but we sensed it because we saw a narrow road on the narrow bank at the bottom of the steepest damned mountain I'd ever seen that still had trees on it.

"That's where the tram thingy goes," Garrett said, pointing to the top of the ridge. "The Mount Roberts Nature Center. Here's your ticket."

I followed a cable from the top of the mountain down behind the *Mirth*. A tram appeared and traveled slowly upward. I guess it was technically a tram, but the incline was so steep that "outdoor elevator" wouldn't have been an off description.

"What's up there?" asked Standard.

"A view."

"Oh, okay."

"Eagles," I said.

"Maybe."

"No. There. Eagles."

Standing on the black wooden posts of the pier were two bald eagles. They just stood there looking majestic and surveying the activity like ambassadors at a May Day parade. The passengers went crazy with cameras and pushed us away and down the gangplank to get at them but only after we'd taken a couple hundred blurry pictures ourselves.

Getting off the ship was an exercise in fluid dynamics. I was told that the ship wasn't full up, but I'd have sworn it was now, maybe having ferried people over during the night just to clog up the hallways and steps leading out. Perry said he had to exit through another door and would wait for us outside.

We pushed our way forward, and I found myself behind Paul and Ashley Vinalez. The bodyguard was a little ways ahead and the manager, ever with a briefcase, was beside him. He was surrounded by pod people eager to be near the great man. In fact, we were surrounded by them.

"Tight as peas in a—"

"Don't say it, Flaner, or I'll punch you in goddamn yarbles," said Dara.

"You know, Dara, one day—"

I didn't get a chance to complete my sentence. My balance was disrupted, and I fell headlong forward down the stairs. Like a row of dominoes, I took everyone down around me. I grabbed Dara's arm and planted her face into somebody's back. My own chin struck Vinalez on his neck and he dragged his wife down, dropping the Nutri-Pod he was at that moment savoring.

Twenty of us surged and stumbled, but since the stairway was so crowded, no one was hurt, just more intimately introduced to their neighbor.

I'd gotten my feet under me in time, and only Ashley ended the push with her head lower than her feet. I saw the Nutri-Pod on the floor at the bottom of the step. It was a green one and looked like a squashed caterpillar with a conical hat.

"Sorry," I said and turned around to see where it'd all started.

Behind me, everyone stood staring. In front of me, everyone picked themselves up and apologized for lipstick smears on strangers' collars.

"That could have been really bad," said Garrett.

"Safety in numbers," said Standard.

"I blame you, Flaner," said Dara.

The crowds pushed by, around, and with us, and I scanned the faces for guilt or knowledge of what had just happened. I saw only glazed lemming stares of inconvenienced vacationers and pod-popping sycophants.

"Have a pod," someone said. "You had a close call. The garlic and cloves will settle you."

"I'm good," I said. But it was a lie. Not a moral lie, more an emotional one. Someone had pushed me. I was sure of it. There were so many people, so many faces and arms that I couldn't tell who'd done it, but someone had. Someone had reached out and put their hand on my back when I was on the steep stairs and shoved me. Had there been no one else on the steps I might have been killed. Hell, if there'd been fewer on the steps, several people could have died.

I worked in a hospital for a while. You know how in the movies people fall down stairs and it's funny? Well, it might be, I've never actually seen anyone fall down the stairs except just then, but I can tell you that the aftermath is not funny. Old people fall down stairs a lot, and if they're lucky they end up in the hospital with people like me offering them Jell-O on a plastic spoon. "Open the hanger, here comes the train." If they were unlucky, they didn't get my mixed metaphor eating routine, they got a dirt nap. Even young healthy lithe athletes died when they fell down stairs. Children, as rubbery as they are, might be the best to survive a stair tumble, but they're not immune to sharp right angles and gravity, just a bit more resilient. No—stairs are nasty. Stairs are dangerous. Stairs kill people.

I got to the bottom of the steps. I moved with the people out the open door, along the roped gangway, and into the gray Juneau sunlight.

My mind was on the stairs and the danger they posed. I felt my heart race with rage against them. Then, I calmed down and thought maybe I was being too harsh on them. Is it sane to be mad at an architectural convenience, no matter how many people it kills? I thought not. Instead I thought that stairs don't kill people, people pushing people down stairs kills people.

9

"I WANT to get a better picture of those eagles," said Garrett, circling around the parking lot.

"I want to get out of this crowd," I said.

"I hear you," said Standard.

"Hey, I forgot to ask you, Standard. How'd it go with your new girlfriend?"

"Not great. I bought her three drinks—three mixed drinks at the bar, on the ship, and only got her name and that she's from a town called Valparaiso, a port city on the Pacific Ocean."

"That's a big ocean," said Garrett.

"The biggest," said Standard.

"You're an idiot," said Dara.

"What's her name?" I asked.

"Camila."

"Nice name," said Garrett.

"She's out of your league," said Dara.

"How can you say that? You haven't even seen her."

"With a name that cool, she's out of your league."

Stan shook his head, but I could tell that he thought she was right.

"Did you get your precious photos?" I asked Garrett.

"They flew away. Too many people."

"There's Perry."

"And these are the buses we'll take to the glacier. Our tour leaves at five. We can't be late."

A row of tour buses was diagonally packed against the curb. Drivers with signs advertising their companies and destinations stood looking shell-shocked as thousands of people passed them.

"What about the tram?" I asked.

"Any time," said Garrett. "You can even save them and use them the next time you're in Juneau."

"How convenient."

Beyond the buses there were taxis and hired cars, bikes to rent, and more people holding signs advertising everything from free Wi-Fi with a minimum twenty-dollar purchase of Juneau Elk cheese, to full-body holistic massage with otters. People held signs up with other people's names, and others just scanned the passersby as if looking for a good mark. Two men in hunting fatigues, camouflage leaf patterns on their jackets, consulted a clipboard and watched us. They looked at Dara a little too long and received from her a finger and a "fuck off, you fuckwads," to which they blanched and looked elsewhere.

"I think we could get them to take us moose hunting," said Standard.

"You mean poach some," I said.

An ambulance sat as inconspicuously as possible near the pier, two technicians leaning against it, patiently waiting for the ship to empty to retrieve a body inside. My heart caught in my throat.

Perry had been to Juneau before and walked us along the touristy cruise ship strip mall beyond the docks.

If Garrett hadn't already arranged for tours onboard, we could have done it on shore. There were kiosks for whale watching and salmon fishing tours, bus tours to the glacier, bus tours to a fish hatchery, bus tours to a garden, to a restaurant, bar and brothel. We could pan for gold and hold a real six-shooter if we dared. We could visit the famous Governor's Mansion where Sarah Palin supposedly installed a tanning bed before vacating it to do whatever it is she does now. The touristy area was busy and lively. Although still surrounded by out-of-town tourists, I'd gauge at five hundred to one local, I was glad to be away from our ship. I was sick of the pushy pod people, plus my paranoia told me that someone on our ship didn't like me and had demonstrated their ill will with a hard shove down steep stairs.

We found a table at a cute cafe and ordered twenty-dollar cheeseburgers and drinks. I could see how a thousand pounds of gold wouldn't last long in Juneau.

While we waited, I excused myself and made the call. Allie answered on the fourth ring.

"Before you hang up or say anything terrible that I probably deserve but will hurt my feelings anyway," I began talking over her, "let me say that I haven't had bars on my phone and I haven't been able to call you until now. I'm hemorrhaging money, and I didn't know what to say anyway."

The message beep came on.

"Damn," I said. "Hi, Allie. It's me. I miss you. I'm sorry. I'll call you later."

My heart sank. I really wanted to talk to her. I imagined that she was standing right there in her kitchen where the old-fashioned tape-recording answering machine was. She hadn't wanted to talk to me. She was there, I told myself, and she didn't want to talk to me. In my imaginings I saw her laughing while she deleted my message, saying, "Loser" and "You don't deserve me."

And I thought she was right.

I called my ex-wife, Nancy.

"Hi," I said.

"Hello, Tony. Where are you?"

"Jou-know where I am?"

"Alaska?"

"Heard that one, huh?"

"What are you doing in Alaska?"

"I took a cruise. It's ten days. Stops all over the place. We're going to see a glacier."

"You and Allie?"

"No."

There was a pause.

"Are you two in a fight?"

"We are now."

"Because you took a cruise without her? Well, I don't blame her. You haven't the kind of money to go on cruises."

"It's worse than you think. I left without telling her I was going."

There was another pause, longer and more painful. Then she said, "And you called me up why?"

"I can't get a hold of Allie."

"Tony," she said with a sigh. "When will you ever grow up? When will you learn? When will you be responsible?"

"I've been meaning to get around to it," I said.

"Allie was the best thing in your life since I left it. What is your issue?"

"I don't know, Nance. I was hoping you could tell me."

"I could, but that's not why you called me."

"Why did I call you then?"

"So I could chew you out. You may be a thoughtless shit sometimes, but at least you have the good sense to know when you need to be punished."

"I thought we weren't going to talk about sex anymore after the divorce."

"Tony, I swear, I don't know how I put up with you."

"So you can't tell me what's wrong with me?"

"You're afraid of responsibility. You're afraid of commitment because you can't keep your mind occupied on the same thing for longer than seven months."

"That's an average," I said. It's true, though. Nancy had famously calculated the average lifespan of each of my many varied and ultimately abandoned careers. I'd averaged seven months per job for fifteen years. A similar number would apply to my hobby interests and most likely my laundry schedule if I hadn't had nice people helping me out.

She knew me. She was right. She was also right that I called her to be yelled at. I didn't like myself. I didn't like that I couldn't give Allie what she wanted. I didn't like that I'd been attracted to Kristen. I didn't like Kristen. I'd broken up with her, if I remembered right. A late paper that dropped my grade dangerously low. She wasn't prettier than Allie, not as interesting, not as fun or lively or wonderfully in love with me—which I found unbelievably attractive. She was rich, but if I cared about money, I'd probably have done something about it before now.

Listening to Nancy lament my adolescent ways got me thinking. I knew why I'd been attracted to Kristen: I'd wanted to break up with Allie. If I'd have gone all the way with Kristen, which I was probably humoring myself into thinking could happen, it would have ended my relationship with my Moab love as surely as me running off with an old flame on a sudden, and as yet unexplained to Allie, Alaskan cruise vacation. I'd never have been able to keep the secret from her because I have a big mouth and the guilt would eat at me. I'd be looking for punishment like I was with Nancy.

"Do you like Allison?" Nancy asked. "Do you love her?"

"Actually, Nance, I do. I think I love her."

She hmphed into the phone.

"Sorry, Nancy. You asked."

"I know I asked. It doesn't mean I like to hear I'm replaced. Do you want to hear about my—"

"No!"

"Well, figure it out, Tony. It's one thing to be irresponsible. It's another to be a jerk."

"Not always."

"Try to keep them separate."

"I will," I said, feeling all messed up and sick inside. Emotions and bile bubbling up like gumbo. "How's Randy?"

"He's trying to get the nerve up to ask a girl to a dance. He's got romance problems."

"What dance?"

"It's the end-of-year farewell dance."

"Oh, maybe I can help him."

"Please," she said.

"Oh. Right. How goes other things?"

"Funny you should ask. Didn't you do the divorce case with Tammy Peigne?"

"Yes," I said. "Her husband, or rather, her ex-husband is actually on the cruise ship with me."

"Small world. Well, guess who got the listing to sell their million-dollar home?"

"Marilyn Manson?"

"Me."

"And how's that going?"

"Tammy got a court order to sell the house. He wouldn't let her do it. Wants to live there one minute and complains about selling it in a slow market another. He just found out today."

"When today?"

"This morning. She got the notice, called him, and then called me to get it listed. She said he went nuts."

"You sound happy about it," I said, not joining in the enthusiasm.

"He's a jerk. Is there anything lower than a cheating partner? If there is I don't know what it is."

"Neither do I." I felt sick. "Is Randy there?"

"No, he's out with his friends."

"Out? Like outside?"

"No. Of course not. They're at some gaming convention. He said not to wait up."

"Tell him hello."

"I will."

"Thanks, Nancy. It's always good to talk to you."

"Call her, Tony. Tell her. She doesn't know you the way I do."

"I gotta go, my twenty-dollar cheeseburger just arrived."

"What? Hey, right, what are you doing about your money problems?"

"The usual."

"Dammit, Tony."

"Bye."

I rejoined my friends, feeling like a heel. I hadn't done anything really, but I still felt bad. I'd thought about doing something wrong, fantasized about it, even worked to make it happen, or at the least didn't resist it. It was a "crime in my heart." Stupidity with intent to harm. I'd have to pay for my thought crime. I let myself brood, hoping that I'd be over it before I talked to Allie. If I weren't when I spoke to her again, I was afraid I'd tell her. I couldn't see anything good coming of that for anyone.

The burgers were all right, nothing to write home about, but the fries were total crap. They dripped forty-weight through the basket and stained the table and concrete beneath.

"Twenty dollars for this burger?" complained Standard. Standard liked to complain. It wasn't the only thing he did, but it was one of the things he did best.

"Twenty-eight with drinks and fries," Dara reminded him. She'd had the kid's grilled cheese and saved five bucks.

"This whole 'all-inclusive' trip is going to break me," he said.

"Hey, have a heart," said Garrett. "Tony's in real financial trouble. You at least have a job."

"I could have a job if I wanted one," I said.

"You have two homes," said Dara. "Forgive us if we don't fall over crying in sympathy for your financial woes."

"Can't you rent one?"

"I'm trying," I said.

"Sell the one down south," said Standard. "No-brainer. What? No free refills!"

"That's what the sign says," said Dara.

"I can't sell the house in Moab," I said. "It has emotional meaning."

Dara said, "Emotions are overrated."

"So says the queen of psycho-therapy-inducing stand-up," I said.

"Hey, that's good. I'll use that." She wrote it down on a slip of paper and put it in her purse.

"The houses aren't the problem," I said. "Well, not all of it. It's the gift tax on the house that's a surprise. I'll get a loan or something. Maybe a mortgage. I'll be all right. I think. Once I get the house in Moab rented, I should be fine."

"You need to get back to work," said Standard. "Do the detective thing again."

"Work is a four-letter word."

"No it isn't."

"Actually, Stan, it is," said Dara.

"Not in that way. Give me a sip of your Coke."

"It's a suicide."

"Whatever. Give me some."

"The problem is I'm between two places, you know?" I said, spooning a french fry into my mouth. No point trying to pick it up, it'd just run between my fingers. "I have my Salt Lake City life with you guys and all my old haunts, and I have Moab with my family's house and my girlfriend. I'm torn between them. Why can't they at least be in the same geographical place?"

"Jesus. What is this?"

"It's a suicide. I told you."

"What is it exactly, Dara?"

"Coke, Sprite, root beer, iced tea, coffee, sugar and Splenda, a little cream, soda water, and Torani's melon-flavored syrup. It's all right there on the counter."

"It's not fair," I said.

"Shit happens, Flaner," said Dara. "Get over it. This is a good thing. You have a choice between two good things. Allison, who's nice and you say you like even though you don't communicate with her, and us, your friends, who're getting sick of hearing your bellyaching."

"I didn't bring it up."

"Whatever."

"We were talking about money," I said. "How much do we owe you for the tickets, Garrett?"

"Oh, nothing," he said. "I got them for doing that kid show."

"Easier than paying you," said Dara.

"It's payment," he said. "Good payment if you see how much these tours usually cost."

"Do you get paid in tours, Perry?" I asked.

Perry was being uncharacteristically quiet and I wanted his help to change the subject.

"Someone's watching us," he said.

"What? Who?" We all looked around.

"God, you guys are the worst," he said. "Over there in the parking lot."

"Isn't that the health guy from the boat? Xavier something?" We all ducked our heads.

"If he sees what we're eating," Standard said, "He'll give us a lecture."

"You've met him?"

He nodded.

Perry said, "Pilates."

"I hate that guy. He gave me such a guilt trip for eating cheesecake."

"Don't tell him which room we're in," said Standard. "I hear he'll personally wake you up to do calisthenics at dawn."

"Not him, you dolts. The other guy is watching us."

"Who?" I said, speaking under my arm.

"The guy by the rusted white truck."

"Which rusted white truck?"

"The one with a medium amount of rust on it."

"The one with more rust on the front or the back?"

"Around the doors," he said.

"Okay, we're down to four now. Running lights or not?"

"God, right there," he said and pointed.

We finally located who he was talking about. He was a tall stick of man in a white sailor uniform. He had an elephant standing on a ball on his cap where our officers had anchors.

Seeing that we were looking right at him, pointing in fact, he walked over. Walk is not the right word. Sidled over, strutted, or maybe slithered. In his hands I saw the cruise brochure from the *Success*.

"You're Perry Whitehouse, aren't you?" said the man.

He wore a crocodile smile under his pencil mustache. He was tanned as an old boot and his hair was either right out of a shower or the source of our French fry oil. He stepped in close right over Perry and glanced around with shifty eyes, keeping his bearish nose pointed straight at Perry. He reminded me of a vulture settling in over a dying prospector.

"Who are you?" Perry said. I sensed his paranoia was up. He's always going on about people following him. It's surprising how often he's right about that.

"My name is Carl Toover. I'm with Circus Cruises. I'm the cruise director aboard the *Clown Car*. How are you all doing tonight?"

"It's not night," I said.

"What's that you say?" he looked over the rest of us as if noticing we were sitting there for the first time.

"It's not night," I said. "Barely past noon. Afternoon would be more accurate."

"Yes. I see," he said never losing his smile. "Are you enjoying your cruise?"

We stared at him. He didn't expect an answer, and we didn't give him one. There was something unsettling and clandestine about the way he moved and talked. His shifting eyes reminded me of a Cylon but without the warmth.

"I hear you do the comedy act on the *Success*, is that right?"

Perry stared at him.

"I hear you're pretty good, is that right?"

"Do you know Dr. Gaius Baltar?" I asked him.

"What's that?" he said, not looking at me. "No, never heard of him."

"How about Apollo or Starbuck?"

"Just up the street," he said. "Look for the green sign with a mermaid."

He was right. There was a Starbucks just up the street.

"You're making scale on the *Success*, is that right? Just started there, right? Like your fifth time out now, isn't that right? Well, I can pay you more on the *Clown Car*, see? I'll tell you what I'll do. I'll pay you double scale and give you a 5K bonus right now if you jump ship and come over to the *Clown Car*. We can use a guy like you. You're really funny, I hear. Isn't that right?"

"I'm a comedian," said Standard.

"Are you working on the *Success*?"

"No."

"I'm not interested."

"Don't you already have acts on your boat?" I asked.

"Of course we do," he said. "All good ones, but we'll make room, right? I'll tell you what, Perry Whitehouse. If you don't want to come over to our side, you don't have to. I understand ethics and all that. I'll tell you what I'll do. I'll give you the five thousand signing bonus if you jump ship here in Juneau. You don't have to go back there, right? I'll even buy your ticket back to Salt Lake City. I'll throw in cab fare from my own pocket. How's that sound? Five thousand dollars and you're off buffet leftovers and back with the Mormons."

"What about us?" said Dara.

"What about you?"

"We're a team," Garrett said.

"I'm actually really funny," said Standard. "Ask anyone."

"Whatcha say, Perry, should I hire your friend? I could bring him aboard tonight, give him a lounge show right away. Or you two can work together. Your other friends can ride for free. I'll get you all a suite. Wouldn't that be nice? What do you say?"

"I can put together half an hour," said Standard.

"Wasn't it a Circus cruise ship that floundered off Florida for a week and the people had to crap in bags?" I asked.

"That wasn't the *Clown Car*."

"Didn't a Circus cruise ship just sink in the Mediterranean Sea?"

"Old news."

"Didn't I see the *Trapeze* in Seattle getting de-molded?"

"Who are you?" he said, finally taking his eyes off Perry and digging them into me.

"I'm Tony Flaner."

"Never heard of you," he said.

"He's a detective," said Garrett.

"Really? I thought you were a comedian."

"Only sometimes."

"And he's not always a detective either," said Dara.

"Well, Tony, I wasn't talking to you, right? I was talking to Perry, making a business arrangement with Mr. Whitehouse."

"He's not interested," I said.

"The man can speak for himself."

"Where's my juggler?" said Perry.

"Not living five to a room in the lower decks of a rat barge," he said.

"Get out of here," Perry said.

"The man spoke for himself," I said. For effect, I stood up and tried to look menacing. Dara stood up too, then Standard and finally Garrett. Perry was seething.

"I see how it is," Toover said. "I see what it's like. Think about it. Maybe I'll see you in Skagway. The airport's not as nice, but it'll do."

10

PERRY WAS THARN—THAT kinda over-extended, short-circuited, fight-or-flight, rigid palsy that happens to rabbits in the beams of oncoming headlights. 'Tharn' is a great word, invented by Richard Adams for *Watership Down*. It amazes me that it didn't exist before bunnies told Adams about it, and it surprises me still that not everyone uses it. Kids today.

Perry had summoned all his courage to tell Toover off and now that he was gone, the sleazy creepiness of the visit gripped him like a straitjacket. His mind had turned off.

"Tharn," I said.

"Delayed tharn," said Dara.

"Tharn," agreed Standard.

We finished our burgers and congealing fries while Perry's eyes watered up, staring into the middle distance.

"That was pretty creepy," said Standard.

"Still better than talking to the fitness freak."

"Oh yeah."

"Without a doubt."

"Lucked out there."

"How did he know my name?" said Perry.

"Yes, he seemed to know a lot about you."

"You're a public figure, Perry," said Standard. "Show business. Remember?"

"Oh, right."

Ever seeking cultural enrichment, after lunch we immersed ourselves in tourist kitsch. We wandered the souvenir stores admiring Chinese-made refrigerator magnets and shot glasses, T-shirts and pocketknives, snow globes, books, back scratchers, postcards, plush bears, eagle puppets, giant mosquito-shaped kites, Seattle smoked salmon, Mexican silver, African tanzanite and Caribbean larimar.

"Do you sell a lot of this shit?" Dara asked a bored Birkenstock-wearing clerk.

"Some."

"Are these stones a good investment?"

"That's what the sign says."

I looked closer at the sign and saw the little registered trademark circle after the phrase: "A good investment®."

"So it does," I said.

Allowing our personal portfolios to go 'larimarless' for the time being, we found a bar and ordered a round. Perry was still shaken up and nothing calms the nerves and erupts the stomach better than beer during a walking tour of Juneau's docks. The drinks were cheaper than on the ship but not by much. Standard swore up and down as we paid five dollars for a good local brew called "Joe's Grubsteak."

"Lighten up, you tight-wadded dick," said Dara.

"The mouth on you."

"Will never touch yours." Dara had a lot of occasions to use that comeback. I expected it. I'd heard it before. Many times.

The beer was cold and hand crafted. Not terrible at all. I considered buying a few for later, but Perry warned me off.

"They're going to search you before getting back on board. No booze allowed."

"Wait," said Standard. "Are they going to take my knife?"

Standard had bought a thirteen-inch antler-handled buck knife, just the kind of thing you'd need to skin a walrus. He wore it on his belt because it was fashionable in a Mad Max kind of way. The weight of it gave him a limp.

"No, the sword is fine," he said. "You can bring guns on and off the ship. Hunters do it all the time."

"How about uranium-enriched hollow-point cop-killer ammo?"

"Since they don't sell those on board, they're fine. Just no booze."

"Glad they got their priorities straight," I said.

"Do you think that was a real job offer? You think I could have gotten on that ship?" asked Standard.

"Please," I said. "He wasn't looking for acts, he was looking for Perry."

"But it could have been my big break."

"Standard, if you were any dumber, I'd have to water you twice a week. Circus is a joke."

"They're huge. They can't be that bad," he said.

"Every time you hear about some terrible cruise, it's Circus Cruises," I said. "They're the K-Mart of cruises, and K-Mart is suing them for the association from the grave."

"Do you think he was trying to sabotage the *Success*?" Perry said.

"Seriously? You're just getting that?" The beer had loosened my tongue. "History will judge me harshly for not killing you."

"When we first met, I thought you were nice, but boring. Now that I know you better, you're just boring," Perry said.

"Zing," said Garrett. "I wish Critter were here. He'd smoke you."

I was up. "Somewhere in this world is a tree that is tirelessly producing oxygen for you, and you owe that tree an apology for wasting its time."

"I'd love to engage in a battle of wits, but you're clearly unarmed."

"You're not being the person Mr. Rogers would want you to be."

A crowd was gathering.

"Your IQ would make a great golf score."

"You wouldn't understand if you stood under it."

"You fight like a cheesemaker."

"Your mother was a hamster," I began, and the crowd joined in, "and your father smells of elderberries!"

We were treated to a free round. Standard was moping.

"Perry, explain it to him," I said.

"The two cruise lines are in a feud," Perry said. "I was telling Tony that Danish swooped in and took the docks from Circus when the *Trapeze* got nabbed for mold violations. Circus has another ship ready to take its place, but Danish got the space since Circus is so badly rated."

"Who's doing the rating?" asked Garrett.

"Rating companies."

"Oh. Them."

After another round of Grubsteak, we headed to the tram ride.

"My head feels icky."

"Icky? Did Dara 'Dirty-Mouth' just say 'icky?'"

"Stan, I'm going to kick you so goddamn hard your grandkids will limp."

When we'd first gotten off the ship, the queue to the tram was out the door and down the street, it being the first "attraction" on the road to town. Hours into our Juneau experience, everyone had wandered off to find eagles and blue rocks to buy, and we had the platform to ourselves. A small group of people got off, some of whom I recognized from our ship, and then we walked right aboard. The car was large, the windows mostly clean. Empty Nutri-Pods littered the floor in what I could only hope was an innovate new marketing campaign and not blatant littering.

Tourist towns are always looking for new attractions to attract tourists. It's the game. The Mount Roberts Nature Observatory had the smell, feel, and usefulness of a gimmicky desperation ride to give visitors something to do while the town tried to figure out why it was still there, with the gold having run out long ago.

The nature we were to observe at the top of the mountain consisted of a souvenir shop, an expensive empty cafe, and a museum of taxidermy mistakes, though it wasn't called that. Outside there were trails and an overlook that overlooked the parked ships and the narrow road leading to town. On the other side, we could observe the other side of the mountain where we could satisfy ourselves that Juneau was indeed inaccessible by road, a feature it advertised like it was a good thing. Story goes there were only three ways into Juneau—boat, plane, or birth canal.

We saw bald eagles and we took pictures of them. A little farther on, we found more eagles and took pictures of them too. They might have been the same eagles, but they were pretty chill, so we took pictures of them just the same.

"Isn't that the pyramid schemer?"

Dara pointed up the trail to a group of folks at a gazebo. I recognized Paul Vinalez's entourage, his wife Ashley, the bodyguard, a couple of zealots with star-struck waxen faces, and the man who acted like a manager. The manager had blood on his face. They were being attended to by two helpers with ranger hats and blue latex gloves. He'd suffered a head injury. Those bleed like mad and his was plenty angry.

"What happened?" I asked no one in particular.

"Accident," said a ranger.

Ashley Vinalez stepped forward. She wore a pink "ski-bunny" snowsuit complete with bibs and a turtleneck. I sweated just looking at her, but she seemed fine, minus the boobs, her body fat index measuring in the negative integers. Her cheeks were pink and her eyes red with dilated pupils. She sniffed often, and though it could have been the cold, I suspected something with more perk at work. I'd never heard her speak before. Her voice was an octave higher than a goosed porpoise's.

"We were walking on the trail, the lower one just under the gazebo here, just minding our own business, you know, looking at the island over there and wondering how far it was and who'd live out here, the usual. We saw some eagles too. Those are so majestic. Majestic," she said again. "Majestic." She liked the word.

"And?" I prompted her.

"Oh, so we were walking and thinking that maybe we should go back soon because it might rain, but I was saying that the sky is always gray in Alaska, and it's the state color. That's pretty funny, isn't it? Gray is the state color of Alaska because the clouds. Get it?"

"And?"

"Oh, we were down there on that trail, it's so steep, even the trails are steep, but not as bad as the mountain, how can trees grow here, it's weird, isn't it? Don't they need soil? This looks like all rock. Maybe it's the rain."

"And?"

"Oh, some rocks fell on us. Smashed Mr. Sennegar on the head, and then we came up here and now here we are."

"Where was this?"

"Right below the gazebo there, see? If you look you can see the rock that hit him. I wanted to kick it down to see if it would go all the way to the water. What do you think that is? Ten miles?"

"A thousand feet." I saw a rock about the size of a cantaloupe on the trail. Half was dark with moisture and mud, but only half.

"So what's that? Two miles? I bet it would have gotten there."

A migration of tourists fresh from the trails behind the gazebo pushed their way forward to snap photos of the bleeding man.

"Was it a bear?"

"Yes," I said. "It was a bear. A bear with a rock."

"Wow."

Among the gawkers, I recognized Oscar, the woman who'd fallen overboard with the short haircut. She'd spiked her hair that morning. I thought that with a little yellow dye, a red shirt and blue shorts, she could pull off a first-rate Bart Simpson cosplay. "Can I help?" she asked. "I'm a doctor."

I could see the rangers' relief when she said that. I could also see that one of the zealots was squeezing a Nutri-Pod onto Mr. Sennegar's hair and trying to knead it into his scalp. "For infections," he said as the doctor pushed him aside. "It'll promote healing and cure his hair loss."

As she inspected the wound, a group of actual EMTs arrived and she backed off.

"Seen enough nature?" Perry asked.

"Yeah, it's time for the glacier anyway."

Joseph Whidbey became the first white European to visit the sliver of flat land later to be called Juneau, Alaska. In 1794, working as master of the *HMS Discovery* with George Vancouver himself at the head, and no doubt sick of the smell aboard the crowded ship, he went ashore to explore. He probably took a lunch. Whidbey noted in his log that there was a glacier stretching out of the mountains and far down the valley. He didn't name it. He'd probably run out of names by then, since they'd been exploring for nearly four years, or maybe he didn't want to name it; it being really just a big pile of snow. I mean, who names piles of snow?

Lots of people, apparently.

In 1888, when the area was being again discovered, if that's a thing, naturalist John Muir learned that the local Tlingit tribe, the Auke, called it "Aak'wtaaksit" which they said meant "the glacier behind the town." No one's sure if that was a proper name or they were just answering Muir's question about what that thing was over there. Muir didn't like the name, however, not having the patience or glottal stops to pronounce it and recorded its name as Auk Glacier.

Muir's locally inspired appellation didn't last long, though. In 1891, to garner political points, the glacier was renamed "The Mendenhall Glacier" after the then-serving Superintendent of The Coast and Geodetic Survey, Thomas Corwin Mendenhall. Not stopping there, they named the lake formed at the base of the glacier Mendenhall Lake. The creek leading out to the lake was naturally called Mendenhall River. All these things are still there today but the Mendenhall Clouds, Mendenhall Light Rain, and Mendenhall Frog Farts have been lost to time. If you're going to kiss some ass, kiss it hard.

Mendenhall is best known today as the man who has a glacier named after him. In his lifetime, he was a scientist and did work in weather and gravity that I don't understand so it can't be important. He's also the guy who finalized the border between Alaska and Canada. That's probably why he got the big snowdrift named after him. I'd like to think it was for that and not his work in stylometry, the pseudo-science of casting doubts on the authorship of literature and music based on the idea that authors never change their style. Mendenhall was one of the first to besmirch Shakespeare, floating the theory that Frances Bacon wrote all his plays. What a dick.

Besides literary libel, Mendenhall is also famous for the Mendenhall Order, which would finally bring the system of weights and measures within the United States away from the quaint English style of feet and ounces and into the modern metric system by the turn of the century. He was talking about the turn of the twentieth century, so you can see how well that went.

Our bus took us alongside the Mendenhall River up the Mendenhall Glacial Valley on Mendenhall Loop Road. The valley was full of houses and new neighborhoods where only two hundred years before there'd been a hundred feet of ice. I wondered if the homeowners had to get special glacier insurance. Glaciers have a history of moving, and if Mendenhall Glacier got uppity, it had only one way down—over those houses. Flat land being rare in the area, I guess people were happy to accept the risk to not have to rappel to work.

The bus ride was short enough to be tolerable and long enough to give us a rest. We were all still half drunk and at that horrible tipping point between tipsy and hungover.

The Mendenhall Glacier Visitor Center is famous for being the first-ever U.S. Forest Service visitor center built in the nation. This happened in 1962, so there's that. The toilets were nice, and I spent a long time admiring them before visiting the exhibits. From the helpful but crowded displays, I learned why the glacier ice was blue—the ice is compressed, how the sand beneath the glacier got to be so fine—it got compressed, and why the souvenir Blu-Ray adventure disk had so much more data on it than the older DVDs. Compression, is there anything you can't do? It was the keyword in the exhibit to be sure. We saw it everywhere as we were pushed and shoved and moved along by the compressed crowd shuffling between dioramas and interactive button-controlled displays. If I'd been a pickpocket, I'd have cleaned up. If I'd been claustrophobic, I'd have been going out of my fucking mind.

"I've got to get away from these people, Tony. I'm going out of my fucking mind," said Garrett.

Critter could have talked him down, but he'd been left on the ship. I grabbed Garrett's arm and together we made a beeline for what we thought was the door but was only a broken drinking fountain. A second attempt found us at the wild birds of Juneau environs display, and Garrett's teeth were chattering. At the third attempt we were downstairs and outside again. The air was cold and bracing, which was a great improvement from the hot, body odor-flavored atmosphere in the visitor's center.

Perry and Dara were already outside sticking quarters into a telescope to see the glacier.

There it was, across the lake, big blue and moving imperceptibly toward us or melting back out of existence, depending on your knowledge of current events.

"Look. Eagles." Out came the cameras.

"There's a path," Perry said. "We should take it."

"We have time," said Garrett.

We saw Standard hitting on a tan-skinned beauty by the soda machines.

"That must be Camila from the Pacific," said Garrett.

"You coming?" hollered Perry, gesturing to the path.

"Not yet," Standard said and winked.

"God," said Dara, disgusted.

Since mostly only Americans on all-inclusive butter-buffet cruise ships visit Juneau and the Mendenhall Glacier, there weren't many people willing to take the two-mile hike to the falls beside it. We weren't alone on our trek, but most of the heaving masses were left at the visitor's center.

I felt every extra pound of my flab a hundred yards in. The sand from the glacier, as I well knew, was fine as flour from compression, and the walking was hard. Since pride goeth before the fall, I soldiered on until, trying to leap over a stream, my legs betrayed me, and I fell in.

My friends didn't see it. They had left me in the dust and were far up the trail.

"Are you a'right?"

I looked up and saw the Oscar doctor from before.

"I'm good. Just tired."

"You need to lose weight," she said. "You're fat."

"Is that your professional opinion, or are you making small talk?"

She looked confused. "I'm a doctor. You're fat. You're not healthy."

"Gee, thanks," I said. "Any opinion on my heroin habit?"

"You're a junky?" her face twisted up in contemptible disgust, or maybe disgusting contempt.

She stormed ahead, leaving me to pull myself out of the stream and pray my socks wouldn't freeze.

Half an hour later, I met up with my friends and the curt doctor at the falls. They stood on a sand bar taking pictures and screaming over the din of the water. The falls had looked small from the visitor's center, and the glacier quaint. Up close, the falls were awesome and the glacier intimidating.

"Calving!" screamed Dara.

"And Hobbes?" I said, coming alongside.

"There you are! Did you fall in?" said Garrett. "Oh. Yeah. Looks like you did!"

"When the ice falls off the glacier, it's called calving!"

"Bullshit!" I yelled.

"You're an idiot!" she screamed.

"The sand tastes like salt!" I said.

"Really?" Dara scooped up some sand and brought it to her mouth. I pushed it into her face and ran.

Why I thought I could get away with that is beyond me. My legs were jelly, but I bolted toward the falls just the same, hoping my head start would save me.

"Mud eater!" I screamed.

"Here's some mud!" She picked up a handful and threw it at my back.

"Ouch!" I yelled. "That hurt."

I put my hand to my side. It was warm and wet. Sticky. Then I caught the smell.

"What did you do?" I asked.

"What the fuck?" said Dara.

I heard the buzzing of the next bullet before I heard the sound of the rifle's first one.

"Get down!" I yelled. "Shooter! Everyone get down!"

My friends hugged the dirt as I'd directed them. There's nothing like frigid glacial runoff mud to get the stains out. The other sightseers ran for cover. That's what I should have said. That's what I should have done: run for cover. Why hadn't I done that? Stress, I guess. But there it was, too late. Cowering there on the sand, soft as flour as it was, we were sitting ducks, and I'd already been shot once.

11

THE PHARAOHS WORSHIPPED it and the Romans bled to conquer it. The British tried to control it, and engineers fought to harness it. I'm speaking of course about denial. Is there a more powerful force on earth for missing the obvious? I think not. I pondered this lying on my belly, my love handle bleeding into the miraculously soft sand. My joke of making Dara eat dirt had naturally turned a hundred eighty degrees, and I was now inhaling it. I had time, however, to let the coincidences of the last couple days gel into a personal affront.

Someone was trying to kill me.

I call myself a detective sometimes. When I'm working, I model myself after the greats, Spade and Marlowe, Hammer and Rockford. Their literary examples have led me to murderers and buried treasure, drugs, spider-ridden video games, and a nice girl in Moab who isn't answering the phone for me right now. Those gumshoes have been good to me. I, however, have not always done my part in honoring their memory.

I can't see Philip Marlowe not having his spidey sense raised by a near-broken neck on a crowded staircase. Sam Spade might have made a mental note that the dead guy whose blood he slept in the night before, bore a striking resemblance to him and taken some kind of precaution. Mike Hammer, be he portrayed by Robert Aldrich, Robert Bray, Darren McGavin, Stacy Keach, Kevin Dobson, Rob Estes, Ralph Meeker, Mickey Spillane—the man himself, or anyone else for that matter, except maybe Daffy Duck, wouldn't be wetting himself while simultaneously kicking himself for not recognizing danger after all that.

I blamed the novelty of my surroundings. I've never been on a cruise before. Never been to Alaska. I must have thought all the weird stuff happening around me, and to me, I remembered, was all part of the grand Alaska vacation adventure.

"Hey, Perry!" I yelled.

"What, Tony?" came the sand-muffled reply.

"Does this usually happen on cruises?"

"No."

"Okay."

My theory was confirmed: I'd been in denial. I could blame Allie too, or my money problems, my ex-wife, the neighborhood watch committee, or my own innate slacker tendencies, but whatever the cause, I had to admit that my mind had been parked in neutral. It took a bullet to the gut for me to reach for the shifter. The clutch was down, my foot over the gas, and my hand on the stick. Something was not right on this cruise, and if I lived past this day, if I got off this glacier-softened sandbar, I might just have to look into it. That's right, world. I might actually do something.

"Let's get out of here," said Garrett.

"Flaner's shot," Dara said.

"I can run," I said.

"No, you can't. On your best days you're lucky to trot."

"Watch me."

I got up and loped for cover.

It felt good to be doing something. It was the right thing to do, and that felt especially good. Not only was I moving to a safer location, I was making myself a clear upright target pulling fire away from my friends.

"What the hell am I doing?" I screamed as I dove behind a tree.

I waited for the next shot. Nothing came. After five minutes, the others got up and ran to the bushes.

"Medic!" yelled Perry.

"This isn't 'Nam," said Dara.

"Right here."

The rude Oscar doctor who'd seen me fall earlier was there now.

"Hi again," I said. "I hope you're having a lovely day."

"What?"

"He's been shot," said Perry.

The doctor said, "He's in shock."

"No. He's always like that," said Dara.

The doctor examined me. "It didn't go in. It just grazed him. 'Grazed' is the layman's term. It would have missed you entirely if you weren't so obese," she said. "Can you walk, or should we get a wheelbarrow?"

"Oh. I get it," I said. "Because I'm overweight. You're making a joke about the wounded fellow being fat. That's wonderful! Perry, I found your opening act. Doctor Derision and the Suck It Up Orchestra."

"He's in shock," she said.

"Still no," said Dara.

"He's not fat," said Garrett. "Sure, he can lose a couple of pounds, but he's not that bad."

"He's raising insurance premiums for all of us."

"Who *are* you?" I asked.

"Doctor Phillips."

"Do you have a first name?"

"Why?"

"Why not?"

"It's Belinda."

"Oh, Belinda? That's a nice name," I said. "Go fuck yourself, Belinda."

"If you won't take your doctor's advice, I can't help you," she said.

"You're not my doctor until I've gone through every other doctor on the planet and most of the vets."

"What does his weight have to do with being shot?" said Garrett. "He's bleeding."

"Apply pressure. Diet and exercise," she said.

"Bring me a carrot and a treadmill and I'll close this wound right up," I said.

"Exactly."

"Let's get back to the bus."

With Perry on one arm and Garrett on the other, we moved back to the visitors' center. Dr. Belinda Phillips power-walked ahead.

"At least she didn't try to pour a Nutri-Pod into the wound," Perry said.

"Small miracles."

Rangers at the center applied a bandage over the graze and took a report. One was nice enough to give me a big white pill out of a paper envelope he kept in his pocket, "For those days when it just doesn't pay to be sober," he explained.

A policeman arrived, examined the bandage and took another report.

"Hunters," he said. "People hunting."

"So, what you're saying," I said, "just so we're on the same page, is that people who are hunting are called hunters?"

"Hunters."

"What were they hunting? Calves?"

"What calves?"

"Glacier calves. That's what it's called when a glacier breaks up like that. Haven't you seen the exhibit?"

"Badgers."

"No, calves. Ask a ranger."

"The hunters were probably hunting badgers."

"From across the lake?"

"Stray bullet."

"Bullets."

"Right."

"Are badgers in season?"

"Maybe."

"Well it's all all right then."

"Good. Okay. Sign this report acknowledging that all this was an accident and that none of it needs to be included in our official crime statistics or requires any further official attention. You also forfeit any right to sue."

"Officer?"

"Yes."

"Do you have a first name?"

The ranger who'd given me the pill volunteered to drive us back to the dock.

"You coming on yet?" he asked me.

"No."

"You musta' had a full stomach," he said. "It will."

"Can't wait."

Garrett said, "That cop was pretty mad."

"Never pass up a good call-back," I said.

Perry nodded. "Well played, but don't expect any help from the Juneau police."

"It's not about Juneau," I said. "It's about the boat. It's about the *Success*."

"You get shot a lot," said Perry.

"This is only the second time," I said. "I get beat up a lot."

"Who'd want to kill you?"

"I'm making a list."

"Standard was surprisingly absent," said Perry conspiratorially.

"I'll add him."

The *Clown Car* and the *Mirth* were already gone. The *Success* was readying to depart. Perry left us to enter the ship through the crew door. We got in line behind a Nutri-Pods cultist carrying a stuffed badger and a family of six wearing matching T-shirts that read, "Jefferson's Bible-Based Lawn Care and Barbecue—Demopolis, Alabama."

Noting the badger, I said, "You hunt that today?" The pill was taking hold.

"No. It's a souvenir."

"Lucky for you."

We took our turn to be manhandled, body searched, screened, scanned, and sniffed for alcohol. They reluctantly let us aboard but only after they'd peeled the tape off my side and examined my wound. I may have been hallucinating from pain and blood loss, but I think they tasted it for alcohol.

"Mr. Flaner?"

A thin man in blue slacks, navy shirt, and a baby-blue tie waited for me beyond the security checkpoint.

"Who are you?"

"I'd like to talk to you."

"I'll ask the questions around here."

"I didn't ask a question."

"You didn't answer one either. I said, who are you?"

"I'm Mr. Kline. I work for the Brors."

"Do we have to be here for this?" asked Dara. "I'm beat."

"We'll stay if you need us to, Tony," said Garrett. "But if you don't, I'd like to hit the buffet before it closes."

"It never closes," I said.

"I still don't want to be here."

"Fair enough. Tell Critter hello."

My friends boarded an elevator, and I regarded Mr. Kline.

"You're the lawyer," I said.

"And you're the detective."

"Do you have a cigarette?"

"No. I don't smoke."

"Neither do I."

"I don't follow."

"That's the way I like it," I said. "Now spill the beans. Who sent you?"

"I told you. I work for the Brors."

"But Vincent Bror is dead, or don't you read the papers?"

"It hasn't been announced yet. It just happened."

"Ah-ha!" I said.

He stared at me. I stared him back. Blood ran down my side and into my pants. My head spun in colors. I pushed the bandage down and winced. The tape that had closed the gash was loose.

"No more games, flatfoot," I said. "You're here to shut me up, right? You've got some form or another, some contract? An offer I can't refuse. What's the deal?"

"Is there someplace we can talk?"

"I can hear you just fine."

"Washy-washy!"

"Not again," said Kline.

"Stay calm," I said. "They can sense fear."

I offered my hands and got a squirt of disinfectant hand sanitizer in each. The giggling attendant saw the caked blood in my palms, giggled again, and gave me another squirt. Then she assaulted another passenger. "Washy-washy!"

"Maybe Mrs. Bror should explain. I'm not doing very well."

"I'm sure you're used to it."

"Let's go."

"Buy me dinner first."

"What? No. To the brig."

"Already greased the coppers, eh?"

"What? No. Mrs. Bror is in the brig. She wants to talk to you."

"Bullshit. She was taken off this morning, right after her husband's body."

"Mr. Bror was flown to Salt Lake, but Mrs. Bror has asked to remain on board until Seattle. She wants to see you."

"She's still on board? Stuck in the brig? Why would she want to spend a week in that tiny cell? Why would they let her?"

"She's rich."

"Which question is that an answer to?"

"All of them."

"Turn around," I said. "Just do it. Put your arms up against the bulkhead. Do it."

He did. It's amazing what people will do if you just tell them to "do it." Nike did their research.

I frisked him. I'm not very good at it, I admit. Mostly I just smeared blood on his chic blue outfit. So he'd know I was serious, I forced myself to jostle his junk and prayed to God that if I felt anything hard it would be cold steel and not hot flesh. I wanted to intimidate, not masturbate. But he was squishy and unarmed. His wallet confirmed his name, height, age, eye color and donor status—not a donor. Typical lawyer. He had five hundred dollars in fifties and a business card I'd seen described in *American Psycho.*

"Lead the way," I said.

He knew the way. He passed through a door marked "Crew Only" and then down a stairway to deck three. He found his way quickly to the security office through the maze of white-walled, conduit-decorated corridors, something I wouldn't have been able to do.

He knocked on the door, and the man I'd seen the night before with the big gun opened it.

"Where's Security Head Ola?" I asked.

"Bright Star," he said.

"Okay, where's Security Head Bright Star? I didn't know he had a nickname. I'd think he'd be more 'Burned-Out Forty-Watt' than 'Bright Star.' Is it ironic?"

"'Bright Star' is the code for a dead body," he said.

"Another one?"

He nodded and opened the door to Kristen's cell.

"Tony!" She hugged me.

"Ouch."

"What happened?"

"Same ol' same ol'," I said. "I got shot."

"Why?"

"I'm not sure yet. Why are you still here?"

"I asked to stay. I can't leave yet. If I leave, everything falls apart."

"But that's good, isn't it?" I said. "If the case falls apart, you go free."

"What?" she said. "Oh, not you too, Tony."

"I didn't mean it like that," I said. "It's a mess but you'll be all right."

"But what about Vincent?"

"What about him? He'll be dead. No matter what, he'll still be dead."

"Someone killed him, and it wasn't me."

"I didn't mean to imply you had." Or had I? Either the ship was moving, or the pill had entered my inner ear and was rearranging furniture. I sat down on the bed beside her.

"You have to believe me. I need you to believe me. I need you to help me."

"What do you need me to do?"

"Find the killer, of course. I've got to hire you. There's something wrong on this ship."

"I'm coming to the same conclusion."

"So you'll take the case?"

"I'm already on it," I said. "I made the decision this afternoon while eating dirt and bleeding into glacier runoff."

"Good. Great actually. Whoever killed Vince is still on this ship."

"You're still here."

"I had to stay," she said. "I can help you."

"You're in the brig."

"I'm not powerless. I can help. I can pay you. At least a little. Once the will is read, I don't know."

"Why don't you know?"

"The last will I saw had very little set aside for me."

"Who benefited?"

"Tommy's Place. It's a poverty assistance organization."

"Never heard of it."

"You will if they get all of Vince's money."

I called in Mr. Kline.

The lawyer poked his head in the cell. The door had been left open. No one ever left doors open when I was in jail.

"Do you know about Mr. Bror's will?"

He hesitated not because he didn't know the answer, but because he wasn't sure if he should say anything. All lawyers answer questions like that. It's why fast-food employees so frequently punch them in the mouth—"You want fries with that?" "I'll get back to you after a consultation." Pow. "Next."

"Answer him," Kristen told him.

"I'm not sure about confidentiality."

"Vincent is dead. It's a simple question."

"Tell him."

"Do it," I said.

"Yes, there's a will."

"Has he changed it recently? Is Tommy's Place still getting all the money?"

"Not all of it."

"Bryce?"

"It hasn't changed since he showed it to you. But you'll get a generous annuity. You'll be comfortable, but not rich."

"So money isn't the motive," I said.

"Money's not a motive for *me*," said Kristen. "You're not doing a very good job of convincing me that you think I'm innocent."

"Sorry," I said. "Detective 101, find out who benefits from the will, and you have motive and usually the murderer. Does Tommy's Place know about the endowment?"

Kline said, "No."

"How can you be so sure?"

"I'm sure. Vincent was adamant about it. I'm actually surprised he told Kristen."

"Why?"

"I don't think—"

"Do it."

"Because," Kline said. "He was going to divorce her."

12

HER EXPRESSION REMAINED calm and determined, unshaken by the news.

I took in the changes since I'd last seen her. There was no longer blood on her hands, which is more than I could say. Her hair was neat and her makeup straight. She'd changed clothes and was now wearing what I'd call "vacation casual"—clean, sensible, and comfortable clothes in layered cotton pastels. Her toilet kit had been brought to her, and a suitcase was tucked in the corner by the sink. A washcloth was taped over the window slit in the door to give her some privacy. It was good to be rich. And the door was still open.

I said to her, "You're not surprised he was thinking divorce?"

"I don't know. Things weren't good."

She struck me as mature, calculating, and a little world-weary. She didn't have a smoldering cigarette at the end of a long holder or shadowing backlight, but I recognized her as the femme fatale she was.

"Do you think that gives me motive?" she said.

"Some might think so. Lovers' quarrels don't need much to get ugly. Trust me, I know."

"But I loved him."

"It wouldn't work any other way."

"Tony," she said. "You have to believe me. I didn't do it. At least I didn't start it. I might have killed him by accident, but I didn't put the knife in to begin with. You have to believe me. You have to approach this as if I'm innocent. You're right. We were married. We had problems. We didn't always get along. We argued a lot recently. We argued the night he was killed. Emotions were high. They often were. I'm sure that any first-year prosecutor can put me away. I need you to believe me so you can find the real killer."

She reminded me then of another time when I'd given nearly the same speech. I wondered if I'd sounded as hollow as she did now. Probably.

"You'll get off," I said. "Even if you did it—which you didn't—you'll be all right."

"But what about the murderer? Should he get away too?"

"So you're publicly minded?"

"Why are you being so difficult? You already said you'd look into it."

"I'm investigating now."

"Oh? Yes, okay," she said. "I'm being interrogated. All right. I loved Vincent. But why should it be strange that I want to find the killer?" She wrung her hands in her lap. "Maybe it is part public safety. Maybe it's part vengeance. I don't know. Why does it matter so much?"

"I don't know. I'm just curious."

"That's it," she said. "I don't know. That's why I need you find out who it was. I need to know what happened. How can I go on not knowing?"

It was the best reason anyone had ever given to hire me.

"I can see that," I said. "I'll do what I can. But this is only a ten-day cruise and we're already three days into it. If I don't solve it by the end, all the clues and suspects are gone, spread out over the world."

"Thanks, Tony. That'll be enough."

"You hope."

"I hope."

"I'd like to see the contract before she signs anything," Kline said.

"Are you still here?" I said. "Beat it."

He left.

"Oh wait," I said. "Mr. Kline."

He came back.

"When did you get to Juneau?"

"This morning around ten. I waited for the ship to come in."

"Do you hunt?"

"What?"

"Can you operate a rifle?"

"I've bagged my buck every year for the past twelve," he said.

"And badgers?"

"What?"

"Never mind. You can go now," I said. "Do it."

It was a little chilly in the room, but I was feeling the happy pill the ranger had given me. My side was warm and soggy but didn't hurt. My mind was surprisingly focused. The room was slightly rubbery, I'll admit, but I could handle that. I'd been to Vegas.

"So what were you arguing about?" I said. "On the night he died."

"I don't know," she said.

"You said you could help me."

"All right. Uhm," she began. She took a deep breath. "He was anxious.

Angry. Something had upset him at dinner, I think. I asked him what it was, and he was evasive. He said his money wasn't well spent. Then he said something about a coincidence. He'd been drinking a lot, and I could see he couldn't focus. I challenged him to explain what he meant, and he told me to mind my own business. He called me a 'gold-digger' and I left. I went for a walk on the deck and then I came back to the suite. He was gone then, so I went to bed. I was asleep before midnight. I woke up to noises and found Vincent with the knife in his neck. That was around two-thirty."

"Could he have been upset about me?" I realized how narcissistic that sounded only after the words were out.

"Maybe," she said.

"Really?"

Awaken O Narcissist! Behold the world really does revolve around thee! Or is it thou?

I'm not immune to flattery. In fact, I'd go so far as to say I'm susceptible to it, like a moth to napalm. I think girls are used to compliments and attention, whereas guys, the typical pursuers in modern romance, are naturally suckers for it, and I'm the worst of the breed. For me, it doesn't have to be actual flattery. Blasé interest is enough to muddy my thinking. It comes from having low self-esteem, a surprisingly common trait among sarcastic attention-seekers like me. I married Nancy because she said she liked me. My mind turned off when Allie said she loved me. My detective skills were dulled by the suggestion, the barest hint, that Kristen held a torch for me. Hell, she'd remembered my name. How was I supposed to deal with that kind of aphrodisiacal distraction? I had to try, though. I had to remove myself from the equation because I was a detective on a case. I was a trying to find a murderer and I'd been shot. I felt my side to make sure the bandage was still there and to help me focus. The bandage, like my focus, had slipped. I recovered both as best as I could.

"You told Vincent about me?"

"I told him I'd run into you," she said. "I'd mentioned you to him before."

I hadn't forgiven myself for not remembering Kristen's name. This didn't help.

"Was he the jealous type?"

"He never needed to be. I'd never given him reason."

I wondered if the kiss Kristen had given me the other night would have given him reason.

"It was on the cheek," I said out loud. I do shit like that surprisingly often. Before I had to explain my Freudian undergarments, I said, "Tell me about your marriage."

"We would have been married nineteen months this week," she said. "We lived together for seven years before we got married, mostly in an apartment so small and run down it'd need a remodel to be called a dump."

"That's a good line," I said.

"I stole it."

"Who from?"

"From you," she said. "I caught one of your open mic's a couple years ago, before I was married. You were good."

I didn't say anything. I didn't know what to say. My mind did a nice loop-de-loop and left me dizzy. The ship shifted under me. The walls wobbled. I forced myself to refocus. I summoned the ghost of Sam Spade and said, "Go on."

I am so good.

"Vince worked at the university and got his degrees. After I got mine, I tutored and flipped steaks for a while. We got by. Then the patent hit, and money wasn't a problem. It all happened so suddenly, like within three months we were juggling car payments and rent and then we had a house and two cars all paid for."

"Good for you."

"No," she said. "The money was bad. It ruined our marriage. It ruined Vincent."

I brushed my side and felt fresh blood pooling down my hip. It didn't hurt, so I ignored it.

"Remember how I told you how generous he was? How he always had a positive attitude? It didn't survive the money."

"I've heard money can change people."

"He was generous at first," she said wistfully. "But then…well, he'd grown up poor and had needed help sometimes. He hated to ask because he told me he seldom got it. Tommy's Place was there for him after his brother died, but there weren't many others. Still, at first he gave to charities and would hand out hundred-dollar bills to those guys under the onramps holding cardboard signs."

"When did he change?"

"It wasn't sudden," she said. "It was a general shift. He grew hard and hateful. He began to remember all the people who hadn't helped him when he'd needed it, when he'd had to swallow his pride and ask for it. That hadn't happened often, but it had happened, and it was the only time he told me he ever actually despaired. Those same people who didn't or wouldn't help him now appeared, he said, asking for favors and handouts. It infuriated him."

"I can see that."

"I could too, but it got worse. He became brooding. He stopped talking about the future and was fixated on the past. Instead of planning the lives ahead of us, he would dwell on how it was when he was growing up."

"Depression?"

She shrugged. "After brooding came secrecy. He stopped talking to me about how he spent his time and after a while I stopped asking. Six months ago, I asked to go on this cruise, and I was surprised when he agreed to come along. He appeared excited at first, but then didn't seem to care. He went back to doing whatever it was that took all his time, and I shared my excitement about finally seeing Alaska from a luxury cruise ship with my Twitter followers and Facebook friends. Hardly a substitute for a loving husband."

"He seemed alright at the dinner," I said. "At first, anyway."

"I don't mean to paint him as a monster. He was a nice guy, and what I'm telling you wasn't out in the open. I doubt Kline knows any of this."

"I bet he does."

"What I'm trying to say is, he wasn't a bad guy. I sensed the change, but I knew him better than anyone."

"Why'd you come see me perform and not say hi?" The detective in me had run out of questions so I let the insecure attention-starved juvenile have a turn. I blamed the pill.

"What? Oh, I was engaged," she said. "And you were married."

"Ah," I said.

The cell became cold. I shivered and felt woozy. I felt moist. I might have been sweating. I tried to concentrate on what Kristen had said about her husband, but my mind was focused on trying recall the show she might have been at.

"Tony?"

"Uhm," I said, snapping back to the present. "I thought I saw Vincent pale at dinner. Did you see anything? You had a better view of everything up there by the captain."

She got up and got herself a glass of water from the sink.

"I don't remember seeing anything unusual. A lot of people coming in, those crab guys, a bunch of Nutri—blood."

"Pods," I said. "Nutri-Pods, the innovative nutritional dietary supplement everyone is talking about."

"No!" she shrieked. "Blood everywhere! You're bleeding. You're bleeding bad."

"Badly. Adverb," I said. "It's okay. It doesn't hurt." I was so dizzy. "Let me lie down here for a second."

"Help!" she cried. "Why didn't you say something?"

Kline appeared in the doorway.

"I'm okay," I said. The look on Kline's face suggested he didn't agree.

I lifted up my arms to see my side. It was pretty red. My shirt was soaked with blood, some of it new over the half-scabbed supply I'd gotten on the glacier. My pants too. Kristen would need new sheets. Maybe a new mattress. A new room wouldn't be out of the question. A power washer would take the stains off the deck. Yes. It's called a deck here, not a floor. I felt the blood. It was warm and sticky, and I was light-headed.

"Guard!"

Kline and the nice security guy picked me up and carried me away.

"I'm all right," I said. "Just a graze. I'm a detective. I'm used to this sort of thing."

"This way," directed the guard. We took a turn and walked past anxious-looking employees with trays of food and armfuls of towels. I expected a minotaur to leap out at any moment. I stopped trying to keep up and let my feet drag on the floor.

"He's passed out," said Kline with some alarm.

"No, I haven't. I'm just lazy," I said. "She came to my show, and I didn't even remember her name."

13

THE INFIRMARY WAS clean but compact, like the rest of the ship. It reminded me of a storage locker but with beds and two round porthole windows through which I saw dark ocean and occasionally bright white foam.

"Why didn't you go to the hospital in Juneau?" said Principal Medical Officer Felix Reyes.

"Just a graze," I said. "In my love handle. Someone gave me pill. It's working. I don't feel a thing. You have lovely eyes."

"You need stitches," he said.

"It's just a graze. Doctor Belinda looked at it."

"Who's Doctor Belinda?"

"Doctor Belinda Phillips. She was there. She said it was just a graze. She's a bitch."

"Oh yes, she is," he said. "You need stitches."

"They taped it up."

"You've bled a lot. What's your blood type?"

"Are you proposing? Don't read too much into that beautiful eyes remark. What am I saying? My mother always wanted me to marry a Principal Medical Officer. I accept."

"Blood type?"

"Oh, I'm positive I can give blood. That's what I say." I don't know why, but that was just too funny, and I broke into hysterical laughter.

A sour-faced female Filipino intern about four-foot-three peeled me out of my clothes. She looked like the evil stepmother of the giggling squirt squads roaming the ship. She unwrapped alcohol swabs and went to work on my flab.

"Washy-washy!" I said.

She scowled.

There were three beds in the infirmary, and with me, all three were occupied. I recognized the man from the tram ride lying on another bed. His head was wrapped in white gauze, and his gown hung open to reveal his Fruit of the Looms. The third bed I could only see between the narrow opening of a drawn curtain. A figure lay there unmoving under a pulled sheet.

"Bright Star?" I said.

"Yes. Mr. Kirby passed away."

"Foul play?"

"Mr. Kirby? No. Not at all. Heart attack."

"Those can be faked," I said.

"He was ninety-two."

"Who benefits from his death?"

"What are you, a detective?"

"Actually, I am. Hey, what gives with all the needles?"

"Blood infusion," he said. "Can't you deduce that?"

"Don't you start. I got the ghost of Mickey Spillane calling me a dimwitted muttonhead."

While Reyes worked on my side, the surly gnome scrubbed down my arm.

"Washy-washy!" I said. Nothing like a good call-back. "Ouch! Are you using a needle or a lawn dart?"

Now she was smiling. "Ready," she said to Reyes.

Reyes hung a bag of what looked like raspberry Jell-O from a steel hook and threaded a tube from it into the already-bruising pipe in my arm.

"I'm going to anesthetize your side with a local. It'll make suturing easier."

"What fun."

"Who shot you, if you don't mind my asking?"

"I don't mind," I said, wincing with each little pinprick. Love handles are as sensitive as the people who have them. "I just don't have an answer. The local constabulary, a.k.a. the Juneau tourist board protection squad, said it was badger hunters."

He snorted and stabbed away. "And they wouldn't take you to a hospital?"

"Didn't even come up. I made them mad."

"How?"

"It's what I do. I had to bum a ride from the Forest Service guys to get back to the dock."

"This may have been a graze, but it'll take five stitches to close. Eight if you don't want a scar."

"Chicks dig scars," I said.

"Okay."

Reyes sewed me up and topped me off with O+. I thought the pill was wearing off, but my equilibrium didn't agree. Then I remembered I was on a ship.

"Rough outside?" I asked. The ship usually rode so smoothly you could stack cards.

"A little," Reyes said. "We should miss the worst of the storm. Should."

Reyes' assistant covered me up.

"Blanky blanky," I said.

She scowled.

"Lie back. I'll get someone to take you back to your room in a little bit."

"Okay," I said.

The guy on the next bed stirred. He made to get up, thought better of it, and reached for a stainless-steel bedpan from a table. He relieved himself and held it out for someone to take. No one was there. He put it back on the table.

"What's your story?" he asked me.

"Attempted murder victim," I said. "You?"

"Same."

"Really?" Reyes had left me a cup of ice chips to munch on. I'd have preferred a beer and another happy ranger pill. "I saw you up on Mt. Roberts. I heard it was an accident."

"I doubt it."

"Go on." Sam Spade was in the house.

"Are you in the Garden?"

"Do you mean do I push vitamin pods to my friends in a multi-level marketing scam that is illegal in every state but Utah? No."

"Good."

"Go on."

"I work for Paul Vinalez, you know?"

"I do, actually. I saw you with him."

"This is the third time I've taken a hit for him. I'm through. I'll take my options and go. Not worth it."

"When were the other two?"

"Brakes in December," he said. "Fire in March."

"Go on."

"I was taking his car to be detailed. Someone cut the brake lines. Zoom—down the end of Wasatch Boulevard," he said. "That's a steep road in Salt Lake. Utah."

"I know it. I live in Sugarhouse. And Moab too. Sometimes."

"Small world."

"Yup."

"Second time. The bus. Someone lit a fire under the Nutri-Pods Good

News Vitamin Energy Bus during a publicity tour. I was the last to get out. I was sleeping."

"Someone's trying to kill Vinalez?" I said. "You're kidding."

"Look at my head. Does it look like I'm kidding?"

"No, it looks like you're concussed."

"I am that."

"I'm Tony Flaner," I said. "I'd shake your hand, but you just pissed on it."

"I understand," he said wiping his fingers on his gown. "Adam Sennegar. Glad to meet you."

"How long have you worked for Vinalez?"

"I was there for the Cedar City condo fiasco and the end of the used car thing."

"Go on."

"I should keep my mouth shut," he said. "He'd kill me if he heard me talking out of school."

"I thought you were quitting."

"I should," he said.

"Couldn't the car and the van be coincidences?"

"And the rock?"

"And the rock."

"It could, but it's not. I don't think so, and neither does Paul. You see that bruiser he hired? That's a bodyguard. A real one. Not just for show."

I'd never thought of anyone hiring a bodyguard as a status symbol, but it made sense, in a paranoid, tough-guy celebrity kind of way. Kind of the male equivalent of a pocket dog. If a non-rapper were to have one, it would be someone like Paul Vinalez. He oozed slime.

"I take it the condo deal left some unhappy investors." Land scams were as common in Utah as pyramid schemes and nearly as profitable.

"Oh yeah."

"Used car buyers too?"

"And wholesalers."

"Nutri-Pods Garden folk?"

"They're coming."

"Someone on board doesn't like him, you think?"

"Looks like it," he said. "Someone sent coffee to his room. It spooked him."

"He doesn't drink coffee?"

"He took it as a threat from some old Colombian investors," he said. "I should shut up now. The hand that feeds me."

"And gets you clobbered."

"Seems so."

"What floor is Vinalez staying on?"

"Deck."

"Deck," I said.

"He and his fifth wife are staying on fourteen."

"That's interesting," I said.

"Denny and I are on five," he said. "Inner cabin. It's like a tomb."

"Denny?"

"The Gold's Gym alumnus. Vinalez's guard."

The conversation ended then when he made a dramatic gesture meant to indicate something important and upturned his bedpan.

He screamed like he was covered in snakes, but it was only piss. People came in looking for vipers and dealt with him until the room stank of antiseptics and I fell asleep.

When I woke up, I was unplugged and my clothes were on the chair. Mr. Sennegar was still on his bed, but the curtains were opened on the third one and it was now unoccupied.

I put my pants on but that's all. Carrying my shoes and second blood-soaked shirt of the trip, I wandered past the sleeping assistant into the hallway. I nearly turned around when I ran into the ship's fitness engineer Xavier Polates coming out of a supply room, marked in black spray-painted stencil. He backed out and pulled the door shut nearly walking into me. He smelled like cat pee.

"Eh, man. Will I see you on deck at dawn?" he said when he saw me. "Just the thing to lose the pounds you'll put on at the buffet, eh?"

"I was shot."

"Eating right and exercising will speed your healing. A jog around the deck and a few pull-ups and you'll be a new man."

"I'd have to be," I said. "I'm injured. There was a bullet involved and everything. See the blood?"

"Excuses are the devil's hors d'oeuvres."

"You weren't burdened by an overabundance of schooling, were you?"

"I attended the University of Cartagena."

"I'm sure that hors d'oeuvres phrase sounds better in Spanish."

"No, it sounds pretentious."

"I thought you were Jamaican."

"I get around, mon."

"Can I ignore you another time? I'm busy right now."

"Procrastination is the devil's favorite carbonated beverage."

"Is carbonation good or bad?"

"It's the devil's own flatulence."

"What's the fastest way to leave you?"

"There's stairs over there but it's Crew Only."

"I want an elevator."

"That way, but it's Crew Only too."

"How about a passenger elevator?"

"Doesn't come down this far."

"So I'm stuck?"

He pinched up his face in thought. "Wait," he said. "You shouldn't even be here. Why are you here?"

"What are any of us doing here?"

His face blanched. "I'm crew." He pointed to his name badge.

"Your elevator doesn't go all the way to the top floor, does it?"

"I think it does," he said. "Wait. Are you insulting me?"

I could think of no answer that wouldn't prolong the conversation or lead to a duel with medicine balls at dawn, and I sure as hell was not getting up that early.

Without another word I left him and followed the corridor a couple of yards until I found the elevator. It opened when I called it. Two crew members looked me over as I got in but didn't say anything. I pressed nine and up we went.

I was all turned around. I consulted a map and realized I was on the wrong side of the ship and set off to find my room. At a cross hall, I saw the Bible-Based Lawn Care guy sleeping against an ice machine. I adjusted his ball cap and noticed the time, half past three. It was late.

Following the decreasing room numbers, I eventually got home. I searched my pockets and possessions for my room key but couldn't find it. I was debating the merits of knocking and waking Dara versus cuddling up with Bible-Based when a door up the hall opened and a tall redhead quietly backed out. She carefully held the handle as she closed the door to minimize the sound of the lock catching hold. Like me, she held most of her clothes in her arms, her underthings and shoes included. She wore slacks and an untucked blouse. She leaned over to pull one shoe on and noticed me.

I smiled.

She smiled back.

"I'm locked out," I said to break the awkward moment.

"Oh," she said. "Wait a minute."

She slipped on her other shoe and walked up to my door.

"This it?" she asked.

I nodded.

I put her in her mid-twenties, with tussled red hair and green eyes. Her makeup had been "rearranged," and she was missing an earring. By her accent she was Australian. By her physique, a bikini model.

"This is your room for sure?"

"Yes."

"You should alert security about your missing card. You don't want people charging on it."

"Okay."

She snapped open her purse and took out a keycard. She slid it into the lock and the light went green.

"There you go," she said and winked. "If I find out this isn't your room, you'll regret it."

"Okay."

She turned and disappeared around a corner. I pressed the door open and stepped into my room.

Of course Dara was in the big bed. She was curled up with a Louisville Slugger. I dropped my clothes and threaded my way to the other bed. There was a folded-towel bear on it. It was adorable. There was also someone in my bed. Goldilocks looked a lot like Garrett and in the dim reflected light of the sea, I felt Critter's appraising plastic eyes on me from the pillow.

"Move over, Critter," I said. "You can explain in the morning."

14

"STAN KICKED US OUT. I had your key from before and just kinda fell asleep waiting."

"You didn't even get a look at her?" said Dara.

"No," said Garrett.

"I smelled her, though," said Critter. "She reeked of perfume."

"No, I smelled that too," said Garrett. "That was Stan's cologne."

I shared a worried look with Dara as Garrett and his hand agreed to disagree on the origin of the strong floral scent they'd both encountered the night before with Standard Flox, gentleman playboy, and last night at least, room hog.

"You should have just waited in the hall. How long would it have been? What? Two minutes, and he's done."

"I didn't want to sleep in there after that."

"Maritime cooties are the worst," I said.

I pushed fruit around my buffet plate and sipped coffee. Garrett and Critter had bagels and lox. Critter didn't like capers, so Garrett had scraped them off.

Dara had three plates in front of her. One with a ten-inch stack of waffles, oozing with butter and syrup, another was overflowing with bacon and sausage, and the last had fried eggs, hash browns, muffins, and even a salted kipper. She wasn't eating any of it. She was instead surreptitiously sliding the plates closer to me when I wasn't looking.

"Why are you doing this to me?" I said, forcing a cube of cantaloupe between my teeth.

"What?"

"You gotta keep your strength up," said Critter. "All that blood loss."

"Oh yeah," I said. "Right."

Dara's face lost its color. "No. Think of Allie. Think of that doctor. You have to be strong. Avoid fatty foods. Don't touch these. These are mine."

I took a piece of bacon, and staring into her eyes, I ate it.

"I scoff at you and your attempt at temptation torture," I said. "Bwahaha!"

"Drama queen," she said.

"How are you going to do this?" Garrett asked. "You only have a couple of days and then, like you said, everything's gone."

"Yeah, but at least now I'm starting with a manageable list of suspects."

"How many?"

"A little less than three thousand."

"That's manageable?"

"I usually start with three billion. I'm ahead of the game."

Dara said, "You shouldn't make promises you can't keep."

"Are you talking about Kristen, Allie, or me?"

"All the above."

I pushed the bacon plate away and ate some grapes. "I gotta get to work."

"This better not screw up our vacation, Flaner."

"Yeah, I got some more passes for a tour in Skagway," said Garrett. "You gotta come."

"We had to fight for them," said Critter. "That grabby brat ratted us out after I threatened to suck out his eyeballs if he touched mine again."

"What happened?"

"Dara saved us," said Garrett.

"I told the cruise director that he'd tried to look up my skirt and nearly got him thrown off the ship."

"Did you even bring a skirt?"

"No," she said.

Garrett said, "Whale watching in Skagway. You'll love it."

"I gotta get to work."

In the center of the ship was a large open area meant to thrill new arrivals with the grandness of the boat. A chandelier big enough to be used as the ship's anchor hung from betwixt the tenth, eleventh and twelfth decks. A winding stairway looped around it, granting access to bars, non-inclusive restaurants, tour planners, concierge services, and of course, shops. There was a big open area at the bottom that could be transformed into a stage for quiz games, karaoke, lounge music, and marketing. Later that night there was to be a "Glamorous Exploration of Tanzanite and Other Luxurious

Investment-Grade Precious Stones" presentation with a drawing for a larimar necklace and "deals galore." Today, however, it was Nutri-Pods.

The previous seminar had been by invitation only, a pep-talk/strategy meeting/brainwashing session for the already indoctrinated. Today's program was a full-on infomercial and recruitment drive. It included music and a slide show, free samples, and of course the energetic and charismatic Paul Vinalez himself.

I'd missed the start of it for breakfast, what little of it I'd had. I found a seat on an upper deck where I could look down on the gathering for an effective and poetic vantage point. I ordered an iced tea with aspirin and scoped out the scene.

On the enormous screen, enormously pretty people showed their enormous happiness with enormous smiles in what I recognized to be a slideshow of the most used stock photos on the internet.

"Health and happiness, the building blocks to the good life, all begin with a pod," said the disembodied voice-over to raucous applause.

A spotlight set up on the deck above me came on, swept the area like it was looking for escaped convicts, and settled stage-left where Paul Vinalez burst out of the wings waving his hand like he was on *The Tonight Show*. I noticed Sandra, the cruise director, with her ever-present clipboard holding open the curtain for him. The screen filled with the scene as a video camera captured the moment and projected it larger than life behind him a moment delayed. While the camera zoomed in, the screen became one of those infinite mirror illusions, each nested scene a second or so behind the last.

Vinalez trotted up to the microphone stand and grabbed hold.

The lights went out. He dropped the microphone like it was hot. Like it had shocked him.

A moment later the lights came back on, and a technician brought out another microphone.

"Your body is made of elements that are stored and spent like food," Vinalez said after clearing his throat.

I've been zapped by a microphone before. Once at Barry's nightclub there was a frayed cable and a spilled beer. I completed the circuit and wet my pants. Urine is a good conductor by the way, and my hand was not the only thing injured that night. I'd run off stage. I had to admire Vinalez going ahead the way he did, with hardly a hiccup. He should have made some reference to the mishap, a joke to break the tension, but I got the feeling he wasn't good at ad-lib.

"When the body spends its nutrients, it must replace them. Will it replace the squandered resources with straw, sticks or brick?" he said. Three pigs and a wolf appeared on the screen. I rolled my eyes.

The pod people held back for the most part, allowing potential customers/marketers to have the seats, but I could see a few were seeded in among them to start the applause and fill the empty seats so it didn't look sad.

My vantage point allowed me to focus on the audience as much as the stage, and I scanned the faces, looking for killers. I had to start somewhere. My little chat with Mr. Adam Sennegar the night before had given me a possible lead: Bror had been killed on accident and the real target had been Vinalez. He'd said there'd been several attacks already. I realized then, like a slow-witted stoned narcoleptic sloth, that I might just have witnessed another attempted murder on stage.

"Coincidence?" I asked my tea.

"Coincidence is something killers want detectives to believe in," answered my drink.

"God, I'm talking to myself," I said to myself. "I'm becoming Garrett."

"And Critter."

"And Critter," I agreed.

"Shhhh," said Bible-Based Lawn Care at the table next to me. He and his wife each had two margaritas and were trying to watch the show.

I saw Standard take a seat in the back beside an attractive tan woman. He tried to put his arm around her, but she shrugged it off and he retreated. He said something to her, and she laughed. Knowing Standard, I figured her for a professional.

I looked for Mr. Sennegar, but he wasn't there. The bodyguard was though, sitting with Vinalez's fifth wife, Ashley. He sat very close to her in fact. Too close for modesty. Not quite the same chair, but nearly. Judging by the restless leg syndrome, I could see from where I sat, that they wanted to share socks.

I saw the doctor who'd told me my weight was responsible for my gunshot wound and I hoped she'd fall off the ship again. Then my attention was drawn to two restless Hispanic guys in the back. They kept mostly in the shadows behind the crowd but moved in nervous circles in front of Abbie's Jewelry Emporium. One of them pulled out a smartphone and tapped into it.

They might have been Colombian hitmen, or they could have been ship waiters on their off day. I kept my eyes on them. Security Head Ola Peterson also had them on his radar. The ship's chief cop was on the deck above mine, watching the crowd as I was. I waved to him. He pretended not to care. He did a good job at it. He had me convinced.

I did my best to tune out Vinalez's sales pitch when he began referring to marketers as "gardeners sowing pods of goodness." He sucked down two or three of the things during the presentation like they were orgasmic heart pills. He did a yellow, blue, and a red—all the primary colors. Behind him, images of multi-cultural health-crazed photo models flashed on the screen, broken up by the occasional scene of waving corn, nuts, berries, tubular roots, and happy Hispanic laborers at the Nutri-Pods plant.

I watched bored passengers wander in, sit down, look interested, lose interest, glance around, get up, and leave with regular frequency. A large contingent of elderly people took up a quarter of the seats. Some slept, some read. A couple knitted. They were dressed somberly for a cruise, I thought, but then remembered Mr. Kirby, the Bright Star, and understood.

I kept my eye on the two guys in the back. They stayed for the entire tiresome, cliched, stock-photo-laced, hard-sell, jingoistic sales barrage and never took a seat.

Just as it was wrapping up, I nearly spit the last of my tea over the railing when a couple wearing "Tommy's Place" sweatshirts sat down.

"Try it for yourself," said Vinalez. "We think you'll agree. The future of goodness is Nutri-Pods!"

There was applause, some enthusiastic, some polite, some sarcastic—that was me—and the event was over. Ushers directed the soon-to-be sickened audience to the free-sample table. By the time I'd gotten down, the crowd was too thick, and I couldn't see the people in the sweatshirts.

I stood on a chair looking for them but couldn't see them among the freebie frenzy. I think it was a man and a woman, both with short hair, but I couldn't be sure. My detective skills were as good as ever. The two men who'd been watching from the back were gone too, or at least were not where they'd been. There was a mass exodus from the lobby led by the patient and polite who had been unable to bring themselves to walk out once they'd been caught looking—the very kind of people whom the Nutri-Pods gardeners were taught to hunt down and make feel uncomfortable in their own living rooms, vowing silently to themselves to never accept another "neighborly" visit from anyone ever again.

I got in line behind a Florida couple anxious to unleash the power of aloe root and ginseng on their unsuspecting Tallahassee Baptist brethren and sisteren and reap the Ponzi benefits.

"It'll cure Belle's gout."

"And Rosalyn's hernia."

"Don't forget Trevor's bulimia," I said. "And Peggy's SAT scores."

"Gladys' kids?"

"You betcha."

I was handed a six-pack of assorted food coloring bottles of differently vitamin-enriched goodnesses. I slid it into my pocket for later disposal and brushed my wounded love handle. The pain reminded me of the personal nature of my investigation, and my mood turned to shit.

"Mr. Vinalez," I said. "Paul. How are you? I'd like to ask you some questions."

"I know you," he said. "We met the other night. You're the jack-of-all-trades."

"You heard that, huh? Well, today my trade is detective and I'm jacked about a murder that happened on your floor. The fourteenth floor, where your room is."

"Deck," said half a dozen people.

Sandra, with clipboard in hand, fluttered toward me, then turned and hurried away.

Ashley Vinalez extricated herself far enough from the guard to say, "Detective? What's this about?"

The question was picked up by the crowd. There couldn't be more than a couple hundred within easy ear shot. They all grew quiet, so I shot.

"Vincent Bror, a passenger on this ship, was murdered the night before last in his suite on the fourteenth *deck*," I said. "I'm Tony Flaner. I'm a detective. I'm making inquiries."

I wasn't a cop but I knew how to act like one. I'd been watching *Inspector Morse* reruns lately.

"There's a murderer on the ship?"

"Are we safe?"

"Who died?"

"Murder?"

"Did he say 'making inquiries?' Is he British?"

"Tosser."

"Stuck-up git."

"Really, Mr. Flaner," Vinalez said. "Can't this wait?"

"Now works for me."

"But not for me," he said. His eyes were dark and angry, his skin shiny from onstage exertion and secreted eel oil. He was working, signing up new converts, and I was upstaging him. It was a tactless, inappropriate move on my part, and I wasn't going to give it up so easily.

"Where were you on the night in question?" I asked.

"Denny," he said. "You can make an appointment with my man, Denny?"

"Why not Mr. Sennegar?" I said.

His eyes flashed on me, and his alligator smile returned. "We'll talk later, Mr. Flaner. Excuse me now."

He shook my hand and pushed me along. I counted my fingers to make sure he hadn't lifted one. I felt the strong hand of Denny, the steroid-enriched bodyguard, on my bicep, pulling me away.

"You're not the police," I said to him. "You have no authority over me."

I felt fingers curl around my other bicep. "No, he's not, but I am."

"Ola!" I said and snapped my fingers.

15

"MR. FLANER," Ola said. "Why do you do this?"

"You told me to sit here. I thought I was doing you a favor. I'll go."

I got up to leave the security office but was pushed back in my chair by one of the two crewmen flanking the door behind me.

I said, "So who narced on me? Cruise Director Sandra?"

"We all have our jobs to do," said Security Head Ola Peterson, doing his job. "I asked you not to start a panic."

"Did I cause a run on pig-belly futures? I'm sorry. Did you get caught short?"

"I can tell you're going to be a nuisance," he said, steepling his fingers. "We don't have a lot of patience for nuisance passengers."

"Who's 'we?' You got a mouse in your pocket? Or maybe a rat. I've seen a few in the halls."

He smirked a pained little grimace that told me I'd struck a nerve.

"Did you notice we have six cells in the brig?" he said. "Only one's being used right now. You could be in one of the others. You could talk to Mrs. Bror with Morse code on the walls. How would that be?"

"Is this part of the all-inclusive package?"

"What is wrong with you?"

"What's wrong with *you*?"

"Childish."

"I know you are but what am I?"

He leaned back, weaved his fingers together and cracked his knuckles. He sighed, "I know Mrs. Bror has asked you to look into her husband's death."

"Actually, she hired me. I'm on the clock. I'm getting paid to deal with you."

"Then we are the same."

"Only if I cut six inches off my penis and you triple your IQ."

A guard chortled behind me. Ola threw him a look that said the brig would house crew as well as passengers.

"Why are you trying to antagonize me?" he said.

"Habit," said I. "This is rerun. It's a cliché—cops warning off private detectives. Are you going to give me the 'jurisdictional lecture' or the 'ongoing investigation' spiel?"

"I'm going to give you the 'don't make trouble' speech," he said. "Again."

"An oldie but a goody. And still another rerun. If you lock me up, I'll have your guts for garters."

"There's a difference, I assure you," he said. "Last time I asked you as a gentleman not to alarm the passengers."

"That was your first mistake."

"You've done nothing technically wrong, so I won't put you in the brig. I'm confident you will though, and I'm asking myself why I don't just lock you up now."

"Because you're a burned out, lazy ex-policeman haunted by the past?"

"What? No."

"Just burned out and lazy then?"

Another sigh. "The captain has given me great license in how I deal with you. I can have you thrown off the ship in Skagway. I can have you taken off the ship now if I wanted to. We are not so far from shore that a helicopter could not be here within the hour."

"A lot of hassle for just little ol' me," I said.

"Not if it protects the line. You're upsetting the passengers. You're hurting our image. Passengers come back and cruise again. They can tell their friends and share photos of their wonderful trip. Alternately, they can complain about unsafe ships and vermin and write negative reviews that can cause some people to get fired and ships to lose their dock space. The line knows this. They'd sooner push you overboard than let that happen."

"Was that an actual threat?"

"No, of course not. It was a metaphor."

"Danish police are different," I said. "I'll give you that."

"I don't want anything from you but your cooperation, Mr. Flaner. If you can be discreet, I welcome your investigation. Mr. Kline has assured me that whatever you discover will first be brought before the captain and the line before going forward."

"He doesn't speak for me," I said.

"He assured me he did. If that's not the case, then you leave me little recourse."

"Let me just go tell Mrs. Bror that you're throwing me off the ship, and I'll go pack my bags."

He squinted at me. I squinted back.

"I will throw you off the ship if you continue to alarm the passengers."

"Okay, maybe I handled that badly down with Vinalez. Using the 'M' word so much. Murder," I whispered in case he wasn't keeping up. "I'm sorry. I'll buy you a donut. Danish cops like donuts too, right? Or do they prefer Danishes? Dumb question?"

"I'd expect nothing else from you."

"Ooo, trying your luck with me in a battle of wits? You brought a melon to a gunfight."

"What does that even mean?"

"Like I'd tell you."

He smashed his hand onto the desk.

"Mr. Flaner, Mrs. Bror is not the only VIP on this ship. Mr. Vinalez and his company are spending a lot of money on this cruise. I cannot allow you to bother him or his efforts. Hecklers will not be allowed."

"What heckling? I waited for his medicine show to end and then talked to him."

"The 'show,'" he said, making air quotes, "as you well know, was not over. You did what you did. You deliberately antagonized him. Tell me, does that kind of behavior work for private detectives in *Utah*?"

I didn't like the way he said Utah.

"It might," I said. "Sometimes."

"Mr. Vinalez was in his room when the murder took place," Ola said.

"How do you know that?"

"I checked the door records. He opened his at 12:45 am, and it didn't open again until 3:15 when I personally talked to him."

"How do you gather door records?"

"The locks are all controlled via computer. They send out signals. We don't need hard wires."

"Which room is he in?"

"That doesn't concern you."

"Okay, I'll go ask him."

"14508."

"Is that on the port or the left side?"

"Port and left are the same. Port and starboard, left and right. His cabin is on the left side."

"Which side was the Brors'? 14500?"

"Port side, but up front."

"Next to Vinalez's, though."

"No, there's a room between them."

"Is his room as nice as the one the Brors had?"

"It's a courtyard suite, not a villa, so no. Not as nice."

"Smaller?"

"Yes."

"How much?"

"A tenth the size."

"So the size of my cabin?"

"Three times that."

"What about larboard?"

"That's port too. Archaic."

"Do you know how to tie knots?"

"Are you going to behave, Mr. Flaner?"

"I thought you said the security system was down. How'd you do the key thing?"

"The camera systems are out." He gestured to the wall of black screens. "The key locks are functioning."

"What about the one in the elevator?"

"What do you know about that?"

"I saw it was trashed the night you took me up to the suite. If I remember right, we rode right up without a keycard. You could have gone to deck fifteen too. What's up there, by the way?"

"Deck fifteen by that elevator is another block of suites. Empty this trip. As for the elevator key reader, that has been repaired."

"How about the one on the Brors' suite? Has that been fixed?"

"You are observant," he said. I hadn't been. It was a hunch. Detectives are all about hunches. I was hitting my stride. "It too has been repaired."

"Same kind of damage?"

I could see the wheels in his blond viking head spinning.

"You'll have an easier time with me if you play nice," I said.

"I should throw you off the ship."

"Whoa there, Thor. I thought you were a cop. There was a murder on your beat. Aren't you at all interested in why and by whom? If only for an intellectual exercise, let alone the fact that it's your fucking job?"

"Don't curse."

"Oh, shit. Did I curse? Fuck me, am I right?"

"My job, Mr. Flaner, is to keep the peace. I'm not a detective. I'm a policeman."

"Come on. You got people dying left and right. Bright Stars all over the place. Vincent Bror, Mr. Kirby. I was shot, Sennegar was bouldered."

"People die all the time on cruise ships. It's nothing new. Mr. Kirby was very old. He'd died *in flagrante delicto*."

"More Latin. Do I need a priest, or can you translate?"

"He died during sex. We have a witness. No foul play. Just a ninety-year-old man going out with a bang."

"That's a good line," I said. "But really, Ola—can I call you Ola? You should say yes because you know I'm going to no matter what. But really,

Ola, don't you think this cruise is a little out of the ordinary? People may die all the time on ships, but millionaires with a steak knife in their necks has to be rare."

"Again, not as much as you'd think. But you have a point. Mr. Sennegar said someone might be after Mr. Vinalez and Mr. Vinalez confirmed that he's received threats."

"Someone tried to kill him today."

"What do you mean?"

"The stage show. He could have been electrocuted. Or are you saying that the lights-out air-raid drill during the Nutri-Pods show was a coincidence?"

"It might have been. I don't know about it."

"Maybe you should look into that. I'd like to know what you find. Now tell me about the keys. What time did the elevator go out?"

He sighed. "The last key signature we had was from Mr. Bror just after two o'clock."

"So the vandalism happened after that."

"No. The card reader was still recording, it just didn't lock out the upper floors. It could have been done earlier."

"That's not a lot of help."

Ola shrugged.

"What about the door on Vinalez's room? What does that tell us?"

"Mrs. Bror can't be sure that the lock hadn't been vandalized when she came in. She says she was upset. She used her key just after midnight. The next actual key insertion was Mr. Bror's, but the door was effectively unlocked once the vandalism occurred."

"Where was Mr. Bror between twelve and two?"

"He spent some time in a bar, some time on deck, some time in the casino. Nobody saw anything unusual."

"You questioned the passengers?"

"I questioned the crew."

"How is it you repaired the two locks but not the cameras?"

"We're still working on the cameras."

"What broke them?"

"Wires were cut."

"You're telling me you can fix an electronic magnetic computerized key reader, but you can't splice wires? I thought they taught you knots?"

"They were cut multiple times. In multiple places."

"How many?"

"I don't like discussing this with you," he said. "I'm not sure I have the authority to, and I know I don't have the inclination."

"Do it," I said, summoning the old ways.

"We have discovered two separate sites so far. There is obviously a third."

"Why do you say separate?"

"Different locations in the ship. One was cut with a knife, and the other looked to have been done with wire cutters. That last one actually removed three meters of cabling."

"Hardcore."

"A slight inconvenience," he said. "I have men. The crew's on alert. Nothing can happen."

"That line might have worked a couple days ago, but it's a hard sell now, don't you think?"

"The passengers are safe."

"What about—"

"The *Success* is as safe as any other city."

"But there's a killer out there."

"As any other city," he said. "Besides, I don't believe Mr. Bror was killed randomly. The rest of the passengers aren't related and so aren't in any danger. Don't you agree?"

"I don't have enough facts to form an opinion," I said. "But don't let that stop you."

"Would you have me evacuate the whole ship? Ruin the vacation of nearly two thousand people? Really, Mr. Flaner, this is not my first murder."

"How many have you committed exactly?"

"You are tiresome."

"But funny," I said. "Okay, maybe he wasn't killed randomly. But how about accidentally?"

"No difference to the average person."

"As in any other city."

"Exactly."

"Who else is on the fourteenth floo—*deck*."

"You can't really expect me to tell you that."

"Okay, I'll ask around."

"There're two fishermen making a reality TV show, their producer, but not the cameraman. There's a banker and his wife and another couple, probably not married."

"Peigne?"

"No. Harrison and Padget."

"Any Colombian drug dealers?"

"None that I know of. No Russian spies either."

"I'd like to get another look at the room," I said. "Can you arrange that?"

He sighed. "Do I have to?"

16

ONE OF THE nice guards put me in an elevator and rode up with me.

"I got shot," I said.

"Doesn't surprise me."

The doors opened on the buffet deck.

"Washy-washy!"

The ship seemed to be hardly moving, and it was raining outside. I was thinking of checking out the exercise room, Allie never being far from my mind. I'd come to a place where I equated my recent weight gain to my insensitivity toward my girlfriend. Wait, hear me out. Both are reactions to my resistance to commitment. My mind, in some juvenile, Neanderthal knee-jerk bid for independence, had put both my responsibility toward my lover and my health on a shooting range and had taken potshots at them. The same phenomenon had also apparently turned off the metaphor-constructing part of my brain.

What I'm trying to say is that I figured if I could get a handle on my weight, I could do the same with Allie. It's about taking the long view. It's using the part of the psyche that puts aside instant gratification for enduring happiness. The part of the brain that shows you why you should skip the cookie, take the stairs, and cherish the beautiful woman in the desert.

I almost made it to the exercise room, but there was a game room in the same hall, and it looked interesting, so I went in there instead.

Shit.

I found a bench and wistfully watched rain streak down the window, hating and feeling sorry for myself. I tried to tell myself—myself myself myself—that my side was injured so I probably couldn't have done real exercise anyway. I clung to that like a life preserver in a sea of self-loathing. Myself.

There were a half dozen tables in the room. There were three card games going, at least two of which looked like poker, some dominoes, and a Dungeons and Dragons session. I put the average age of the gamers at about eighty-seven, including me, and just over a hundred if I left.

I recognized the same gray-haired, black-clothed folks who'd sat through the Nutri-Pods presentation with knitting needles and crossword puzzles. Now they were throwing chips into the pot and rolling a d20, hoping for Critical Damage. They ignored me.

There was hardly a boundary between the sea and the sky. I could see whitecaps between breaks in the drizzle, but the cloud making the rain was parked right on top of us, and the mist made everything blurry. If not for a slight tinge of blue, the whole of the outside could have been rendered in black and white.

I felt very alone.

I closed my eyes, took a deep breath and tried to focus. There wasn't anything I could do now for Allie. Might as well be useful for Kristen. And myself, I remembered. I was involved in this. Someone had tried to kill me.

Assuming all the weirdness happening on the *Success* was related, and only a brain-dead, non-detective, brush salesman from Poughkeepsie would think otherwise, I pieced together what I knew about my recent attempted assassination.

I'd not actually taken the case when I'd been shot, but I had talked to Kristen. I'd been shown the murder scene, albeit briefly, and had had an interview with Ola Peterson, the Security Head himself. This was as far as the killer could have seen me progress. Not far, but apparently still enough to warrant shooting me in a national park.

Why shoot me, though? Did they think I was Vincent Bror? From a distance, through a scope, I could definitely be mistaken for him. We looked a lot alike up close. It wasn't a far stretch. The killer might not have known they'd succeeded the other night. The news of the murder had only gotten out this afternoon, about an hour ago, by me, when I blabbed it to the whole damn ship.

Then again, maybe the shooter was really after me. Maybe Bror was killed in my place. That was a sobering thought. I guess it came down to how much planning had gone into the killing. I'd only been booked on the ship the day before it sailed. If the killer had been after me, he or she had been quick or lucky to find me. I thought that a steak knife and a vandalized lock didn't require much planning.

I didn't know if Vincent Bror had any enemies, but I knew I did, and I knew that one was on the ship: Bailey Peigne who just happened to find out his ex-wife was selling his house through my ex-wife after I ruined his life. Even without the house, he had reason to want to get even. I tried to think if he was the violent type. I wasn't sure. He wasn't the intelligent type, that I knew, so I had to imagine he'd put his stat scores into violence.

Then there was Vinalez on the fourteenth floor.

Deck.

He had enemies. A killer could easily have mistaken the rooms. Bror didn't wear his wealth the way Vinalez did. Anybody looking for the big shot would naturally think he had the bigger room. The room could have been dark, and again, the wrong man had been killed. The killer figured out his mistake and by all appearances was still trying finish the job.

But what about me then? Me me me.

I had to assume that the killer knew who I was. I have a reputation in Utah as a reasonably successful detective. We weren't in Salt Lake City now, but we might as well be. As near as I could guess, about half the ship was from Utah with the Nutri-Pods thing. Hell, even the ship's doctor was a University of Utah alumni. Then there's the internet. It never forgets. Even if they didn't know me from before, one 'Googling,' and the killer could assume I'd been brought on to catch him. Thus, and therefore, quid pro quo, caveat emptor, id est—the push down the stairs and the shooting on the glacier.

"At least I know how I figure into it now," I said.

"Don't talk to yourself, young man. Unless you mean it. They're liable to put you off."

A blue-haired woman in yellow slacks and sunglasses was speaking. From my angle I could see she had two pair and a king kicker.

"Put me off?"

"Don't listen to Susan. She's demented," said the man sitting across from her. He had a one-piece gray jumpsuit with a built-in elastic belt and red tennis shoes. Also a black armband.

"I am not, you dumb fossil," Susan said. "I'll call."

"Queens full," he said, smiling.

Susan threw her cards at him. "Go change your Depends," she said.

"I'm Arnold." The man offered me his hand to shake before scooping up the chips.

"I'm Tony Flaner."

"I'm Roxanne Hunter," said the other woman at the table. "You can call me Roxy. Do you want to sit in a game?"

"What are the stakes?"

"Nickel, dime, quarter," said Susan. "Otherwise, we'd be put off for gambling outside the casino."

"Okay."

"Ten-dollar buy-in," Arnold said, shuffling the cards. "Put up or shut up."

I gave him a ten. He put it in a box and gave me chips.

"Texas Hold'em," he declared, and dealt.

"What does 'put off' mean?"

"What do you think it means?" snapped Susan, scowling at her cards.

"I'm going to bury you, Susan," said Roxy. "You're on tilt."

Susan snarled and looked at her chips.

"The cruise line is looking for excuses to put us off the boat," Roxy explained.

"Why?"

"Because we won't leave otherwise," said Arnold. He turned over the flop.

"We did the math," said Roxy. "It's cheaper to live on board than in a nursing home."

"You've got to be kidding," I said.

"Are you calling us liars?" said Susan, staring at me behind cataract glasses.

Sensing a bluff, I called her raise with an open-ended straight possibility. "You are," I said.

Roxy tossed in some chips. "If we become too much of a burden, they'll put us off."

"What does that mean?"

"Diapers," said Arnold.

"Dementia," added Roxy.

"Too many doctor visits," said Susan.

"Only for you because you're a drug seeker," teased Roxy.

"I have glaucoma."

"Pothead."

I missed the straight but thought my kings were good. No one else acted like they had anything. I bet into it.

"They wouldn't really put you off, would they? I mean, not in Alaska."

"Oh yes, they would," said Roxy. "Mr. Turner was put off in Nassau for pooping in the casino."

"Twice," said Susan.

Arnold tossed in his cards. "They'll put you off too, Mr. Flaner, if you keep it up."

"I can control my bowels."

"Not your mouth, though," said Roxy. "We heard you blabbing about that man's murder before."

I turned my kings over. They were better than Susan's tens. I won the pot.

The deal moved to Roxy. "Seven card Chicago," she said. "You know that one, son?"

"Seven stud, with a high hole spade splitting the pot with high hand?"

"We got a ringer," said Arnold.

Roxy dealt cards.

I said, "You don't sound surprised to hear about a murder aboard ship."

Arnold squinted at his hole cards. "It's happened before."

"And we already knew about it," said Susan. "Everyone important already knew. All you did is scare the little people. I'll see the quarter and raise a dime."

"How'd you find out?"

"She has a carpet cleaner who does double-duty as a plumber, if you know what I mean," said Arnold.

Roxy glared at him. "Arnold, I swear I'll throw you overboard like the fish bait you are if you don't mind your manners."

He winked at her and said, "Susan's been on the *Success* the longest."

"I sailed with it through the Panama Canal on my third trip. How many times have you been, smart-ass?"

"My canals are my own business," said Arnold. "Your sixes bet, son."

I bet a dime, hoping to confuse the other players.

"He doesn't know what he's doing," said Susan. "He's trying to slow play a spade."

"He doesn't have it," said Roxy. "I'll raise."

"I got shot, you know," I said.

"Are you looking for mercy?" asked Susan.

"No. Just making conversation."

"We know about that too," said Roxy. "Sorry to hear it. There are lots of gun nuts in Alaska."

"That's why I don't leave the ship," said Susan.

"You don't leave the ship because you're afraid they'll leave you, like they did in the Caymans. That's why she went through the Panama Canal—hid on board."

"Call the bet or stick your head in a toilet, Arnold," she said. "Better yet, do both."

"You seem to be doing pretty well for someone who got shot," said Arnold. "Must not have got ya' good."

"I got lucky. And now it'll cost you." I'd been dealt a third six and bet it.

"I hear that man's wife is still on board," said Roxy. "I take it you're working for her. Trying to clear her name?"

"Yes."

"Waste of time," said Susan. "She did it."

"How can you be so sure?"

"Who else would?"

"You have a mind like a sieve, Susan," said Arnold. "I'll bump it again. That'll be two to you, Flaner."

"That got big."

"Try and keep up," said Susan. "We're on the clock."

"I'm sorry to hear about Mr. Kirby," I said, pondering my chances at a full house. The other six was in front of Roxy, and nothing else would carry me except a lucky spade on the last card.

"Did you know him?" asked Roxy.

"I heard about it," I said. "All the important people know he passed last night. During sex."

"Oh," said Roxy. "That I hadn't heard."

"I knew it," said Susan. "He's got no one to blame but himself."

"Who was it?"

"One of the working girls," she said. "The new Chinese one, I bet."

"Oh, I gotta try her," said Arnold.

"You should," said Susan. "Be done with you once and for all."

"But what a way to go." He grinned. "Down and dirty."

I peeked at my last card. It was a spade, a middle one, an eight, just the kind of card that's not good enough to bet and not bad enough to fold. I bet the sixes and the eight of hope. I lost all but three dollars of my ten.

"I hope you're a better detective than you are a card player."

"I lost one hand."

"You were crushed," said Roxy piling chips. She had had a straight and the ace of spades.

"Don't you miss your families living on the ship?"

"Look here," said Susan, handing me her passport.

"You travel quite a bit. Are you saying your life is fulfilling without family?"

"No, you idiot, look at the picture page. See that there? Those initials, DNR—it means 'Do Not Resuscitate.' It means that if something happens to me, doctors will see that on my ID and won't try and revive me."

"That's pretty brave," I said.

"Shut up, you idiot. I didn't write that. My kids did."

"Oh."

"Show Flaner the picture of your kids, Arnold," said Roxy.

He tossed me his wallet. I opened it and found a book of double-stitched plastic photo pages. Unless his kids were multi-ethnic wallet models, there were no pictures of his kids at all, just the place holders that came with the wallet.

"I told 'em I'll carry their pictures when they fix their faces."

"Piercings," said Roxy.

"Tattoos," said Susan. "And ugly. Oh god, they're ugly. They look just like Arnold."

"Susan's deal."

"Five card draw, jacks or better to open, quarter progressive."

She tossed cards.

"You guys notice anything weird about this cruise? Something out of the ordinary?"

"Are you kidding?" said Susan.

"No, if I were kidding, I'd compliment your social skills."

Arnold hit the table laughing. Roxy grinned. Susan glared.

"Yes, detective," Roxy said. "This cruise is one for the books."

"No caviar for one," said Susan.

"You eat caviar?" I said.

"How else am I going to go through my kids' inheritance?"

"The lights going out was unusual," said Arnold.

"And the rats," said Roxy. "Never seen as much as a bug on the Alaska cruises, and now there're white lab rats everywhere."

"Half the passengers canceled when the squirt people booked," said Arnold.

"Food order got shorted, and we had to pick up supplies in Juneau," said Susan.

"Security system got cut," said a man from behind Dungeon Master's screens.

"You aren't supposed to know about that," I said.

"When I'm not DM, I'm a fifteenth-level rogue," he explained.

"Someone fell off the ship," said a domino player.

"Someone else was shot," said another. "A detective no less."

"Oh, and someone was murdered in the best suite on the ship."

"Yeah, we got that one."

"The ship is littered with food coloring bottles."

"The internet is out."

"The juggler jumped ship."

"We sailed on a Friday."

"We're taking on water."

"What?"

"Just a little."

"The comic stole a lifeboat."

"And he's sleeping on deck."

"Perry Whitehouse?"

"That's the one. Funny guy, but crazy."

Just then the cruise director appeared in the doorway. Our eyes locked. She raised her hand and with a curving finger beckoned me over.

17

"CAN YOU TALK TO PERRY?" asked Sandra, the cruise director. "He's scaring the passengers."

"We wouldn't want that now, would we?" I said bitterly.

Some of the sparkle left her omnipresent smile. "You're mad that I called security on you."

"They beat me with rubber hoses and sodomized me with a masthead."

"What?"

"Just kidding," I said. "But yeah. You got me in trouble."

She sighed. "I was doing my job."

"Only following orders," I translated.

"You don't understand. Do you know how hard it is to get a job like mine? Do you know how hard it is to keep it?"

"I heard there's actually a lot of turn over on cruise ships."

"There is, and that's half the trouble. I have a thankless job. I'm underpaid, overworked, and the easiest to blame if something goes wrong. I hear every passenger's complaint and most of them are aimed at me as if I had something to do with their towel monkey not hanging properly on their shower curtain."

"Why don't you leave?"

She sighed. "It's not without its perks. I see the world. I'm in entertainment. I'm the highest-ranked officer on the ship that doesn't actually know how to sail."

"But you're not paid much?"

"No," she said. "Not a lot of respect for the position. I make it look easy, so they think it is."

"Like comedy."

"The last cruise director stormed off the ship in Juneau last year after being accused of helping passengers sneak booze onboard."

"Did he?"

"Yes."

"Cost him his job, huh?"

"No, he quit. People want to work where they're appreciated. He didn't feel appreciated, so he left."

"And then they hired you?"

"Yes, and I like my job."

"But you don't feel appreciated?"

"I feel appreciated," she said.

"Then why are you telling me all this?"

"I don't know," she said. "Yes, I do. I'm telling you why I called security on you. You were disrupting the cruise."

"Disrupting the cruise or disrupting the show?"

"No difference," she said.

"I guess I can understand that."

"So you'll help me with Perry?"

"What about Perry?"

"He's in the hot tub. Go talk to him. Calm him down."

She pointed to the door leading outside and I knew I was dismissed.

I found Perry on deck in the hot tub in the drizzling rain. He had the tub to himself, because, like I said, it was raining. And we were in Alaska. Since I was already in my workout shorts, I joined him. It was that or freeze to death. I regretted my decision the instant the hot water hit my stitched wound.

"I think I just bought myself an infection," I said.

"No, the hot tub water is from the ocean like the pool, but they chlorinate it when they warm it."

"Still, this can't be good for me."

My bandage bobbed up to the surface like a breaching whale, only to be swept away in the Jacuzzi current.

"Fire and ice," he said. "It's primal."

"If you mean my head's frozen and my feet are boiled, I agree."

"That's sorta close," he said. "I heard you got in trouble for inciting panic."

"News travels fast."

"Roxy told me. The only gossip chain faster than the crew's is the Grays'."

"They told me you stole a lifeboat."

Perry paused.

I said, "Is it true?"

"No, of course not. I didn't steal a lifeboat. It's still on the ship. I simply moved it. A little. To where I could find it more easily."

"Where is it?"

He pointed to a tarp under the stairs that led up to the next deck.

"It's not an actual lifeboat. No one's assigned to it. It's a spare. An inflatable covered arctic-approved life support pod."

"Don't say pod."

"It'll hold twelve people and survive a gale."

"What if it's popped?"

"Redundant systems. It can take lots of pops."

"But what if?"

"Then it'd sink," he said. "But I couldn't exactly take one of those." He pointed to a huge fiberglass-hulled lifeboat hanging on a crane over the deck.

"No, I guess not."

"I hardly stole it," he grumbled. "Busybodies."

"Yeah, I figured they exaggerated. They said you were sleeping out on the deck. That can't be true."

"I can sleep outside if I want to."

"But you aren't, are you?"

"Only last night," he said. "And tonight."

"Isn't it cold?"

"Oh god, yeah."

I chipped ice off the tub control and switched the bubbles back on. I dunked my head to melt my eyebrows, and when I came up, Perry had submerged himself to his eyes.

"Perry. Why are you sleeping on deck? No, wait. Let me re-phrase this. Are you taking your meds?"

"Someone stole them."

"Stole them?"

"Right out of my room. Gone. Happened the first night of the cruise. I didn't say anything because I thought they'd turn up."

"You just misplaced them."

"Nope. Stolen."

"How can you be so sure?"

"It fits the pattern," he said. "The juggler, the wine, you being shot, the murder. This ship is cursed. Absit omen."

"You were fine yesterday," I said. "This is too quick."

"The ship's sinking," he said.

"Only a little. The Grays told me so."

"I know you think I'm paranoid, but I have good reason. Tony, this cruise is messed up."

I squirted bath water at him with my hands, but it froze midair, and I hit him with an ice cube.

"Sorry," I said.

Perry was unfazed. "You haven't seen my room," he said. "It's down on the second deck. Below the water line and an inside cabin to boot. If shit happens, I'll be dead. No getting out of there. I'd be a fourth-class passenger on the *Titanic*."

"Nothing's going to happen," I said. "Is it?"

"Why take the chance? I'm sleeping on deck until they fix it."

"If the ship were sinking, wouldn't they pull into port and fix it? This is a business, and killing customers, unless you're the cigarette consortium, is usually considered a bad business model."

He didn't look convinced, so I went on. "They say there isn't a modern dam in existence that doesn't leak. I'm sure big ships like this are the same."

"Don't be stupid. They have a word for a ship with a leak—sunk. This is new and recent. It happened after we left Juneau. Nobody's saying it—well at least none of the officers, but it appears to be sabotage."

"Why?"

"My best guess is that someone's trying to kill someone else on the ship and will go to great lengths to do it."

"I'm not saying you're wrong," I said.

"What are you saying?"

"I'm saying that I may need you, and if you got too nuts, they'll toss you off the ship. After talking to the Grays and Security Head Ola, it sounds like they toss people off pretty regularly for doing less threatening things than screaming the ship's sinking."

"Rub a dub dub, two jerks in a tub," came a voice from a terrace above us.

We looked up and saw a man in white pants and a plaid flannel hunting jacket. The PETA-enraging fur hat finished the schizophrenic ensemble with flair. Cradled in the crook of the man's arm was a gun, the barrel pointed down and at us in the pool.

"Are you talking to me?" said Perry.

"Any friend of Flaner's a jerk in my book."

"A book?" I said. "Bailey, I didn't know you could read. Will wonders never cease?"

"I hear someone shot you," he said. A smile spread over his lips like crude oil on a migrating pelican. "I wonder who'd want to do a thing like that. You're such a likable fellow, soft-spoken, minds your own business."

Perry said, "Who is that?"

"Let me introduce you to Bailey Peigne, unemployed, divorced, and indicted."

Perry waved. "Hello."

"Didn't know you were queer, Flaner, but I should have guessed."

Nodding at the gun, I said, "On your way to blow your brains out? Need any help?"

"Always the smart-ass, aren't you, Flaner? Someday someone's going to get real sick of your lip and shut it for good."

"I heard you had an open house today," I said. "How'd it go? Get any offers?"

Even from twenty feet away I could see his face grow red. He said, "Isn't it just funny how much misfortune you can cause me? You cost me my marriage and my house, my business and savings, and now your whore wife is there to get a commission. You're a goddamn racket."

"You'd know about that," I said.

"You better stay away from me, Flaner, if you know what's good for you."

"We were here first."

"Yeah, you started talking to us," said Perry.

He took up his gun in both hands and racked a shell into it. Another one popped out and splashed into the tub. The gun had been loaded all along.

The bimbo I'd seen with Peigne before appeared beside him. "Come on, Bailey, I'm freezing. Let's shoot these skeets and get inside. I'm cold. Who're ya talking to?"

She had on a white snowsuit, and unless the pants were lined with NASA-grade thermal reflective Kevlar, she was losing more heat out of her ass than the rest of the outfit could contain.

"I'm talking to a dead man," he said.

"Who's dead?"

"Him." He pointed the gun at me.

I peed a little and waved.

"He doesn't act dead."

"Looks can be deceiving, Candy."

"Can you point that gun somewhere else?" said Perry.

"I could."

We waited. He didn't move.

"I'm freezing, Bailey," Candy whined.

"Candy? Is your name really Candy?" asked Perry.

"Yes," she said. "What's wrong with that?"

"Nothing," he said. "It's sweet."

She wrinkled up her nose and panted a series of short snorts that I took at first to be a sudden allergy attack before realizing it was her laugh.

"Oh, you're funny," she said.

"I'm performing day after tomorrow in the Nautilus."

"Is that in Skagway?"

"No, that's the big theater at the front of the ship. It's after Skagway. I'm doing two shows."

"Oh, we'll be there, won't we, Bailey?"

"You're ruining the mood, Candy," he growled. "Go wait for me by the skeet."

"But it's cold."

"Candy," he said more sternly.

She shuffled off in little steps, which told me she had on heels.

"You ruined my life, Flaner," Peigne said. "I can ruin lives, too. You just remember old Smitty Young."

"Who's Smitty Young?" asked Perry.

"Flaner knows."

I shrugged. Peigne's face grew angrier.

A scream and a crash and then a string of curses told us that Candy's heels had succumbed to the ice on the deck.

"Bailey!" she cried. "I hurt my bum."

He threw one more malignant glare into the pool, turned, and left.

We listened to muffled crying, muffled talk, and then after a few minutes, the sound of a muffled shotgun blasting clay pigeons over the Chilkoot Inlet.

"I didn't like him," Perry said. "I take it you've met before."

I told him about his wife hiring me and my subsequent discoveries of his many affairs and financial malfeasances.

"He's not blaming himself for being a douche, but you for catching him?"

"That's how things work."

"Damn," Perry said. "You really don't know who Smitty Young is?"

"I do," I said. "He was Peigne's partner. He died in a car crash a few years ago."

"Was he involved?"

"I didn't think so before now."

"Sounded like he was bragging about killing him."

"Yeah, it did, didn't it?"

"You should tell Ola or the captain that he threatened you."

"His word against mine."

"And mine," said Perry.

"You're my friend, hardly an objective voice."

"But—"

"And you're sleeping on deck under a tarp with a stolen life raft," I said.

Perry sulked.

"He's just acting tough," I said. "He's a jerk, not a killer."

"Are you sure?"

"No."

"Sucks to be you."

"I'm used to it."

It started to snow, thought better of it, and then sent wind instead. I could see green mountains in the distance. The crack of gunshots rolled across the water to the hills and came back in muted echoes. My side stung with each one.

"Perry, what do you know about Bror's invention? The microchip thing. You said it could be used for evil. What is it?"

"It's a power regulator. It's used in all kinds of electronics."

"So are LEDs, and you don't say they can be used for evil."

"LEDs can be evil."

"What's the deal with Bror's chip specifically?"

"Have you seen cable-less charging stations?"

"Yes."

"They use NFMR, 'near field magnetic resonance.' Basically, you just put your device in a field and it charges."

"Neat."

"Yeah, it's pretty cool and also pretty evil."

"Of course. Bror's chip does this?"

"No. I don't think so," said Perry. "Or maybe it might."

"You are a font of useful information," I said.

"What Bror's chip does is allow very tiny itty-bitty devices to regulate their power so well that it can pull power from these devices or other magnetic fields so effectively that under certain conditions and certain applications, it's a permanent charge."

"What conditions and what applications?"

"Around magnetic fields, so anywhere in the industrialized, 'electroniced' world would be the right conditions."

"How's that evil?"

"The nefarious application is active-RFID."

"Do I need a dictionary?"

"Radio frequency identification," he said. "Basically a chip that emits a radio frequency that can be picked up, monitored, and tracked. Right now it can track people, but soon it will be able to listen in too."

"So basically a cell phone?"

"Worse. It can be embedded into your body, and it's so small you don't even know it's there. It could charge itself by being near a light switch so it's always on."

"And Bror invented this?"

"No, but his patent is making it happen."

I sat and soaked and thought about what I'd heard.

"But the cat's out of the bag now, right?" I said.

"You mean did Vincent Bror's death affect any of this?"

"Right."

"Well, the patent is surely in Bror's name, issued and perfected," said Perry. "He could have suddenly grown a conscience and tried to revoke his technology from the Pentagon, but dead, that's surely not going to happen."

"That does get in the way of things. But wouldn't they use it anyway?"

"It's the military *industrial* complex," he said. "Business runs it, not the military. He could have thrown a hammer in it."

"If he'd grown a conscience."

"If," agreed Perry. "But it might have been the other side."

"What other side?"

"Groups like THAFF—The Humanist Alliance Freedom Foundation. They threaten industrialists and inventors who let their work be subverted to evil purposes."

"Do they really talk like that? 'Evil Purposes?'"

"Why not?"

"Melodramatic."

"If the word fits, use it."

"Have they killed anyone?"

"They did a half-day DDoS—that's a Denial-of-Service attack—on Google that increased their search time by nearly a whole second."

"That's hard core," I said. "But no actual violence?"

"They said on their blog that they were going to make an example of someone."

The sun broke out. It was still cold, but it looked nice at least.

Perry said, "The group mentioned Vincent Bror's patent."

"Really?"

"Yeah, they're kinda mad that Bror got to keep the patent since he was working for the University of Utah when he developed it."

"The U of U?"

"Yes. THAFF was started there."

"By whom?" I love it when I get that word right.

"Get real, they're on the US terrorist watch list. They don't post resumes online. No one knows who they are."

"But they're Utahns?"

"Yeah, I think so. They know a lot about stuff at the university and around the state."

"Great," I said.

A group of dedicated vacationers came on the deck for the sunshine. Two had University of Utah sweatshirts, one had a Utah Jazz windbreaker and one a Greenpeace-stenciled duffel that held towels. They stripped off their clothes and dove into the unheated ocean water pool.

For five full minutes, their screams drowned out the sound of the shooting and calmed my nerves.

18

I'D BEEN DOWN to deck three so many times that the crew no longer batted an eye at me.

Ola hadn't complained or been an officious butt-munch when I appeared at the brig and asked to see Kristen again and reminded him I still wanted to visit the crime scene.

"Okay," he said.

"And I'd like to talk to the guy who fixed the door."

He rolled his eyes but got on the phone.

"Busy?" I said.

"I have a real job, Mr. Flaner. It's an interesting experience. You should try it sometime."

"Ha," I said. "I've had more jobs than you've had teeth."

"Why doesn't that surprise me?"

"No imagination?" I enjoyed pushing Ola's buttons, but to be honest, he was probably the easiest cop I'd ever worked with. He hadn't once beat me up, shot me, arrested me, or even lied to me. He had threatened me, but that was required or he'd lose his pension. I couldn't hold that against him. I thought maybe I was getting a rapport with him, a relationship where I needled him to distraction, and he took it without violent retribution. It's a common basis for my relationships.

"Is it true the ship is sinking?" I asked as he got his keys out of his desk.

"No," he said. "One of the engines failed. The intake valve let some water in. It's nothing."

"Okay," I said.

"And if you say a single word about it to anyone, I'll have you airlifted off the ship in a body cast."

"I understand," I said. "I swear by Odin, Freya, and Thor to keep silent. Ja?"

He sighed and let me into Kristen's cell. She was reading a psychological thriller about a modern cult of Kali in America: *What Immortal Hand*. It looked great. I'd have to check it out.

"What's the news?" she said.

I got right to it. "Did Vincent ever mention a group called THAFF?"

"No. I don't think so. But remember, he wasn't talking to me about important stuff. Actually, he wasn't talking to me much at all. Is it important?"

"I don't know. Probably not," I said. "How're they treating you?"

"Fine, really. I think they'd let me have the run of the ship if the police weren't waiting for me in Seattle."

"They still might. Money buys privilege," I said. "What does Kline say?"

"He says not to worry. The broken lock is enough for reasonable doubt."

"That's good."

"Have you found *anything*?"

"I've picked up some information, but I don't know what to do with it yet. Ola is taking me up to look at the room here in a bit."

"I don't have to go, do I?"

"Was anything taken?"

"I didn't see anything missing, but I didn't look very well."

"You should come up then," I said. "Just look through your stuff, see if anything's gone or moved."

"Okay," she said.

"Ola!"

"Yes?" came the security head's voice.

"Ola, Ola," I said. "That's Spanish for 'hello, you.'"

"Stick it up your ass," he said.

Yes, we definitely had a rapport.

"Let's go and see the room."

Ola didn't balk at bringing Kristen along. I guess since he got to bring two people, security officers with guns no less, it was only fair I got to bring a friend. To even the odds, I asked him to invite Kline too. Kristen's lawyer should see what he was up against.

There was a tall man, black as wet coal, waiting for us when we got out of the elevator on the fourteenth flo—*deck*.

"Mr. Flaner, this is our electrician, Peter Samson."

"Danish?"

"Yeah, can't you tell?" he said. "By way of Miami, Jamaica, and the Congo."

Ola slid a card into the door of 14500, and the green LED lit up as the lock snapped back. He went in first.

"Did the Juneau police come aboard and look around?" I asked.

"Yes," said Ola.

"Did they make a report?"

"Yes."

"Can I see it?"

"No."

"Can Mr. Kline threaten you enough that you'll change your mind on that?"

He rolled his eyes and said, "I'll see what I can do."

"Thanks."

"The blood's been cleaned up," I said.

"Yes. We have people who clean. They're good at it."

"Did they clean the whole place?"

"Yes. We pay them to do that."

"This is terrible. What about fingerprints and all that?"

"The real police handled that."

Kristen called from the back of the suite. "Everything's been moved."

"How moved?"

"Put away. Like maids were here," she said.

Ola nodded.

"Well, this is a waste of time," I said.

"I couldn't find Vincent's briefcase," she said. "Or his computer or wallet."

"Mr. Kline took possession of those," said Ola. "He's on his way."

"Tell me about the doors," I said to the engineer.

"The panels had been pulled up and the sensors re-wired. It wasn't hard to put it right."

"Was it hard to do?"

"Not if you knew what you were doing."

"Who'd know how to do it?"

"It's old technology," he said. "Been around for decades. Anyone with a knowledge of locks or electronics could have done it."

"Which would you say it was?"

He looked at me slyly. "I'd say it was an electrician trying to cover his tracks."

"Go on."

"The front was all scraped up. There was no need for that. Whoever did it knew how to pop off the plate and had the tools to do it. Once on the board, the wires were pulled, stripped and replaced exactly where they needed to go so they'd stop receiving but not sound an alarm. Plus, in the elevator at least, it had to be done fast. People use those nonstop."

"Was there similar 'covering up' with the cut security camera feeds?"

"No," he said.

"Is the system up now?"

"No. We spliced cables, but our computer's damaged too. It could be coincidence, but it got short-circuited and power-surged those boxes to slag."

"That big?"

"Uh-huh."

"When?"

"I just found it yesterday after we got all the splices done. It could have happened any time between then and when the system first went dark on boarding day."

I walked to the window and looked out on the freezing bathers. The pool had two or three men doing uncomfortable laps, their skin blue as parrot fish. The tub Perry and I had been in was overflowing with folk now, as were the three others just like it. The clouds had broken up a little, and sunlight slipped between them like frozen sand between your toes. I noticed the hot tubbers had only their heads above the water, and not much of that either. I'm sure I could have made a killing selling snorkels.

Kristen came out of her room and shrugged. "Except what Kline got, I don't see anything missing," she said.

"Show me where Vincent was when you came out," I said to her.

"He was right there by the couch."

I walked over to where she pointed.

"Where were you when you first saw him?"

"I was here in the hall. I saw him in silhouette against the windows there."

"So the lights were out?"

"Yes."

"What happened? Did you say anything?"

"I asked him if he was ready to apologize. I told him if he wasn't, he'd have to sleep in one of the other rooms."

"Is that it?"

"I suggested he sleep in the ocean," she said.

"A threat?" asked Ola.

"A lovers' spat," she said.

"What happened then?"

"He turned to look at me and staggered forward. I switched on the light and saw the knife. I ran to him."

"Show me where," I said.

She came over.

"I screamed, and he pulled me behind the piano by the shoulders."

I took position where she indicated.

"Did he say anything?"

"No. The knife, was uhm…" She pointed to her neck.

"Right. Then what?"

"I pulled the knife out and got sprayed with blood. He staggered backward a step and I put the knife back. He pushed me away, staggered forward and then fell over right there, where they found him."

"There was blood splatter all over the floor and furniture," said Ola indicating the path. "It fits with what she said."

I moved as she described. It was five or six steps from where Kristen said she'd pulled the knife out to where he'd fallen.

"Why didn't he sit down? Where was he going when he fell?"

"The bar?" offered the engineer. "Maybe he wanted a drink."

The bar was set in a corner just inside the hallway. It was a chest-high, curved-top bar with five steel barstools bolted into the deck around it.

"Where'd he push you?" I said to Kristen.

"That way. Just here." She moved to the windowed wall that looked out onto the atrium.

"What did you do after he fell?"

"I ran to the bathroom. I guess I was looking for towels or Band-Aids or something. I came to my senses and called the front desk from in there."

"We had people here within three or four minutes," said Ola. "A medical team and a cruise officer."

"Which bathroom did you call from?"

"The one across the atrium."

"How long were you in there?"

"Not long. A minute. Two?" she said. "I came out and saw he was dead."

"How'd you know?"

"I knew. I just knew. I stood here and stared at him until the people arrived."

"Did you let them in?"

"No. They just came in."

"The door couldn't lock," said the engineer.

"They'd have had a key in any event," added Ola.

"What did you hear from your bedroom that woke you?" I said.

"I'm not sure," said Kristen. She sat down on the edge of the couch.

"Try to remember."

"She said before—"

"Shhhh," I shushed Ola. "Let her tell it."

"Voices," she said.

Ola raised an eyebrow. "She didn't say anything like that before."

"I might have been dreaming," she said. "But I might have heard a conversation, a murmur. An argument. What finally woke me was the sound of furniture moving."

I walked down the corridor to the entrance way.

"Where were you sleeping?"

"The master bedroom, right here." She opened the door and showed me.

"Was the hall door open here into the entranceway?"

"I think so."

"Was your bedroom door closed?"

"Yes," she said. "I remember yanking it open. It bashed the wall."

I pulled the door open, bashing it against the wall.

"So you heard furniture move," I said. "And it woke you up?"

"Yes."

"Did you come right out?"

"From the sound, I knew Vince was back. I got out of bed and went straight out. I didn't even bother putting on my robe. I guess I was looking for a fight. I was pretty alert."

"How long between waking up and opening the door here?"

"Ten seconds," she said. "Maybe less. Probably less."

"So you'd have seen anyone leaving if the door was open here."

"She isn't sure the door was open," said Ola. "And she could be lying."

"No noise from the peanut gallery," I said. "It would take a few seconds to open the door. With that and the distance, I figure it would take maybe eight, ten seconds to leave the suite from where Bror died."

"At least," said Ola. "Unless the door was already open."

"Was the door open to the parlor?"

"No, it's on a spring," said Kristen. "It closes automatically unless it's propped open. It wasn't propped open."

I went back out into the big living room and looked around. I paced a couple of steps forward and back, squatted to get another vantage point and crossed to the glass. I touched it with my fingertips and pressed my ear against it. I hummed twice and went back to the piano and tapped a couple of keys. I gave it a little shove. It resented the assault and said so with a sour, melodious pulse. I went to the meeting table and shifted a chair. Then I shifted another.

"Is that what you heard?"

Kristen nodded. "Maybe."

I paced the distance from the chairs to couch and then to the door. Then I did the same from the entrance room and the door. I tried the locks and tested the noise. I went back inside and flopped on the couch.

"The killer didn't have time to leave the room," I said. "He was hiding there behind the bar. He only slipped out when Kristen went for towels through the atrium. If she'd gone to a different bathroom, he might have had to kill her too. She'd have seen him."

"What? How are you getting that?" said Ola.

"The table is as deep into the room as you can get and not have to put on swim trunks or a parachute. The piano blocks a straight run out of the room. Even a fast trot will result in a hip-check into the Steinway there. If that had happened, Kristen would have heard a pissed piano. Did you hear this?"

I bumped the piano with my tush. The strings complained. Ola grimaced. Maybe it really was a Steinway.

"No. Not that."

"Okay," I said. "So after hearing Kristen's door bang against the wall, the killer had barely enough time to get to the other side of the room. If he'd had tried for the door, he'd have been caught. There's no other hiding place except behind the couch, and had he been there, Kristen would have seen him reflected in the glass."

They nodded. I was on a roll. I trotted to the bar and ducked behind it.

"Can anyone see me?"

"I can," said the engineer.

"Can anyone not standing right next to the bar see me?"

"No," said Kristen.

"He'd have been visible from the side when she first came in," said Ola.

"It was dark. And she wasn't looking this way. She was looking at her husband, who was right there, big as life against the lights of the foredeck. By the time the main ones were on, she was already past the bar and into the room."

I came out and switched the lights off to prove my point. Then I went back behind the bar.

"So the only hiding place is behind here," I said. "That's where he was. When your husband pushed you into the wall, Kristen, he wasn't mad at you, he was trying to protect you, to get you as far away from the killer as he could. I suspect he was heading to the bar to deal with him when he died. He might have been in shock at first but seeing you here, he went into Man-Mode and made to kill his killer. Kristen, Vince died trying to save you."

My stellar deductions didn't have the effect I thought they would. Though Ola looked at me with what might have been new respect or bad oysters—hard to tell, Kristen crumbled to the floor and wept into her hands.

Just then a Filipina maid with a bottle of hand sanitizer escorted in Mr. Kline. "What'd I miss?" he said.

19

JUST TO CHECK MY THEORY, I verified that there was no other way out of the parlor or the room than the front door. There was of course the patio and the two balconies, but to escape using those would have required an invisibility cloak, paraglider, and waiting speedboat with a space heater.

After his initial reaction, Ola was indifferent to my theory. The murder really wasn't his business. The killer would be gone in a few days no matter what. I think the engineer was impressed, but once Kristen had melted down, he excused himself.

Kline was angry at me. He blamed me for upsetting Kristen. She was inconsolable for a good ten minutes, which I figured was about eight minutes longer than she'd been in the same state the night Vince had been stabbed. The doctor was again called in and brought pills and a warm blanket, a cup of tea, a magazine with the new fall lineup from Paris, and eventually she was escorted away and back down to her cell—where I'm sure a masseuse was waiting to work the kinks out of her shoulders and send her to bed with a happy ending. It's good to be rich.

"Are we done here now?" asked Ola.

"Did you take a briefcase out of here?" I asked Kline.

"Yes, it's in my room."

"Let's see it."

Kline slipped into his legal concern face.

I turned to Ola. "Yeah, we're done here," I said. "But I don't want you leaving town."

He rolled his eyes and led us to the hall.

He pushed the passenger elevator for us and waited. I timed it. It took thirty-five seconds to arrive. When it did, it was full of people who rubbernecked to get a look into the hallway, gawking at the bubbling fountain and Italian sconces. Kline and I got in but not Ola. We'd been set free among the passengers.

One floor down, everyone else got out and Sandra got in.

"Hello, Mr. Kline," she said. And then to me, "How'd it go with Perry?"

"Oh, fine, fine."

"You talked him down? He's normal again?"

"Sure."

"Is he better or not?"

"Oh, you know." I shrugged.

"Does he still think the ship's sinking?"

"We talked about that, and I told him it wasn't."

"And he believed you?"

"He might have."

"Is he going to sleep on deck again?"

"Oh, you know."

"You didn't do anything, did you? He's going to be weird, isn't he?"

"See, you do know."

"If he upsets the passengers—"

"It's part of his act."

"No it isn't. I've seen his act."

"Not this one."

"So, I shouldn't worry?"

"Oh, you know."

"Flaner—"

"Gotta go."

The door opened and I pulled Kline out with me. I took him to the Eye Patch Lounge hoping to get some free drinks out of him.

"I'll have a double bourbon with a chaser of bourbon," I said. "And you, Kline?"

"Nothing for me," he said.

"Lighten up. You're buying, might as well enjoy one."

"Coke," he said.

I mouthed "and rum" to the waitress before we slid off to a side window for some privacy.

"I can't keep calling you Kline," I said. "What's your first name?"

"Cephalus."

"Wow."

"Yeah. My parents didn't think that one through."

"Kline it is."

It was prime drinking time on a cruise ship, which is really any time, but it was coming on dusk when the habituals slinked out for nourishment and ethanol, yet the bar was empty. The reason was obvious. There was a singer.

She was a big-haired blonde woman, base-caked and over-eye-shadowed, falling over the wrong side of fifty. Her keyboard accompanist was barely twenty, tanned to leather, black hair, combed part, bow tie tuxedo and a smile that included a gold incisor. By the sound of it, they'd started drinking in Seattle and hadn't stopped. Between missed keys and sudden music stops, the singer barked out lyrics to disco hits like Ella Fitzgerald strangling a basket of cats.

"Stay-in alive, stain alive. AHHHHHHHHH stain alive!"

I ground my teeth, but Kline stared out the window, his jaw set but not against the music.

"Why'd you have to do that? Why'd you have to put her through that?"

"She said she could handle it."

"And you believed her?"

"Should I not believe her?" I said.

Kline flashed at me. He sensed the double meaning. I may have discovered a plausible scenario to allow for a killer to escape the room without Kristen seeing him, but it was based on Kristen's story. If she were lying or wrong, then it was nothing. It was at best a tenuous explanation when the more plausible scenario was and continued to be that she'd done Vincent in herself.

"No," said Kline. "You can trust her. She just doesn't recognize her own frailty."

"And you do?"

"Better than you," he said. He scooped up his rum and Coke and drained half of it before he noticed the rum. He winced, pulled another swallow, and said, "I hate that she's upset about Vincent. He was a jerk. He didn't deserve her."

This was interesting.

"How long have you worked for the Brors?"

"He hired me a year ago. After the money came in."

"Why would you work for a jerk?"

"Capitalism."

"Oh, right."

"And he wasn't a jerk at first," he said. "Well, maybe he was and I couldn't see it."

"When did you see it?"

"It's really none of your business." He'd finished his drink and signaled for another.

"You don't want to help Kristen?"

"Of course I do."

"Then tell me. I'm helping her."

He weighed the scales of justice in his mind until his drink arrived.

"Won't you shimmy to a funky TOOOOOWN!"

"What did you do for Vincent Bror?"

"All kinds of stuff. I helped him find tax people, and I insulated him from problems. It's what lawyers do."

"Kristen said he got mean."

"Yes," he said. "He was furious with people asking him for money. He blamed them for neglecting him when he needed help and wanted to teach them lessons."

"So he was a tightwad?"

"At first, no. Then he was. Then he was worse. He started a list and—" He stopped short.

"Gotta go go go! Dum de dum de dum DUMMMMMM."

"Just not the same without the horns," I said. "What did he do with the lists?"

"I really shouldn't—"

"Shut up and tell me," I said. "You know what I mean."

He sucked an ice cube for a minute. "Different things," he said. "He tried to, eh…make the punishment fit the crime, you know?"

"No, I don't."

"Okay, well, there was a landlord who threw him out once. He bought his mortgage and foreclosed on him when he was three hours late with a payment."

"Oh."

"Two professors lost their tenured positions the day after Vincent Bror made a big donation to the college."

"I see."

"Cops raided a banker's house and found drugs he denied having. He got a maximum sentence for a first-time offense, and the DA is a cinch for re-election."

I sipped my drink. Seeing I had room, I poured in the chaser.

"He was the most vindictive man I've ever met," Kline said.

"Was he really going to divorce Kristen?"

"He began to see everyone as a chiseler. I swear his mind was going. When he asked me about the divorce implications, I encouraged it."

"Why?"

"To get her away from him."

I dumped the ice from Kline's drink into mine and let it melt. The singer finally left Funky Town and headed for the YMCA with some creative license.

"Young man, please don't be a dumb clown!"

"What do you know about the patent itself?"

"He developed the idea while working at the University of Utah in the electrical engineer laboratory as a graduate assistant. Most of his time was spent calibrating machines."

"Did the university have a claim on the patent?"

"They couldn't prove they did, but they didn't try very hard. They got a donation and the fact that he came from there was enough esteem. Plus, I guess, it was only theoretical until recent innovations made it practical. When he filed the patent there was no way to prove it would work. It came out of his head, he said. One day he just thought of sharing electrons like sharing a pizza, without actually eating it."

"That is the dumbest thing I've ever heard," I said.

"I don't understand it either," Kline admitted. "There were people who came forward challenging the patent. Several nearly identical ones had been filed, and no one noticed the similarities because it was so technical. I helped Bror's patent to primacy by virtue of age. And he got rich."

"Would any of the sore losers be out to get him?"

"Corporations and think tanks," he said. "Murder isn't their kind of thing. Plus it's over. Killing him does nothing to get the rights. They all flow into a foundation with or without him. No one can touch it."

"And the foundation is going to benefit Tommy's Place?"

"Yes. A tiny little shelter in North Salt Lake. They won't know what hit them. Twenty million dollars from nowhere."

"What was Bror doing with the money himself?"

"Petty revenges," he said, his tongue thinking with the booze. "He bought nice things. This trip, for example. A couple of cars, but mostly he hoarded it."

"What does Kristen get?"

"A couple million and money until she dies. She'll be all right. Considering how little money they spent, she'll hardly notice a difference."

"So one bit of philanthropy and a slew of malevolence. Sounds like there are people out there who'd hold a grudge against the man."

"No. It was all done in secret. Tommy's Place has no idea. Neither did any of his victims. That's what they were, you know. Victims. He wanted it to look like the Hand of Fate. 'Just give them their desserts, and don't let them know who baked it,' was his line."

"He said that?"

"Yeah."

"It's 'kay to stay the Y–M–C–A! That's what I say, Y–M–Say–A!"

"I saw somebody wearing a Tommy's Place shirt this morning," I said.

"Yes, I arranged for two ex-volunteers to come on the cruise. They think they won a contest. It took a lot of convincing to get them to come."

"Ex-volunteers?"

"They don't work there anymore, but they did once. I tracked them down from Tommy's Place's records. He only remembered their first names."

"It's gay to be at the Y–M–C–A!"

"Who are they?"

"Jim Harrison and Holly Padget."

"You ever hear about a group called THAFF, The Humanist Alliance Freedom Foundation?"

"Yes. They sent us a couple of letters. Polite and threatening all at once."

"Did Vincent go after them?"

"I don't think so. They were pretty low on the list, if they were on it at all."

"Was there an actual list?"

"He said there was."

"He said that?"

Kline nodded.

"What a guy," I said. "Real saint."

"I did bad things for that man." Kline began his third drink.

"But nothing illegal," I said.

"Borderline. I think he was doing some himself."

"What do you mean?"

"It was just a suspicion I had. She's better off without him. She shouldn't be crying over him. He wasn't trying to save her up in that room like you said. He was just so mean he went after his killer out of spite."

"Stay on point," I said. "Tell me about your suspicion."

"There was a transfer of money to Santiago, Chile, last month. Twenty thousand dollars to Flores Limited. He sent it through a dummy corporation. It was suspicious as hell. I asked him what it was for, and he told me to mind my own business. He'd said that to me before, but the way he said it this time really unnerved me."

"What'd you do?"

"Why do you think I did anything?"

"So you did nothing?"

"I brought it up again, after he'd had a few drinks."

"What'd he say then?"

"He said it was for his brother."

"His brother lives in Chile?"

"No. His brother is dead."

20

I LEFT Kline drinking and burning in a butchered *Disco Inferno*. He said he had some information about Vincent Bror's brother and would have it faxed to him in Skagway.

"Burn burn burn mother burn, burn burn down baby that!"

I didn't mention the tab. The waitress would give him the bad news later. No need for me to be there. I took a drink for the road and found an elevator. I needed to see the primary medical dude Reyes about my bullet wound. It hurt like hell, was red as hell, and hell if I could find a bandage for it. As I made my way to the concierge desk for a chaperone to Sick Bay, I couldn't help but notice other passengers pointing at me and talking behind my back. A bigger man would have ignored them, but that's not me.

"Hey. What'd you say?"

"You're the detective, right?"

"Oh. That. Yes."

"You look like a bum in a dirty shirt."

"That's blood."

"No, there."

"That's Alfredo sauce."

"Was there really a murder?"

"I'm not supposed to talk about it."

"Right," he said and slid a finger down his nose.

I returned the signal. The concierge was not happy.

Since I knew the way and didn't feel like being tattled on, I found my own way down to the secret decks through the "Crew Only" doors and elevator, rushing in before the door closed behind a maid. After a few minutes of drunken lost stumbling, my hands were made "washy-washy" and I was led to the clinic.

Principal Medical Officer—don't call him "Doctor"—Felix Reyes was in the office. He was talking to someone I couldn't see, but I recognized the severely short haircut and curt tone of voice.

"The internet's out on the ship," said Dr. Belinda Phillips erstwhile Oscar, my personal glacial fitness consultant and medic. "I'm asking you."

"What's up, Docs?" I said, pushing my way forward.

She whirled around at me, and I could see displeasure in both her beady eyes.

"Don't interrupt," she said.

Reyes lifted a plastic bag out of an ice cooler. There was a brown pea inside it that he looked closely at.

"It's a spider," he said. "A dead spider. What do you want me to say?"

"Is it poisonous?"

"All spiders are poisonous," he said.

"You don't recognize this? From your Third World home?"

"From my Third World home? You mean my ancestral villa overlooking the bay? I had servants to deal with spiders."

"Let me see it," I said.

Reyes handed me the bag.

Inside was a half-squashed, reddish-brown-tan icky insect. It looked like a spider, but it didn't have all its legs. Even counting the two in the bottom of the bag, I could only account for five.

"Hurm," I said. "I think it was a spider."

"What kind is it?"

"It's a thin spider," I said. "You should like it."

She glared at me. "I heard you're supposed to be a detective. Is that right?"

"I'm supposed to be."

"I'm not impressed."

"You're supposed to be a caregiver. Is that right?"

She turned her back on me and regarded Reyes.

"Keep it and ask your staff," she said. "See if anyone recognizes what kind of spider it is."

"No," he said. "I have important work to do. I still treat people. I don't have time to research every little gnat that flies into your cabin. Call housecleaning. Have it fumigated."

"It was in my bed. Who do I blame for that?"

"It was probably attracted to the smell of moral decay," I said.

"What?"

"Your bodily funk. That's what probably attracted the bug."

"The sheets were cleaned."

"Some stains can't be washed away."

She fumed. Reyes stepped in. "What do you need, Mr. Flaner?"

"My side is angry." I pulled up my shirt to show him.

"Yeah, let's get you some antibiotics."

"You put stitches in that?" Phillips said. "Why?"

"It needed them," he said. "Does this hurt?"

"Only when you poke it like that," I said.

"It was nothing. A scratch. I was there. He's faking it. He's a drug seeker. I see them all the time."

"He lost a lot of blood to this wound," Reyes said calmly.

"You gave him a transfusion?" She laughed. "How would it be not to have a budget?"

He rolled his eyes and pulled a set of keys from his top drawer. He opened a heavy metal cabinet affixed to a wall and came out with a small glass vial. He peeled back a foil lid and deftly filled a syringe.

"Bend over, Flaner," he said. "This goes in the ass."

"Fitting," Phillips said and stormed out.

"Don't forget your spider!" I said.

"You eat it," she said and laughed.

"She's funny. Ouch," I said. "That burns."

"She's the worst doctor I've ever worked with," he said. "The stories I could tell. Pull your pants up."

"Tell," I said.

"I can't. Professional courtesy."

"I sensed no courtesy from her."

"Good point. Plus, who are you going to tell?"

I pulled my pants over my cheeks. "How long has it been since your last confession?" I said and steepled my fingers at my chest.

"She got herself a reputation for being so efficacious that she endangered lives."

I raised an eyebrow.

"She'd decide when someone was abusing the hospital system by counting bandages. Some people said she'd triage based not on who needed the help the most but by who'd use the fewest supplies."

"You're kidding."

"That was the rumor. And God help you if you were in pain. Everybody was a 'drug seeker' and they'd be lucky to get an aspirin. After residency, and private practice, she got picked up by some big hospital in Salt Lake, where she's in administration. She's still counting bandages but well away from patients."

"Patients who can complain."

"Or sue," he said.

"And she's afraid of spiders," I said to round out her character.

"Here she had a reason, though. This little beast is *araña de rincón*, a corner spider. *Loxosceles laeta*, of the family *Sicariidae*."

"That's just what I was thinking," I said. "But I didn't want to say anything to alarm anyone."

"It's a brown recluse," he said. "We had them in Utah. I remember them."

"And black widows too, but I don't remember them having travel agents."

"This is a stowaway, of course. We get them once in a while."

"Like the white rats?"

He sighed and shook his head. "No, not like that. At least I hope not. The rats are ugly, but they're not wild rats. They're pets. Nobody would keep a spider this poisonous as a pet. This is the worst kind. South American. Chile if I'm not mistaken. Must have come aboard with the bananas."

"Remind me to stay away from the fruit."

"I can't do that," he said, looking at my ponch. "How's the pain?"

"I'd seek a pill, if you were offering."

Back in the cabinet he poured out a half dozen white tablets and slid them into an envelope.

"Take as needed, no more than one every four hours. May cause drowsiness. Avoid alcohol."

"Thanks Doc."

"PMO," he said.

I was conscious and I was dieting, so I was hungry. I knew we were going to arrive early in Skagway, and I had one more visit I wanted to make before landfall.

I found Paul Vinalez in the Rollin' Weed Sushi Bar. It was a small but crowded restaurant with booths made into separate rooms by the efficacious use of sliding paper scrims. I caught sight of Vinalez when a waiter slid out of his space. He was flanked by his wife Ashley, bodyguard Denny, and malcontent manager Sennegar, whose head was still bandaged. The lighting was just a tich brighter than I imagined a coffin to be. Shoes were optional. Chairs too.

"Hey Paul. Mind if I join you?" I said, sliding in.

"The more, the merrier," said Ashley and snorted a laugh.

Denny made to get up, but Vinalez held him back with a hand on his shoulder. He had to be content with flexing his biceps and scowling.

"That was an inconsiderate thing you did today, Mr. Flaner," Vinalez said. Instead of squeezing a pod into his mouth, this time he mixed it with his orange juice. Orange and blue make brown.

"Is that the California roll?" I said to the dish. "Mind if I try it?"

"Go right ahead."

I borrowed Sennegar's unused chopsticks and shoveled in three pieces. I was hungry. It tasted like every other California roll ever made—rice, seaweed, avocado, cucumber, and for me at least, enough wasabi to blow open Superman's sinuses.

"Yeah, I'm sorry. I got in trouble for doing that." I helped myself to some tempura.

"The security man, Peterson, talked to you then?"

"Oh, yeah. I got a time-out and everything."

"You did?" said Ashley. "I used to get those."

"Spankings too?"

She snorted another laugh. "You're funny."

I wasn't sure if she'd been drinking or drugging. I noted her inability to sit still or completely upright and figured it was both.

"Tomorrow we're back on shore," I said. "I thought I could ask you a few questions now."

"Sure," he said. He squeezed a Nutri-Pod into a dish and dipped salmon sashimi in it.

"What flavor was that?" I asked.

"Soy," he said. "It was the first flavor manufactured."

"The eel oil. Makes sense."

"Try these shrimpies," said Ashley.

"Thanks. Don't mind if I do."

The table was festooned with overflowing plates of Asian chow.

"Aren't you hungry?" I said, noting Vinalez more poking than eating his food.

"I'm having something special made."

"Sounds great. What is it?"

"Sushi," he said. "Your questions?"

Paul Vinalez had struck me as a professional con man. However, here at dinner at least, he'd dispensed with the steal-the-rings-off-your-fingers ingratiating charisma I'd expect from a classically trained swindler, and I sensed a tired man waiting for a specially prepared seaweed wrap.

"Had a hard day?" I asked.

"Actually, I have. I was half hoping that you could help me, but after the disrespect you showed today, I'm not sure I even want to help you."

The blue tuna melted in my mouth. I could taste the heavy metals and Fukushima radiation. Delicious! I chewed and considered what he'd said. I'd hurt his feelings, I could tell. I tried to see beneath the corrupt charlatan exterior to the fragile flower beneath.

"Suck it," I said. "Bring me a beer."

"Oh, I don't drink beers," he said, looking askance. "They're fattening."

"You had to go and remind me," I said. "Water then."

"Are you on a diet?" said Ashley conspiratorially. "Because if you are, I know just the thing." She winked.

"Nutri-Pods?"

"No," she whispered and winked again. Then she sniffed and mouthed the word "drugs," winked again, and squeezed my leg under the table. Vinalez rolled his eyes.

"How's your gunshot?" he asked.

"Healing."

"Did you get any pills?"

"Ashley!"

The paper door slid open and the bald mustachioed man I'd seen personally distributing menus to the captain at the steakhouse the night Bror died appeared with a plate of food. He wore a sparklingly bright white cook coat with the snazzy double-button front. He had an epaulet on his shoulders that made him a ship's officer.

"There you are, Mr. Vinalez. I made it myself."

"Hi, I'm Tony Flaner," I said. "Who're you?"

"Marvelous Martin McGuire. Ship's cook."

"Glad to meet you."

"Enjoy your food," he said and slid the panel closed behind him.

"Aren't you special," I said to Vinalez.

"Paul's got the worst allergies," Ashley said. "He has to be very careful what he eats. It's why he made the poddies."

"It's just a peanut allergy." He dipped rice into the dish of black pod juice. "It's made me the man I am, made me careful and curious and given me the inspiration for my business."

"Would that be the condos or the used car thing?"

He glared at me but didn't stop chewing. "What do you want?" he said.

"Who's trying to kill you?"

He blanched at my bluntness. "How do you know about that?" He glanced at Sennegar, who held a glass in front of his face.

"I'm a detective," I said. "Plus, you're a celebrity."

Vanity is a common trait among people like Vinalez—vain people. I used it.

Ashley went for a shrimp strapped to a Lego of rice on Paul's plate, and he slapped her hand away.

"You have your own," he said.

"I'm working on the theory that whoever killed Vincent Bror might have actually been trying to kill you," I said.

"A great man makes great enemies," Vinalez said smugly, but I could see the wheels in his head spinning. "That has occurred to me too," he said.

"Who might have it in for you?"

"It's probably an old girlfriend," said Ashley. "Or maybe an ex-wife. He has a few of them. They're all skanks. There's that Kelly girl. She's all bent out of shape because she didn't have a pre-num, pre-null, pre-nakookoo. You know, one of those marriage contract thingies. I got one. She should have thought about that."

"Are you rich?"

"I'm not, but Paul is. Thanks to Kelly the skank."

"Shut up, Ashley," Vinalez said. "Denny, maybe you should take her upstairs."

"No." She folded her arms in a pout.

"Would this Kelly want to see you dead?" I asked.

"Hell hath no fury. But no. Not like this."

"What do you mean?"

"She wouldn't need to drop rocks on people or light trailers on fire. Her family has some influence. She'd use lawyers."

"Kelly Vinalez?"

"No, she went back to her maiden name. Black, Kelly Black."

"So who do you think might be trying to kill you?"

"I've a had few businesses go sour. Some of my investors lost money. I did my best to repay them, but there could still be hard feelings."

"Colombians?"

He stopped chewing. Stared at me a second then shrugged. "Could be," he said.

"Tell me about the night before last, the night Vincent Bror died."

"We had the seminar that day," he said. "It went very well. I understand you were escorted out."

"Had I known you were ducking drug cartel hit men, I'd have been more subtle."

Again, I got him to stop chewing. I have powers.

"I had dinner with the captain," he went on. "Bror and his wife were sitting on the other side of the table, if I remember correctly. I remember also seeing you there. Bror left suddenly, rudely even. I finished my meal, went dancing with Ashley, and then we went to bed."

"When did you get to your room?"

"Quarter to one," he said. That fit with what Ola had told me about the keycard log.

"You didn't leave your room?"

"Not until Mr. Peterson knocked on the door."

"Were you still awake then?"

"Yes."

"What were you doing?" I asked before my brain kicked in.

"You were?" said Ashley. Her brain was working better than mine. "Did I enjoy it? I must have blacked out."

"It was wonderful," Paul said. "You were great."

"I always am, aren't I, honey?" She gave his knee a squeeze and them moved up his thigh. He winked at me. I gagged. The sleaze on these people was so thick, I swear I could see it pooling around them.

"I don't mean to brag," she whispered loudly, drunkenly, "but Paul's very big. If you know what I mean?"

I waited for someone to quiet her for decency's sake. No one did.

"He tires them out," she cooed. "Four other wives couldn't keep up. Isn't that right?"

Paul smirked.

"One even hanged herself when she couldn't have him."

"One of your wives killed herself?" I said, sensing a rattling skeleton behind a cupboard door.

"Not a wife. A friend in college," he said. "Someone I knew."

"Someone he dumped," Ashley said. "Some people are too frail."

"But not you," Paul said, winking at her.

"Not me," she said and went to lick his face.

From behind a napkin held over my eyes, I said, "How long have you been planning this cruise, Mr. Vinalez?"

"Three months," he said.

"That would have given your enemies time to prepare." I tried to force greasy pictures out of my head.

"Yes, it would have," he agreed. Ashley's hands were back on her champagne flute. Her tongue made an obscene show for her husband. Sennegar found something interesting to study on the opposite wall and Denny just continued flexing. His face was red and liable to pop.

"You ever hear about an organization called THAFF?"

"Who are they?"

"A people's rights group out of the University of Utah," I said.

"I went to the U of U, but I don't know them."

"You didn't strike me as a man over-burdened with education," I said. "What'd you study?"

"Like you," he said, ignoring or missing the insult, "I was a jack-of-all-trades. I studied a bit of everything. I finally graduated with an MBA."

"I guess they don't teach business ethics anymore."

"They did then," he said. "I excelled in them."

"Really?"

"You're judging me," he said.

"Am I that obvious?"

"You're in no position to judge," he said sourly. "You're not better than me."

"I didn't know I had to be."

"Of course," he said. "That's the burden of quality. The world is full of little people, Mr. Flaner. People like you. People who are small and think they're big. People who are lucky and think they're smart. People who steal but are too stupid to see they have."

"You're not that stupid?"

"No, I'm not. I know the rules. I know how the world works. I know how to use the rules and when to bend them. You might not like what I do, or how I do it, but I'm within my rights, and since the world is ultimately just, every day I excel."

"How so?"

"Money is power, power is privilege. Privilege has perks," he said.

"Now you're just sounding like a Bond villain. Where's the button that blows up your laboratory?"

Sennegar coughed, I suspected to cover a laugh. I like to think things like that. Denny squeezed his buttocks to send blood to his steroid-shrunk testes.

"I've made many enemies, Mr. Flaner," Paul said, sliding his hand under the table onto Ashley's knee. "Whoever is after me is taking a terrible chance. I solve my own problems in the old way. My people are from Sicily."

"I thought you were from Utah."

"Originally," he said.

"Wouldn't that be Africa then? In the Awash Valley? Modern Ethiopia? You know, Grandma Australopithecus?"

"What I'm saying is that I get even with the people who've wronged me." A shadow crossed his face. "When I find out who's to blame, I'll mess with them."

"Maybe someone has the same attitude with you," I said. "Maybe you'd be better off playing nice. Maybe you should find a legitimate business and work on making the world a better place instead of looking to rob people."

"There's a sucker born every minute."

"So you're admitting you're suckering people?"

"No," he said indignantly. "I was talking about…you're tiring me. Mr. Flaner, you find out who's messing with me, and I'll make it worth your while. In the meantime, take your middle-class moron morality and stick it."

"Such hostility."

"Denny." The bruiser got up with a gasp. The veins in his neck throbbed and his legs cracked with the movement.

Just before Denny put his beefsteak mitt on me, I said, "Who are the two Latino men I saw watching your presentation today?"

The bruiser hesitated.

"Why don't you find out who's to blame," he said. "Make yourself useful. Now if you'll excuse me, I'm expecting a guest."

Without assistance, I got up and opened the door.

"Thanks for dinner. Good luck with the medicine show."

"Nice talking to you," said Ashley and I genuinely think she meant it.

As I was leaving, I passed Bailey Peigne and his living sex doll, Candy. He pretended not to see me, and Candy was as out of it as Ashley was, struggling to count her fingers. I shouldn't have been surprised to see them escorted to Vinalez's table, but I was.

21

SKAGWAY in its day was called "little better than a hell on Earth" by people who actually believed in hell and were not unfamiliar with hard living and trouble. They were people to whom dying by Indian raid, cholera, smallpox, dysentery, gun shots, stampede, starvation, lead poisoning, drowning, cave-in, black lung, salmonella, or cooties was a real and probable outcome to their short, miserable lives. These things were all accepted as normal parts of their daily existence. For them to pick out the little town of Skagway for such a brutal and Biblical appellation says something.

It didn't have to be that way. On paper, from a distance, through beer-colored glasses watching from the deck of a cruise ship, Skagway was a great place. It was the first incorporated town in Alaska, beating Juneau by a day, and unlike the state's capital, you can drive to Skagway. There's a road right up through Canada connecting it with the rest of the United States. Well, the lower forty-eight anyway. It's a long and lonely road, a bit round about, but it's there. You can drive it. Go ahead and see.

Also, Skagway had the good fortune of having a prescient town father. Much of a town's character is usually cast by its early citizens. It's amazing that Skagway isn't remembered as the town that saw it coming. But nope. That's not how it went down, not how the little slice of hell is remembered. That town father, the prophet? He got screwed and no one remembers him. Instead, the town's history is all about a crook and a conman. It seemed fitting, after my previous day's encounters with Peigne and Vinalez that we stopped in Skagway next.

The story goes like this. The ground where Skagway is now came first to the attention of white folks during a boundary survey expedition in 1887 by William Moore. William Moore was a restless steamboat captain. His friends called him Billy, acquaintances called him "Buddy"—no doubt having forgotten his name—and the papers called him The Flying Dutchman. Moore was from Germany, so you can see how far the media has come in a hundred fifty years.

In the 1880s, Canada, feeling neglected and always in competition with its southern neighbor, tried several times to have a gold rush of its own. It saw how well the California strike of 1849 had worked out for the US. From that, the country got rich and powerful, got to wear nice things, and San Francisco was born, which would later give rise to the Summer of Love, Jefferson Airplane, the Grateful Dead, Dirty Harry, and Monk. Billy Moore had chased the Canadian gold discoveries up and down British Columbia with steamships and barges, a gaggle of children, a stable of goats, and one very patient wife.

Skagway is located at the head of Taiya Inlet, at the north end of the Lynn Canal, which means as little to me as it does to you. There's a relatively flat piece of land between a couple of mountains at the end of a river that flows into a protected bay that just happens to be deep enough to accommodate cruise ships. Moore arrived at the spot, and with the help of a guide called "Skookum Jim Mason," saw that there might be an overland trail to the interior from there and thus provide a close—well, "closer"—port for the gold fields.

Skookum Jim Mason's real name was Keish, and he was of the Tagish First Nation in the Yukon territory. His hunch about a path over Chilhook Pass to Bennett Lake connecting to the Yukon might have been influenced by the fact that an Indian trading route had run along that path for a couple centuries already. But that day, he was a fucking genius, and Billy and Jim "discovered" Chinook Pass. To celebrate, they immediately renamed it White Pass because Thomas White was the Canadian Minister of the Interior and you're never too far or too cold to kiss some ass.

Here Moore is shown as the visionary the world should remember him as. Immediately after the discovery of the pass, he took his sons and high-canooed it down to Juneau, where they made official claim to 160 acres at the head of the Skagway River. They named the place Mooresville and patted themselves on the back. Moore said that he'd seen enough gold strikes to know that the next one was going to be in the Yukon, and he just claimed himself the door to it. He and his family set up a sawmill, built a cabin, and started work on a dock for all the stampeders that were surely on their way. They probably set up snow cone kiosks and sled dog racetracks in anticipation of Jack London's later visit, but we can't be sure.

All this happened in 1887. It was a busy year.

Moore's prophecy, like the ancient Delphic Oracles', wasn't too clear on details, and the Yukon Gold Rush didn't begin for a decade. It happened it 1897. But Moore was ready. When the first steamships sailed up to his dock, there he was with hot chocolate and roadmaps. "Close as you please. A quick five hundred miles over glacier, rock, and ice hell, and you're there."

Overnight, Moorseville went from a population of a dozen anticipatory Germanic folk and natives to a couple thousand, then tens of thousands of stampeding prospectors.

They don't call them gold rushes because people are patient. When you're blood-crazed for gold, there's no time to wipe, let alone the niceties of land claims and deeds unless you have the muscle to back it all up, which sadly, Moore didn't. I'd like to think he wiped though.

There were immediate problems. People started squatting on his land, building houses, brothels, bars, and churches on it. Just kidding about the churches. Moore held up his deed, showed them the diagram, the signatures, and seals. They smiled and nodded and called him Buddy, then renamed the town after the Indian name, Skagway, which means either "a windy place with white caps on the water," or "place where steamboat captains get shafted," depending on the dialect.

At one point, surveyors were laying out the lines for new roads and discovered that Moore's house lay right in the middle of one they wanted to make. Moore held up his deed, showed them the diagram, the signatures, and seals. They smiled and nodded and prepared to push a road through his living room. With the help of a few friends, he managed to move his house just in time. Moore was pushed aside, not unlike the Native Americans watching from the periphery of the Skagway city limits.

Enter the villain of Skagway. Jefferson Randolph "Soapy" Smith II. If you've ever seen a black and white melodrama with a twisty mustachioed villain and Klondike setting, you already know something about Soapy Smith. An unabashed self-proclaimed conman, Soapy Smith was fresh from his recent ouster as two-time all-star crime boss of Denver. He'd honed his skills of fleecing prospectors in Creede, Colorado, during a short-lived silver rush there and arrived in Skagway in 1897, ready to do crime.

Soapy earned his nickname by a scam where he'd set up a table of soap in a public space and then dramatically hide cash among the bars, wrapping ones, fives, tens and even a hundred-dollar bill around the soap before wrapping them again in paper, thus creating a lottery out of the soap and ensuring that anyone who bought a bar was sure to get cleaned. A loud and dramatic accomplice would find money in a bar, make a big deal of it and Smith would sell penny bars of soap for a dollar each and auction off the rest when he had only a few remaining and the hundred-dollar bill yet to be claimed, which always happened. A little sleight of hand and a shill or two kept the con going until the cops chased him out of town. He got rich and helped to bring about "no purchase necessary" provisions in business-sponsored giveaways we all know and love today.

Soapy arrived in Skagway in 1897 but was quickly and firmly sent away after robbing people in a three-card monte game on the White Pass Trail. Yep, right on the trail.

Undeterred, he returned in January 1898 with some muscle and this time took root. Between charging five dollars to send a telegram to anywhere in the world three years before there were actually telegraph wires to Skagway, to soap, three-card monte, and of course the old-fashioned muggings, Soapy Smith and his gang of criminals found easy marks among the tired, gold-rich, gullible prospectors. Within a couple of months, he was running the town and the marshal was on his payroll.

Though Skagway was a lawless hellhole before Soapy, his arrival put molten pain-flavored slagma on the heaping pile of frontier villainy for frosting. Muggings turned to murders and mayhem to madness. A bunch of fed-up miners got together and formed a 101-man vigilante committee. Soapy gathered 317 men and told the miners to stick it.

In July 1898, six months after Soapy arrived, concerned citizens finally gunned the fucker down on the dock Moore had built with his sons and proclaimed the town "a little better than a hell on Earth."

The Klondike Gold Rush petered out the next year when gold was discovered near Nome. Moore finally got some satisfaction in 1901 when he received a twenty-five percent reimbursement for his lost lands, now not so valuable. Except for the honest work he did at his lumber mill, he got nothing out of Skagway's golden heyday. Today, the most famous person in Skagway is still Soapy fucking Smith, and prescient Billy Moore's name is all but forgotten beyond tour bus drivers killing time in traffic for tourists. A hundred thousand people went through Skagway during the few years of the Klondike Gold Rush—miserable, tired, smelly, greedy people. They didn't stick around. In 1900 there were only 1,800 people in the town. In 1930, that number was 492.

Skagway would be a footnote in a Jack London compendium had it not been for cruise ships. There are still fewer than a thousand permanent residents of Skagway, but the tourist rush today eclipses the gold rush of yesterday by a factor of ten—a million people per year travel to Skagway for an afternoon of Alaskan folk tales and temporary Wi-Fi.

We arrived at Moore's renovated dock at seven in the morning, though I wasn't awake to see it. I'd crawled into the big bed after hiding Dara's baseball bat in the shower and was asleep before she got in. I was woken up by Garrett at the door at seven-thirty.

"Dammit, Tony!" he yelled. "If we miss our trip, I'm blaming you."

"Dara, get up," I said. "It's time to have fun."

"Ugghhh," she moaned.

We left the ship without breakfast. We caught snippets of four different walking tours embellishing Soapy Smith's six-month criminal career in Skagway. A guidebook left at the cafe where we had our lattes advertised Moore's homestead house and sad history.

"We should see it," I said. "It looks cool."

"How far is it?" said Standard.

"How far is anything in the town?" I said. "You can throw a rock from end to end."

"I hope we'll have time to climb the Golden Stairs," said Garrett.

"The what?"

"Up there in the pass. They cut stairs for the prospectors to use on their way to the gold fields," Garrett said. "And charged them, of course."

That was a theme in Skagway. Times hadn't changed that much. It was still a feeding frenzy on visitors. Between the boat and café, we'd been propositioned by fifty people offering tours of a lifetime, gold panning, hang-gliding, gambling, and whores. Our lattes made the ship's restaurant prices seem reasonable. Dara had slipped into French to discourage pushy salespeople with fliers until someone from Quebec asked her why she kept talking about bathrooms and youth hostels.

"Where's your girlfriend, Stan?" asked Garrett.

"She said she had work to do here. We're going to try and meet up later."

"What does she see in you?"

"I'm funny."

"She obviously hasn't seen your act."

"She knew about you, Tony," Standard said. "I guess you made a scene in the lobby."

"Nothing that won't get me thrown off the ship," I said.

"I talked you up. We should double date."

Dara looked at me with accusing eyes.

"Allie," I said. "I gotta call Allie."

22

"SO, hun, I'm in Skagway. It's not as bad as the name sounds. It's kind of pretty. Very rustic. Touristy. No one lives here. It's like Disneyland but colder. Look, there's an eagle."

She hadn't picked up. I was talking to a machine. Somehow that made the distance seem much farther away than the few thousand miles it was.

"I'm on a case," I said. "There was a murder on the ship. I know the victim's wife. I'm doing the detective thing. I'm working. I'm going to be paid and everything. Oh. I've even been shot too. A rifle at a glacier. It was cool. The glacier, not being shot. That hurt. I bled a lot. It was just a graze, don't worry. I got stitches and pain pills. A shot of penicillin in my ass. I haven't been arrested yet, but I know my way around the jail. They call it a brig. I came close though, to being arrested I mean. You know. It's me."

It was agony. I should have just hung up, tried later but I couldn't release the phone. I realized that while my mind had been occupied with asking dick-head pod salesmen about shady humanist pseudo-terrorists organizations, my subconscious had been focused on Allison Braise and my inability to deal with my relationship with her. I was racked with guilt. My mind punishing me for putting its energy toward Kristen and not Allie.

"The case could be a big deal," I said. "It's like destiny that I'm on the ship. You know? It was meant to happen. I was meant to come with my friends on this cruise and not even call you because, you know? Destiny. I'm not doing myself any favors, am I? Listen, Allie, I'm sorry. I know I screwed up. I miss you and I hate myself. I know I'm to blame. I'll find the flaw and I'll fix it. I'm sorry. I miss you. I—"

Yeah, I left it hanging. I could have, maybe should have, said I loved her, but I didn't. I felt too ashamed of myself to say it. I didn't want Allie to think

I was saying it to gain favor or manipulate her into forgiving me. I didn't deserve it.

"I gotta go," I said. "I'll try and call you later. Bye."

I called Nancy.

"Hey Nance. How's the house selling?"

"I presented an offer on the Peigne place. It's an insultingly low offer. If I hadn't been contractually obligated to present it, I wouldn't have."

"She took it, didn't she?"

"Yes. How'd you know?"

"Lucky guess. I know Bailey Peigne will be pleased to hear it. No, wait, the other thing. It'll put him in a rage. Lucky me. Does he know yet?"

"He'll probably get the news today."

"How low is the offer?"

"They're losing money."

"They don't have to take it then?"

"It's her call and his wallet. He's still paying on the remodel. Hell hath no fury like a woman scorned."

"Speaking of hell, ever been to Skagway?"

"No. Is it nice?"

"A little lonely."

"You haven't talked to Allie yet, have you?"

"Have you talked to her?"

"Why would I talk to her?"

"I don't know," I said. "I thought maybe you might have called her to patch things up between her and me."

"Tony, you are too much. Man up and call her."

"I tried. No answer."

"She's probably working."

"Probably avoiding me."

"Or that."

"I feel terrible."

"You should," she said. "It's your fault. All this is your fault. When you talk to her, fess up and take the blame. If you whinge, I will personally slap you."

"It's not easy, you know."

"What?"

"To take responsibility for something bad you've done."

"This isn't like you, Tony. As long as I've known you, you've been a pretty good judge of your own staggering limitations."

"It was easy to admit when I only had to answer to myself, when I wasn't afraid of losing anyone's respect."

"What about me?"

"Our marriage was hardly textbook," I said. "Besides, you accepted me and had your plan. I enjoyed trying to mess it up and never had any fear of actually doing it."

"In your own stupid insulting way, I think what I'm hearing is that you think Allie will think less of you if you confess to having done what she already knows you've done."

"Does that make sense?"

"No."

"But you said—"

"I understand it because I understand you. No rational person can think that way. You've got to take responsibility. Don't equivocate. Don't put your failures and failings on someone else."

"Is that what I'm doing?"

"Aren't you?"

"I might if I had a good target," I admitted. "I've blamed Perry and my friends for my alcoholism."

"You're an alcoholic?"

"No, but I'm thinking of trying it on to help me through this."

"Tony…"

"I've never done anything so thoughtless in my life as going on this cruise without as much as a phone call to Allie."

"You didn't call me or Randy either."

"That's not the same."

"No, but it's something."

"Ahhhhh," seemed like the appropriate response. "What's wrong with me?"

"For one thing," she said. "You're asking your ex-wife this question."

"But you know me."

"These are new problems with you. I'm happy to see you're growing up, Tony, but I'm not your babysitter. I'm not your mother. Be a man and work it out with Allie."

"No. You can't make me."

"So much for growing up."

"Is Randy there?"

"If you dump your emotional garbage on him, I'll murder you."

"Come on. Would I do that?"

"Yes."

"Well," I said. "Well. I won't. How's that? Now whatcha gonna do, huh?"

"And to think you're having relationship problems. Randy! Your teenage father's on the phone for you!"

I heard the line pick up.

"Hello," I said to my son.

"Goodbye, Tony," and Nancy was gone.

"Hey, Dad."

"So I hear you're having relationship troubles."

"It's nothing."

"It's about a dance, right?"

"Yes. I want to ask Julie out, but I don't know how."

"What's the dance?"

"End of the school year thing," he said. "How'd you get Mom to go out with you?"

"I'm charming," I said.

"Does that work?"

"It used to."

"I don't think it'll work here. I have to think of a clever way to ask her. That's what it's all about."

That's not what dances were all about when I was in school, but times change.

I said, "I read about a boy who used fireworks to ask a girl out. She used melted crayons to accept."

"Everyone's read that book," he said.

"Put balloons in her car."

"She doesn't have one."

"Sing under her window. Do you play guitar?"

"No, of course not."

"Do your drums, then."

"I want her to accept the invitation."

"Oh, right," I said. "Well, do what you do best. Use your computer."

"How?"

"Don't do anything creepy. No viruses. Maybe a Photoshop thing."

"Maybe," he said. "Yeah, okay. I have an idea."

And Nancy said I couldn't help my son.

"Hey, Randy," I said. "While I've got you, can you do me a solid?"

"What?"

"I need you to do some research for me. There's a guy named Bror, Vincent Bror. B-R-O-R. He went to the University of Utah and he invented a microchip. He's got a patent for it."

"Dad, I got stuff to do."

"I'm on a case, and someone cut the internet on the ship."

"Oh right. You're in Alaska. Mom mentioned it."

A wave of guilt for not letting my son know I was gone stood up, brushed itself off, and got in beside its twin from Allie.

"Yeah. Sorry, son. I should have told you."

"Why? You're a grownup."

"I think I came up here to hide," I said.

"Oh. That doesn't sound very grownup."

"No, it doesn't. Anyway, Vincent Bror was murdered on the ship, and I'm looking for clues. I have to crack it before we land back in Seattle in four days. I need help."

"What do you want to know?"

"Whatever you can find would be helpful."

"Is that all?" He didn't hide his sarcasm very well. I think it was intentional.

"Flores Limited in Chile."

"A company?"

"I don't know. Seems shady. Whatever you can find."

"Whatever," he said with a sigh. I heard the tell-tale clicks of his keyboard in the background and knew I was losing him. "Anything else?"

"Well, yeah. Okay. Dig up what you can about a guy named Paul Vinalez. He owns a company called Nutri-Pods that sells—"

"God. Those things are disgusting."

"You know them?"

"There's a kid at school who sells them. He's a pushy creep."

"Yeah, I'm on a boat full of them."

"Bummer."

"See what you can find," I said. "Oh, and a group called THAFF. And a homeless shelter called Tommy's Place."

"Come on, Dad," he whined.

"That's all," I said. "And a girl named Kristen—"

"I gotta go, Dad. I'll talk to you later." He hung up.

I went back to my friends at the cafe.

"I'm hungry," said Garrett. "Let's find some chow."

"Aren't we going to wait for Perry?" I said.

"I don't think he's coming," said Standard. "He said not to wait for him. He was hunting for supplies."

"What kind of supplies?"

"An arctic sleeping bag, MREs, and a waterproof satellite transponder."

"Let's go," I said.

We walked up the narrow main street of Skagway along wooden boardwalks past souvenir shops, taffy makers, and precious metal stores with grandiose displays of blue stones that at once reminded me of glaciers and Caribbean seas. "Now on sale!"

We found a crowded cafe that offered "Chowder and Muffins" and ordered some of both. We sat on a bench to eat and people watch.

The storm that had buffeted the buffet the day before was out to sea, lurking. A broken gray cloud cover shaded the town and made it cool enough to require a jacket that I had of course left in the cabin.

The pier lined right up with the street making our ship look like a grand mansion at the end of it. The Circus cruise ship *Clown Car* was pulled in behind our *Success* and was disgorging passengers like a cat ridding itself of hairballs.

"Do you think that Circus Clown Toover will be here?" said Standard.

"He said he would," Garrett.

"Threatened," corrected Dara.

"Here comes Perry," I said, seeing him down the boardwalk, hood pulled over his head.

"Hey don't we know those guys?"

The two men we'd seen in Juneau walked by us on the sidewalk. They still wore the same hunting fatigues but didn't have the clipboard this time. They did a double take at Dara and were rewarded with another view of her middle finger. They hastened away before she could follow up verbally.

"Are they on our ship?" I asked.

"I haven't seen them."

Perry sat down and took half my muffin.

"They look local," said Standard.

"Local to Juneau and Skagway?"

"They're not that far apart," said Garrett.

"They seem to be looking for someone, don't you think?"

"Dammit, Flaner," said Standard. "Turn it off. Enjoy your cruise. You blew us off all day yesterday."

"What did I miss?"

"Dara got hit on," said Standard. "That fitness guy, Xavier Polates."

"Oh my god," I said. "I can't stand him."

"Neither can I," said Dara.

"What happened?"

"I went to his aerobics class, and he talked me into going to his secret cabin."

"And you went?"

"It was a secret cabin," she said with a mouthful of muffin. "I was curious."

"How was it?"

"It was a storage room on deck four. It stank like a pet shop. Boxes and cans and shit. He'd set up a hammock. Expected me to climb aboard."

"Tell me you maced him and ran away screaming," I said.

"He's not that bad looking, Flaner," she said. "Maybe he doesn't have your girth or your idiot haircut, but some girls might find him attractive."

"He's the ship gigolo. I know the type," I said. "I've run into them before."

"He's been around," she said. "I'll give him that. He's got more sea miles on him than the Spanish Armada."

"It was built and then sank," said Garrett. "The ships were brand new. They had hardly any miles on them at all."

"I'm saying he's worked cruise ships forever."

"Always for Royal Danish?"

"No. He just got hired on."

"Didn't the ship already have a male prostitute/fitness instructor?" I asked.

"The last guy jumped ship in Seattle. Didn't show up to work. I'm not surprised," said Perry. "He was sick of it and met a rich widow from San Diego. I'm sure he's there now, playing pool boy for six figures a year."

"Good work if you can get it," said Standard.

"Don't hold your breath," said Dara. "You gotta be good-looking."

"That's all it takes?" I asked.

"Being romantic doesn't hurt," she said. "Xavier said his arrival on the ship was destiny. It was written in the stars so he could meet me."

"Tell me that didn't work," I said.

She shrugged.

"Really?" said Garrett. "If I'd known corny worked so well on girls, I wouldn't have studied fine arts."

"It helps if you have six-pack abs," she said. "Not the twelve-pack that Flaner has."

"Why does everyone call you fat?" said Perry. "You're not fat."

"He says he is," said Dara. "We're just encouraging him."

"Hey, I've been dieting hard. Don't give me that shit."

"How's your chowder?" asked Standard. "The extra-large, double-oyster cracker chowder and chocolate chip muffin?"

"And Diet Coke," I added. "Delicious."

"Xavier knows you, Tony," Dara said. "I guess you guys met."

"Briefly."

"He asked me if you were a real detective."

"What did you say?"

"I said you have your moments."

"Really? Thanks."

"A rare instance of charity. It won't happen again."

"So did you, uhm..." asked Garrett.

"A lady doesn't kiss and tell."

"That's why he's asking," I said.

"Fuck you guys. There's our bus," said Dara.

"What bus?"

"Didn't I tell you? Xavier gave me passes for the Golden Trail Panning Iditarod Adventure Bus Tour."

"No, you didn't," I said.

"But we have whale watching," said Garrett.

"We'll be back in plenty of time."

"Why'd he give them to you?" I asked.

She scowled. "They were a cruise promotion. He was to give them to a lucky attendee of his 'Sweat Out the Dawn' class."

"Why didn't he?"

"No one showed up to sweat at dawn."

"Sounds like there was one person," I said and got slapped.

23

PERRY SAID he had things to do and left us at the bus stop like children on the first day of school and headed for a survivalist store that sold MREs by the gross.

A handwritten sign on a torn piece of brown cardboard proclaimed "Welcome Danish Success Passengers" in stringy black Sharpie letters. Dara handed over our tickets, and we got on the bus.

It was a repurposed school bus. The top had been covered in corrugated tin, and the outside was paneled in wooden slats making the whole thing look like the love child of the Brady Bunch station wagon and an aircraft hangar. The seats were original issue, built when padding meant springs and Naugahyde was traded on the New York commodities exchange. A small flat-screen television hung on hinges and was secured to the roof with a bungee cord so it could be lifted out of the way while moving about.

We were the first to board. A red-bearded lumberjack who smelled of strong weed and dogs sat in the driver's seat and welcomed us by repeating, "Where ya' from? Really? Far out," as a single slurred statement. Since we were comics and thus ex-juvenile delinquents and troublemakers by nature, we took our assigned seats in the back of the bus as was tradition.

A parade of familiar faces boarded after us in small straggling groups. Roxy, Arnold, and Susan from the Grays' poker game presented laminated passes and took the second-row seats like they were assigned pews. Paul Vinalez boarded the bus with Ashley in matching fluorescent pea-green nylon Nutri-Pods windbreakers, which I'd noticed other cultists wearing that morning. Denny joined them, but Mr. Sennegar was left on the curb and ducked into a bar the moment the party was aboard. Dr. Belinda Phillips paid cash and took a brochure from the lumberjack. A gaggle of pod people tried to trade sampler boxes of assorted flavors for a ticket to ride with their guru but were refused.

Candy burst onto the bus like she was crashing a bachelor's party. Three steps behind was Bailey Peigne with a toothpick in his teeth. He took the seat behind Vinalez and they passed a flask back and forth. The two Hispanic guys I'd seen at the pod presentation tried to get tickets, but the bus was full by then, the Alabama Bible-Based Lawn Care conglomerate having taken the last six seats.

The lumberjack closed the door with a steel mechanical arm and saluted the ticket-taker who went back to her kiosk and changed departure times on a chalkboard. He undid the bungee, lowered the screen, turned it on, and started the motor.

The bus spurted to life with a raspy mechanic smoke-cloud that even I knew meant gasket failure. He turned the bus around, nearly taking out a pack of mountain bikers with moose antler helmets and headed out of town. The television came to life, and a drawling actor with a handlebar mustache, bowler hat, and a gold pan told us about the Golden Stairway and the Klondike Gold Rush.

The sound wasn't great, or it might have been, but we couldn't hear it over the sound of the engine, bad roads, squeaky suspension, and complaining seat cushions. Close captioning was on, so if I was willing to risk car sickness, I could watch the movie.

The gist of the show was that White Pass, formerly Chinook Pass, was easier than other routes to the Klondike gold fields, but still a total pain in the ass. In fact, it was a terrible trip. The steep pass was known as the Golden Stairs and took all day to climb. I assume the name had to do with the final goal of the miners, not the condition of the steps after so many half-drunk urinating miners had climbed them.

We were told lots of miners died on the way or starved, which seemed a bit redundant, but made for a good segue into all the dead livestock. So many horses died along the trail that the trail was nicknamed "Dead Horse Trail," as if it didn't have enough names—local color at its finest. The starving miners were so hungry, since they were starving, that they sometimes ate the dead horses. Many prospectors went insane on the pass. Some think it was from eating dead horses, others say there was an Indian curse, science suggests scurvy, but I personally think they were insane to begin with. The trip to the gold fields from Skagway was over five hundred miles. True, you could build a raft at Bennett Lake and float some of it, but only after you made the terrible trip across the pass multiple times. So many people were dying of starvation along the path, that officials mandated that you had to bring a year's worth of rations or they'd turn you away. That's over nine hundred pounds of trail mix, and the road was single-file, steep, and crawling with thieves. After you purchased your grub in "little better than a hell on Earth" Skagway from the villains there for twice what you were likely to pay an armed extortionist, you had to get it up the hill. Many local Indians got rich carrying crates to the top of the pass and retired as wealthy men while prospectors ate two-year-old rotting dead horse meat, danced with sticks named "Matilda," and wondered why their teeth fell out and old scars reopened.

Our road paralleled the narrow-gauge train tracks that were laid to take miners up the pass after the tram didn't work out. The completion of the rail line coincided with the end of the Klondike Gold Rush, which led to a domino of bankruptcies in Skagway that continue to this day. We waved at the tourist-packed train as it chugged past us.

The television switched to general Alaskan history and then to the Iditarod race and what makes for a good sled dog. Spoiler: it should be able to handle cold temperatures.

The jostling bus and TV attention made me queasy. I turned my attention out the nearest window in case my chowder and muffins needed a quick exit.

Dara nodded off and flopped her head onto my shoulder. Standard played with his phone and didn't even glance out the window. Garrett took flash pictures with a little digital camera.

Vinalez had bullied his own seat and was talking across the aisle to Peigne. Behind him, Ashley and Denny tried to trade foot fungus. Paul sucked down plastic bottled grease and dropped the empties on the floor where they rattled all trip.

Candy turned in her seat and waved at me. I waved back. Bailey elbowed her and she scowled. Roxy had a book and Susan brought knitting. Arnold had his walker turned upside and was prying the rubber feet off. Once they were gone, he reached inside the legs and withdrew a length of clear tubing. He did this for all the legs. When he was done, he had four five-foot sections of three-quarter-inch clear tubing closed at each end. He put the rubber feet back on the walker, turned it upright, hung the tubes around his neck and winked at me when he caught me looking.

The bus turned off the Klondike Highway and drove down a gravel road through stunted pines to a creek. It crossed the water, made a right, and we were at the "Golden Trail Panning Iditarod Adventure Park." A sign told us so.

The Adventure Park was attached to the "Klondike Adventure Hunting Lodge," where for "reasonable rates," you could rent a wooden shack a little smaller than our shipboard closets. We passed a row of them just beyond the gate. They were rustic in a *Li'l Abner* kind of way, with a wood stove and chimney, crooked shingles and a porch decorated with jarringly modern plastic lawn chairs and bear-proof garbage cans.

The bus pulled in beside the "General Store," so labeled in Old West script, complete with a disembodied cuffed hand pointing a finger at the door.

"Enjoy your visits," the driver said. "Buses leave every half hour. Far out."

"Far out," I said.

The bus passengers dispersed to explore the ranch. I wandered into the general store for some relief. Away from the shore, the mosquitoes were thick enough to spread with a knife. I couldn't find a knife I liked, so I bought a can of bug spray. I picked up a sweatshirt that depicted a hunter on a dog sled shooting a bear eating an eagle grasping a salmon with a gold nugget in its mouth.

"Check it out," Standard said. "Bear scent."

"Great," said Dara. "Just what you need: novelty bear stink."

"It's not novelty," said a cashier, a pale-blonde twenty-year-old girl in a silk-screened Kurt Cobain T-shirt and minimum makeup.

"Here's cougar musk," said Standard. "And badger."

"What does it do?" I asked.

"It has a lot of uses," said the cashier.

"Chili seasoning?" I suggested.

She smiled. "I wouldn't go that far. Hunters use it to attract prey. Farmers use it for discouragement."

"I'd think the three-week growing season would be enough for that."

"We grow crops here," she said. "The ranch is a co-op, kind of a commune. We use those musks to keep deer and rabbits away from our vegetables."

"Don't bears eat anything? Aren't you pulling them in?"

"We use fences against the bears, but stink against the smaller things. It works. Deer and moose are the worst."

"Aren't they just?" I said.

"Is that how you got Camila, Standard? Using cougar musk?"

"Shut up, Garrett," he said.

"Here's some slug repellent for Dara," I said, not knowing she was standing right behind me. She made her presence known by slapping the back of my head.

"Is that the bus we rode in?" asked Garrett, pointing to a book, *Into the Wild*.

"No," I said. "That's another one."

Another bus arrived, and more people got out.

"If we want to do anything here, we better hurry," said Standard.

The two Latinos had arrived. We passed them slapping their own faces in the doorway to the general store. They went straight for the mosquito spray.

The crab fishing mayhem was there as well, bright lights following the two brothers as they argued about which attraction to visit first.

"You're just a hateful, useless, lazy sack of shit!" the first said, giving post-production something to bleep out.

"You have no respect for your elders," said the second. "Dad was an Iditarod fan. We should see the sled dogs first."

Before they came to blows, we steered clear of the blinding spotlight.

The panning trough line was filling fast with other reality show refugees, but we were closest to that, so we started there.

"Howdy, folks. You're not from around here, are ya?" said a costumed prospector complete with scraggly white beard, suspenders, holes in his hat, front teeth missing and halitosis. He sat on a three-legged stool surrounded by earthen jugs marked with triple X's.

"What gave it away?" said Standard.

"Ain't nobody from around here!" he hollered and slapped his knee. Then he grabbed a jug, and tipping it with his elbow, took a big drink.

"Moonshine?" said Dara.

"Don't mind if I do!" He took another drink from the jug.

"Touristy novelty bullshit," she said. "Give it here."

He passed her the jug. Dara took a mouthful and screamed.

"What the fuck is that?"

"Moonshine," said the prospector. "What'd you expect?"

"It's not even noon yet!"

"What's your point, lady?"

I took a pull. It was clear as spring water and as potent as charcoal-filtered rocket fuel. Just a mouthful cut through the chowder and muffins to my central nervous system, and I found it hard to stand.

"How much?" I rasped.

"Them's fightin' words!" he proclaimed, standing up suddenly. "Come on back roun' here and we'll settle this."

He stormed away behind an authentic functioning outhouse. I pinched my nose and followed.

I found Arnold with his walker sitting behind the building on a stool. His walker was again disassembled. Using a funnel, with the help of a ranch hand, he carefully poured moonshine into the plastic tubes I'd seen him with before. Several other plastic tubes were already full and ready to be re-inserted into the walker to be smuggled aboard.

"What ship ya on?" the prospector asked me.

"The *Success*," I said. "Royal Danish."

"A hundred, and it'll be in your room when you get back. Thirty-five and you can take it with you. Take your chances with the cruise ship gestapo."

I didn't have a walker, so I gave him my last two hundred-dollar bills for two jugs. He wrote down my room number in a moleskin book with a two-inch knife-sharpened pencil stub. He gave me another shot from a dented metal cup to seal the deal and my esophagus fused shut.

"Thanks," I squeaked.

Dara's tour passes only included getting us to the ranch. The amusements were extra. We forked over twenty dollars each to learn how to swirl mud in a tin pan over a trough of freezing water and sand.

"This is fun," said Garrett.

"I can't feel my fingers," said Standard.

"My mouff is still numb," said Dara.

"I can sense the gold in the water," said I. "It calls to me."

"You guys are taking too long," said the not-still-so-patient panning instructor. "We got people waiting to get in."

"You said we got to keep whatever gold we find," said Standard.

"So find some," he said. "You only get one scoop."

"And we're making that scoop count, buddy."

"I can hear the *Call of the Wild*!" I shouted. "It sounds like indigestion and heart palpitations."

We swirled moist dirt for a while longer. Finally the instructor took our pans one at a time and with a couple quick twirls found color in the dirt. He tipped each into a little glass vial and handed them over.

"Thanks for coming—next!"

"Dog kennel? Dog racing? Dog feeding? Or the 'Forty Below Experience?'"

"I like puppies," I blabbered.

"Dogs it is."

Dara led me to the kennels, where huskies yapped and jumped around for the tourists, who bought biscuits from a bubble-gum dispenser and tossed them through holes in chicken wire.

For five dollars I got to hold puppies for as long as I wanted or fifteen minutes, whichever came first. Garrett splurged and got to ride on a converted Iditarod sleigh. At the magic word "mush," a string of nine dogs pulled him across a racetrack faster than I thought a non-freefalling sled could go. He failed to brake in time and took another trip around the course. A tense moment erupted while drunk Dara explained to them in language that would be forever etched into their subconsciousness' why Garrett was not going to pay for the "extra fucking dog ride lap, you motherless goat-raped fellatio spit-takes."

The conversation ended with a drawn-out silence wherein many inner children silently wept.

"What's the 'Forty Below Experience?'"

"I'm ready to go," said Standard, pulling his baseball cap lower over his eyes. "That was ugly."

"Could have been worse," said Dara.

Since the tourist season no longer included the opportunity of freezing to death while picking horsehair out of your teeth, the ranch did their best to provide the service. Instead of horse meat, they offered boxed salmon. For the cold experience, they had a bank of walk-in freezers decorated as nineteenth-century rustic shanties. It was free to go in and pose in front of the thermometer where an automatic digital camera would snap a souvenir photo you could buy for twenty dollars. What a deal.

There was a line to get in. Our bus wasn't back, and we'd had enough of the dogs, so we waited.

There were two freezer photo booths operating. A third shack identical to the other two, but set off a little, had a "no admittance" sign hanging off the stainless-steel handle. The kennels were right behind us, and the barking dogs made it difficult to think, let alone talk.

"I would go crazy here," said Standard. "The noise is terrible."

"We're in a sound pocket," said Garrett. "It's a natural feature of the landscape and the huts. It's not so bad in other areas."

"Between the dogs and the pounding and the screaming, I don't know how they do it."

Garrett was right, though. The sound from the entire ranch was focused right into the line to the freezers. The Alabama group went in ahead, and we were next.

A tourist musher flipped his sled and there was an abrupt silence before the dogs went wild. The air was double full with the sounds of injured yips and apologies from the idiot who'd leaned too far over in the turn. Cursing handlers rushed in before he was eaten by the pissed-off huskies.

I put my hands to my ears and tried to shake off the 120-proof alcohol. Something was wrong. There'd been something in the silence. In that brief split second before all hell broke loose, I'd heard something I shouldn't have.

I stepped away from the line.

"What are you doing, Tony?" said Dara. "We're finally fucking there. I'm not saving your place."

"What's wrong, Tony?" asked Garrett.

"Shhhh," I said.

Standard laughed. "Are you kidding?"

"Shush them, Dara," I said.

Dara, diminutive elfish drunken Dara, could probably scale Everest without oxygen and hold her breath for a fortnight. Such were her lungs. She took a deep breath, cupped her hands over her mouth and yelled.

"All you limp-dicked losers need to shut the fuck up now!" she hollered.

Like magic, the ranch fell silent. Even the dogs paused, sensing the primeval power of a scrappy, underestimated blue-streaked comic in their midst.

The screams were muffled, the pounding far away. I tilted my head, turned around in a circle and traced the sound. I took a step, checked my bearings, and then approached the locked freezer. I pressed my ear against it.

"Help us!"

I pulled the handle, but it didn't move. It was locked down by a rusty sixteen-penny nail attached to a chain on the door and threaded through a hole in the handle. I lifted the pin out and the door flew open.

Paul Vinalez and a tight red sweater on a buxom brunette tumbled out into the yard. They were red as cherries, covered in frost and shaking like silenced pagers.

"So that's where you got to," said Ashley Vinalez, coming up behind me. "I thought you had a headache, Paul."

24

"ANOTHER MINUTE and I'd have been dead," Paul Vinalez said through chattering teeth.

"We'd have both been dead," said his freezer buddy.

"No. It takes longer than that," said an official representative of the Golden Trail Panning Iditarod Adventure.

"No, he's right," said the younger crab fisherman. "You lose consciousness in seconds and are dead as an iceberg in five minutes even if you have a survival suit."

"That's for water temperatures," said the representative, a black-bearded, middle-aged man with biceps as big as boulders and a red bandana around his forehead.

"How long were they in there?" asked someone.

The brunette in the nippily red sweater said, "Ten minutes."

"Then you're dead!" said the crab fisherman.

She started to cry.

"You'll be fine," said the representative.

"Can you repeat that?" asked the cameraman, pushing a lens into his face.

"They'll be fine. No harm done."

"No harm done?" said Paul. "We could have died."

The representative looked down at Vinalez's open fly and the camera followed his gaze and zoomed in. "Looks like you two found a way to keep warm," he said. "What were you doing in that locker anyway? It's not part of the tour. We store meat in there."

"I think they were looking for sausage," said Ashley, popping her gum. I could sense she still had a little buzz on, but it was fading fast and her sobering eyes were ablaze. The Vinalezes hadn't struck me as the jealous types, but commitment of any kind brings obligation and exceptions. Don't I know it.

Denny moved behind Vinalez and adjusted the blanket to cover his boss' open pants.

"Where were you?" he spat at his bodyguard.

"You told me you wanted some time alone," he said. "You said to keep Ashley distra—"

"Oh, shut up," he cut him off.

The woman in the sweater was vaguely familiar to me. She'd sat up close to the stage during the seminar, and I only saw her back then. I'd seen her in the audience acting as an attractive shill for the Nutri-Pods presentation in the manner of Soapy Smith's street antics. Once her face warmed up, it was easy to match up the color of her smeared lipstick with the stain on Vinalez's pants.

"You shouldn't have been in there," the representative said. "There was a sign and everything."

"Didn't want to wait in line," he chattered. "Someone locked us in."

"If one of my people saw the chain undone, we might have locked it," the representative conceded.

"It was attempted murder," Vinalez said.

The camera was right in his face. He squinted from the floodlight.

"I mean, I could have been killed in there. Lucky I was saved."

"*We* were saved," said the brunette.

"Yes, me and this young lady here. Curiosity got the better of us. Thank the good Lord we're safe. God bless everyone."

He sucked down a pink Nutri-Pod with his patented "good medicine" show and nearly chipped his teeth trying to smile.

While Vinalez massaged his public persona, I examined the storage shed where he'd been trapped.

It was a walk-in freezer like the ones we could have our pictures taken in but without the mural of mountain sluices under clear blue skies. There was, however, a thermometer. It read just below freezing, not forty below as the others. There were shelves of supplies, boxes and wrapped meat, and pallets of dog food marked *Dog Food–Elk, Dog Food–Moose, Dog Food–Deer,* and *Dog Food–Badger*. I could see where someone had laid out burlap bags of coffee beans into a kind of mattress by the wall. The lack of frost was a giveaway, even if the unopened condom on the floor hadn't been there. I suspect Vinalez and his "date" had had bigger plans than a blow job in the closet but had underestimated the cold and shifted their plans to a faster, more clothed coital encounter. The love nest was as cozy and romantic as a frozen dog food storage locker could be.

I examined the door. The latch was solid and sealed the airtight door effectively. There was a handle on both sides, but the simple mechanism on the front locked it tight with just the single metal pin dangling under the handle. The hole was large enough to accept a padlock coil, and I couldn't help thinking that if the Golden Trail Panning Iditarod Adventure hadn't been a half-hippy co-op where trust was assumed and honesty expected, Vinalez might still be in there behind a real lock.

After the cameraman relented, Vinalez retreated with Ashley for some uncomfortable damage control.

I followed the ranch representative through some trees and came up on him beside a stream as he was bringing fire to a fat six-inch reefer. He looked at me once and offered me a toke. To put him at ease I took one. Or two. I gave him my new business card, *Tony Flaner, Private Detective—I'm not after you, unless I am.*

"So did any of your people lock the door?" I grunted in the time-honored manner of stoners everywhere. Had to put the man at ease, didn't I?

"It'd served them right if they had," he said. "But no. I asked everyone. No one had been near there since breakfast."

"How long would they have lasted in there?"

"Hours if they had half a brain between them. Days, really. Maybe weeks. Plenty of food in there."

"How long if it had been one of the forty-below lockers?"

"The way they were dressed? Permanent damage, ten minutes. Death in less than half an hour. Not as bad as water, but water doesn't get as cold as the Alaska tundra, and that's what we're imitating in those lockers. They really had no business being in there."

"Can't fault them for having too much intelligence," I said.

"You buy that sweatshirt here?"

"Yep, and two jugs of your finest."

"Don't be telling anybody where you got that. And don't bogart the joint."

"Wouldn't think of it," I said.

The stream was idyllic, and had it not been moving, bending light as it tumbled over stones and around fallen limbs, I'd have sworn the water was blown glass, so unbelievably clear was it.

"This is great grass," I said.

"Keeps us in business."

"And the moonshine?"

"Yeah."

"Is it really going to be in my cabin when I get back?"

"What line are you on?"

"Royal Danish. The *Success*."

"Not as easy as the Circus line—they're a joke, but we'll get it to you."

"How?"

"Dock workers get paid shit. Ship cleaners get paid worse than shit. How much you pay for delivery?"

I did the math in my head. “Well, let’s see. It was thirty-five if I took it with me, a hundred if it was delivered. So eighty bucks a bottle.”

“Sixty-five.”

“Oh, right.”

“It’ll be there.”

“I should go while I can still feel my internal organs.”

“Good luck, Tony Flaner,” he said. “Love what you did in Thailand.”

“You get internet out here?” I said.

“Not much else to do in the winter.”

“Cool.”

The group was waiting for me at the bus.

“We gotta go, Tony,” said Garrett. “We still have whale watching to do.”

“Lord knows those whales won’t watch themselves,” I said and climbed aboard.

The driver, the same lumberjack as before, smelled the pot on my clothes as I got on. “Far out,” he said.

“I am indeed.”

“You’re too much, Flaner,” Standard said. “You disappear on us to do ‘detective work’ and you come back smelling like Cheech and Chong.”

“Did you want some?” I said.

“That shit will ruin your brain,” said Standard.

“You gotta have one to lose one,” I said. “You’re safe.”

The bus filled up with more or less the same people who’d arrived in it. Ashley and Paul Vinalez were in separate seats, Denny in between them. Bailey Peigne and Candy were still in line for the freezers and called up to the bus that they’d take the next one, as if anyone cared. Doctor Phillips boarded late and had to sit in the back by us. She slid in beside Dara across from me. The fishermen left the way they’d come—in a pair of hired cars. After the first car sped away with the producer and cameraman, I overheard the two fishermen talking outside the bus.

“Where do you want to eat?” asked one.

“Oh, anywhere you want to go,” said the other.

“No, you decide. It’s your turn.”

“But you’re hungrier,” came the reply.

“We’ll find a nice place in town.”

“Sounds great. I’m buying.”

“You’ll have to fight me for it.”

The younger one held the door open for the older who tickled him as he climbed in.

“That,” I said, “tells you all you need to know about reality television.”

“What was it?” said Garrett. “I missed it.”

“People getting along,” said Dara.

“How’s that good television?”

“Exactly,” I said.

The television screen was lowered as before but I tuned it out and watched the countryside. My stomach was already doing calisthenics from shots of moonshine and tokes of Alaskan grass. I didn't know if I could actually throw up, but I didn't feel like taking up the challenge, so I avoided carsickness as much as possible.

"How's your side?" said the lady doctor, not looking at me.

"Do you care?" I said.

"No," Belinda Phillips said. "You were over-treated. That would never happen where I work. It's wasteful."

"Where do you work?" asked Dara.

She turned in her seat and smiled warmly at Dara. "Wasatch Medical."

"For how long?"

"A few years," she said politely. "A long time, actually. I'm rising up."

"Ever been in private practice?" I asked.

"I tried after ER work at the U, but it didn't work out. Too many needy people expecting things just because they're paying you."

"Imagine that," I said.

"That's what they don't teach you in medical school," she said to Dara. "It's so messy dealing with some people. Most people."

"Most people are messy," Dara said.

Dr. Phillips laughed, a forced mirthy giggle. "Yes, so true. Where are you from?"

"Utah," said Dara.

"Are you with the Nutri-Pods group? I think I'd have seen you there."

"Hell, no," said Dara.

"You're with the group?" I asked.

Still not looking at me, she said, "I'm investigating it."

"Like for the law?"

"No, for an investment."

"Is he looking for investors?"

"By 'he' I assume you mean Paul Vinalez. I don't know."

"So what are you doing here? Don't you make enough seeing patients?"

"Oh, I don't see patients anymore. I'm in administration."

"I thought you were a doctor."

"I am a doctor."

"Licensed?"

She turned to look at me then, with her cold, appraising, compassionless eyes more fitting for a used car salesman with a crack habit than a healer. It was a good thing, I decided, that the public at large didn't have to deal with her in a clinical setting.

"Yes, I am licensed," she said. "I finished in the top five percent of my class."

"Grenada?" I said and got another withering look.

"University of Utah."

"Ah, right. They have a good program there. How'd you ever—"

Before I could insult her again, she cut me off for Dara. "Have you been to the Twilight Bar on the ship?" she asked. "It's really a nice place."

"I'll have to check it out," said Dara.

"I'm Belinda. Hello."

"Dara. Hi."

They shook hands, Belinda cast a don't-even-think-of-talking-to-me-anymore look at me, and I settled into the scenery as the television explained how desperate men had eaten dead horses.

Back in Skagway I broke my shattered diet with bag of chocolate chip cookies and a box of ice cream sandwiches. To be fair, I shared with my friends, and they ate most of them. I forced myself to eat slowly, enjoying the calories, buying time for the food to register in my craving centers.

"You look like a cow," Dara said.

"Shut up. I'm dieting."

We'd found a picnic table outside a quaint convenience store. It was a good place to people-watch. The weather was gray and uncertain, but the air was still and the ice cream ambrosial. Thousands of people walked up and down the street, an unbelievably thick and steady stream to and from the colossal moored cruise ships at the end of the road.

The ground was sloped on a river delta that had a history of destroying the town at regular intervals. I couldn't help noticing that the air smelled of mosquito repellent but also that if a sudden flash flood were to hit from the mountains above the town, down White Pass, it would toss all those dead horse parts and tourists through town and deposit everything neatly on the decks of the waiting ships.

"That'd be cool," I said.

"What?"

"You're mumbling, Flaner."

"It's like none of you is listening to a word I'm thinking," I said.

"We gotta work on that," said Standard.

"Dara, there's your boyfriend," I said.

The ship's fitness instructor, Xavier Polates, moved past us across the street on the boardwalk. He was in street clothes, with a cap pulled low over his eyes. His hands were in his pockets, and he walked at a decidedly hurried place.

"He couldn't look any more guilty if he were covered in blood," I said.

"What's up with him?" said Garrett.

"That?" said Standard. Flox pointed to a store advertising "deep-fried breaded chocolate bars and butter." The sign showed they could deep-fry Three Musketeers, Snickers bars, Almond Joys, Butterfingers, Krackels,

Hershey's—dark and milk chocolates—Twinkies, Ding Dongs, Zingers, Mr. Goodbars, York Peppermint Patties, and two flavors of butter—"salted" and "unsalted." They had scones, elephant ears, fried ice cream, and breaded deep-fried thick-cut bacon. A wind blew from behind the shop and I nearly orgasmed.

"Let's go!" I said.

"Hold it, Flaner," said Dara. "Think of Allie. You said you'd come back a new man. You asked for our help to diet."

"Breaded bacon," I explained. "Deep-fried butter."

"Grab him," said Garrett.

I don't remember standing up, but I was up and three steps toward heaven when Standard grabbed my arm. I pulled him with me a couple of steps. Dara got her fingers around my hair, and that stopped me.

"You'll hate yourself," Garrett said.

"I'm used to it."

"We'll hate you."

"No, you won't."

"Allie."

"But…butter…"

"Allie," Garrett said again.

"You don't want to go over there anyway," said Dara. "Look."

My head was craned upside down, Dara not having let go of my hair yet. So upside down that I saw a slit of dental clean white in a round plate of tan gravy. The man looked over, craned his head, smiled even more broadly, and crossed the street.

"Shit. He's seen us," said Standard.

"I wonder how. We weren't acting conspicuous or anything." Dara released my head, and the guys let go of me.

Mr. Toover, cruise director of the Circus Line *Clown Car,* strolled up to us behind a toothpick-enhanced grin.

"I was hoping to run into you," he said. "I said to look for me in Skagway, didn't I? It's good to see you. Enjoying your cruise? How's life aboard the *Success?*"

"Perry's not here," Garrett said.

"So where do you think he is?"

"Maybe he stayed on board."

"I thought I saw him in town," Toover said. "You think he's interested in my bargain? Are you guys?"

"I'm a professional comic," said Standard. We rolled our eyes. He had worked for money at clubs for a while, testing out the circuit until his temperament got the better of him and he called everyone cheating, stealing jerks and came home.

"I'm not looking for just any comics, see?" he said. "I'm looking for Perry Whitehouse. You understand?"

"You want to steal the act off the *Success*," said Garrett.

"It's not stealing," he said. "It's business."

"Why do you care?" I said. "Why do you smell so good?"

"Did you know you can deep-fry M&M's?" he said. "I'll tell you why I care. I'll tell you what I'll do. The Danish line isn't even American. That ship is a place-holding for my sister ship. It's not fair, see? A little mold and a multimillion-dollar boat gets taken out of the rotation. We're talking about people's lives here—income, investors, shareholders. It's probationary, though, see? We get another chance if the *Success* is not a success. Hey, see what I did there?"

"You said words?"

"I'm saying—try and keep up—that if the Danish line is embarrassed, then we, the *American* Circus Line, might get another shot. An appeal, you see what I'm saying? It's a long shot, but it's only fair, don't you think?"

"Do you have any of those M&M's?" I asked.

"You get Whitehouse to jump ship, and you guys maybe even file a couple of complaint forms. I'll get them to you. Just sign the bottom—they're already filled out, see? Keywords and such, like 'shortages,' and 'rats.' That sort of thing, see what I'm saying? You do that for me, and you'll get money for M&M's. Plenty of them, see?"

"We could include the murder."

"I heard about that," he said, shifting his toothpick to the other side of his mouth without unclenching his teeth. "Do you feel threatened? Endangered? That'd be a plus. I could add that. Good thinking. Now, where's Whitehouse?"

"We don't know."

"I understand he has a good act. If we can't have it, you know, it'd be a shame to let the *Success* keep it, you see what I'm saying? It doesn't matter to me if he skips his show because he's on the *Clown Car*, or an airplane back to Utah, or locked in his cabin, or in the infirmary. You can tell him that, see? It's all the same to us."

"Is that a threat?" I asked. "I'm a detective. I'm usually good at detecting threats."

"He gets them all the time," said Garrett.

"You're not helping," said Dara.

"Nothing of the kind," Toover said and grinned. "It's all business, see? Things happen all the time, and it's all business."

25

TOOVER SLITHERED AWAY with a tilt of his invisible fedora. That's my schtick and I was angry that he'd used it. I told myself that I looked much cooler when I did it than when he did it. Much cooler.

"I don't like that guy," said Garrett.

"Flox would have blown him for a midnight show," said Dara.

"That's not true," said Standard. "I was just trying to draw out information. You know? For Perry."

"Right," she said.

"Maybe we shouldn't tell Perry about this," I said. "You know how he gets. He's already rattled. He thinks weird things are going on."

"And he'd be right," said Dara.

"I kind of agree with Tony," said Standard.

"Really? Now I'm not so sure," I said.

Standard glared at me.

I said, "We'll see how he is."

"Oh, we gotta go," said Garrett, looking at his watch. "The tour's leaving."

At a rush, Garrett led the way to a kiosk advertising Klondike Whale Watchers.

"Isn't the Klondike inland, strictly speaking?" I asked the man in the booth.

"No, it's a region," he said.

"No, it's a river," said I.

"I don't think so."

"Then you'd think wrong."

"Whatever. Do you want to go on the boat or not?"

"Yes, we do," said Garrett, handing over the passes.

"This way."

The Alaskan tour guide who knew less than I did led us to the end of the dock, where a fleet of over-sized Jacques Cousteau surplus zodiac rafts were tied up.

To my chagrin we were not alone on the tour.

Dr. Belinda Phillips waited in line behind a sober but not very happy Ashley Vinalez with her shamed husband. The two Latino guys who reeked of hitmen waited behind a pod of Nutri-Pod-slurping pod people waiting behind them to buy passes. The reality show cameraman and producer craned their necks to locate their missing reality stars.

"We won't all fit," I said.

"That's why we have many boats," said the guide.

"Which one are you driving?" I asked.

"That one. The first one," he said.

We all got in the second.

The sky was gray and threatening. The sun hadn't peeked out since before we left the ranch. It could rain any minute. A typical day in Alaska. Our boat guide, a fifteen-year-old Nebraskan runaway, adjusted her hat, tossed us each a life preserver and said, "Don't fall in." Safety check complete, we pushed off from the dock and bobbed like a rubber duck.

In our boat we had our group, Standard, Dara, Garrett and me, plus Dr. Belinda Phillips because of reasons, and Ashley Vinalez who refused to get into the same raft as her husband.

In his boat, was Denny, whom I noticed hung pretty close to his boss and kept his gaze away from Ashley. Mr. Sennegar, complete with head bandage, got in beside his boss and checked the clasps on everyone's vests like it was his job.

The Latino guys were going to ride with them but got out when the camera crew and fishermen got in. The two brothers laughed and joked until the camera light went on and then were at each other's throats, threatening to drown each other before the raft untied. The Latino guys got their money back and left.

"Hey, there's Camila," said Standard as we set off. "Is there room for anyone else?"

A stunning raven-haired woman stood on the dock watching us float around.

"She doesn't want to go," said our guide. "She didn't think much of my route."

"She's just sick of Flox drooling on her shoes," said Dara.

"I wish I could get that close," said Standard.

"Out of your league," said Garrett.

"There aren't a lot of singles on the ship," said Dr. Phillips, watching the woman on the dock.

"Lucky for you, Stan," said Garrett.

Eventually a conga line of six boats pushed off from the dock as a drizzle began. We waved at the towering cruise ships looming above us as we passed them.

From a door in the side of the Circus *Clown Car,* two men were shoveling trash into the harbor with red snow shovels. A frenzy of waiting aquatic life splashed like blood-crazed piranha beneath them. They waved back at us and tried to hide their shovels behind their backs.

"That can't be legal," Garrett said.

"Not a fucking chance," said Dara.

"What's that?" said Standard, pointing to the side of the *Success.*

We'd each been issued a pair of hard-worn binoculars with our life vests. We pushed them to our faces.

"It's a man on the last rung of a ladder," said Ashley Vinalez. Her eyes were wide and dilated, a little dreamy and far away. She dropped an empty Nutri-Pod into her purse.

"He's going to fall," said Belinda.

Garrett said, "Is that..."

I screwed my lenses into focus.

"Yes," I said. "That's Perry. And—there he goes."

Perry tumbled in majestic cartwheels down the side of the ship and into the water below.

"I thought there'd be a bigger splash," said Garrett. "That was pretty high."

"Whatever was tied around his ankle broke the water for him," said Dara.

"Suicide?" said Standard.

"Murder?" said Dara.

"Perry," said I.

"Hold on," said the guide.

She might not have had her driver's license yet, but the girl driving our boat knew how to steer a gray triangular rubber raft like a trained Navy SEAL.

We all held on to ropes and bent in against the windblown rain as she made a beeline for the side of the *Success.*

Perry had been hanging from a rope ladder dangling from the front section of the ship, forward of the outside cabins with the balconies. He'd been in obvious distress, a large orange bundle tied to his leg pulling him down.

"Code Oscar, port side. Code Oscar, port side." The voice echoing from the ship's PA was different from before, a caricature of the one I'd heard the day we sailed. The voice seemed muffled, but the alarm was clear enough; somebody had seen Perry fall. The upper rails filled with crew looking down and then passengers seeing what they were looking at. There was a sudden volley of spilled drinks and dropped cameras as they gawked at Perry in the water.

Perry was easy to locate. He was in a bright orange arctic survival suit and hanging on to a floating duffel bag. I glanced at my compatriots and put a finger to my lips for them to keep quiet about Toover. They nodded in agreement.

We came alongside.

"Cancel code Oscar," came the final announcement from the ship.

"What is wrong with you, Whitehouse?" I said, grabbing hold of him.

"The raft was heavier than I figured," he said.

"What raft?" I said, reaching for him.

"This." He pushed the duffel ahead of him, and I pulled it aboard. It took up a good portion of the available space on the raft.

"We can't take that," said the teenage guide captain.

"We're just going to run him to the dock," I said.

"No, we're late."

"Late for what?"

"The tour, silly," she said.

"What are we going to do with him?"

"Take him along," she said. "And charge him, of course."

"But he's freezing," said Dara.

"No, actually, I'm okay," said Perry, settling in beside Standard. "It was a good test of the suit. So worth the money."

"I'm afraid to ask."

"Seventeen hundred," he said. "And I got a good deal on the raft since it's Korean army surplus." He patted the duffel.

"North or South?"

"North," he said.

"They saw you coming," said Dara.

"We can't take the raft," said the captain.

"I'll sit on it," Perry said. "You others move up, and I'll sit back here on top of it. We'll all fit. It's Jake."

"Who's Jake?" asked the captain.

"Can we just get going?" said Dr. Phillips. "The smell from the garbage is making my eyes water."

We'd drifted beside the *Clown Car,* into the shoveled trash that had made a slick out of the harbor. The smell was indeed something to fear. It was a sweet, pungent stench like vanilla-frosted roadkill.

Perry adjusted his cargo in the back section with our teenage captain and tried to strap a regulation life preserver over his insulated arctic-sea survival suit.

"The tour's fifty bucks," she said.

"Not a problem."

"We don't take checks."

"I don't use them."

"Now would be good," she said.

"Oh. All right." Perry fumbled through the layers of watertight zippers for his wallet.

"Here," Ashley said, handing over the cash and holding her nose. "Just get the boat moving."

A grouping of eclairs bobbed in the garbage slick beside islands of wilted lettuce and stained napkins. A fish sucked down half a tortilla shell and churned the water into a broth of stench that plumbed the depths of our imagination and made me think that the kitchen waste was a cover for the emptying of gray water at the same time.

"Go!" I yelled.

The boat turned and sped away, sending a spray of polluted seawater into the side of the ship.

"I can't believe they get away with that."

"They'll be fined," the girl said. "They usually do it farther out."

The other rubber boats were far ahead of us and spread out by then.

"Okay, I'll bite," said Dara, turning to face Perry. "What the fuck were you doing?"

"Safety test," he said. "I had to check the gear."

"Off the side of a cruise ship? Dangling off a ladder over raw sewage and hypothermic water?"

"People think you can just jump off a ship if it's sinking, but that's wrong. You've got to be very careful when leaving a sinking ship. It can pull you down. There could be fuel in the water, fire, debris, dead bodies—"

"Buffet desserts," I added.

"Exactly. Plus it's a long way down. The fall can hurt you bad even if you only land in water."

"Did it?"

"What?"

"Hurt you—falling in the water?"

"Yes, it did," he said earnestly. "I fell on the raft. The ladder is too short, obviously. I'll need to exchange it for a longer one or plan on waiting to evacuate the ship only after three decks are already filled with water."

We stared at him.

"My room is on deck three," he said. "See?"

"You're off your meds again, aren't you?" said Garrett.

"You'll thank me."

"Did you buy us all a suit?" asked Standard.

"No. They're expensive."

"I don't think we'll be thanking you then."

Perry furrowed his brow in a sulk.

The weather hadn't decided what to do yet. It experimented with drizzles, and mists, sudden gusts, and calms. The only thing it was sure about was that the sun would not be making another appearance around Skagway for a while.

The boat zipped across the mostly calm water at speed with remarkably little sound, but still created a brisk breeze without the help of the uncertain storm. I tucked my hands under the life preserver and used Standard and Garrett for a windbreak as much as I could. Dara did the same behind the doctor and Ashley. Perry, beside the teenage tour guide in the back, faced directly into the wind, tilting his back and forth, obviously measuring the thermal qualities of his suit's hood.

"Is that a whale?" asked Ashley.

"No. That's just a white cap," answered the guide.

"Then why is that other boat going over there?"

"Because they're stupid," she said.

We sailed for a while in the wind, conversation fading with the heat.

We came out of the relatively narrow channel into a broader one. The water was dark, the sky making it so. White caps popped up as the wind tried on "steady miserable" for a while. Pieces of ice broken from glaciers floated by in lonely groups, reminding us of the water's deadly temperature.

"That's Haines over there," the guide said, pointing. "It's a town. I bet you didn't know it was there."

"I knew," said Perry.

"Well la-dee-da," said Dara.

"Where are we going?" I said over my shoulder.

"We're looking for whales," said the guide.

"How far are we going from Skagway?"

"An hour," she said. "Twenty, twenty-five miles."

"Isn't that a long way?"

"No."

"Seems like a long way," I said.

"Don't be stupid. Whales are out here. You want to see whales, don't you?"

"Do we?" I asked the passengers.

"We're this far," said Ashley. "I wanna see a whale."

"Hell, yes," said Dara through chattering teeth. "Garrett worked for this trip. Quit your bitching."

"Critter too," said Garrett.

"I can't feel my nose," said Standard.

"It's still there," said Dara. "Looks like it sprung a leak, though."

Standard wiped the snot off his face with his sleeve.

"How about you, Doctor? Are you still good with going on?" I asked.

"Where are the other boats?" she asked.

"Dicking around," the guide said.

"And we're not?" said Dara.

"No."

"But we're getting—"

"Shhhhh," said the guide, and we fell silent.

The only sound was the low purr of the engine and the wind in the trees. We'd stayed near shore, a stone's throw from land. Eagles perched on trees up the steep hillsides, but no one even bothered to point them out to the others, let alone wrestle a camera out to take yet another picture of them. I still thought they were cool but kept it to myself, conserving warmth.

"There!" called the guide and pointed out into the bay. Before we could swivel our heads to look where she was pointing, the boat banked ninety degrees and we sped to the middle of the channel.

We all squinted to see what had drawn the guide's attention but saw nothing but dark water. The only distinguishing thing between where we were and the other bank, miles distant, was one patch of sunlight streaming through the clouds. The rays were brilliant in the drizzle, and the pool of light made a strange oasis on the black water. Just as we were all staring at it because nothing else was interesting enough to look at, a whale breached there. It shot out of the water, did a half turn and fell back in a dramatic frothy splash.

"Holy shit!" someone yelled, probably me.

The boat cruised forward, the motor noise barely above a hum.

Another whale, or it might have been the same—not to be a speciesist, but they all looked alike to me—rose to the surface slowly and rolled on its side.

"What's it doing?" asked Ashley.

"It's checking out the light," the guide said. "They're curious."

It waved a flipper and finished its roll, then spouted a jet of water.

The boat coasted into the circle of light and stopped.

We fell over ourselves reaching for cameras. Time seemed to slow. We all held our breaths and peered over the sides, expecting one to rise up either right in front of us like in a travel show or under us like in *Moby Dick*. Perry gripped his duffel raft with both hands, expecting the latter.

It was the travel show. A whale breached again and splashed down like its friends had dared him to do it. We all cheered. Standard dropped his camera into the water and started to go in after it. The guide grabbed his belt and pulled him back.

"Let go," he said. "I can get it."

"No," she said. "I haven't lost a man yet, and I'm not about to start now."

The camera fell to the depths.

"Garrett, take good ones," Standard ordered.

"If you insist."

The circle of light moved with the clouds. The whales followed it, and we followed the whales. For twenty minutes we watched whales come to the surface and check out the sky and us. We got to where we named one Cut

Fin and another, a juvenile we were told, Junior. Standard called a big female Camera Thief.

The little boat, so fragile and cramped, cold and exposed, was perfect. We might have been able to feel closer to the whales if we'd been in the water with them, but according to our guide and seconded by Perry, we'd not be able to talk about it afterward. So the little boat was just the thing.

Standard sulked, but even he had to admit that the experience was transformative. After a while he started explaining how he was happy to have lost his camera.

"You guys are missing the real experience," he said. "You're all too interested in catching the moment on film, whereas I am experiencing it right now. I'm absorbing it, not just watching it. I'm the lucky one."

"Shut up, Stan," said Dara.

"Hear, hear," said Belinda.

"I'm in *The Now*. You're not."

"You're going to be in the Chilkoot Strait in one second if you don't shut your trap," Dara said. "I'm trying to enjoy this."

"But you can't, at least not as much as me."

That was it. Dara lunged at him. She'd caught him off guard and tackled him to the floor of the boat before any of us could react. It's not often one of us tests Dara's patience. Usually she just cuts us down with a verbal quip, but she'd gone postal a few times. I think she takes pride in surprising us with over-the-top reactions. They were memorable when they happened and served as a lasting reminder that she was not to be messed with. Standard should have seen it coming; he was asking for it.

Garrett and I pulled her off him but not before she'd gotten her knees under her and straddled him. His back was in water, splashed in over the side during the ride. His hands were over his face, protecting his eyes while she sissy-slapped him. She wasn't hurting him; the worst he'd get was a wet ass, but the shock of the sudden attack was terrifying, and he was suitably terrified.

"There's another one," said Ashley, pointing to the water.

We all turned to take pictures and watched as a humpback whale slid effortlessly through the water, sending up a sudden tall geyser before rolling downward.

"It's going to dive," the guide said. "Watch for the flukes."

"What's a fluke?" said Standard, getting to his knees the better to absorb the moment in *The Now*.

"Your career," said Dara.

"The tail," said the guide. "It's called the flukes."

"I knew that," said Ashley.

"Me too," said Dara.

"I knew about Stan's career," said Garrett.

Standard glared at him.

"Me too," I said. "About Flox; not about the tail. That's new."

Right on cue, the tail rose up out of the water. The guide had maneuvered the boat so close we could practically touch it. Ashley pulled back, afraid of a splash. Perry gripped the side of the boat, ready for it to be upturned, but the rest of us stared stupidly in awe of the massive blue-gray flukes as it rose and then slid silkily and silently into the water.

"Wow," I said.

"Wow," said the others. "Wow."

Then we were quiet for a moment, all experiencing *The Now* when the solitude was interrupted by the blaring of other boats. The other rafts we'd left behind were all now converging on our spot. They'd been joined by twenty others with less environmentally silenced motors. Trollers and charter boats, speed boats, and fishing skiffs bulging with passengers were heading toward us from all directions. I hadn't seen them before. I'd felt we'd had the inlet to ourselves, that the world was empty but for us and the whales, but I'd been wrong. It'd been an illusion. Even as we watched, our prime spot was being stalked by other tourists. We were now in the center of an aquatic stampede of camera-crazed whale watchers.

The clouds closed, and the pool of light that had attracted the whales disappeared. Our guide pushed the boat forward, getting away from the others as quickly as she could. It wasn't just aesthetics she was trying to preserve, giving us the best lasting memory she could, but she was afraid of the wakes. The big charter boats sent waves outward that surfers could ride.

"Hang on," she said and crested one. We flew up into the air, not more than fifteen or twenty feet, just enough time and distance to give us all free-fall nausea and test our dental work.

Dara screamed before we landed. Perry moaned after we hit. Garrett whimpered, and Ashley giggled. I let out a "Yippy ki yay! Ride 'em!" which got me a smirk from the guide.

We passed the boats at speed who passed us chasing the pod of whales who were already gone. We were a few hundred yards from them when the boat shuddered and spun a bit to the left.

"What was—" the guide's question was cut off by the sound of an echoing rifle shot.

A hiss burned past my ear and a moment later another report echoed over the water sounding like thunder, just a little sharper and shorter than it should be.

"Hey, somebody's—" began Ashley.

"Get down!" I yelled, throwing myself onto my friends. "Badger hunter!"

26

THE GUIDE PUSHED the throttle to the limit and hunched down beside Perry, who'd begun chanting *Dune's* Litany Against Fear.

"I shall not fear. Fear is the mind-killer. I will face my fear."

"I pissed myself!" yelled Standard.

"I will let it pass through me" recited Perry.

"Standard just did," said Dara.

"How do you know he's not talking about bullets passing through us?" shouted Ashley.

"Good point," I said.

The water splashed up in a minigeyser to the right, and the guide cranked the boat the other way. The sound of the shot followed a moment after.

"There shall be nothing," chanted Perry. *"Only I will remain."*

"Not if I can help it," I said, assuming the role of action hero. "Stay down, everyone."

"It's coming from one of those boats," said Dr. Phillips.

"That's what I think," I said.

Another hiss and a splash. Another delayed bang, and the boat went on.

The sky was darkening, and the rain was beginning to get serious.

We sped at full throttle while we got acquainted with the wet sloshy rubber floor of the boat. After a few minutes the shooting stopped, and the boats behind us were all just Pink Floyd's distant pinpricks on the horizon.

"What the hell was that about?" said Dara. "Turf wars?"

"Who were they trying to kill?" said Garrett. "You, Tony?"

"Me?"

"Yeah, you, Flaner. You make friends like cholera."

"Me?"

I looked at the other people in the raft. Standard, Dara, and Garrett joined me in looking at Perry in his bright orange survival suit, all weighing Mr. Toover's threats.

Dr. Belinda Phillips looked confused and concerned. Ashley looked down at her outfit, the bright green Nutri-Pods windbreaker, the exact match for the one her husband was wearing on another identical boat at that very moment. She looked up and our eyes met. I knew she was thinking the same thing I was. First, that it was very unfortunate that Standard had pissed himself, and second, that the killer might have made a mistake and was shooting at the wrong boat.

"Mayday, Mayday," said the guide. "Mayday, Mayday." She had a telephone receiver pressed up to her ear. The motor still buzzed smoothly, but I noticed we weren't making much headway.

"Mayday, Mayday. Does anyone copy? Coast guard? Over? Hello? Anyone there?"

"Is that a bullet hole in the radio?" I said.

The guide tossed the handset over her shoulder and lifted the radio set off the floor. The side of the plastic housing had a jagged rip in it, electronics and wires spilling out if it like viscera.

"Uh-oh," she said. "Maybe we can make shore."

"I'll just call Sennegar," Ashley said. "He'll get this straightened out."

She tapped on her phone and sighed. "No bars," she said.

"Maybe you have to turn on roaming," I suggested.

"Mine's showing no signal," said the doctor.

"Mine too," said Dara.

Same with mine. We were in a data hole. You'd think there'd be cell towers in the farthest reaches of Alaska by now, but you'd be wrong.

Shore seemed very far away at that moment. The evasive maneuvering had led us away from it.

"How'd that get hit?" said Dr. Belinda. "It was in the bottom."

"Must have been hit when the first shot hit us," I said. "You know, the one that's sinking the boat."

The first shot had entered in the right rear pontoon, pierced the radio, then the middle seat and exited through the left forward pontoon, effectively taking out half the craft. The boat was deflating like a popped beach toy.

Perry tried to readjust himself on the seat and fell back into the flattened quarter, then over into the sea. His leg dragged behind him, and I grabbed it. I had him, he wasn't going anywhere, but the positioning meant seawater was spilling into the boat.

"Let him go!" ordered the doctor. "You'll kill us all."

"Don't panic," said the guide.

Perry panicked. He thrashed and kicked and fought his way back on board. He got hold of the back of my vest and pulled it to lift himself up. As

I was going overboard, I reached back and blindly grabbed a handle of the first thing my hand found. It didn't hold me, and I was tossed over Perry headfirst into the water.

I remembered the screams the swimmers had unleashed when they'd dove into the ship's pool and did my best to match their tone and volume. I bobbed up and howled.

"Help!" I said as calmly as possible.

Perry pushed an oar to me. The rest of the passengers were retreating to the front of the boat, whose sinking end I could see was near.

"Where's the emergency kit?" asked the guide. "Where's the box with the flare gun and emergency radio?"

I looked down where'd I dropped the weight into the abyss and saw the sinking emergency box as a momentary flicker of reflected lightning just before it disappeared forever.

"Haven't seen it," I said.

The boat drifted away from me. I began to swim toward it with varying degrees of success as one by one, each appendage turned in its resignation.

Eventually, I reached the boat, though I think it had come to me more than I to it. Perry pulled me in. I managed to help for the first little bit, but then my hands stopped working, feeling it a better use of their time to turn into numb flippers than dexterous fingers. I couldn't blame them. My legs had decided to do the same a few minutes earlier but only after sending a series of crippling painful jolts up my spine as a farewell gesture.

The board of directors in my mind had taken up the debate of whether or not to continue oxygen intake with scabs or let the striking internal organs have their way and destroy the company. I'm not usually on the side of management, but I thought the organs were out of line this time and seconded an emergency initiation of heating procedures by chattering my teeth and unleashing violent muscle spasms that made me look like a grounded epileptic fish.

"He's hypo-dynamic!" said Standard.

"Thermic, you idiot," said Dara.

Lightning crashed above us. The boom of thunder was instantaneous and deafening. I tasted ozone and saw the hair on the guide's head stick straight up.

"That's not a good look for you," I said.

"He's delirious," said Dr. Belinda.

"No, he's right," said Dara. "It doesn't suit her at all."

"Hey, spaceman," said the guide said to Perry. "Time to open your present."

"What? Oh right, yes! I told you you'd thank me."

I was pushed and pulled and moved aside. I tried to see what was happening at the back end of the boat, but I couldn't get my muscles to do anything other than shake.

"We gotta get out of this boat before we're all wet," the guide said. Her young voice was strained, and her syllables had extra vibrato from shivering. I managed to turn my head a little and saw that she was sitting in water.

Perry unzipped the duffel and bright orange fabric poured out of it like the rain poured down on us.

"Where're the instructions?" he asked. "Oh. Here they are. Does anyone read Korean?"

"Give me that," the guide said. She threw the duffel out of the boat and held on to a leader rope. She gave it a hard tug, which initiated a slow, steady hiss. The rain was half snow now and little warmer than the water beneath us.

The little lifeboat inflated rapidly. It was upside down but flipped itself aright when it reached about fifty percent.

My teeth were playing teletype, and I could feel my testicles pulling back up into my abdomen.

"Oh, look. Whales," I said.

"He's delirious," said the doctor.

"No," said Dara. "Look."

"Wow, cool," said Garrett, taking pictures.

"Ah, shit," said the guide.

"What? Why?" said Standard.

"Orcas. Killer whales."

"That's just a name, right?" said Ashley. "They're not really dangerous."

"Not usually, but I know that one with the hole in its tail. He's nasty. Stay out of the water."

"You know him?"

"It's Pepehi Kanaka."

"That's Pepehi Kanaka?" I said.

"Yeah, he was raised in OceanWorld where he…uhm…did some…"

"Murders," I interjected.

"A couple of trainers. He was released here after that documentary. He's half insane, all pissed off. Very dangerous. Only whale I know that actually hates people."

"But I wanted to practice my water ballet," I chattered.

"He's going into shock," said the doctor.

"This day just keeps getting better and better," said Garrett.

"You're channeling Critter," I said.

"I wish he were here," he said. "He'd think this was cool."

"You don't?"

"I did until the shooting, the sinking, and now the impending whale attack."

"Downer?"

"A little," he said. "I arranged for the trip, and now it's all ruined."

"Don't blame yourself," I said, going into grand mal convulsions. "You meant well."

"Thanks."

"I blame him," said Dara.

"Me too," said Standard.

Ashley said, "You did this? What a jerk."

"You're a menace," said Dr. Phillips.

"Get him in," ordered the guide.

"But I didn't—" stammered Garrett.

"Not you. Him. Get him in the raft."

"The whales are coming."

"Hurry."

I was shoved, pushed, pulled, rolled, and kicked out of the boat. They could have just directed me with fingertips, and I'd have spasmed across the boat like a set of wind-up chattering teeth, but I guess they needed to stay warm.

"Don't drop him in the water," someone said.

"It's warmer than the air," said I.

"It just feels that way."

"So doesn't that mean it's warmer? Isn't that feeling? What are you using to measure?"

"He has a point."

"No, he doesn't."

"It's all about windchill," I said.

"Doesn't he ever shut up?"

The rain stopped hitting my face, but I could still hear it. I focused my eyes on the grayscale clouds overhead, which had changed to white and orange stripes. I was in Perry's surplus life raft. It was like a floating tent, with a reinforced elevated nylon floor over a hexagon pontoon ring. My feet stuck out the little triangular door. I was missing a shoe and a sock.

Doctor Phillips crawled in next and bent over my face.

"I don't like you," I said.

"You're in shock."

"No, I think he means it," said Standard, coming in. "He's mentioned it before."

"We've got to warm him up," the guide said. Ashley was wiggling in, Dara ready to follow her.

"It's hopeless," said the doctor. "There's nothing we can do for him."

"What about Perry's suit?" asked Dara.

"No," said Perry. "I'm naked under this."

"All our clothes are wet," said Dr. Phillips. "It's a shame, but we have to triage for survivors."

"I know what to do," said Ashley and took off her jacket.

"That's not going to give him enough warmth. He's going to need direct warmth. He needs—"

Ashley wiggled out of her pants. She'd gone commando that day. After removing her sweater and black lace bra, she pulled off my sweatshirt and T-shirt, then pants and Fruit of the Looms. Draping the green windbreaker around her waist, she cuddled up with me.

"I'm cold too," said Standard.

"And me," said Garrett.

"The whale is circling us," said Perry.

We were all inside in the lifeboat now. It was cramped, people practically lying on top of other people, literally in my case.

"Hi, I'm Tony," I said.

"I'm Ashley," she said and giggled. "Oh, looks like you're getting some circulation back."

"Oh for Chrissake!" said Dara.

"Is there a radio in here?" asked the guide. "A beacon? Flare gun or flashlight?"

"Here's something," said Perry. "It's a packet of some kind. There's something written in Korean. Who speaks Korean? Nobody? That sucks. What are the chances?"

"Give it to me."

Perry passed the bundle to the guild who tore it open with her teeth. She dumped it out and dug out two flares and a strobe light. No radio.

"Is there any food?"

"Here's a thermal blanket," said Perry.

"Mine," called the doctor.

"Ours," said Ashley.

"Maybe we should all get naked for warmth," said Perry.

"That's not going to happen," said Dara.

"Maybe." The doctor stole a glance at Dara.

"Still not. If I see anyone's dick, I'll cut it off with this knife."

"You didn't see mine, did you?" I asked through chattering teeth.

"Where'd you get a knife?" asked Perry.

"The bag."

"There's a whistle on it," said the guide. "Give it here."

"Then how will I cut off dicks?" asked Dara.

"No one's getting naked," said the guide. "Well, no one else."

Dara handed over the knife and the lanyarded whistle hanging from its handle.

The guide stuck her head out of the opening and gave a three long blasts of the whistle. They were loud. I reached up to cover my ears and brushed Ashley's breasts. She giggled. I stirred.

"What about your husband?" I asked.

"He had his fun in the freezer," she said.

"Are you having fun?" I asked.

"It's not bad," she whispered in my ear. I stirred a little more.

Before you blame me, let me remind you I was half dead from hypothermia. An attractive, fit, sexually enhanced, middle-aged woman had come to my rescue with personal body heat at great personal peril to herself. My mind was not all there. I was still feeling the effects of the marijuana and the moonshine and the cold, and I hadn't had sex in a while and my mind wasn't working right, and I'm actually usually pretty good in bed, with staying power and tenderness and vigor, and what happened in that lifeboat when she whispered in my ear and ground her naked thighs into my naked penis under the silver reflective blanket, can in no way be used to condemn me now. I was not in control. It was not my fault. I am not to blame.

"Oh." She giggled as it happened.

"Oh god," I grunted.

"What?" said Perry.

"A whale," I said. "I think I felt a whale."

"Your face is red," he said. "Are you blushing?"

"Heat's returning," I said.

"Some's leaving," Ashley giggled. "I can feel it."

"I don't want to be eaten by a whale," said Dr. Phillips.

The guide was about to say something, probably something calming and comforting, but then Pepehi Kanaka breached and flashed his damaged fluke. She nodded to herself and scanned the horizon with sharp eyes then blew three more blasts on the whistle.

The rain came down hard and loud. The guide pulled her head inside and zipped the door shut. Moisture beaded on the stitching and then ran down the sides in rivulets.

"Isn't this supposed to be waterproof?" said Dr. Phillips.

"Supposed to be."

Ashley shuddered.

"I'm sorry," I said. "And thanks."

"You're welcome." She giggled.

"I have a girlfriend," I said.

"And I'm married."

"Who's trying to kill your husband?" I asked, feeling I could broach any subject imaginable at that point.

"I don't know," she said.

"Are you?"

"No," she said without insult. "I'll divorce him later. Or him me."

"What kind of relationship is that?"

"What other kinds are there?"

I thought of Allie and suddenly really missed her. I felt sorry for Ashley for thinking that relationships were always temporary but held back saying anything because my entire life was an example of temporary jobs and hobbies. I was divorced. I was in no position to judge.

"What about the prenup?"

"I'm not worried about that," she said, digging a pod out of her purse. She flicked off the lid, shook a white tablet out, and popped it in her mouth. "Want some?"

"What is it?"

"Xanax," she said. "For nerves."

"I really shouldn't," I said. "Interesting bottle."

"That's to hide it from Paul," she said. "He thinks five drops of ginseng and clove will fix everything. Don't tell him."

I was sure he knew about this wife's habits, but I promised not to mention it.

"So why aren't you worried about the prenuptial agreement?" I asked.

"He's put so many things in my name, I'll be fine. If it gets too ugly, I know where all the bodies are buried. I could make life really hard on him. But he won't as long as he comes out better than me. That's a thing with him. He hates to lose. No, that's not it. He hates to be *bettered*. I've seen him lose before, but he really hates it when someone beats him without trying and especially when his efforts aren't noticed. If I ever have an argument with him, if I expect to win, he's got to have his pound of flesh too, no matter what." She popped another pill and swallowed. "That's why he can't have any partners anymore. He never feels appreciated, never feels like he's getting his fair share. Even on deals he's no longer a part of, or never was a part of, he expects to be recognized. Like when he gave a tip to an oil guy that Sanpete County had oil in it. He drilled and Paul expected a cut. He sued but was humiliated in court. The guy finally named a well after him just to shut Paul up."

"When was this?"

"Years and years ago. I know it still gets to him."

"I'd be afraid of divorcing someone like that," I said. "Sounds like he has a temper."

"Who says I'm divorcing him?"

"You did."

"Not right away." She giggled. "He's going places I want to see first."

The guide stuck her head out and blew three more blasts. She held the light out too.

"What is the whale doing?"

"Eating the old boat," she said.

The rain lessened for a second, just long enough for us to hear the terrible thrashing and tearing of our old boat being devoured by a traumatized child star. The most unsettling noise, even more than the sound of the metal motor housing being shredded by sharp ivory whale's teeth, was the high squealing and clicks he was making. It sounded like a nursery full of babies with squeaky dog toys and maniacal laughter all at once. It would have been a nice addition to the whale watching tour, hearing actual whale noises, if we didn't think he was talking about how he was going to kill us and eat us.

The wind pushed away from the wreck of the old one. The waves slapped the floor from below and brought screams of terror from someone believing the whale was biting through. The others asked me to be quiet.

The old wreck was finally pulled beneath the surface, and we never saw it and Moby's little brother again.

We settled in. The guide blew the whistle in regular intervals and shined the light into the rainy gloom. Our breath and body heat soon heated the inside of the shelter to a point that we were gasping from the stuffiness. Ashley put her clothes back on and I wrapped myself in the silver blanket.

"The boat's leaving at seven," said Garrett. "What time is it?"

"Seven-fifteen," said Dr. Phillips.

"They wouldn't leave without us, would they?" said Garrett.

"Of course they would," said Standard.

"But they won't, will they?"

"I wish I had some cookies," I said to no one in particular.

"I have some Girl Scout cookies back at the dock," said the guide. "Ten dollars a box."

"Thin Mints?"

"I got about five boxes left."

"Samoas?" asked Dara.

"No. I don't have Samoas," she said.

"No Samoas?" said Standard. "What kind of Girl Scout are you?"

Just then a loud horn blasted. The guide whistled long and hard and flashed the light. We heard a rumbling motor and the splash of an oncoming wake.

"A damn good one," she said.

And we all had to agree.

27

THERE WAS a machine gun mounted on the front of the Coast Guard boat that picked us up. It was an updated modernized orange version of the one we'd sunk, and a whale had eaten—the boat, not the gun. Instead of rows of seats, there was a steerage shack with a skyline of antennas and a flat rescue deck where we could huddle together against the wind while they debated whether to sink Perry's boat on the spot or drag it back.

"It'll blow into the rocks and be an eyesore. We can't leave it."

"It's still watertight. It might could be used again."

"But I want to use the machine gun."

"There is that."

"Hey, it's not yours," said Perry. "I paid a fortune for it."

"You're in shock," one of them said. "Machine gun?"

"Machine gun."

Perry's mouth hung open as the crew skipped to the front. The driver steered the ship around and pointed the boat at our erstwhile savior.

There was a loud click, a muffled "damn" and a rattle of cans. Three of the four crew were up with the gun arguing over who got to shoot first. The captain, a guy with a fancy hat, was in the boathouse, watching them through the window.

I was wrapped in a wool blanket, as were the others. I'd pulled my pants on but had left my sopping sweatshirt off. I had my one shoe on, but my last sock had gone missing, probably still in the boat.

Click.

"Someone was shooting at us," I said, my teeth chattering but not life-threateningly so. Ashley cuddled up to me like I was a needy child. She barely knew me but had sized me up pretty well.

"I'm sure it was an accident," the officer said. "Stray bullet into the inlet. Happens all the time."

"People in sightseeing rafts are shot at repeatedly all the time?"

"You weren't being shot at," he said.

"Yes, we were," I said.

"Hell, yeah," said Dara.

"Without a doubt," said Ashley.

"I was there," said Garrett. "It happened."

"You're all in shock," said the captain.

Click.

"We'll get you back to Skagway, and everything will be fine."

"How can it be fine when our ship left us?" said Dr. Phillips. "It left nearly two hours ago."

"Which ship?" asked the Captain.

"The *Success*. Royal Danish Line."

"No, it's still there," he said.

"They waited for us," said Ashley.

"No," he said. "Well, yes. Kinda."

Click.

"Damn."

"You're not making any sense," I said. Ashley slid her hand down the back of my pants.

"I'm a volunteer," he said in way of explanation.

Click. "Damn."

"It's the thingy there. Pull that thingy."

"What about the *Success*?"

"Oh. It's still in Skagway. Some kind of mechanical problem. It's delayed."

"Well, that's lucky," said Garrett.

"Unusual," said Perry. "It's never been a minute late since I've been on board. The line prides itself on that."

"Didn't Toover mention delays?" Standard asked.

"When?" said Perry.

I shot Standard a look.

Click.

"Give it to me."

"You guys saw him in Skagway, didn't you?" Perry said. "Why didn't you say anything? What did he say?"

"Nothing good," said Standard. "He's a dick."

"Dara said Stan was going to blow him," said Garrett.

Click.

"Guys, can't you just tow it in?"

"It's a one-use thing," the captain said. "It can't be recharged, or at least I don't think it can. If we bring it back to the dock, you'll have to pay to have it tied up, ultimately disposed of. The cruise line wouldn't let you bring it aboard in any condition."

"Perry had it on board," said Garrett.

"Ixnay on the on oardbay," said Perry.

Click.

"Is the safety on?"

"I don't think so."

"Could be rust."

"Wait," I said. "I think my wallet's still on the raft. And my phone."

As if I'd said the magic words, the air exploded in gunfire. The rapid reports rolled over the water and echoed back at us from the steep mountainsides of the inlet.

The crew yipped and hollered and took turns riddling Perry's surplus Korean lifeboat with fifty-caliber bullets until it was a flat orange disk.

"It's not sinking," said a crewman.

"Tie it up," said the captain. "We'll have to drag it back."

Perry's lucky lifeboat became Perry's perforated parachute and slowed the Coast Guard boat considerably as we steered back to Skagway. It was late, but the sky was still bright, being so far north.

The Circus ship was gone, but the *Success* still sat where we'd left her in a pool of chum thrown overboard by the *Clown Car*.

"You'll have to make a report," said the Coast Guard captain to our tour guide. "Do you have any Samoas left?"

Skagway at night was a picturesque little town, all lit up, and the crowds gone. Cruise ships came in the morning and left in the evening, so there was no tourist night life. It was still pretty, though. The smell of deep-fried breaded bacon wafted down to us on the dock, and I moaned.

A couple of Nutri-Pods cultists had set up a concession table on the dock and were taking it down for the night.

"How'd you do?" I asked.

"Really well," said one of the young entrepreneurs. "We pretended to put a hundred-dollar bill in one of the packages. People were buying them five at a time."

"You think of that yourself?" I asked.

"Just came to me. Inspiration."

Soapy Smith's spirit roams the streets of Skagway to this day.

We looked like hell. What the wind hadn't done to the girls' hair, the tent roof had. We were sore, wet, and cold and looked like we'd just been saved from an Alaskan shipwreck.

Dara, bless her immortal soul, bought the last five boxes of Thin Mints and gave us each one. We munched them on the dock while we filled out trip evaluation forms and suggestion cards for the tour group. They wanted to know how they could improve the trip and wished to send us a monthly newsletter. The guide seemed nonplussed about the whole thing, bored even, and filled out her official Coast Guard incident report with a pink pom-pom topped pen.

Ashley tipped the guide a hundred bucks with a wink, and my opinion of Paul Vinalez's future ex-wife rose a little higher. She might be a lifesaving, sex-starved, drug-addicted, gold-digging bimbo, but she was a good tipper.

"Where's your husband?" I asked her. "You're the only one who had anyone who'd miss them. Where's Paul?"

"Good question," she said. "What room are you in?"

"Nine-five-seven-eight," I said before I could think. I do that a lot, speak before I think. My brain was warming up by then, and the drugs and alcohol were gone, so the only excuse I can use is surprise. Yes. Surprise. I blame surprise.

She got in close, real close, rose on her tiptoes and kissed me full on the mouth. She surprised me again. Her tongue parting my lips surprised me too, and my mouth, opening in surprise, let her tongue dart in and touch my surprised one. My surprised hands wrapped around her shoulders, in a surprised reflective embrace while her hand surprised my penis by rubbing it through my surprised pants.

I coughed a surprised exclamation and we broke apart. She winked at me and marched away to the ship.

Dara gave me a surprised, raised judgmental eyebrow.

"She saved my life," I said.

"That's not what I meant. Remember Allie."

"Right. Of course," I said. "Allie."

"Allie," said Garrett.

"Allie," I said again. "Allie."

"Allie," said Garrett.

"Allie," I agreed.

"No. Allie," said Garrett again.

"Allie?"

"Allie."

"Allie—"

"Hi, Tony."

"Allie!" I screamed.

There she was. No doubt about it. Allison Braise, my girlfriend I'd left in Utah, and left badly at that. The one who I didn't even tell I was leaving for a week in Alaska. The one who'd asked me to help her with the summer season at her ranch and I'd ignored. The living, breathing, staring, glaring symbol of my inadequacies as lover and boyfriend.

"Allie," I said. "You're here."

"Miss me?" she said. There was an edge in her voice which surprised me. Surprise.

"Uhm," I said, remembering Ashley's kiss.

"Wrong answer." Her tone was ominous and hurt. I braced for the slap. I had it coming, I wanted it. I needed it. It would be big and hard and teach me a lesson I sorely deserved. It might knock me down. It would certainly loosen a tooth and bring stars to my eyes. I needed those stars. I waited, eyes clenched in that anticipatory waiting that's worse than the blow itself.

It didn't come.

When I opened my eyes, Allie was gone.

"Where'd she go?"

My friends all pointed in unison up the road.

I ran the way they sent me, but barefoot and with only a silver reflective blanket around my shoulders for clothing above my waist, I couldn't go fast. As I rounded the corner, I just managed a glimpse of her before she disappeared up the gangway leading into our cruise ship.

"You're on the boat? That's great," I called. I caught my foot on a raised plank on the dock and pulled up a toenail. I pressed on.

"Allie! I can explain," I shouted. "Allie, wait!"

The security folks stopped me. They stopped me cold.

"Are you smuggling in alcohol?" they asked.

"Yes, I've got a bottle of vodka up my keister," I said. "Move."

"You'll have to remove it before coming aboard," the worker said. "Room key?"

"It's at the bottom of the inlet with my phone—drowned, whale-bitten, and machine-gunned."

"And you say you have alcohol?"

"No, I was lying," I said. Allie had disappeared beyond the security checkpoint onto the ship.

"Lying about your room key?"

"No, that's real."

"Whale-bitten?"

"Could have been."

"Machine-gunned?"

"Almost certainly."

"But you don't have alcohol in your bum?"

"Let me on. That's my girlfriend."

"I think you have alcohol."

"Get out of my way!"

Security arrived. I didn't recognize anyone. It wasn't Ola or the happy guards I'd seen before. I think they were just crewmen who drew the detail.

"Am sorry. No stow-ways," one said in broken English.

"I'm supposed to be here!"

The screener said something unintelligible, and the "guard" looked at the seat of my pants. My ripped-up toenail trickled blood under my foot in a little red pool.

"Allie!" I yelled. "I didn't have twice-fried breaded bacon!"

I could write love sonnets.

I pushed past the guard and made three steps beyond the x-ray machines when I felt the familiar dual stabs of a Taser strike my back. Most people would not be able to identify a Taser shot unseen. They might think they'd pissed off a hornets' nest or were having sudden and extreme muscle spasms. That's what most people would think until the electricity hit them and they stopped thinking all together. I am not one of those people. I'd been shot by a Taser before, several times actually. That as much as anything probably explains why I was being shot then. I do dumb things.

I tried to spin out of the wires, and maybe I did, but it didn't help. Perry's metallic reflective blanket conducted stun-volts as well as my back would have, and I was flopping on the floor like a fish before I could yell "overreaction."

My consciousness was shocked out of me, and I went happily into oblivion. It was easier than facing Allie.

28

I WOKE up in the ship's medical bay. I was covered in blankets and lying on my side. I felt a new chipped tooth in my mouth, another dreaded rough spot on my molar, which meant a six-hundred-dollar crown if it didn't have complications. My toe throbbed, and by wiggling it I felt a bandage around it. My side was its usual post-gunshot ache and I was hungry. And Allie was somewhere on board, hating me.

"Fuck!" I said.

The Filipino nurse appeared in my line of sight, as surly and unhappy to see me as I was her.

"How's it going?" I said.

She snarled and choked my bicep with a blood pressure cuff going about three pumps beyond the required tourniquet strength to 'I-don't-like-you' strangulation levels.

My hand went cold. Two more pumps and she put her stethoscope in her ears.

"Pumpy pumpy," I said.

That got me three more. My fingers went blue and tingled.

"How are you feeling, Mr. Flaner?" asked Dr. Reyes, coming in.

"Igor, your assistant here, doesn't have much of a sense of humor. Does she even speak English?"

"Why don't you ask her?"

"Do you speak English?"

She ignored me and produced a thermometer from a metal tray, rolled me over and took aim at my ass.

"Whoa!" I said.

She laughed, a hyena cackling laugh. She got right up in my face, three inches away and cackled. I'd never been more creeped out in my life.

"What? You don't like jokes now?" she said.

"On your planet, that may be a joke. On mine, it's sexual assault," I said. "And I've had enough of that for one day."

She scowled.

"Can dish it out but not take it, huh?" I said. "Jokey jokey."

"You've had quite a day," Reyes said as the nurse left in a huff. "Fell in the sea and Tasered."

"Got high with hippy-hillbillies and saved myself from freezing to death with a chippy, but I didn't eat the fried ice cream."

"I know that place. It's decadent."

"Are we still in Skagway?"

"No, we finally set sail an hour ago."

"How long have I been here?"

"Here? About an hour. On the loading deck, about half an hour. Being dragged down here maybe another fifteen minutes, give or take."

"That long?"

"I think you were in shock."

"I'm hearing that a lot," I said. "Maybe I'm just tired."

"Tired of what?"

"Physical and mental stress. Blood loss."

"That's shock."

"Really?"

"Yes."

"That reminds me. What about the shock of the stun gun? I want to issue a complaint."

"Go ahead."

"You're not going to try and stop me? You're not going to send Ola in here to lean on me to keep quiet for the good of the cruise line?"

"No."

"But it'll be embarrassing to the line. Don't you care?"

"*I do,*" said Captain Finn on cue in the doorway. Beside him was Security Head Ola. They both looked like they'd just come from dinner. Italian by the smell.

"Marinara?"

"Chicken parmesan," Captain Finn said with an accent less pronounced than Ola's but still discernible.

"We have you on video," said Ola. "A half-naked man chasing a guest onboard, without papers, ticket or ID, claiming to be smuggling alcohol in his rectum, making no sense at all. 'I didn't have bacon in an alley?' What does that mean, exactly? How was shouting that supposed to calm down the guards?"

"I've had a hard day."

"We're sorry about that," said the captain.

"You're forgiven," I said. "Can I have a pain pill? My arm hurts. I think it's bruising."

"We didn't do anything to cause you to have a bad day," said Ola.

"Hello? Shot in the back?"

"They were only reacting to your—"

Captain Finn cut Ola off with a raised hand.

"The others told us about the whale watching tour," the captain said. "And Mr. Vinalez himself told us about the freezer incident. You were involved in both."

I'd been expecting to see the inside of a jail cell since I began the investigation. It's an inevitable part of every case. I could see where this was going and sat up to face the music.

Captain Finn looked tired. He ran his fingers through his hair and sat down in a steel chair facing the table. Ola did the same. Primary Medical Dude Reyes stood behind me. I swung my legs over the gurney and heard my bare bum squeak on the vinyl. I was wearing nothing but a skimpy half-paper hospital gown that would barely reach my thighs if I stood up in it.

I don't like being arrested. It's not good for me. It aggregates my tendency to do stupid things. When I feel like I have nothing to lose, I lose some of my charm.

Facing them, I opened my legs and let the air get to my privates. They'd had a hard day, what with the cold water sucking my testicles up into my shoulders and Ashley drawing them out again. A little air would do them good.

My soon-to-be jailers didn't agree. Captain Finn glanced at my junk and rolled his eyes. Ola glared at me. I fanned the gown to encourage airflow and Reyes snickered behind me.

"Mr. Flaner," Captain Finn said. "What are you doing?"

"Demonstrating my feelings about this bullshit scapegoating you're about to pull on me."

"I'm told you are a detective, but I didn't know you were a mind reader."

"It's not hard to guess what you're going to do," I said. "Vinalez is making a stink. He's the biggest living, unarrested, VIP on the ship. If he's unhappy, the Royal Danish Line is unhappy. He thinks that someone is trying to kill him and he might be right. I ruined his show the other day. I saw his wife's boobs. Touched them even. You need to show him you're not impotent and are taking him seriously because, after all, this is a business. You're leaning on me now because Ola's earlier chat had no effect. I spend a night in the brig—maybe the rest of the cruise, and as long as nothing more untoward happens, everything is hunky dory. Did I miss anything?"

"Close your gown, please," said Finn.

"It's my patented response."

He sighed and shook his head.

"Mr. Flaner," the captain said. "We're not here to arrest you. We're here to ask for your help."

"What? You're not? You are?"

"Yes," he said. "I've been talking to Mr. Kline, and he tells me that you're something of a big deal, back wherever it is you're from. He said you've cracked some big cases."

"A couple," I said.

"I need you to find a saboteur on board."

"I'm actually already on a case," I said.

"I think it's the same case," the captain said.

"How?"

"This ship is under attack," he said. "Today's delay in Skagway was just the newest thing."

"Are you talking about the shooting on the whale tour?"

"No, the navigation computer."

"What happened?"

"The navigation computer was damaged with magnets. Big magnets on the side of the machine. Rare earth, big as your hand. We kept reinstalling software until we figured it out. It put us five hours behind."

"Lucky for me," I said. "You'd have left us."

"Lucky," said Ola.

"You're right," said the captain. "This is about business. The Royal Danish Line is trying to get another ship for the Alaskan cruise season."

"Yeah, I know. The Circus *Trapeze* fell out."

"Impressive," said Finn.

"I have my moments."

"Will you please close your gown?" asked Ola.

"Oh right," I said and covered up.

"Circus has doubtlessly put someone or someones on my ship to embarrass us so they can appeal the *Trapeze* ouster and get their spot back."

"Corporate espionage?"

"Yes. But at sea, it's called piracy."

"Yo ho ho."

"We hang pirates," said Ola.

"You're funny," I said.

They weren't laughing.

"What are you saying?"

"I'm saying that messing with a ship's navigation computer, cutting the security feeds, disabling elevators, releasing rats, and dumping storage lockers can carry the same penalty as murder."

"You think whoever's messing with your ship killed Vincent Bror?"

"Don't you?"

"It's crossed my mind, but it's good to hear you say it. Good for Kristen Bror anyway. How much is on the line here?"

"Millions of dollars," said the captain.

"Two or three?"

"Fifty or sixty," he said. "Net."

People have been killed for a lot less than that, I thought.

"Your killer is a member of my crew," he said. "It is someone who knows their way around the ship, knows where to cut wires, has access to the bridge. The security scanners would have picked up the magnet in a passenger's luggage. It's clearly a crew member."

"I don't know," I said. "It could be a passenger."

"How could they smuggle the magnets on board?"

"Please," I said. "I used to work for an airline. It's not hard to get stuff by the security pantomime stations. But it would be easier if there were an inside contact."

"We don't allow passengers on the bridge," said the captain. "Not since 9/11."

"Really? Not even for a tour?"

"Not anymore."

"Even if Bruce Willis is on board?"

"Not even then."

"Isn't Ola working on this?"

"Yes, but he's not a detective like you are."

If Ola was insulted by his captain's low opinion of his police work, he didn't show it.

"Okay, I'll look into it," I said. "The mastermind is a sleazeball named Toover. He's the cruise director aboard the Circus *Clown Car*."

"How do you know this?"

"He tried to hire Perry Whitehouse off your ship. The comedian."

"Oh, did he?"

"Oh, yes, he did."

"That's interesting," said the captain, "But Mr. Toover is not aboard my ship. I need you to find who his agent is."

"Right," I said. "I'll get right on that."

"Thank you," said Captain Finn. "I'll leave you now. Mr. Peterson will help you." Finn lifted himself out of his chair like he was battling twice gravity, giving me some idea of the strain he was under by having his ship "attacked."

"Your friend dropped by some clothes for you," said Reyes.

"What friend? A girl?"

"Yes."

"Laser straight light brown hair, chestnut eyes, healthy tan?"

"No. Short and abrupt."

"Oh," I said, wondering why I'd thought Allie would have brought me my clothes and not Dara.

"I'll wait for you in the security center," said Ola and took his leave.

I got dressed in front of a mirror over a stainless-steel sink and admired my bandages. I had a nice new pad on my love handle covering up my bullet wound, two matching squares of taped gauze on my back for the Taser holes. My big right toe looked like a golf ball, and I had a neon purple Coban around my arm where an IV had been. That's what it's called, the scrunchy elastic self-adhesive bandage. Coban. Don't ask me why.

I felt my chipped tooth and flexed my sore, thawing muscles and stared at my windblown hair. I pulled on a T-shirt, squeezed into my undies, and cinched up my pants. My shoes were gone, but I had sandals, and Dara had delivered those. I considered how terrible I looked, but it was nothing compared to how I felt.

It was midnight. Ola could wait. I found my way off deck four easily this time and went to the upper ones looking for Allie.

The buffet was midnight snacks and drunk food. A pile of bacon, nachos, grilled cheese sandwiches. Bagels. Lots of water and orange juice. They knew their trade. I went to the bar and ordered a sandwich to go with my Red Horse beer. The beer arrived immediately and went straight to my head. When the sandwich came, I'd lost the willpower to ignore the chips that came with it. I ate them all and the Reuben and the pickle and licked the plate I was so hungry. Another beer to settle it down and two more aspirin to thin my blood for the alcohol and I was good to go.

I watched ice floes through the window, set aglow by the ship's lights. Our next stop was Glacier Bay. The ship would spend the day leisurely admiring the view there. It was booked as the most romantic day of the cruise.

And Allie was here somewhere.

I figured she came out to surprise me. I don't know how she did it, what strings she had to pull back home to arrange to fly to Skagway and meet our ship, but it couldn't have been easy. It was a grand gesture, and I'd screwed it up. I screw up a lot of things.

I nursed this last beer and tried to put Allie out of my mind for a second. I was running out of time. The cruise would end soon. A murderer was running loose, and I hadn't a clue who it was. I'd told Allie that I'd been distracted by the investigation. Maybe it was time I was.

Vincent Bror was dead. His wife, in the brig, waited for me to do something.

Since the violence had not ended when Bror was killed, I had to figure that Bror was not the actual target. Either that, or he was and there were more to follow. I'd been attacked three times: the stairs on leaving the ship, the glacier, and the inlet. Vincent looked like me. Was I the real target?

But then what about Vinalez? The rock was real, Sennegar would swear to it. There'd been several incidents in Salt Lake before the cruise. Had that followed him? I half assumed that Ashley had locked Paul and his tryst in the freezer in Skagway, but I couldn't be sure. Had she been trying to kill him? Did she know how dangerous the freezers could be? Did she know the freezer Paul was in was not as dangerous as the others?

The pod people were creepy in an excitable capitalistic greed-crazed kind of way. None of them had struck me as a killer, but I hadn't gotten to know many of them. Why would any of them want to kill Vinalez? But one might.

Or maybe all this had nothing to do with any of the passengers and everything to do with the ship.

Captain Finn was sure it was all connected and all aimed at him and the cruise line. It stretched my sensibilities, but I'd been wrong before. I stared at the water and tried to imagine tourist magnates jockeying for advantage in out-of-the-way ports.

How did it all connect? How did I manage to be a target on this boat? I'd told no one I'd be here, not my son, ex-wife, or best friend. Yet I had the wounds to show that I'd gotten someone's attention.

The ship was practically another Salt Lake City suburb with all the Utahns on board, and the University of Utah in particular was well represented.

I was failing hard as a detective. I didn't even have a suspect yet because I hadn't the slightest idea what was going on. I'd blown the day sightseeing and demonstrated my failures as a partner for good measure.

I ordered a water and rubbed my eyes.

Assuming that she wasn't lying and hiring me wasn't some kind of a killer's sick joke, Kristen had been in the bedroom asleep when Bror came home. The door may have been unlocked, but Bror had seen and talked to his killer, again assuming that Kristen was being straight with me.

I tried to remember when the vandalism on the ship started, thinking for a minute that the killer was using it as a distraction to hide his identity, hoping the murder would be ascribed to corporate sabotage. No. That didn't work. It fit more easily the other way around. The killing was part of the wreckage. The attack on the ship started before the cruise began. Shipments were lost, people went AWOL, and the security feeds were cut—cut in several places in fact—and vandalized electronically. The saboteur had used several levels of technical assault to disable it. He'd been thrice redundant, a practitioner of overkill, if ever there was one.

It wasn't important. Kristen would be fine. If Kline ever grew a pair, he might even ask her to marry him. Did that make him a suspect? He'd be my first and best if he'd been on board, but alas, he was back in Utah when Bror was stabbed. He'd make Kristen a good mate, I thought. He was smart and nice, whereas Vincent was smart and may have been nice once, but not at the end. Who was to blame for that?

I know the captain believed it was all Circus Line, but I couldn't help thinking that Bror's recent obsession with getting even wasn't at work here.

What would be perfect was to find out that he'd declared war on Circus Line, and they'd heard about it and then sent hired hitmen to off him in corporate self-defense. It was my first real theory, and I ran with it, as totally shitty as it was. I'd see Kline in the morning, but first I'd get some sleep and hunt down Allie and try, somehow, to get back in her good graces.

I got up to leave before realizing I didn't have my key card to pay the bill, let alone get me access to my room.

I scanned the bar for a friendly face and saw Bailey Peigne in a dim booth across the lounge. He was staring at me with alcohol-fueled malevolence. Candy was at the bar, chatting with a group of people I recognized: Dr. Phillips, Ashley, and the girl who opened my door for me the night I was locked out.

I was wondering how I could separate the one from the herd when I saw Sandra, the cruise director, come in. I almost didn't recognize her without her clipboard. Her hair was down, her shoes were high, and her backless silver dress drew stares from everyone as she came in.

Except Bailey Peigne. He never took his eyes off me.

I formed a possible alternative theory about the murder based on Peigne's expression and my likeness to Vincent's Bror. I turned to Peigne, locked his eyes in mine, and stuck my tongue out.

"Sandra," I said when she came close.

"Sandals?" she said.

"Am I under-dressed?"

"Am I overdressed?" she said. I could smell alcohol on her breath and feel her arm slide into mine. "You should buy me a drink."

"Actually," I said. "Can you buy me one?"

"Don't make a girl do everything, Tony."

She remembered my name. That's flattery. I'm prone to do stupid things when I'm flattered. Things I regret later. Things that destroy other things.

"Can't do it," I said. "Let me tell you about my day."

I escorted her to the brightest table in the bar which was still dim, but still the brightest. I told her my tale of woe and she drank fuzzy navels that were delivered to the table without her having to order them.

"I saw Perry fall. That was frightening. What the hell was he doing?" she said.

"Preparing for when the ship sinks."

"The ship's not sinking," she said, her eyes big and blurry.

"No. Well, I don't think so. Actually, are you sure? There's all the weird shit happening on board. Perry's spooked. The captain has me looking into it."

"He does? Well, tell Perry everything is okay," she slurred, patting my hand. "Just inconveniences is all."

We talked Alaska and the Caribbean, blue precious stones and helicopter tours until I felt I could ask her for help.

In the end, she gave me a passkey to get into my room and made me promise to bring it back to her first thing in the morning.

"Don't get me in trouble," she slurred. "Promise me."

"Okay."

"Sure you don't want some company?" she asked.

"Good night, Sandra," I said and paid the bill with her card.

29

DARA WAS in the room when I got there, and luckily for me, she was alone. She was, of course, in the big bed. I slid into the other one. Today the bath towel was folded into the shape of a whale and was perched upon two white earthenware jugs of moonshine on my pillow. I hid one jug for later and tried to spoon with the other. No good. I took the towel animal instead. It was easier to spoon with. Not easy, just easier.

One of the things I dislike most about myself is my inability to complete difficult tasks. Lying there in the dark, I felt all the wounds on my body but fretted mostly over the painful one in my gut that was Allie. I knew that this flaw was ultimately at the root of my problems. Before, when I'd faced identity issues like this, I actually managed to do the hard work and see it through. That one superb moment in my life gave me a career and carried me on. It got me the job I was on now and a girl who'd come to Alaska for me. Most importantly, it'd given me confidence, which was probably the catalyst of everything else.

I didn't like myself. The push and the pull of my life wasn't working. I had to take action and do something. I promised myself, there in the dark with the whale towel in my arms, that I would make it up with Allie and I would actually solve Kristen's case.

I'd taken the case, but let's be honest, not seriously. If I'd been serious, would I have gone sightseeing in Skagway? Would I have gotten drunk and stoned behind an outhouse like a sophomore on Spring Break? Probably, but I'd have felt bad about it sooner.

The truth was that this mystery had too many moving parts for me, and I'd shut down. It was, in a word, hard. And that was all the reason my subconscious needed to distract me. It was the same evil subconscious mechanism that had distracted me from my Moab lover.

The usual push and pull of my life was not here. Damn it all, I had to grow. I had to prove something to myself and with it, hopefully, something to Kristen and ultimately—most hopefully to Allie.

———

Dara was gone when I woke up, and so was much of the day. Through the window of the balcony, I saw ice floes and blue mountains. We were in Glacier Bay.

I wandered up to breakfast through the buffet, looking for Allie and didn't find her. I made a tray with three cups of coffee, a bowl of grapes, a piece of toast with more nuts in it than a gay squirrel video, and a kipper. I'd never had a kipper before. I didn't like it.

I used skim milk in my coffee and wondered how anyone could drink it black. I think if the Old World had had coffee, we'd have called it "bitter" and let the Germans figure out another way to say "Please."

Naturally, I couldn't get a seat by the window to look at the breathtaking views. I had to take my own breath away in a booth facing the kitchen. I recognized the ship's cook, Marvelous Martin McGuire, by his reflective scalp before I saw his *Mythbusters* mustache. He wasn't actually cooking. I'm sure his rank was too high to actually get his hands dirty. He supervised. Today, he appeared to be leading a private tour. Belinda Phillips pointed with plastic gloved hands to boxes and bottles while McGuire nodded. She bent over a cutting board to sniff, and he pulled her away, offering her a hair net, which she reluctantly put on. She spoke to him, and he produced a first aid kit from under a counter. She inspected it while he rolled his eyes.

I knew the kitchen behind the buffet wasn't the real kitchen. The real buffet kitchen was below the buffet, deep in the lower decks. Maybe the expensive restaurants had real grills and artisan chefs, but most of the millions of meals served on the cruise were mass-produced in the cooking factories I'd glimpsed under deck four. I'd seen lifeboat-sized vats of bubbling gumbo and industrial sized deep fryers that, after a suitable coating of batter, could cook a Honda Accord to golden brown perfection. The ovens ran on conveyor belts, and the juicers could juice a moose to varying levels of pulp: none, little, or extra-pulpy.

I fought off the urge to go back for bacon and sausage, ham, boiled eggs, scrambled eggs, fried eggs, poached eggs, eggs benedict, omelets, pancakes, waffles, french toast, muffins, croissants, bagels, cream cheese, butter, jam, jelly, honey, whole milk, half and half, breakfast shakes, breakfast burritos, breakfast sandwiches, cheese sandwiches, ham sandwiches, turkey sandwiches, club sandwiches with bacon on San Francisco sourdough bread and extra bacon—

"There you are," said Kline. "I've been looking for you. What are you doing?"

"Starving. What are you doing?"

"Hey, have you seen these? They're called Nutri-Pods, the innovative nutritional dietary supplement everyone is talking about, now with more ginseng, aloe, and turtle root."

"Turtle root? That's a new one."

"Would you like to try one? The first one's free. I can hook you up under me, like in a garden."

"Or a pyramid," I said. "No thanks."

"They're really cool. They'll lubricate your joints."

"Is that why you were looking for me?"

"No, I wanted to know how your investigation is going. You only have a couple of days left. Do you have any clues?"

"Clues? Do I have clues? Kline, all I have are clues."

"What do you have?"

"I have no idea. I have more attempted murders than a crow singles bar."

"A what?"

"Never mind," I said. "I don't know what I have. I don't know how it all figures in, but that's the magic of it. When I figure it out, I'll know I'm right because there could be no other way for all the shit to fit together."

"You're not making sense." He opened a purple pod and poured it into my coffee. "Try it," he said.

"I have Bror's murder," I said, ignoring the cup of eel juice. "I have the clues around that. The broken electrical lock and the strong possibility that Vincent knew his killer."

Kline laughed.

"What is it?"

"It's stupid," he said. "I was just thinking that if Vincent were alive, he'd be able to tell you everything you wanted to know about the locks, and how to defeat them most effectively."

"Funny you mentioned that," I said. "The ship's electrician thought that the locks were defeated by an electrician and then made to look hacked up."

"That's interesting."

"I'm glad you think so," I said. Kline poured a pink pod into my second coffee. I curled my lip. It curdled the milk.

"What do you have to lose?" he said.

"My life, apparently. I've been attacked multiple times, as has the ship. There are rats in the equation."

"I saw those."

"That's just the tip of the iceberg," I said. "And on top of that, I'm missing them."

"What?"

"Icebergs," I said. "Listen, I need to know more about Vincent. I need to know who he punished."

He gave me the lawyerly pause, and I waited.

"If it makes you feel any better," I said. "I work for you. I'm an extension of you. The same lawyer-client privilege connects to me."

"Really?"

"Yes," I said. It sounded good. It could have been true. Maybe it was. But I didn't think so. I was working on a verbal contract. We hadn't even discussed money yet. In retrospect, that was probably an early indication that I wasn't going to take the case seriously. "And I want to be paid," I said.

"Of course," he said. "Whatever you and Kristen agreed upon."

We hadn't agreed on anything. "Tell me about Vincent. I need names of the people he hit."

"You really think one of them killed him?"

"It's a theory," I said. "Maybe The Humanist Alliance Freedom Foundation—THAFF for the thick-tongued—did it."

"I don't have a list," he said, looking around to be sure that no one was listening. "I told you about the big ones. Everything else was little and petty."

"But you didn't do them all?"

"How would I know?"

I took a sip of coffee, forgetting what Kline had done to it.

"Oh my god," I said. "What was that?"

"Eucalyptus surprise."

"I think I hate you now."

"It's pretty good, isn't it? Finish that cup and you'll have energy all day."

"Really?"

"Yes."

"I could use energy." I pinched my nose and drained the cup.

"Pretty good, isn't it?"

"No. Did you get that information in Skagway about Bror's brother?"

"Yes," he said.

"So give it here."

"I don't feel right about it."

"Come on. I'm an extension of your arm. Kristen hired me."

"Vincent made it clear that I worked for him."

"And not Kristen?" I completed his thought.

He nodded.

"You know he's dead, right? Vincent Bror? I saw him recently. He didn't look good. He's dead."

"I know."

"You're going to do it eventually," I said. "I drank your nutrition-enriched slime, now give it."

He reluctantly pulled an envelope out of his back pocket. I grabbed it out of his hand like it was his lunch money and opened it.

It was a report from another private investigator, a competitor of mine in Utah, Chris Traard. He was a straitlaced, by-the-book PI who had a knack for following the rules and wearing ties. I hated him and I'd only met him once.

"What'd this cost you?"

"A thousand dollars."

"I'd have done it for five hundred," I said, though to be honest I really had no idea how to charge for a report like this. I'd have billed hourly and guessed.

"I wanted it done right," he said.

I glared at him.

The report was as dry as my toast but less interesting. Traard made such liberal use of the words "subject" and "alleged" that my mind finally rebelled against it and replaced the word "Daffy Duck" for the noun, and "frothy" for the adjective. So embellished, I had to read it several times to understand the salient parts.

"The frothy Daffy Duck was involved in a frothy car accident on the fourteenth of June, frothily. Daffy Duck was rushed to the University of Utah Medical Center trauma unit where he later died of his frothy injuries. Daffy Duck may have been the frothy cause of the frothy accident and two other Daffies were killed in the frothy collision, bringing the frothy death toll of the frothy Daffy Duck's accident to three, frothily."

"You paid money for this?"

"What's wrong with it?"

"Nothing, if you like Disney porn."

"I don't follow."

"You obviously haven't heard a thing I've thought."

He looked at me bewildered. I let him.

"Save my brain," I said. "What's the gist of it? What got Vincent's toga in a knot? Besides the obvious?"

"It was a head-on, late at night. No witnesses. No survivors. The cops couldn't put together a good scenario of how it happened. It looked as if the couple veered into traffic, but Brad was under the influence. They called it a wash. Three dead kids. It all happened before I met Vincent. Long before," Kline said. "All he'd ever say is that Brad was a good kid and died too young."

"How young?"

"Nineteen. When Vincent was in his twenties. I know that Vincent worked to support both him and his brother."

"Didn't his brother work?"

"The report says he didn't."

"You commissioned this report because you suspected Vincent was up to something?"

"Yes, with the Chilean money transfer. It was creepy."

"After reading this, what do you think now?"

"From that report, not a lot."

"Whoa, do I detect legalese for 'there's something I'm not telling you'?"

"No," he said. "But I couldn't find anything about Flores Limited. That in itself may be suspicious."

"Don't worry. I've got my best people on that."

"Who?"

"A sixteen-year-old boy."

"Oh, good for you." He wasn't being facetious. He knew the power of a teenager with a computer.

I tried to read the report again, looking for keywords and saw Tommy's Place mentioned.

"Daffy Duck's frothy residence was 148 M Street but frothily he'd formerly resided at Tommy's Place, a frothy homeless shelter."

"Why is Tommy's Place mentioned here?"

"Read it."

"Save me," I said.

"You're not very thorough."

"Do it."

"Since Brad was unconscious when they brought him in, the hospital called Tommy's Place. He had a card in his wallet."

"Not his brother?"

"No. There was no ID, no way to connect Vincent. It's all in the report."

"Good to know."

"Any idea who came down from Tommy's Place?"

"No. The report doesn't say."

"What were the names of the two Tommy Place volunteers you arranged trips for?"

"Jim Harrison and Holly Padget," he said, then catching on. "You think they're involved?"

"It's a coincidence, don't you think?"

It was an easy jump, one I should have made before Skagway, but it dazzled Kline. I wasn't as impressed. In fact, I was embarrassed at how long it had taken me. I knew the names of two key people and I hadn't even found out what room they were in yet.

"Now I know what to ask them," I said to make myself feel better.

"How's the pod working for you?"

"I'm hungry," I said.

"I'm not sure if that's a side effect or an indication."

"I gotta go," I said. "Have you mentioned any of this to Kristen?"

"Nutri-Pods?"

"No. Vincent and his campaign of vengeance."

"Kristen? Hell no. And I'm not going to. Why ruin her opinion of her husband now? He's dead."

"That's why," I said.

30

THE STORY of Glacier Bay is most interesting if you're a geologist. If you're the kind of person who gets excited hearing the words "igneous" and "sedimentary," and get all hot and bothered when someone whispers "metamorphic" on the bedsheets, you're going to get the most out of Glacier Bay. If you're not that kind of person, you're just going to have to do with the breathtaking beauty of an Alaskan wilderness complete with bears, whales, wolves, and eagles. Lots of eagles. I was getting sick of eagles. But the bears were neat. And the water was black and dreamy under the overcast sky with chunks of ice floating on it, some with eagles on them. Fuck those guys.

The ship had sailed to the end of an inlet and was making slow stationary circles at the mouth of two glaciers. We were scheduled to be there for hours, just spinning around slowly with the ship's lateral thrusters.

I went up on deck to get a look. My shorts, T-shirt and sandals meant I wasn't going to stay there long. The wind blowing off the glacier was, well, glacial. I stuck my hands in my pockets and looked for people I knew. I was of course distracted by the glaciers. One was snow white over tanzanite blue ice, the other was black as coal. From the orientation lecture I knew that the black one was "dirty." Thanks for that orientation lecture. The black one picked up more debris than the white one. The white one was a wall of snow; the black one a freight train of cracked rock and ice. And also snow. Separate they were breathtaking, while together, side by side as they were, they were spectacular.

There is some human history around Glacier Bay that I find interesting. It's a little geological but exciting anyway. It's a story of native peoples getting screwed over by white folk, so a true history of the American West.

When the first white people visited the area, Glacier Bay wasn't Glacier

Bay but a glacier. It was one big, miles-deep wall of ice pushing into the sea from the coast in the 1790s. Now, as the Royal Danish Line so admirably shows, it's a deep bay with many little glaciers feeding into it.

The glacier has receded in modern times.

That's interesting, you might say. Thanks for that, Tony. But wait, there's more. It also proceeded in modern times. Here's the rub: archaeologists have confirmed the oral history of the Tlingits that they were chillin' in the glacier-less bay for thousands of years. Three thousand years ago they were making huts and totem poles, eating salmon, and burying their folks up on the hills right in the bay.

All was going splendidly in the picturesque retreat until one day they noticed this glacier barreling down on them. It's hard to imagine a glacier barreling down on anyone, but that's what happened. Overnight, their village was being run over by a wall of ice a mile thick. They had to run. They left their poles, homes, salmon riches, and dead folks, jumped in their boats and got the hell out of there. The glacier wrecked everything, met up with a few friends, and took over the entire valley for hundreds of years.

As near as we can figure this happened in the late 1500s. The Tlingits returned in the mid 1800s, when the glacier had retreated. The dates of the glacier's advance coincide exactly with what's called "The Little Ice Age."

Now it gets weird and cultural, and global, and sorrowfully, genocidal. There are some people who'd disagree with me and the scientists I'm paraphrasing here, but they're wrong and we don't need to think about them anymore.

Some scientists, the better ones, think the Little Ice Age happened as a direct result of white European contact with the New World. Here's how it worked. Before the whites showed up, the contingent of North America was crowded with people. Millions and millions and millions of natives. Some say tens of millions. That's a lot. They had roads and trade routes, languages and wars, religion, festivals, holidays, traffic jams, and slow internet—the whole bowl of maize. I don't think they had balls of wax, but I could be wrong. But what's most important is that they had huge portions of the land under cultivation because they wanted to eat, and like I said, there were lots of them.

Then came the whites and their nasty little diseases. In the course of a hundred years the population of North America plummeted because of disease. This made things easier for the colonists, who remarked how nice it was to arrive at a new place and have the crops already sown and no one there to tend them. Ironically they still managed to starve anyway.

As the coastal areas were slowly filling with new white religious extremists, the dead continued to pile up, and all the land that had been used to grow crops went fallow. Trees returned—and boy, did they ever return. There was a sudden and drastic return of oxygen-making, heat-absorbing, canopy plants on the grounds that had been peas and beans. So much so in fact, that the new re-forestation of North America caused the jet stream to shift a little to the right and a degree to slide over on the Fahrenheit scale, which butterflied a thousand miles away into angry glaciers chasing away whole Tlingit villages.

By 1880 when the Tlingits felt it safe to return, the ancient farmlands of North America were once again being used, and those pesky trees had been pushed back to the forests where they belonged.

I remember this story and share it because it says something sobering about human impact on the planet, but also because I love the ironic image of people actually running for their lives from a glacier.

As I stood freezing my ass off on the deck of The Royal Danish *Success* thinking these things, I got to see a chunk of ice "calve" off the white glacier in a spectacular splash that brought applause from the sightseers. I smiled with my chattering teeth and slapped my frozen fingers together like mother nature needed the attention.

Too cold to feel my lips, I ducked into the first door I came to and ran headlong into the two Hispanic guys I'd seen watching Vinalez's pod presentation before.

"I—I-I-I I've been lookin' feryu guyzzz-z," I mumbled.

They stared at me.

"Enjoyin' the the the the cruise?"

They nodded.

"Who're you g-g-guyzz?"

They looked at each other.

"I'm T-T-T-T-T-T-T-Tony Flaner," I said to put them at ease.

"The detective?"

"Y-Y-Y-Yes."

"I'd like to shake your hand," said the first, offering me his. I offered him my shaking one. He shook it more.

"Let's go someplace w-w-w-warm," I suggested.

"We're heading down ourselves for a soda. Wanna come with?" said the one.

"Yeah, it's fetchin' cold out here," said the other.

They were Utahns; "soda," "with," and "fetchin.'" I felt like I was at a mall in Salt Lake eavesdropping on a gaggle of high schoolers at the food court.

The lounge was packed with people wanting the view but not the cold. Today was the day the balcony upgrade would be most useful, but I pushed that out of my mind. Hopefully Dara was using it, sharing it with the gang, while I was trying to gain control over my life.

I ordered three cups of coffee. They warmed me up but did nothing for my shaking. In fact, I think they made it worse. Go figure.

"We're out of bunco," said the one called Barker. The other was Sanchez.

I signaled the waiter. "More bunco, please. My friends are out." Never miss an opportunity for a joke.

"No," Barker said, confused, putting his hand over his Diet Coke as if the waitress were going to pour Jack Daniels into his glass. "I mean, we're in fraud. We work to catch fraudsters, con men."

"Maybe he thinks we're talking about the game," said Sanchez.

"Bingo?"

"No, Banco," he said. "My sister plays it every Wednesday."

"I know what you guys meant," I said, admiring the view through a briefly unobstructed window. "I was just razzing you."

"Razzing us!" said Barker slapping his knee. I didn't think people actually did that, slap their knees, but he did. "I gotta tell the office that we were razzed by Tony Flaner."

"You ever see McGraw?" I asked. He was a cop I'd cut my teeth on.

"Sometimes. He's not too bright, but he's getting better."

"Unlike you fellas."

"Exactly."

"So are you two, like, dating?"

They glanced at each other, just realizing for the first time that they could be perceived as a gay couple.

"No," they said in unison and scooted their chairs apart.

"Nothing wrong with it," I said. "It's the twenty-first century."

"We're not…" said Barker.

"He's not my…" started Sanchez.

"What?" said Barker, his wide eyes softening a little.

"We're here following Vinalez," Sanchez said quickly. "For the department."

"Immigration?"

"No, Salt Lake Major Crimes. Bunco," said Barker casting a sidelong glance at his partner.

"The state has the kind of money to send you two on a cruise?"

"It was cheap," said Sanchez. "They were practically giving the rooms away."

I couldn't argue with that. That's how I got on the boat.

"Plus, we got to use Police Clout."

"Is that a new charge card?"

"Kinda," laughed Barker. "You'll be surprised at the discounts you get flashing a badge."

I remembered that I had a badge too. I'd never tried to get discounts with it. Maybe I would.

"It's a plumb assignment," said Sanchez. "It's a reward assignment for breaking up a nanny ring."

"People being brought in illegally to tend kids," explained Barker.

"Thank God you stopped the babysitters."

"It was a ring," Sanchez said in defense.

"It's Vinalez you're after, right?" I said.

"He's got this pyramid thing going," said Barker, drinking his Diet Coke like it had a bite. "In any other state but Utah, he'd be arrested on the spot. We're wondering if we can't arrest him in Alaska for this scam."

"Soapy Smith is the hero of Skagway," I said. "They won't blink an eye at Paul Vinalez. If he dies in a blaze of glory, they'll name a street after him and show tourists where it happened."

"Probably right," said Barker.

"Look. An eagle!"

I didn't even turn my head.

"Is someone trying to kill him?" I asked.

"Why do you want to know?"

"I'm working the murder case on fourteen."

"There was a murder on fourteen?"

"Deck fourteen."

"When?"

"Didn't you check in with security when you came aboard?"

They looked sheepish.

"Were we supposed to?" asked Barker.

"We're undercover," said Sanchez.

"Yeah, that's it. We're undercover."

"Vincent Bror was stabbed to death with a steak knife second night out. His wife's in the brig. I'm looking for the killer. It happened on fourteen."

"So you think Vinalez did it?"

"No."

"But he's on fourteen," said Barker.

"Have you been up there?"

"No," they said. "The elevator has a lock."

"How do you know?"

"Hey," said Sanchez. "We're cops."

"Ashley told you, didn't she?"

"Maybe."

"How long have you been shadowing Vinalez?"

"The department, a long time. Us, about a year. Since he started the pod thing."

"And is anyone trying to kill him?"

"You think whoever killed Bror was really after Vinalez?"

"You're good, Sanchez," I said. "You answer questions with questions. I bet you're hated in the interrogation room."

"I am."

"Answer the fucking question," I said.

He blanched.

"There have been a couple of things. A suspicious fire."

"Who's doing it? I heard he'd been involved with Colombians. Are they out for blood?"

"Don't be a racist," said Barker.

"Excuse me?"

"Just because someone's from Colombia doesn't mean they're mobsters and part of a drug cartel."

"So Vinalez wasn't involved with gangsters?"

"Oh, he was, just not a drug cartel."

"I stand corrected."

"But they're not after him," said Barker. "No. He paid them back everything with interest. They like him now. They want to invest in the Nutri-Pods."

"How about other business partners? I heard he pissed off a lot of people."

"He has, but we don't think it's any of them. Most of the bad ones got put away already, and the other bad ones are too smart for such thuggery. I wouldn't discount the stupid ones, except, you know, they're stupid."

"Ex-wife?"

"The last one was pretty upset. He put her into bankruptcy," said Barker.

"He put them all into bankruptcy," corrected Sanchez.

"Any of them mad enough to kill?"

"At the time, I'd say yes, but they're all remarried and happy and doing better than ever."

"So no theories?"

They looked at each other and shrugged.

"We're bunco," said Barker. "Homicide is another department."

"Plus there really hasn't even been a homicide."

"Vincent Bror," I said.

"But that happened here, on a cruise ship. We don't have jurisdiction here," said Sanchez.

"Who does have jurisdiction on a cruise ship?" asked Barker.

They looked at me.

I shrugged.

"So what about the Nutri-Pods?" I asked. "Anything fishy about it?"

"You mean besides eel oil?" They both laughed.

"Yeah, besides that."

"He's treading the law carefully," said Barker. "He's hired good MLM lawyers. There are a lot of them in Utah."

"Makes sense. It is the multi-level marketing capital of the world."

"MLM," I said.

"And the fraud capital," said Barker proudly. I'm not sure why.

"I've heard that."

"He's nearly crossed the line, but we haven't caught him yet. I think he will, though. He's in too big of a hurry."

"Most likely it'll be another bankruptcy because the FDA will shut him down," said Sanchez, a little discouraged. "We might catch something in money laundering, but it'll be after the fact. The pyramid scheme is legal."

"In Utah," I said.

"Yes. In Utah."

"Is the FDA really going to shut him down?"

"We think so. His claims are getting too far afield of even unregulated dietary supplements. The FDA will get involved and then the deal will be over."

"And he knows it," said Sanchez. "That's why he's in a hurry."

"And why he'll stash money."

"Would any of this make someone want to kill him?"

"Maybe when it all goes south," said Barker. I could tell he was trying to be helpful. "But not yet. I just don't see it."

"Right now the Nutri-Pods folks are happy as clams," said Sanchez. "Their gardens are growing."

"And their skin is breaking out," I said.

"There's a Viking over there staring at you," said Barker. "I think he's coming over."

"Do you want to meet the ship's Security Head?" I asked without looking back.

"No," they said. "We're on vacation."

"You mean you're undercover."

"That's what we meant."

"Mr. Flaner," said Ola Peterson behind me. "Didn't we have an appointment?"

"Enjoy your trip boys," I said. "I gotta go to work."

31

IT DIDN'T SURPRISE me that Ola didn't want to talk in the bar, the standing rule about not spooking the guests with reality and all. But we could have started a fire in the middle of the lounge and no would have noticed until the smoke obscured the windows. All eyes were pointing outward. It was times like this when I really wished I'd followed my father's advice and become a pickpocket.

Security Head Ola Peterson was either a super laid-back cop or he just didn't give a shit. He didn't seem at all upset that I'd ignored him the previous night. Most cops I know would have taken that as an insult, a deliberate show of disrespect. It was a sign of disrespect, I'll admit, but not deliberate. Well, it was deliberate. I didn't accidentally ignore him. I just did my own thing. But it wasn't a deliberate attack on his authority. It was a deliberate reaction to my having other things to do. Like sleep. He seemed to understand, but for all I knew he was luring me into a padded cell with rubber hoses and a waterboard.

I followed him, confident that he was in fact a laid-back ex-cop who didn't give a shit. He was jaded. He didn't once glance out the windows as the majestic glaciers panned by. Like me, he ignored the omnipresent eagle sightings, but where I shuffled a little and tried to get to a window when someone called "bear," he kept walking. At the door he turned back, surprised I hadn't followed him. I'd wormed my way to a window to see the bear on the ice, but when I got there, it was gone, if it had ever been there. Throngs had rushed to the window where the sharp-eyed Munchausen had claimed to have seen it. At the other window, someone cried "wolf," and the throng sped the other way like a tidal current. I rejoined Ola, who stared into space patiently waiting.

"Where are we going?" I asked him.

"The captain thinks you should see the bridge," he said.

"Really? That'd be cool. Very nice of him."

"That's where the navigation computer was tampered with."

"Oh," I said, following him into a crew elevator. "Still kinda cool, though."

He inserted his card into the slot and pushed twelve.

"Is the regular crew locked out of twelve?" I said.

"Yes," he said.

"Who can get up there?"

"Only people who are supposed to be up there."

"Which are?"

"All senior officers and staff have access since the captain's office is there. Technicians and sailors who steer the ship. People who belong."

The door opened, and we passed through a short hall with doors to a glass one at the end which led to the bridge.

"By the way," said Ola. "The microphone cord was cut and deliberately cross-wired."

"Which one?"

"The one used by Mr. Vinalez at his ship presentation. I'm told by our electrician that it was a deliberate act of sabotage."

"Expertly done?"

"Clumsily."

The bridge was a modern-day cross between 60s *Star Trek* and an IKEA garage sale—flashing lights on smooth surfaces. The crew stole glances at me, a look of nervous discipline on their faces. Maybe they were just sick of all the eagles too.

I'd found the best seat in the house to see the glaciers and sat in it. I had a hundred-eighty-degree panorama of the inlet looking over sunken ship stations like Captain Kirk in the command chair of the *Enterprise*.

"Don't sit there," Ola said.

"Please," I said. "It's such a cool chair. Warp nine, Ja?"

"This way."

Reluctantly I got up and followed him to the left side of the ship where the deck actually extended out from the hull like a walk-in bay window. From there I could see the entire left side of the ship, forward and back—*aft*. The glass was raked, so by leaning I could also see down into the sea. It was another great view, and I sat down in the swivel chair to enjoy it.

"Is that a bear?" I pointed to something on the glacier.

"That's a rock," Ola said.

"This is where the computer was tampered with," Ola said, pointing to a console. "There was a magnet stuck behind it. It played havoc with the screen and hard drives."

"Permanent damage?"

"No," he said. "But very inconvenient. It caused us hours of delay in Skagway."

"Who found it?"

"The ship's electrician. You met him."

"The Black Floridian," I said. "Yeah. I should talk to him again."

"I think you need to call him 'African American,'" Ola said. "The other word could be construed as an insult."

"Okay," I said. "The black African American. I didn't know 'Floridian' was an insult outside of the United States."

Ola shook his head.

"When did it happen? When did the computer go out?"

"We don't know," said Ola. "The bridge was skeleton crew."

"But someone was here," I said.

"We had two crewmen on watch, but they left for an hour for dinner and when they came back, it was done."

"When did they come back?"

"It was right after the Oscar alert."

I looked out the port side of the ship, remembering Perry hanging from a rope between this window and the cabin balconies.

"Who calls 'man overboard' by the way?"

"Whoever sees it," said Ola. "The alert goes out, it's picked up here by the bridge until the emergency is handled. We have a female officer on staff to do it."

"Why a female officer?"

"It's calming."

"Psychological tricks?"

"People don't like being reminded that they could die on vacation," said Ola. "That's why we don't publicize these things. By the way, the captain is pleased that except for the one encounter with Mr. Vinalez, you haven't alarmed the passengers. He was afraid you'd hang posters in the elevators asking for leads."

"Don't mention it," I said but was really thinking, damn that was a good idea.

"So who called Oscar in Skagway?"

Ola shrugged and looked to a female officer in one of the sunken chairs. She was blonde, young, and Nordic. She looked sharp and sexy at the same time in her white naval uniform. She referenced a clipboard and then a computer display and said, "No report."

Ola shrugged and translated. "There was no report made."

"That doesn't sound very shipshape. Can't you be fined for not keeping good records?"

Ola rolled his eyes but the other officers looked terrified.

"I'm sure someone will complete the report," Ola said.

"When you find out who gave the report, I'd be curious to know. Whoever it was saved my friend's life."

"The call was made from that the port observation station," said the Nordic girl, reading off her computer screen. "It lasted only three and a half minutes."

"Right there, huh? Right where the computer was sabotaged?"

The officer shrugged. The question was obviously above her pay grade.

"It was your friend who fell over?" said Ola. "Who was it?"

"Perry Whitehouse."

"The one approached by Mr. Toover?"

"Yes."

He nodded as if he'd just remembered which side to put the jam on a sandwich.

"So who came up here during the lunch break?" I asked. "I assume you checked the elevator lock records."

"The elevator lock doesn't keep records like the rooms," he said. "It's a dumb lock. No records, just access."

"That's not great security," I said.

"I didn't design it."

"So anyone who could have gotten up here could have gotten up here," I said. It sounded smarter before I said it. Ola gave me of one his patented eye rolls, and I couldn't blame him for that one.

"Show me the magnet," I said.

From a drawer in the back of the bridge, he pulled out a rectangular magnet and handed it to me. I thought better of asking about fingerprints but did anyway.

Ola shook his head.

"We found the same kind of magnet on the security system."

"What?" I said. I felt he was holding something back because he'd made eye contact with me.

"It's nothing," he said.

"I'm the professional. Let me decide."

He narrowed his eyes at me. I may have been pushing him a little hard, but I thought we had chemistry, and I knew I had the captain on my side, so I needled him.

"This magnet wasn't in the same place as the other one," he said.

"Of course not," I said. "This one was on the bridge."

His eyes narrowed even more, and he swallowed before speaking again.

"The one we traced in the security system was better placed," said Ola. "Mr. Samson found this one right away."

"He knew where to look?"

"He did, but it was just right here under the console, not along the subsidiary systems like the last one."

"So it was meant to be found?"

He shrugged.

I tried to imagine Lief Ericson shrugging his way across the Atlantic. I could, easily, thanks to Ola Peterson.

"Anything else?" I asked.

He shrugged.

"Oh my god," I said.

"What?"

"Isn't that the fitness jerk?" I pointed to the forward deck.

Ola squinted through the glass. "Yes, Xavier Polates. Not my department. What's he doing?"

"Standing next to my girlfriend," I said.

Ola looked at me, then Xavier, and then back at me. Then he shrugged just to needle me.

Touché.

The bridge elevator didn't need a key card to take me off the command deck, and I was down and out before I realized how down and out I was.

On the forward deck at the rail was Allie in a sweater and Xavier Polates offering her his coat.

"Don't you do it!" I said.

They turned and looked at me.

"Mr. Flaner," said Xavier brightly.

"Tony," said Allie coolly.

"If you need a coat, Allie, I'll give you one."

She looked at my sandals, T-shirt, and shorts and shook her head.

"I'll go buy one and give it you," I said. "At least I would, if I had my wallet."

She stared at me. Xavier was finally feeling the awkwardness. My hateful glare must have given him a hint, my balled fists and shaking shoulders a clue, and my low subsonic guttural growling was the final tip he needed to beat a hasty retreat.

"If there's one thing I really hate," I said as he left, "it's cruise ship gigolos."

Allie looked from me to the tan athlete and back. I tried to look confident, sexy and manly. I was still wired from coffee, and the wind blew across the open deck like a wind tunnel. I felt the goosebumps rise on my legs and necks and tried to smile warmly with chattering teeth.

"You look stupid," she said.

"You look great." She did.

Cold as I was, seeing her there made me warm on the inside. Metaphorically speaking, I was fucking freezing again. Over her blue jeans and boots, she wore the chocolate-brown knit button sweater I gave her for Christmas that matched her eyes on cloudy days like this one. Her straight brown hair fell into it from under a new wool cap I figured she got in Skagway or at the airport on the way. It was blue and white and had a stylized salmon design. Her cheeks were tan from desert work and ignored the wind that dug divots in mine. Her lips would never chap. So mine did the work for both of us. I gave her the warmest smile I could muster and split my lips open in six places. Blood dripped down my chin and onto my shirt. I hardly felt it.

"I came all the way to Alaska to surprise you," she said.

"I was surprised. Well done."

"So was I. Who was that woman?"

"A suspect in a murder investigation," I said. "Or a witness. No—a suspect."

"Why'd she kiss you?"

"She felt close to me after lying with me. That was not the right thing to say," I said. "What I meant is that, for warmth, you know, to fight hypothermia, like I'm getting now, she let me borrow her body heat."

"That's a story."

"Isn't it? It's not like we were alone," I said. "Perry and the gang were all there watching."

"Tony," she sighed.

"Would I make up such a stupid story as that?" I asked. "Have I ever lied to you?"

She chewed on that for a minute. "How did you share body heat exactly?" she said.

A better man would have lied, a smarter man too. I'm not that man. I said, "Well, when she was naked and I was naked—and in shock—and you know…"

"Oh god," she said and turned to the rail.

"No, it's not like that," I said. "We didn't do anything. I just popped. You know? On myself. And her." When will I ever learn to shut up?

A mother grabbed her daughter and marched her off the deck. I then became aware of all the people watching us. Something more interesting than breaking ice was happening. I could have sold popcorn.

I stepped closer to Allie.

"Look at me," I said. "I was shot. See?" I lifted up my shirt. The wind froze my side.

"Actually I was shot twice." I took off my shirt to show her the Taser wounds. The wind hardened my nipples into ice picks. "I fell into the ocean and nearly died."

"What happened to your toe?"

"I stubbed that chasing you. That's when I got shot too. The one in the back, not the one in the side. That one happened before, from a badger rifle. Though to be honest, the day you came and I was so surprised, I was also shot at. Probably another b-b-badger."

"Tony, you expect me—"

"I'd like you t-to."

The deck fell silent. Everyone watched. I thought I felt eyes on me from the command deck above me and from the cabins below.

"This is all just one of those s-s-s-silly misunderstandings," I said through chattering teeth. "It's really not m-m-m my fault. Let me tell you about it. I'm not t-t-t-to blame. Not me."

"No, it's not you," she said. "Everything is not about you, Tony. This is about me too. It's about when I want to talk to you again."

"When m-m-m-might that be?"

"I don't know."

A hard gust of wind pushed me to the right but didn't sting. I think that was a bad sign.

"I didn't have any b-b-bacon," I said.

"You didn't call me either," she said. "That hurt."

"I know. I know. B-B-B-But…"

When I couldn't finish the sentence, she turned and walked back inside. The wind whipped my hair into my eyes and chewed at my extremities like a wolf on a caribou hoof.

"That was great," said someone with a laugh, then slow sarcastic clapping. "Hope your heart's broken, Flaner. Hope it burns."

It was Bailey Peigne. I hadn't seen him on the deck, but I'd had eyes only for Allie. Some of the old people, Perry's "Grays," were on deck as well in warm coats, sweaters, and shawls.

"I'd have paid money to see that," said Bailey. "Does the little lady know about you and Kristen Bror?"

"What do you know about that?"

"I know you and Kristen used to knock the nasties," he said. "Does your ex-girlfriend know about that? Mind if I tell her?"

"Who told you?"

"Vincent Bror himself. I ran into him the night before his wife killed him. He mentioned it."

"Why would he talk to a gutter turd like you?"

"We go way back. He taught at the university. I took a class. We reconnected."

"Small w-w-wwworld."

"I'm connected, Flaner," he said. "I know a lot of people. I know people who can mess you up six ways from Wednesday."

"I don't believe you," I said.

"You don't believe I can?"

"No, I don't b-b-b-believe you ever went to s-s-s-s-school." It was a good jab, considering I was chipping my teeth to Chiclets.

"Your girlfriend just dumped you, Flaner. You got no reason to live. You want me to help you over the railing? It'd be my pleasure."

My face was numb and my muscles unresponsive, but I managed to say, "Heard you s-s-s-sold your house."

It wasn't a great comeback, but it did the trick. His eyes narrowed and filled with hate. More hate.

"One day you're going to go too far, Flaner," he said. "One day. One day soon. It's coming. Be sure of it."

He left the deck through the same door Allie had taken.

"Poor dear," said Mrs. Hunter, covering me with her shawl.

"Thanks, Mrs. Hunter."

"Call me Roxy."

"Th-Th-Th-Thanks Roxxxxxxy."

"Come inside and have a shot of shine. Arnold's opened up his walker."

Too cold to argue, too numb to think, I followed Roxy inside.

"And don't let that man get you down," she said. "He's a fucking asshole."

32

THE LIBRARY WAS the least used room on the ship so the Grays congregated there to drink. It had a wall of windows opposite a loaning library of paperbacks that offered excellent views, but the idea of reading on an Alaskan cruise was so abhorrent to the average tourist that it was never even explored. The game room might have someone pop in asking for the blackjack tables or looking for a free deck of cards—they were five dollars in the gift shop—but the library was a lonely retreat.

Arnold had his tubes of Alaskan moonshine over his shoulder like a boa and was rationing out shots. The age of the participants belied the atmosphere, which very much reminded me of a frat party in college, real or Hollywood-depicted. Just to be safe, someone had pulled down the shade on the door leading to the hallway and hung a homemade "closed" sign on the door.

"No need to get kicked off the ship for this," said Arnold.

"Surely they know," I said.

Roxy brought me a pot of coffee, the sight of which churned my already acid stomach, but I drank some just the same.

"Some might know, but they don't care," said Roxy. "And don't call me Shirley."

The group laughed.

"We chipped in for a bottle of vodka," said Arnold. "If the fuzz break in, we show the bottle and they go away."

"You can get a bottle?"

"Oh, you can buy a bottle of liquor and drink it in your cabin," said Susan.

"I didn't know."

"Eighty bucks for a twenty-dollar bottle," said Arnold.

"You buy one in the duty-free shop on deck six, but you can't drink it on board unless you pay another sixty."

"Seems like a dumb investment."

"It is," said Roxy, sipping moonshine. I could see fumes rising out of her shot glass like heat from a desert highway.

"Then we discovered that you don't have to drink it all on one cruise. We bought the bottle last year and we've been 'drinking it' ever since," said Arnold, adding air quotes with his fingers.

"Last year?"

"Only had to open it once," he said. "In Kingston."

"Coming from Kingston," corrected Susan.

"Right."

"This is the real deal," said Arnold, passing me a shot of shine. "Put this in your coffee. It'll warm you up."

"I got a jug," I said, topping off my mug with it. "I got it delivered to my room."

"I got some hosing from a hydraulic shop in Miami," Arnold bragged. "I can get a gallon in my walker every week."

"One of us can usually get a pass to the gold panning ranch," said Roxy.

The shot helped the coffee. Anything would have helped the coffee. I'd had so much of it, that I thought of the bathroom as my cabin, the shakes as a natural palsy, and the churning in my stomach a long-suffering ulcer.

"How goes the hunt for the killer?" Roxy asked me.

"Not great."

"I bet it was that man you got in an argument with. Why does he hate you?"

"I caught him cheating on his wife."

"And you told on him?" Susan asked, horrified.

"It was my job. I'm a detective."

"You could make a fortune on this ship," said Arnold. "Everyone's sleeping with everyone."

"I thought that's how cruise ships worked."

"In the Caribbean, everyone's single," said Roxy. "There we see it all the time. In Alaska, with upright married folks like this cruise, you'd expect it to be otherwise."

"It's the head of the snake," slurred an unintroduced woman, an African American with a million-dollar smile and about that much in diamonds on her fingers. What is it with jewelry and old ladies? The room sparkled with it. The woman said, "That Nutri-pug captain has snuck out, what? Every night?"

"Every night?"

"Maybe not every night, but plenty."

"With the big-boobed brunette?" I didn't know how else to describe the woman who'd been locked in the freezer with him.

"The tramp from Skagway?" said Susan. "Her, a couple of times, but also others."

"How do you know?"

"You don't need as much sleep when you get old," said Susan. "Haven't you noticed all the housewives throwing themselves at him?"

"He has a fan base," I said, feeling warmer. Roxy's shawl was warm and wonderful. "Can I have another shot, Arnold?"

"Sure thing, Columbo."

"And that wife of his," said Susan. "What a tramp she is."

"Is that the one who got you in trouble with your sweetie?" asked Roxy.

I nodded.

"She spends more time with that no-brain bodybuilder than she does with her husband."

"How about the night that man was killed?"

"Not that night," said Roxy.

"You sure?"

"I asked around for you," she said with a knowing wink. "But I did find something I've been meaning to tell you."

"What?"

"You tell him, Melva."

The black woman poured a can of clandestine Coke into her glass of lighter fluid and said, "The night Mr. Bror was killed, there was one woman in the elevator trying to get up to fourteen. She rode the elevator for ten minutes trying to figure out how to get it to go up that far. She didn't have a key. She asked me if I could get her up there. I said no. That's when I knew there was some kind of hanky-panky going on. I thought maybe it was those handsome crab fishermen from that TV show, and figured they could handle their own business, so I didn't get involved. I told her to call up and have them meet her."

"Did she?"

"Nah," she said. "She went to The Two Olives."

"What's that?"

"It was Kirby's hangout," said Arnold. "A place to go if you're lonely."

"And have money," said a man in a golf shirt I thought had been asleep.

"That's Drew," said Arnold.

"That story is nothing," said Susan. "Every cruise it's the same thing. People want to explore. They figure out which decks they can't get to and try to get to them. She was just curious."

"What'd she look like?"

"A dyke," said Melva.

"The politically correct term," said Arnold, "is 'lesbian.' I have books on the subject. Lots of them."

Roxy blushed.

"A lesbian?" I said, feeling the whiskey in my veins like electric eels. "Why would you say that? Did she hit on you?"

Susan roared in laughter. The man who'd been sleeping whooped as well.

"Susan sees lesbians everywhere," said the man. "She's homophobic and swears everyone's looking to get into her pants."

"You are," she said.

"So?"

"So, they are everywhere."

"It was one night," said Roxy. "In college. I shouldn't have said anything. I was curious. Sue me."

"I'm not talking about you, Roxy," Melva said. "I'm talking about sinners."

"Another drink?" offered Arnold.

"Hell, yes," said Melva. "God, that's good."

"Why do you think she was a lesbian?" I pressed.

"She looked like one. She had short hair."

I waited for a better description, but it didn't come.

"Was she white?"

"Of course," she said.

"Black people can't be lesbians?" said Drew.

She sniffed for a response and sipped her drink.

"They can," said Arnold. "I have photos."

Roxy blushed again.

"Can you tell me anything else about her?"

"She said that having so many elevators was a waste. That at her job, she'd managed to get half of them turned off."

"Did she say where she worked?" I asked, but I already had a pretty good idea who she was talking about.

"Wabash," she said.

"Wasatch?"

"Yeah, that's it. Wasatch Medical. She was a doctor."

"Dr. Belinda Phillips," I said. "I'm going to have to have a word with her about what she was doing on fourteen that night."

"She didn't get up there," Melva said. "I told you."

"You don't know," said Drew.

"I told her she couldn't get up there without a key and she left for The Two Olives."

"What time was that?"

"Around midnight," she said. "Maybe one."

"The killing happened after two."

"Well, I can't speak to that," she said.

"That's what I was saying," said Drew.

"Shut up. You're drunk."

"What are you going to do about your sweetie?" Roxy asked me.

I sighed. The banter of the Grays had distracted me from my real problems.

"I don't know," I said. "She asked for time. I'll give it to her."

"You can't re-fry an egg, son," said Drew.

"What does that mean?"

"I don't know, but my dad always said that to me when I was having girl problems."

"It means you had one chance to fix things," said Roxy.

"How are you getting that?"

"I know how to cook," she said.

"I've still got to give her time," I said. "If you love something, set it free."

"Did you set her free?"

"No. I took her for granted, but there's not a catchy phrase about that."

The group fell silent trying to think of one but couldn't.

"Don't wait too long," said Roxy with a pat on my warming knee. "Girls like to be chased."

Susan said, "And they like heartfelt apologies."

"Take the blame," said Arnold. "Even if it's not your fault."

"No," said Melva. "Be honest."

"Never," said Drew. "Lie. Girls don't want to hear the truth."

"We're called women," said Susan.

"I wasn't talking about you," Drew said. "I was talking about the pretty ones."

"Tell her how you feel," said Roxy.

"You go, *girl*," said Drew, winking.

Susan glared at him.

"I should go. Thanks for the hooch," I said.

"Put some clothes on," said Melva. "We're in Alaska."

"You tell him, *girl*," said Drew.

On wobbly legs, I left the library and went into the ship. My stomach was a churning cauldron of caffeine, worry, and high-proof poison. My diet would have to make allowances. I needed something heavy and soothing to settle it. Bread sounded good. Bread always sounds good.

The little cafe overlooking the lobby was packed with afternoon drinkers admiring the still majestic ice outside. I traipsed down to the buffet and prayed I'd have strength enough to not overeat but still settle my stomach.

I was accosted at the door by the washy-washy women, who aimed bottles of hand sanitizer at me like fire hoses at an Alabama peace rally.

"Washy-washy!"

I opened my palms and got my squirts.

Speaking of Alabama, at the buffet I fell in line behind the Bible-Based Lawn Care family who were rubbing their sanitized hands together like they were hatching a terrible plan upon Gotham. I was rubbing my sanitized hands too, and we looked like a row of minions. The people in front of them were rubbing their hands together and the people lining up behind me for lunch were doing the same. I continued to rub and noticed the rubbing was easy and ongoing. The line had stopped. The people in front of Bubba's family were too busy bubba-rubbing their hands together to collect a tray and move in.

"Speed it up," I said working my fingers.

"Sorry," said the couple.

The woman picked up a plastic tray only to drop it. The man reached for a white plate and it shot out of his hands like a squeezed marble. The woman picked up the tray, lost it again and kicked it across the floor. The man tried another plate and it squirted out under the counter with a crash.

I'd moved up to my elbows and was trying to work the squirt into my forearms. It wasn't being absorbed.

"Honey Pie," said the Alabamian, "I'm slippery."

"Me too."

"What is it?"

I examined my fingers, scrutinized my hands, and smelled the soft floral scent rising from the goo.

"Oh god," I said. "This isn't hand sanitizer. It's sexual lubricant."

33

THE WHOLE SHIP had been hit. All the sanitizer dispensers had been refilled with "Long Happy Nights Sexual Extending Lubricating Gel." I knew the brand. Don't ask me how. Someone had changed the labels on the cases in the hold after Skagway and every single dispenser in the ship was now an exercise in frictionless sensual gliding. The Royal Danish Cruise Line prided itself in never having had an outbreak of Norovirus, or "cruise ship flu." Reyes told me that when the virus first appeared on cruise ships, Royal Danish Line went to extraordinary lengths to protect its passengers, thinking that people would notice how clean, safe, and conscientious the line was. No one noticed since you can't prove a negative. 'Hey, I didn't get sick on the cruise.' 'Were you supposed to?'

"Of course no one knows one cruise ship from another," he said, examining my toe. "As long as Circus Line continues its shenanigans, the rest of us all suffer."

I'd left the buffet line to talk to the washy-washy girls about their wares, and accidentally kicked the doorjamb, reopening my toenail wound and spilling blood on the deck. I'd limped down to Reyes, leaving a trail of gore and slippery handprints.

"There are thousands of sanitizer bottles on the ship," Reyes said. "The ones in the halls and provided by the restaurant staff are just the most obvious. There are two in every room."

The word had got out and bottles of love slime were being replaced as quickly as possible. Crew members passing the clinic popped their heads in and gave Reyes updates of the disaster.

"We don't have a single untainted bottle on the ship," someone said.

"Like a college practical joke," said another.

"This couldn't have been cheap."

"Pretty hilarious."

And so on.

It took me half an hour to scrub the lubricant off my hands with the individually packaged wet wipes the doctor provided me.

My gut was still awash in acids, but with my toe bandaged up and being so close, I thought I'd drop by Kristen and see how she was holding up and tell her about my breakthrough. Then I remembered I didn't have one. I went anyway.

"Where's Ola?" I asked the guard.

"Other duties."

"He's a slippery fellow," I said and waited for applause.

"What do you want?"

"I want to see Kristen Bror."

"No," he said. "Only one visitor at a time. Mr. Kline is with her now."

"How long can he be?"

"He's been there all morning. We had to chase him out last night. He could be a while."

"I'll just poke in," I said.

"No," he said, but I was already poking.

"Hey, guys," I said. "How goes it?"

"Any luck, Tony?" said Kristen.

Kline sat on the cot Indian style, a hand of cards in his lap.

"Actually, I have bupkis," I said.

The guard popped in beside me. "You can't be here."

"Did you hear that, Kristen? You can go."

"Not her."

"I heard about the lifeboat," she said. "You must be getting close if someone's trying to kill you."

"But who on board knew both me and Vincent and might have a motive to want one of us dead?"

Kline glanced at Kristen.

"Oh, right," I said. "That's not helping."

"Security Head Peterson—"

"Is up to his elbows in lube," I said. "So, Kline, you were here all day yesterday?"

"Yes, most the day."

"How'd you hear about the lifeboat on the inlet unless you were there?"

He stared at me. Kristen raised an eyebrow. I had them.

"Ola told us," Kristen said.

"Did he? Did he really?"

"Yes," said Kline. "Yes, he did."

I nodded slowly. "Okay, you win this round, Kline."

"Tony, tell me you're actually working on this," said Kristen.

"It's a mess," I said. "But I am trying. There's so damn much happening on the ship. Vincent's death is just one thing. You'd think it would be the only thing, but it's not. There's a triple attack on security that I thought was about your husband, but it appears to have been done by someone who wanted to put lube in the hand sanitizer bottles."

"Did that really happen?"

"Oh, yeah. And the ship's being messed with in other ways. And there's someone trying to kill me and maybe also Paul Vinalez too."

"Paul?"

"You know him?"

"Yes," she said. "He and Vincent worked together briefly at college. He was a lab assistant."

"Who, Vince or Paul?"

"Paul was under Vincent. It didn't last long."

"Does that name mean anything to you, Kline?"

He got my hint and said, "Vinalez? No. Never heard the name before this trip."

"Still, it's a good lead," I said.

"You have to go," said the guard. "I could lose my job."

"I'm working for the captain," I said. "Me and the captain are close. I call him Finn and he calls me Flipper. Go ask him. We're good."

"How is that a good lead?" Kristen said.

"I just have to find someone who knew Vince and me and Paul Vinalez, and I have the killer," I said.

Kline glanced at Kristen again.

"Oh, right. Not helping."

"Do you have anything more?" asked Kline. "Something that doesn't direct all attention to Kristen here?"

"Don't sweat it, Kline," I said, trying to act cool. It's not easy to do with a toe bandaged big as football in sandals while in shorts and a T-shirt. "Motive is just one element of the case. Means and opportunity are just as important."

"I have means," Kristen said. "I have money."

"But not the opportunity," I said. "At least for the inlet."

"I could have hired agents."

"Who's your go-between to continue your reign of terror from this cell?"

Her eyes fell awkwardly on Kline.

"Right. Not helping."

"Did you update my Facebook, by the way?" she asked Kline.

"I forgot," he said. "I got the Twitter post out, though."

"You're posting about the cruise?"

She shrugged. "It's not as fun as it was supposed to be, but I made a big deal out of it before and feel the need to keep up the momentum."

The guard kept looking up the hallway as if expecting gunfire.

"That's right," I said. "You had a big lead-up to the cruise. You publicized it."

"I'm not sure if publicize is the right word."

"Facebook? Twitter? Yeah, publicize is the only word."

"Is that important?" asked Kline.

"It meant that someone had notice to buy a ticket to be on the same cruise."

"The ship's half empty," said Kline. "I heard they were practically giving tickets away to bums on the street so Alaskan officials wouldn't notice the empty ship."

"Who are you calling a bum?"

"Please, Mr. Flaner," said the guard. "You have to go now."

"One more thing," I said. "Man, I get distracted easy. I have one lead. A doctor. Dr. Phillips was seen trying to get up to the fourteenth floor on the night of the murder."

"Deck," corrected Kline.

"Dr. Phillips?" said Kristen. "Not Dr. Belinda Phillips?"

"You know her too?"

"Yes. She was in my sorority. I haven't thought of her in years."

"When you didn't think of her, what was it you weren't thinking?" I asked.

"She was weird. I think she was a lesbian. She had crush on a girl who died and went into dramatics."

"Who was the girl?"

"I don't remember."

"Was the girl her girlfriend?"

"No," she said. "I didn't even know they knew each other. In fact, the rumor was they didn't. It made the dramatics so much sadder. Sick even. That's when we decided she was a lesbian. She left the sorority shortly after that."

"Did she leave badly?"

"No. She graduated. She paid dues and came to some functions, but she was never really part of it. She tried her hand one year as treasurer but was too officious. We had to ask her to step down and I took over."

"Could she have a vendetta against you or the sorority?"

"After twenty years? For kicking her out as treasurer? I doubt it."

"What does she have against you?" asked Kline. "How does she fit into that? And the ship? And everything?"

"I don't know," I said. "But this is interesting. A good lead."

"Swell."

The guard glared at me. I could tell he wanted to use his baton to hurry me out, but hesitated because me and the captain were so close.

"Bailey Peigne," I said. "Ring any bells?"

"No," said Kristen.

"Great."

"I know him," said Kline.

"Ugh."

"Not closely," he said. "I have an offer on his house. It's a lowball."

"I think you bought yourself a home," I said.

"How do you know?"

"I'm a detective. I have to know these things."

I left the security center before the guard had a conniption. I suppose it said something that I was allowed in at all. It said more that Kline had been allowed to stay there all day.

Kristen was recovering well from the shock of the murder and the charges. The cell was just a boring apartment for her. Kline had eased her crisis admirably, affectionately. Lovingly.

The washy-washy women were back at the door of the buffet. Their line had changed from "washy-washy!" to "You should wash your hands before eating. There's a bathroom around the corner." It wasn't nearly as catchy, and they were already hoarse from saying it over and over again. To the people like me who knew their hands were clean—well, clean enough to feed me with, they just sent silent stares.

I felt a caffeine crash coming on and got myself another cup of coffee to hold it off until I could get cover. I collected a plate of twigs and sticks, a nut, a piece of kiwi fruit, and a banana, trying not to smell the fried chicken.

"Hey, Tony," called Standard. "We saved you a seat."

They hadn't, but they made room. Critter was there enjoying the ambiance, people watching while Garrett ate like it was a race. Dara looked distractedly out the windows and Standard was buoyant.

"Where's Perry?"

"Tonight's his show," said Standard. "He's backstage getting ready."

"We're opening," said Critter. "We gotta hurry."

"You getting paid in coupons again?" I asked.

"No," said Critter shaking his head and making his eyes rattle. "This time I negotiated. Real money."

"What's wrong with Dara?" I asked. "And Flox?"

"It's just so fucking beautiful here," said Dara. "It's all so fucking beautiful, and there are people who want to fuck it up."

"That's poetic," I said.

"Guess what happened to me?" Standard asked.

"You got laid?" I said.

"Who told you?"

"One of the four horsemen."

"We gotta go," said Garrett. "You want to finish my steak?"

"Yes," I said. "But I won't."

"Allie?" said Critter. "I heard what happened."

"Who told you?" I asked the puppet.

"Dara."

"You still haven't made up?" said Standard. "Didn't you tell her about falling in? Saving Perry and being shot at?"

"She's still mad. I'm working on it."

"See you guys in thirty," said Garrett. "Come on, Critter."

"Wait a minute," said the puppet. Garrett stopped and looked impatiently at his hand.

"Come on, Critter," said Garrett. "We gotta go."

"I told Garrett he can't go on tours with you anymore," the puppet said to me with eye-goggling sagacity. "It's too dangerous to be around you."

"I might hold back too," said Standard. "See the rest of the sights with Camila."

"Dara?"

"God help us if there's any goddamn oil out there," she said, staring out the window.

"Thanks, Dara," I said. "I knew I could count on you."

"Oh. No. I'm ditching you too. You're like the plague."

"My friends."

"Thirty minutes," Garrett said and ran out of the restaurant.

"I hear you, Dara," said Standard, stretching out like a cat. "This Glacier Bay has got to be the most romantic place on the planet. Camila has a balcony and after, uhm, you know, we watched the ice under a blanket together. We fell asleep in each other's arms."

I ate my tray of sticks and eyed Garret's half-eaten egg roll.

"Where's your dude?" I asked Dara.

"How'd you know?"

"Detective."

She shrugged. "He's out chasing your chick," she said without looking away from the window.

"Ahhh," I said.

"Or another chick," she said.

My thoughts swam and my hands shook. The caffeine crash had broken through the last-minute coffee dam and was making a beachhead for a full-on attack with moonshine reserves on the flank.

"I'll see you guys at the show," I said and left.

I took the stairs down to nine, thinking the exercise would do me good but only managed to jog my headache into high gear. With my palms to my temples I got to the door and went into my cabin.

Towel animal of the day: salmon.

I kicked off my sandals and shorts, pulled my shirt off and turned on the shower. One of the best things about hotels—and cruise ships are most definitely hotels—is the instant hot water. I pulled the spigot and stepped in.

The shower in our room was a fully contained plastic cubical set about four inches above the rest of the deck for drainage. It was cramped but serviceable. The water hit the wall and filled the air with a soft familiar perfume I recognized but couldn't place in my caffeine buzzed brain. I remember I didn't give a thought to my bandages as I stepped in. I led with my injured foot in fact, but it wouldn't have mattered which one.

In the moment before I concussed, while my feet were sliding out from underneath me with preternatural speed, time slowed for just a tick, just long enough for me to wonder why my shower stall was completely coated in a uniform layer of Long Happy Nights Sexual Extending Lubricating Gel.

34

I HAVE no memory until the next morning.

Dara pieced together what had happened and told me later. Apparently, I got out of the shower, turned the water off, and proceeded to use every towel, washcloth, tissue, and scrap of toilet paper in the cabin in a vain attempt to mop up the blood pouring out of my head wound. I ended up bandaging my head with one of Dara's bras and a wad of tube socks. It wasn't a big cut, just a half inch gash behind my right ear, but it was a head wound and I was concussed, so therefore, as it was, the cabin looked like the elevator from *The Shining*.

I awoke to the distant song of an Alpha Code. It was calm and soothing but even half asleep and concussed, I knew Alpha Code was a euphemism for something terrible.

Voice at the door: "Is this the Alpha Code—oh, God Jesus! What the fuck happened here?"

"What's that smell?"

"Lube," I moaned. "Lots of lube."

"Not another one of those," said another voice.

"I want another room," said Dara.

"You'll have to talk to Sandra," said the voice. "Cruise director."

"Get her the hell down here, then," she said.

"All right."

"Can you hear me, Mr. Flaner?"

"Hey, Reyes," I said. "We've got to stop meeting like this." I rolled over. I was in my cabin. I was in the big bed, and my head was scabbed to the pillow. It cracked when I turned.

"What happened?" we said in unison.

"You don't remember?"

"Surprise me."

"Let me through," said Ola. I couldn't see him. The room was small and now crowded.

"What happened?"

"I think he fell in the shower," said Dara.

"That's right. Lube."

"I think you have a concussion," said Reyes.

"You think?"

"Why do you have so much lube in your shower?"

"My girl dumped me; I was feeling unloved. What's a guy to do?" I said.

"What?"

"I don't know," I said. "It was just there. I remember stepping in the shower and slipping and then now. It was there when I got here. Ask the fish. He saw the whole thing."

"What fish?" asked Ola.

"The towel salmon," I said. "He was here. Where is he? I don't see him. Maybe he left. That's pretty suspicious, don't you think?"

"You pulled him apart and covered him in bodily fluids, you monster!"

"What's going on?" I recognized the cruise director.

"I want another room," said Dara.

"What happened?" said Sandra.

Reyes answered. "He slipped in the shower."

"With a little help," I said.

"Someone pushed you?" said Ola.

"Greased floor."

Sandra said, "Is he hurt badly?"

Reyes was matter of fact, Ola Peterson uninterested, Dara pissed off, but Sandra sounded genuinely worried about my well-being.

"He's all right," said Reyes. "If he made it through the night, he's through the worst of it."

"Don't you share this room with Tony?" said Sandra.

"Yes," Dara said. "That's why I fucking want to be moved."

"I'll get you a new cabin," said Sandra. "It'll take days to clean this mess."

"I did my best," I moaned.

"Let's get him down to the infirmary," said Reyes.

One of the EMTs who first came in, tried to pick me up but I was as slippery as a greased pig and he couldn't get a hold.

"Why did you get it all over you?"

"If I had to guess," I said. "I'd say I liked how it felt."

"We're going to have to peel him out of the sheets," said the EMT. "Like a banana."

"Speaking of which," said Dara. "Put some pants on him."

"When did you find him?" asked Ola.

"Right before I made the call."

"You didn't sleep here last night?"

"Nope. I had other plans."

"Let's get him in the shower," said the EMT. "Hose him off a bit."

"It's greasy."

"Told you."

With medical gauze they scrubbed the floor and the walls a bit. Then Reyes and the EMTs got me in the shower. Sandra dropped off more towels, and I was de-greased in short order. I rubbed the scab off my scalp and it started bleeding again.

"Damn," I said. "Give me a wad of socks and a brassiere, stat!"

"Funny," said Reyes.

I collected some clothes and rode a wheelchair down to deck four. It was just after dawn. I could tell Dara hadn't slept and was pretty pissed not to have a bed. A small army of maids descended upon the room while Sandra gave them orders in quiet tones so as not to wake the rest of the passengers. Dara collected her things and glared at me.

I got six stitches—two layers of three, a shaved scalp, and another bandage. Before I got my clothes on, I examined my wounds, admiring my gauze.

"You're accident-prone," said the Filipino nurse.

"Yeah, well, you're short," I said. At least my rapier wit was undamaged.

I'd not seen the ship this early. It was mostly deserted, mostly cleaning people and carts of things being moved around hither and yon. Just for giggles I went up to the exercise deck to see what sweating with the dawn was like.

Xavier Polates sat alone on a windswept deck, a towel around his shoulders, glancing at his watch and yawning.

I read a lot into that yawn. First my insecurities read Allie in it, then my mind replaced Allie with Dara and my guts churned in a similarly disgusted way, just not as personally.

I walked up the stairs along the jogging path and saw Paul Vinalez through a window in the exercise room holding an icepack on his knee.

I came in from an outside door to the earnest strains of Abba earnestly asking someone to take chances.

I looked around the empty weight room. To the right were free weights against the wall. In the middle, where Vinalez was, were machines. On the left, set in front of a bank of windows overlooking the outdoor track, were treadmills so stationary that walkers could more easily imagine actually walking.

"Hey, Paul, need a spot?"

He jumped when I spoke. "Don't sneak up on me like that," he said. "Jesus."

"You've mistaken me for someone else," I said. "It happens all the time."

"What happened to you?" he said.

"Pick a wound and I'll tell you a story."

He tossed me a red Nutri-Pod before squirting one in his mouth. "Take it, it'll help you heal."

"I'm trying to cut back," I said. "Hurt your knee? That's why I don't exercise."

"I hurt my knee because someone pushed me down a flight of stairs yesterday."

"Did you see who it was?"

"No, you idiot. If I'd seen who it was, I wouldn't have said 'someone,' now would I?"

"I don't know," I said. "Maybe, with your people skills."

"Someone tried to kill me again," he said. "What are you doing about it?"

"I don't work for you," I said. "I'm working for Kristen Bror."

"Bror is dead. I'm alive."

"You are a master of the obvious," I said. "What's your business with Bailey Peigne?"

"I have no business with Bailey Peigne," he said too quickly.

Just then two joggers circled the track in front of the window. Their breaths came in little white puffs. It was only when they turned the corner that I could read the writing on the back of their sweatshirts: "Tommy's Place."

"I gotta go," I said. "I'll figure out your lies later."

I ran back out the door and hobbled after the two joggers. I'd put pants on that morning, but I was still in sandals and a T-shirt. My side still hurt from the gunshot, my back from the Taser, my foot from missing a toenail, and now my skull from an intimate night with a soap tray. And I was fat. With their head start, there was no way I was catching up.

I searched my mind for their names to call but couldn't remember them. They looked to be about my age, a little older perhaps. They were physically fit and able to get up in the morning without medical assistance and with energy enough to run around the ship like they enjoyed it. They were strange and alien monsters and I could only hope that if I ever caught up with them, I'd be able to communicate with them somehow. I'd start with prime numbers and go from there.

I skip-waddled twenty or thirty yards before giving up. My lungs were burning in the cold morning air and my parade of injuries was demanding attention like a line of bead-tossing Mardi Gras floats. I found a bench and watched them disappear around the aft quarter to my left.

Breathing hard, I turned my attention to the right and hoped my quarry's mutant constitutions would carry them around for another lap. I did not hold out a lot of hope. No human could jog that long.

They were Kryptonians, cousins of Jor-El. I saw them round the front of the ship and come toward me. They were laughing, carrying on a conversation as if air were free and came easy.

"Wait!" I held up my hands to stop them. "I need to talk to you."

"Us?" said the girl.

"You," I gasped. One of us needed to.

"Why?" said the man.

"Murder investigation."

"What happened to your head?"

"Do either of you know Vincent Bror?" I asked.

"Yes," they said in unison.

"We need to talk."

They promised to meet me in the lobby bar for an orange juice after they showered. I was happy to get out of the cold and went there first for some coffee. Sandra had not come looking for her room key, but I still didn't have mine. I wanted a latte but worried about using Sandra's card too liberally. In a rare moment of restraint, I contented myself with the ship's free drip caffeine. It was practically running in my veins anyway.

When they appeared, they were neither tired nor in bad spirits for having endured a morning of exercise.

"One, three, five, seven, uhm…eleven. Ah…thirteen," I said.

"What?"

"Never mind. I'm Tony Flaner." I offered them my hand to shake.

"I'm Jim Harrison and this is Holly Padget," said the man of steel.

"Hello," said Holly with a lilt in her voice.

"Who told you we knew Bror?"

"I'm a detective," I said. "I've got to conceal my sources."

"Don't you mean 'protect'?"

"Not in this case. I'm trying to look smarter than I've been. How do you know him?"

"I only met him once," said Jim.

"I knew him and his brother. Mostly his brother."

"Oh, yeah, his brother I knew. Brad Bror. He stayed at the shelter."

"Tommy's Place?"

"Yes," said Jim. "But that was years and years ago."

"But you still have the sweatshirt."

"I used to work there," Jim said. "Now I donate to them, and they gave me the shirt."

"I used to work there too," Holly said.

"Did you know that Vincent Bror paid for your cruise ticket?"

"No," they said. "Why would he do that?"

"I had no idea," said Holly.

Jim said, "When I saw him on the cruise, I thought it was a coincidence. I was going to approach him, but he saw me and looked right through me. I heard he was a rich guy now, and since he didn't remember me, I left, not wanting to look like a creep."

"He remembered you," I said.

"Then why did he ignore me?"

"He liked to act anonymously," I said. "For his good deeds and bad."

"I wish I could thank him," said Holly.

"He didn't want to be," I said.

"We were there when his brother died," said Holly.

"But we'd also kicked him out of the shelter," said Jim.

"Tell me about it."

"The Brors were poor," said Jim. "Vincent was the only earner of the two. Brad did his own thing. Vincent tried to keep him off drugs, but how could he, when he made them?"

"What?"

"We shouldn't talk about this," said Holly.

"Yes, you should," said I.

"We shouldn't speak ill of the dead."

"Do twenty Hail Marys later. Talk now."

"Vincent Bror made meth. His brother, Brad, sold it. At least, he sold what he didn't use. Vincent had a little apartment. He'd stayed with us off and on for a couple years before he got his lab job up at the University."

"That's where he developed the patent that made him rich," said Holly. "I read it in the paper."

Jim said, "When he wasn't in the electrical lab, rumor was, Vincent was in the chemistry lab making meth. The landlord demanded Brad leave Vincent's apartment after a series of police calls for public intoxication. He moved in with us at Tommy's Place and stayed about six months before we had to kick him out for selling drugs. A month after that, he died in a car crash."

"Did Vincent know you kicked him out?"

"Yes," said Holly. "I know he did."

"What happened when he died?"

"Well, Brad didn't have any contact information on him except for a card to our shelter. We were called and went to the hospital."

"It was horrible," said Holly. "They had all the bodies there."

"I could tell Brad had been using. He looked like hell. He didn't have disfiguring injuries—his back was broken. His face though was a lunar landscape of speedbumps, those delightful sores meth-heads get when they use constantly. His fingers were burned from the pipe, his teeth were rotten and falling out and I could smell it on him. He was high when he died."

"Without a doubt," said Holly.

"We found Vincent and called him. When he got there, he accused the hospital staff of letting him die. Doing it on purpose somehow for some reason. He broke down and cried. We didn't see how it ended."

"Was there any truth to that?"

"I doubt it. We beat Vincent there by hours and he was dead when we arrived," said Holly. "They all were."

"Meth-heads often display persecution complexes," said Jim. "They see conspiracies where there aren't any, feel like everything is about them. I suspected at the time that Vincent might have been a user too. Of course, he was overwhelmed with grief, but still, it made no sense to blame that doctor when his brother was responsible for not only his own death but of several kids. I was glad to get out of there."

"It was so long ago," said Holly. "I don't think I've thought about this in ten years, maybe twenty."

"I don't mean to speak so badly about Vincent," said Jim. "He was upset. And the doctor was a shit. I remember that. She was overly officious and had terrible bedside manner."

"Yeah, just awful," agreed Holly.

"Do you remember her name?"

"No," they said.

"What'd she look like?"

"I don't remember," said Jim.

"This is going to sound crazy," said Holly, "but now that you mention it, she looked like someone I saw on the ship. One of the Nutri-Pods conventioneers."

"Overly thin, short hair, pinched face, lifeless eyes? Looks like Bart Simpson?"

"That's her."

I finished my coffee in a gulp. For the first time since I took the case, I had a full-fledged actual suspect.

"Thanks, guys, I gotta go," I said.

"Did we help?"

"Before I talked to you, the best I had was The Humanist Alliance Freedom Foundation."

"THAFF?"

"You know them?"

"I heard of them," said Jim.

Holly said, "I heard it was one guy with carpal tunnel syndrome on a computer in his mother's basement."

"I heard that too," said Jim.

"It can't be him," said Holly.

"Why not?"

"The ship has no internet."

35

I LEFT Jim and Holly in the cafe with their chilled orange juice and bullet resistant abs. I knew I had half a day before the ship arrived in at the private island for a "bear watching expedition," an onshore activity that for once was included in the all-inclusive cruise.

"Tony."

I looked around. I was alone in the corridor.

"Tony."

"Perry? Is that you?"

"Get in here."

A side door opened in the hallway on the way to the buffet. I was always on my way to the buffet.

"What is it?"

"Come with me."

I met Perry in a secret crew-only parallel corridor that ran behind the restaurants and shops. It was narrow, overly bright, and had a lingering smell of Long Happy Nights Sexual Extending Lubricating Gel.

"Where are we going?"

"I'll show you."

We hurried down a side stairway. He carried a black steel crowbar at his side as nonchalantly as possible while we raced down the nine flights of stairs. Eventually, with some panting and great discomfort, I was in my home away from home in front of the the infirmary.

"Dara mentioned it to me," said Perry.

"Have you slept?" I asked him.

"No."

"Oh, how'd your show go?"

"Great, actually. Not a hiccup. Good crowd. Garrett was all right. Critter killed."

"Sorry I couldn't be there."

"I heard you got attacked over the PA," he said. "When I heard Alpha, I knew it was you. That's how I found this."

He led me past the security office toward the back elevators. He stopped in front of a door and looked down the hallway, casually whistling the theme from *Mission Impossible* until people passed.

"Guess where Dara spent last night before she found you?"

"With Xavier Polates?" I said.

"You know?" His eyes went big.

"I figured she was with her itinerant boyfriend."

"She was. I asked her."

"At least it wasn't Allie," I said.

"Yeah, the Grays told me about that, too. Sorry."

"My own fault."

When the coast was clear, Perry pushed the door. It wouldn't open.

"Damn," he said. "It was open before."

He slid his key card in and nothing happened.

"Here, let me try." I pulled out the key Sandra had given me. The light went green, and Perry opened the door.

There was a faint smell of sweat and a strong one of rodents; not a good combination but it was better than the lavender Long Happy Nights Sexual Extending Lubricating Gel the whole ship now reeked of. Or maybe it was just me. I hadn't gotten it all out of my hair.

"Wait, I know this room," I said. "I saw Xavier coming out of it my first night in the infirmary."

"Exactly," Perry said, pulling the door shut and turning on the light.

It was an overflow storage room that someone had made into a love nest. Behind a wall of wooden crates marked "fragile" and covered in Chinese lettering, there was a mattress, pillows, candle, ice chest with empty champagne bottle, and knotted sheets.

"Why not just get an empty cabin? The ships full of them," I said.

"He's your man," said Perry. "The killer. Didn't I hear that the captain thinks whoever's been doing all the crap to the ship also killed your friend's husband?"

"The gossip on this boat…" I said.

"Is it true?"

"Yes. He said that."

"Look." Perry pulled down one of the Chinese crates.

It was lighter than it looked. He put it on the floor and pried up the lid with his crowbar.

"Rats."

The inside was filled with moving shredded newspapers. I lifted up a tuft and there was a single white rat rooting around the bottom.

"This is how Polates got them on board," Perry said.

"Couldn't they have just crawled in there?"

"The box was sealed. The others are empty, but this little guy got left. He's hungry."

My mind went back to the night the rats first appeared on the ship. It was the same night I'd seen Polates in this room. I remembered his cool Jamaican accent and his moves on Allie. I'd not seen him with Dara but that didn't matter. I couldn't imagine him taking advantage of my poor, helpless vulnerable friend. Well, I could, so long as I didn't remember it was Dara.

"Dara said he was curious about my investigation," I said.

"He tried to kill you, dude. You gotta tell the captain."

"Holy shit," I said, remembering the brief chat I'd had with him. "Where's Cartagena?"

"*Romancing the Stone.*"

"No, in real life."

"Oh, uhm. Colombia. Why?"

Xavier Polates mentioned he went to college there.

"Why's that significant?"

"There was some talk about Colombian hitmen."

"There you go," Perry said. "We got him."

"No. Wait. The hit men were for Vinalez. Plus I was told by cops that the Colombian thing was a dead end."

"Cops don't know much," he said.

"That's true. But for Bror I was chasing a Chilean connection, not a Colombian one."

"They're neighbors," he said. "Chile and Colombia share a border."

"No they don't."

"They don't?"

"No. Not at all. There's a whole Peru between them."

"Well, the same language, right?"

"I think so."

"So it'd be a good cover."

"Maybe," I said.

"Are you kidding? We've got him. Look at that rat. Look at his little red eyes and his little twitching nose. He wants some love, and he's ready to testify."

I thought of Polates putting his arm around Allie and nodded.

"I'll tell the captain."

"Don't tell him how you found this, okay? Keep me out of it. I'm already a hunted man."

"Who's hunting you?"

"NSA," he said. "I did an internet search before we left port. I was so stupid. I'm sure I was flagged."

"What did you search on?"

"The NSA."

I wanted to tell him he was being paranoid, but alas, I could not.

"I'll keep you out of it."

I left him on deck four, encouraging him to get some sleep, and took the elevator up. I thought I'd put my plan together over a breakfast that required some chewing.

What bothered me most about Xavier Polates was what bothered me most about the case as a whole. I couldn't fit the pieces together into a single picture. Was Polates an agent or the mastermind? Was Bror's death an accident? A hit meant for Vinalez? For me? Had the cops been wrong? Perry was right, cops are often wrong. Was it all just a big terrible bloody show to humiliate the Royal Danish Cruise Line?

I remembered Toover, and with a start I recalled that both times we'd run into the Circus line cruise director we'd seen Polates nearby as well.

That was the theory then: all this was Circus Line created chaos. It's the only thing that fit all the messy pieces of murder, mischief, and mayhem. I'd lump it all together under "created chaos" and blame Polates.

I was chewing on a banana and how to present the story to the captain at the buffet when I saw Belinda Phillips carrying a tray of food. She passed me and cornered Sennegar at a window table. She reached in her purse and pulled out two of boxes of Nutri-Pods samples and gave them to him.

"I don't need them," she said. "Give them back to Paul."

"Hey, Belinda," I called. "Sit here."

She stared at me like I'd just offered her malaria.

Not wanting to be nicer than I needed to be, I said, "You can talk with me here now or later in the brig."

"What?" she said.

"Come here. Sit down."

She gave me a look that had malpractice insurance premium increase written all over it. Attitude is so important.

She reluctantly came over when Sennegar didn't offer her a seat.

She compared her plate to mine. I'd have thought she'd have been pleased and supportive of my choices; fruit, oatmeal, fat-free plain yogurt, tomato juice, while she had toast, scrambled eggs, and bacon—yes, bacon. Three slices. Instead, she raised a suspicious eyebrow at me, noticed my weight more than my bandages, and shook her head. It was hard to like Belinda Phillips.

"What do you want, Mr. Flaner?"

I got right to it. "Here's how it comes down," I said. "You killed Vincent Bror."

"What?"

"Don't try to deny it. I have motive, means and opportunity." I held up three fingers.

"What?"

"Means," I said, picking the middle finger to highlight. "You're a doctor. Steak knives are easy enough to come by."

"What? How are those related? What does that mean?"

"You knew where to stab him to kill him."

"Where was he stabbed?"

"The neck."

"I'd have gone for the heart," she said.

"You were obviously trying to conceal your knowledge of anatomy."

"You are an idiot," she said, eating a piece of bacon—sweet, delicious, forbidden bacon.

The bacon calmed her down. I didn't like that. I liked her upset and defensive; it meant I was getting to her. Though I had a suspect in Xavier Polates, I also had reservations. Just to cover my bases, my plan was to blame the doctor for everything and have her confess to it while filling in all the missing pieces for me. It was a bold plan, one I'd tried before without success. I figured I was due.

I'd rattled her at first. She'd shown a nearly human reaction, but it faded fast. She was cold-blooded, of that I was sure. Whether she was a cold-blooded lizard or murderer remained to be seen. And proven.

"I know about your relationship to the Brors," I said.

"I've heard the name," said the doctor. "On the ship, but I honestly never met the man."

"How about his family?"

"I have no idea what you're talking about." She ate a forkful of eggs. I'd have put a dash of Tabasco on them, maybe a little salt, and a touch of pepper. I felt drool at the corner of my mouth and stirred my oatmeal.

"You were the doctor on duty when Bror's brother was brought into the ER after a car crash."

"When? I haven't been in an emergency room in a quarter century."

"It was about that long ago." I felt a little flustered.

"And?"

"And uhm, Bror's brother died."

"Did I kill him?"

"No. He died of injuries from a car crash, but you were there."

"And that's why I killed the other brother?"

"It's uhm..."

"It's uhm..." she mocked me. "You're an idiot. I don't know the man. He doesn't know me. What would I gain?"

"Aha!" I said. "You knew he didn't like you."

"How would I know that? Did he send me hate letters?"

"No."

"Then ESP?"

"Uhm, no," I mumbled. "But you're from Salt Lake and went to the University of Utah."

"Half the damn ship is from Utah," she said. "No—more than that. I'd go so far as to say eighty percent of the passengers are from there. There's a Nutri-Pods conference on board, or haven't you noticed, detective?"

"Are you saying that's why you're here?"

"You saw me in the seminar."

"Then why aren't you eating them?" I asked. "Where's your breakfast pod?"

She hesitated. I could tell I'd hit a nerve. What nerve, I didn't know. I was no doctor.

"I'm a doctor," she said. "I'm not convinced of the science behind the pods."

"But you're in The Garden," I said.

"Business is another thing."

"Don't you make enough money being a doctor?" I asked. "Wait. You're not a real doctor anymore, are you? You're in administration."

"I am a doctor, you idiot. I still have my license. Just because I don't want to spend my time with idiots like you doesn't mean I don't know how the body works. And I make plenty of money. A thousand times what any of the Gardeners will make. A million times what you'll make in your life."

"I'm house poor," I said.

"You mean, 'poor house.'"

"So, Miss Money Bags, why are you doing Nutri-Pods?"

"Why not?"

"You don't believe in them and you have money. Why Nutri-Pods?"

"I said I wasn't sure, you dolt," she said. "And who ever has enough money?"

"Money can't buy happiness," I said to be flippant. I hit another nerve. This one a wistful one. She stopped chewing and found the middle distance behind my right ear to study something meaningful to her but invisible to the rest of us.

"No, it can't," she admitted.

My theory was falling apart. I could see Bror having a reason to kill Belinda, but nothing the other way around. Kline had made it clear that those at the end of Bror's beneficence or malice were unaware of the source, so even if Bror had had it in for the rude doctor, she'd never have known it. Her being here on this ship in Alaskan waters could be a coincidence, but not as unlikely as it appeared because the ship was indeed "little Utah" with all the pod people. Plus, I'd seen her in the marketing class taking studious notes. She needed more classes on salesmanship, marketing, empathy, civil discourse, and common courtesy, but she was there listening. I don't think she'd be selling many pods to her friends, if she had any, but bully for her thinking she could.

"You were trying to get to the fourteenth floor the night Bror was murdered," I said. "Don't try to deny it."

"Deck."

"Calling me names won't help, you jerk."

"I said 'deck.' They're decks on a ship, not floors. I was curious and wanted to see what was up there. I was just getting my bearings."

"You were very persistent," I said.

"I was bored. And I never got up there. You can't prove I did because I didn't."

"Because you covered your tracks?"

"No, you idiot, because I was never up there."

"I have a witness who'll place you in the elevator around midnight trying to get to fourteen."

"That stupid old woman, right, stupid?"

"Don't try your charm on me."

"I never went up there. When was he killed?"

"After two. Giving you plenty of time to find a way up."

"At two?"

"A little after," I said. "You could have bribed your way up, stolen a card, or just ridden the elevator all night until someone finally went up there."

"I was in bed at two," she said, eating another piece of bacon. She ate it slowly, rolling her eyes in pleasure as she crunched the strip of heaven, knowingly torturing me. I took a spoonful of oatmeal. It was cold. I tried to pretend it was bacon. You can imagine how that went.

"That's very convenient," I said. "In bed with no witnesses is no alibi."

She stopped chewing and thought for a minute. I had a piece of melon. It wasn't bacon either.

"You really think I'm a suspect?"

"Until proven otherwise," I said. I wasn't about to tell her I had my doubts.

"I wasn't alone in bed."

I nearly said, 'who'd sleep with you?' but shortened it to the less incendiary, "Who?"

"Chris," she said.

"No last name?"

She shook her head. "No."

"Where can I find this Chris? He left the ship I suppose?"

"Try the Two Olive lounge," she said. "*She* costs three hundred dollars for the night."

36

THE TWO OLIVES was one of the bars you have to go looking for. It wasn't on the main tourist decks but hidden out of the way in the darker reaches of the ship. Cruise ships accurately bill themselves as floating cities. I'd seen Main Street; The Two Olives was in the red-light district.

At eight in the morning, the place was dark as midnight. No beautiful vistas here, just dim light, red candles, loosened smoking regulations, and barflies who'd not be out of place in a Scorsese movie or AA poster.

There were only four people there when I came in—a bartender, the disco duet, and a single woman on a barstool drinking a Bloody Mary.

"You know where I can find Chris?" I asked the barkeep.

He shrugged his shoulders, not taking his eyes off the glass he was polishing. There's something about bar beer glasses that require hours of polishing.

"Who wants to know?" said the woman. She was familiar. Her dress was evening wear and looked like she'd been in all night. Her makeup was worn but not off. I squinted at her profile as she took a long drag on a cigarette. She blew the smoke up in a purple cloud.

I couldn't help it, the scene was too perfect; dim light, seedy bar, tickling piano keys in the background. Ignoring my sandals, I slipped into Noir.

"Hello, doll, I'm a gumshoe looking for a snitch to put the finger on a canary. A dish called Chris, charges three yards a night, that's three Cs to you and me in the cheap seats."

She laughed. "Nice hat," she said, admiring my shaved scalp and bandage.

"Don't try any funny business," I said. "You gonna sing, or do I have to get rough?"

"You got a gat?"

"You mean a heater, a rod, a Roscoe, a shooting iron?"

"Yeah."

"I got one," I said. "Somewhere. I think it's in the kitchen. No. I remember now, I loaned it to Colonel Mustard when he lost his candlestick in the conservatory. But yeah, technically, it's still mine."

"You're too much," she said.

"I really am a private dick, though," I said.

"I've seen a lot of those."

"Do you know a girl named Chris?"

She nodded. "She'll be here. Have a seat."

"How long?"

She shrugged. "What's this all about?"

I took the barstool next to hers and recognized her then. She was the woman who'd let me in my room after my first night in the infirmary.

"Where did you get your key?" I asked.

"Connections."

"Does the captain know about this?" I gestured to her in a roundabout all-inclusive gesture, sure to take in the stiletto heels.

She nodded.

It made sense. The ship was meant to entertain. Once out to sea, away from port where the casinos could operate outside jurisdictions, why not have a few working girls? If they keep it on the down low, it'd be an asset to the cruise.

"You're Chris."

She nodded.

"Thanks again for your help the other night," I said.

"Not a problem. You're kind of cute."

"Please. No flattery. I'm a sucker for it, and I'm already in dutch with my girlfriend."

"I'm just saying."

"Does your key take you to the fourteenth floor?"

"Deck."

"Does it?"

"Yes."

"Will it open any door?"

"Not always, but often. Every cruise when the keys are reset, it changes things up," she said. "So you think I went up to fourteen and killed someone, huh?"

"Where were you that night around two o'clock?"

"I had two calls," she said. "One at ten, another at eleven thirty. I was back here by twelve thirty. Young kid, no stamina. Hard to give him an hour, but I tried."

"I wouldn't have lasted five minutes," I said.

"Now who's flirting?"

I laughed. "If that works for you, I may be in love."

"Don't get in more dutch."

"Right," I said. "So what happened after twelve thirty?"

"I picked up another call at one and spent the night, what little of it there was left."

"With whom?"

"A girl doesn't kiss and tell," she said.

"It's important," I said. "Someone claims to have been with you and I need to check it out."

She sipped her drink, took another long drag, blew it out and shook her head.

"It's a murder investigation," I said.

"I know."

"The captain himself asked me to look into it."

"I heard."

"He could get mad if you don't help me," I said.

"Are you muscling me?"

"I am, doll, I got a stiff but no story. You can crystal it up."

"All right," she said. "Let's play twenty questions."

"Do you go both ways?" I asked. The bartender suddenly found the other end of the bar more interesting.

"Yes," she said. "That's one."

"Did you spend the night in question with Dr. Belinda Phillips?"

"Yes," she said. "Nice work. Got it in two."

"It should have been one, but I wanted to see the expression on the bartender's face."

"Where does that get you?"

"He just seemed like a prude. I like making prudes uncomfortable. How'd he get this job?"

"No, Phillips. Where's that get you?"

"Are you sure she was there the whole time? You didn't fall asleep or anything?"

"I'm sure. Playtime until four. I was out of the room at six-fifteen. She was sleeping then."

"That's a lot of playtime," I said. "Makes my five-minute promise seem a little weak."

"We talked a lot," she said. "Pillow talk."

"What'd she say?"

"Usual tourist stuff. I told her about the ship, things to do, places to go on shore. The usual."

I sensed hesitation.

"Go on," I said.

She smiled and shrugged. I could tell she was pulling some kind of client privilege thing.

"She'll be off the ship in a couple of days," I said. "I've got to clear her. She sent me to you. Help a guy out. Don't be a sap. I'm no sharper; I'm a shamus. It's all Jake."

She smiled. "What do you want to know?"

"Did she say anything like, 'Thanks for giving me an alibi for the murder I'm about to go commit with your keycard'?"

"No. Nothing like that," she laughed. "She just wanted company."

"So you didn't…"

"Oh, we did," she said. "I got the feeling she doesn't get a lot of affection."

I didn't offer any theories as to why that might be, though I had a few. "Is she skipping out on anyone back in Salt Lake City?" I was grabbing at straws.

"I don't think so."

That's straws for you.

Chris said after a drink, "She kept talking about a girl who died in college."

"Yeah, I heard about that."

"You know as much as I do then," she said.

"What else she say?"

"Her friend committed suicide after being jilted at the altar. Some creep dumped her for someone who had money. Typical melodrama."

"Did you believe it?"

"I don't know. Sounded like it happened a long time ago, but she acted like it was yesterday. She read me poetry she wrote for her."

"Did you get a name?"

"Patricia Wohler."

"You remember?"

"*Patty Wohler, woe is me, You left at the University, How I wish you knew my love, But you can see it from above*," she recited.

"Three hundred wasn't enough."

"Usually isn't," she said.

"What room did you use, if I might ask?"

"Hers."

"On the fourteenth *deck*?"

"Sorry, no. Deck eight. Cabin 8044."

"Balcony?"

"Yes," she said. "Like yours but only one bed."

"How do you know which cabin was mine?"

"I opened the door for you, silly."

"Oh, right."

"Flatfoot."

"You got the chin wag to go with the getaway sticks," I said.

"I'm beat." She sighed and finished her drink and cigarette in turn. "If you mention me to the captain at all, you'll say only nice things, right?"

"Right," I said.

She stood up, collected her handbag, said, "Ciao," and left.

I watched her go. She drifted away with a slow easy sway to her hips that promised to put a guy in a spot, behind the eight ball, maybe send him to the hoosegow. It took your breath away like Nevada gas in the big house.

I let her exit have some to time to settle, giving it the proper respect it deserved before I left. The bartender was unhappy. I hadn't ordered anything but I think he was pleasantly relieved to see me go. I have a gift.

Ola was waiting for me out in the passageway like he was on a stakeout.

"You are accident-prone," he said.

"I'm a marked man, copper. Someone's got it in for me in a big way, see?"

"Why are you talking like that?"

"You trying to be wise?"

The ship was coming alive, but the life was all on the upper decks. Down here, barely above the storage lockers, in the hidden seedy corners of the city called *Success*, it was the slow time. The piano player and singer passed us to disappear deeper in the ship.

"The captain wants me to ask what happened to you and see if you are making any progress."

"What does it look like?"

"It looks like your girlfriend dumped you, you got drunk, fell down, got hurt, and are now looking for company," he said.

"It does not."

"Kinda does."

"Well, that's not what's happening," I said. "Someone spread my shower with sex gel and I slipped. It was a trap."

"I was there, remember?" he said.

"Oh yeah."

"Some detective. How exactly does one not notice a shower covered in gel?"

"It happens."

"Maybe you have sexual issues," he said, casting a glance at the Two Olives.

"And I spread my bathtub with lube for some crazy frictionless self-sex thing?"

He shrugged. "It makes more sense than someone trying to kill you with it."

He had a point. I've read many mysteries, seen many movies, watched many TV shows where someone is trying to off someone else, and nowhere could I remember Long Happy Nights Sexual Extending Lubricating Gel or the like being used as a weapon.

"Lots of people die in bathtubs," I said. "They're deadly. Every year more people die in their bathroom than in all the quicksand in all the world."

"Have you found anything?" he said, unimpressed with my encyclopedic knowledge of quicksand deaths.

I hadn't all the connections yet, and that bothered me. My theory of "Cruise Chaos" seemed like a cheat, but it was the only thing I had. He was demanding answers, and I had a suspect. I even had some evidence, which was more than I had on anyone else.

"Xavier Polates," I said.

"The new fitness instructor?"

"Yeah." I told him what I had and took him to the locker. He used his keycard to open it. I still had Sandra's key but didn't want to show it.

"You saw him with Toover in Skagway?" he asked again. "And Juneau?"

"Not with him, per se, but close enough to make the connection. Toover was trying to enlist Perry pretty hard. I doubt he'd miss a chance to talk to Polates if he knew who he was."

"Polates served on a Circus ship," he said. "The *Trapeze* no less."

I opened the box where the rat waited in shredded rat pee-soaked newspapers. It looked up at Ola and me and sniggered his nose at us, wanting to be held.

"Disgusting thing," said Ola.

"It's a white rat," I said. "Show some respect. This is a medical professional."

It squeaked in agreement.

"I saw Polates coming out of here the other night," I said. "And I smelled a rat."

"How did you get in here today?"

"It was left ajar," I said. "He uses it for his liaisons."

"With your girlfriend?"

My gut wound up like an over-tightened watch before I realized he was probably talking about Dara and not Allie. I felt ashamed for making assumptions.

"Dara isn't my girlfriend," I said.

"I wasn't talking about her," he said. "I'm talking about the girl you talked to on the deck."

"Go on," I said as calmly as I could.

"I saw her and Polates having breakfast together."

"He's your man," I said. "Let's go arrest him now."

37

WE FOUND Xavier Polates in the exercise room leading an aerobics class for a dozen guilt-ridden buffet junkies like myself and a handful of hardcore exercise freaks who think it's something you should do every day. I know, right?

Allie was not there, and for that I was grateful.

Ola signaled Xavier over, but he lifted a finger for us to wait.

He was going through a cool-down routine of stretches. The buffet refugees couldn't come close to matching his flexibility and dislocated their shoulders and pulled their groins trying. Everyone was bathed in sweat. I was sweating just looking at them. The smell of exercise alone is enough to make me sweat. It's a sympathetic reaction, like catching a yawn, but without the calorie burning.

Xavier Polates was a fit man, so I naturally hated him. He wasn't bulked up like a bodybuilder, nor did he have the long-distance stringiness of a marathon runner. He was fit and proportioned. His sweat-shimmering muscles glistened with an Olympian ideal sculptors had been trying to mimic for millennia. He had the obligatory six-pack abs but didn't flaunt them as much as he could. Don't get me wrong, I noticed them; his tank top wasn't a dress, but he didn't stick them in my face the way commercial beer-shilling volleyball players did. His skin was dark and his smile a natural gleaming white rich people pay thousands to fake. It came easily to him and naturally put you at ease. The middle-aged, white-bread, plump housewives found much to admire, and possibly lust after in Xavier Polates. He was handsome, cheerful, and sexy. If he'd set his eyes on Allie, I was indeed in trouble.

I banished the thought. Allie wasn't rash or vindictive. That was me. I hoped I hadn't rubbed off on her. I'd not cheated on her, but to be honest we hadn't a formal arrangement to forbid such acts. We were just seeing each other seriously, if the adjective has any special meaning. I felt my insecurities rise like nausea and changed the subject.

"How do you deal with the working girls?" I asked asked Ola while we waited.

"You mean the call girls like Chris?"

He knew her name. "Yes. Is there some arrangement?"

He looked at me disgustedly. It was better than the uninterested look he usually gave me, but not much.

"We're not pimps," he said.

"But you know about it?"

"We do, but we look the other way. We can't come out and condone it."

"But why have it?"

"We're not the moral police. They pay full price for each cruise, and we get to know them. They make the cruise better for some people."

"Like the Grays?"

"The Grays?"

"The old people who live on the ship."

"Yes, the Grays. There is your answer," he said. "It's a service. Put your bourgeois sensibilities away, Mr. Flaner."

"I'm not judging. It's kinda what I thought. I think it's cool. 'Legalize Adulthood' is what I always say."

"In most countries it is legal," he said.

"I'm an American, remember?"

"Yes, of course," he said. "You have my sympathies."

Polates clapped his hands in applause for the workout effort and said, "Good work, class. Go make this the best day ever!"

They clapped back and teetered on unsteady legs to their gym bags where they guzzled from plastic water bottles or sucked Nutri-Pods like it was morphine. Several compromised and squirted the pods into their water bottle before drinking it.

"What's up, Cap'n?" Polates said.

"Where's Allie?" I blurted out.

"Oh mon, no," he said. "Mr. Peterson, I dunno what dis man's sayin' but it got no cause to bringing in the officers. It's a misunderstanding."

"Where is she?" I said. Ola didn't try to stop me.

"I left her at the buffet having orange juice."

If you don't know, one of the most traumatic times in my life involved a cruise ship gigolo. I won't pretend that I didn't have a prejudice against the profession. It earned it. Also, I'm envious. Polates was beautiful, and I was just adorable. He was fit and I had an American paunch I was trying to diet away on a cruise ship. Ironically, Polates should have been my mentor on the cruise, giving me advice and exercise to return me to Allie a reformed Adonis. Now I was getting him arrested.

"It's not about Mr. Flaner's girlfriend," said Ola. "It's about your storeroom."

"I'm not harmin' no one," he said. "Everyone needs a place to get away."

"We'll talk downstairs."

I'd been to several arrests, and not just my own. I'd put bad guys behind bars. I'd orchestrated the grand finale of a long investigation with fanfare and gun battles. Each had been a moment of closure, however uncomfortable and dangerous. In each case, I knew the answers, had solved the riddle. I always knew I had the right guy. As Ola marched Polates out of the aerobics room, I didn't have the certainty I'd had before. I knew that my personal feelings had a lot to do with what was happening. Usually that's been a good thing, but this time I had my doubts. I didn't have all the pieces, or I did and didn't know how they all fit together into a single solution—how they all made the case against Xavier Polates.

Ola and the captain were keen on my theory of Cruise Chaos. Actually, in remembering my interview with Captain Finn Olsen, it wasn't my theory at all but his. He'd had the idea that everything that was happening on his ship was actually an attack on his ship. He took it all personally. I guess that's what captains do. If they're going to go down with their ship, they might as well get butthurt when the internet goes down and people grease up their hands before dinner.

"Tony." It was Allie coming into the aerobics center. She was dressed in an exercise leotard and running shoes.

"Hi, Allie."

"I just saw Xavier," she said. "He looked like he was under arrest."

"You look great," I said. "Can we be friends now?"

"Did you have something to do with that?"

"With what?"

"With Xavier being arrested?"

"Uhm…I didn't arrest him."

"But you set him up."

"Whoa there, Allie. Why would you think I'd do that?"

"Because you're jealous."

"You know me. Would I do that?"

"Yes," she said. "You'd feel bad about it later, but you'd do it. You have no self-control, the emotional maturity of an infant, and a hatred of cruise ship fitness instructors that borders on mania."

"Don't forget I'm fat," I said.

She looked at me hard, saw the tears welling in my eyes, the quivering lip, and the breakdown bubbling up.

"You're not fat," she said.

"I've been dieting."

"I can see it. What happened to your head?"

"Being a detective."

"Tell me about Xavier."

"I will, but only if you call him Mr. Polates, or 'the guy I'm not sleeping with.'"

"Really, Tony?" She threw her arms up. "You can be so insecure."

"Some women might find it flattering."

"What happened to Mr. Polates?" she said. "Please. Tell me. Or I'll wring your neck."

"Does he really mean so much to you?"

My charm offensive was failing. She rolled her eyes frustratedly and turned around to leave.

"Peterson is going to talk to him about what's been happening on the ship," I said to stop her.

"Is he a suspect in the murder?"

I nodded.

"Why?"

"Operation Cruise Chaos," I said. "The theory is that all the mayhem that's been happening—the murder, the mice, the shooting, stair pushes, gel in the bathtub—is all about embarrassing the cruise line."

"That's stupid."

I shrugged.

"Someone tried to kill me," I said in a petulant attempt to win her sympathy and affection.

"Are you sure you just didn't slip in the tub?" she said. "It's not always about you, you know."

"But sometimes it is. Allie, can we be friends?"

"Xavier didn't hurt anyone. He's a nice guy. How could you do it?"

"How do you know I had anything to do with anything?"

"You didn't?"

"No, I did. But you don't know."

"You are so aggravating sometimes," she said. "Why can't you give me a straight answer like you used to?"

"Because I'm afraid of saying something wrong and pushing you further away. You made the effort to come to Alaska to see me even after I was a jerk. Some guys might think you were stalking them, but I know better. I know you really just missed me."

"No," she said. "I was stalking you."

"Well, then, I'm flattered."

"I was afraid I'd find you with another woman. And I did."

"But it's not how it looks," I said. "It's the quantum physics thing. You saw what you were looking for."

"It's an old joke, Tony. 'Am I going to trust you or my lying eyes?'"

"Just because it's funny doesn't make it untrue."

"You obviously don't think much of me, Tony. That's what I've been wrestling with. It wasn't cheap to get up here, but at least I learned—"

"No. No no no. Don't. Don't make assumptions." My lip quivered to cement the point.

"Xavier?"

"You know that love nest he has on deck four?" I asked.

"Now who's making assumptions?"

"No, uhm. I mean, yes. What I'm saying is that he has a room he uses on deck four. There's a bed in it. Dara's been there. She's uhm…and I'm glad you don't…or if you did, it's okay…because I'm a mature human being, and I'd understand—that is, I'd have to, really, if I—"

"Tony!"

"Right," I said, rubbing my eyes. "Someone let a bunch of rats loose on the ship a couple of days ago, and we found where they'd been kept—in a room Mr. Polates has been using."

"That's it?"

"It's a lot," I said, not really believing it. "He also worked for the Circus line before."

"So?"

"So, they're the only ones with a motive for wanting the cruise to be a failure."

"And?"

"And uhm," I stammered. "Xavier is a crew member, so he could have done all the other stuff too."

"There are a thousand crew on this ship," she said.

"The room…"

She waited for me to finish my point. I thought I had. "He's awfully suspicious," I said.

"Quantum theory," she said. "Who was the ship cop?"

"Security Head Ola Peterson."

"Is he a good cop?"

"Average," I said.

"So not great," she said. "Can you prove he killed Vincent Bror?"

"I haven't checked Ola's alibi, but his motive is weak."

"Polates! Can you prove he did it?"

"No," I had to admit.

"Can you prove he let the rats loose? That he tried to kill you?"

"Circumstantial evidence is still evidence." It was a quote that'd been used on me plenty of times and I felt dirty saying it.

"I can see it in your eyes," said Allie. "You got the wrong man. You're blaming him because he showed affection toward me."

"How much affection?"

"There, you see?"

"Uhm…"

"He was so excited to get this job. He told me how shitty the last ship he worked on was. He was trying to make this a career, and you throw blame on him just because he offered me his coat and invited me to aerobics."

"But he might be a villain," I said. "You don't have all the pieces. There's this guy from Circus scurrying around."

"If he is a villain, then okay. But you better be sure, Tony Flaner, because I will never speak to you again if you destroy an innocent man."

"I'll never speak to myself either," I said.

"Good."

"Good."

We stood together both with our arms folded on our chests, looking determined.

"What are you going to do?" she said.

"I was going to grovel at your feet and beg you to give me another chance, but I'm not anymore."

"Why?" she said. I liked the tone of concern in her voice.

"Because actions speak louder than words. And I'm running out of time."

Before she could stop me, I leaned forward and kissed her. She didn't kiss back but she didn't kick me in the jewels or cry rape. My sexual assault complete, I left Allie in the aerobics room and marched away as if I knew what I was doing and had a plan. She might have even bought it.

38

I THINK DISNEY STARTED IT. After they got in the cruise business, because their parks were overflowing with people and their pockets with money, they found themselves down in the Caribbean buying up big ships and competing for tourist money with cruise lines that'd been doing it for years. Just in case sweaty employees in full-body Goofy suits weren't enough to attract vacationers, Disney went into their petty cash and bought an island. Take that, you non-multibillion-dollar, market-manipulating, media-controlling, entertainment conglomerate mega-corporations!

Disney's private island getaway offered family-oriented vacationers with round plastic ears stuck to their beanies, a safe, non-threatening environment to sunburn and swim. The Caribbean on the whole is hot and smelly and has flies. There are real people there with real problems—economic, political, personal—the very thing middle-class American vacationers would rather not see. They'll take the climate but could do without the inhabitants always having revolutions and such. It messes up their Midnight Minnie Mouse Margarita Marathon.

Alaska didn't have the same problems as the Caribbean. It wasn't a third world country. Second, maybe. It was after all a piece of the United States in its fading moments of empire in the twenty-first century, but it wasn't about to spark a revolution. The attraction of a private island wasn't as clear, but the land was cheaper.

Royal Danish Cruise Lines had purchased a little piece of forested rock in the leeward side of the Inside Passage north of Glacier Bay. The island boasted "scenic beauty," "natural wonders," and "abundant wildlife." There was also an all-you-could-eat lunch buffet that I suspected would look a lot like the shipboard all-I-could-eat-anytime buffet but with "abundant wildlife." I remembered the mosquitoes in Skagway and hesitated getting off the ship.

Nutri-Pods was the official sponsor of "Adventure Island" and had a plastic banner over the dock to prove it. Anyone who had not already been forced to drink a dollop of vitamin-enriched eel oil would have their chance at the free sample kiosk you had to pass to get off and back on the ship.

I wasn't sure what my next move should be, but damn it I wasn't going to make it. I wanted to clear Kristen, but now, I needed to either clear Xavier Polates or put him down for good. Either would be fine with me. Actually, that's not true. I wanted it to be him.

I saw Garrett get in line to leave the ship and joined him. It wasn't such a big deal leaving the ship as it usually was since there were no stores where you could buy cheaper alcohol to sneak aboard. The island was an extension of the ship, and we could come and go all day as we pleased.

"Hey, Garrett. Sorry I missed your show."

"You've seen it before," he said. "That looks nasty."

"Six stitches."

"You're not going out in sandals, are you?"

"I don't have anything else," I said. "It's not like I'll be running."

Along the line out of the ship they'd set up a wall of vacation photos. They were the ones that were taken when we first got on board and had been displayed with pride on a lower deck by the shops since the cruise began where you could buy them for twenty dollars. Though only the best looking had been printed and displayed, by the lists I could see there were hundreds as yet unbought. I think the photographer was getting worried. Utahns are known to be cheap, so I wasn't surprised to see so many still unpicked. The faces all looked burned out and tired for having stood in line for so long on the first day, and the unchanging background in each made for a hypnotic mosaic.

"Don't bother looking for ours," said Garrett. "I bought it."

"You'll have to give us all copies," I said.

"That would be illegal," he said. "It says so on the back of the photograph."

"I won't tell," I promised.

I knew enough to get my pullover and wear long pants, but Garrett's warning about the sandals was right on. No sooner had we stepped foot off the ship and onto the island than my foot was a nest of hungry mosquitoes. I jogged in place the best I could to keep them off.

"You're really serious about losing weight," said Garrett.

"Oh yeah," I said.

Off the dock, there was a stairway leading up to an overlook where lunch was being prepared. To the right, around the hill, the sign promised nature tours every half hour. To the left along the beach a sign offered "scenic beauty at your own pace."

"The tour?"

"No," I said. "Too many people. Let's get a beer."

"It's a little early, isn't it, Tony?"

"Nope."

"All right then," said Garrett. "As long as it's not too early."

The hike up was more exercise than I'd had in days, but it kept the mosquitoes away. Large tents like modern longhouses were set to view the ocean. Behind them, running along a ridge, I could see a chain-link fence. It was disguised, but it was there. I assumed it was for the roving herds of mosquitoes on the wilder part of the island.

The sun had burned through some of the clouds, and it was actually a nice day by Alaskan standards, and after I got Garrett to buy us drinks, we sat down and people watched.

"There's Dara," said Garrett, seeing her on the 'at your own pace' beach. "Isn't that Allie with her?"

"Oh shit."

"What? Why?"

"You know that guy Dara was seeing on the boat? I kinda got him arrested."

"For the murder? You solved it?"

"I might have," I said.

"So tell me how it all fits together."

I sipped my beer and watched the two girls below us.

"'Might' might be too strong a word," I said.

"What's a better word?"

"'Didn't?' 'Haven't' is good," I said. "I *haven't* it figured out. I didn't."

"So why'd you get a guy arrested?"

"I'm ready for another beer," I said. "Give me your card."

The buffet line was filling, but the drink line was clear, so I went there and got another round. When they asked for a card, I slipped them the one Sandra had given me as a test. The light went green.

Standard Flox and Camila, the petite raven-haired tan beauty he lusted after, crested the hill. I waved them over.

"Want a drink?" I said. "My treat."

"Drunk already?" said Standard.

"No."

"Wow, you must have really hit your head hard."

"Are you going to introduce me to your friend?"

"Tony, this is Camila. Camila, this is Tony."

"I've heard a lot about you," she said.

"I've heard snippets about you."

"You have a head injury?"

"I do," I said. "I assume you do too, if you're seeing Standard."

Standard slugged my arm.

"That hurt, you little shit," I said.

"Some hard-nosed detective."

Camila laughed. "You two are like brothers."

I paid for their drinks, or rather, Sandra's magic card did. We left the line and headed to our table. I dropped the beers in front of Garrett who winced. "Don't sweat it," I said, giving him back his card. "You didn't pay for them."

"I thought you lost your card," said Standard.

"I'm borrowing one."

He slugged me again.

"Why'd you do that?"

"You're running up a bill on someone else's card? That's low."

"No, it's a crew member's."

"Don't you think they have to pay for drinks?"

"Uhm, I don't know."

They all glared at me.

"Okay," I said. "I am a shit."

I excused myself and went back to the line to see if I could get the charges sent to my room. On the way, naturally, I ran into Sandra, the cruise director herself. She saw me before I could dive off the cliff onto the rocks below, so I pretended to be happy to see her. I quickly prepared a lie and was ready when she came up.

"It's all a misunderstanding," I said.

"What is?"

"You know."

"Polates?"

"What about him?"

"I heard you got him arrested for the killing."

"That and the mischief on the ship," I said. "More the mischief, really. But it's all connected."

She looked sour.

"I have a question," I said. "Do the crew have to pay for drinks?"

"They're not allowed to drink while on duty."

"Even you?"

"I'm different," she said.

"Do you have to pay for your own drinks?"

"I don't," she said. "It's part of my promotion budget. I give free drinks to people all day. Why, you want one?"

"Please," I said, feeling a little less dirty overall. A little.

She ordered a silver pail of bottles in ice with a souvenir bottle opener. She handed over a card from her pocket and they slid it for a green light.

"Why even bother with the card?"

"It shows I'm doing my job," she said. "And budget control."

"Cool."

"Tell me what you have on Xavier," she said.

"Rats in his love nest." Then, thinking of something new, I said. "Plus he tried to kill me in a lover's triangle thing last night. That's how I got this." I pointed to my head.

"That wasn't a murder attempt," she said. "That was a practical joke."

"I could have died."

She looked sour.

"Does Xavier have a lot of friends on this ship?" I said. "Lots of people worried about him?"

"He's a nice guy. I'd hate to see him railroaded. Nothing serious has happened on the ship. It's all been minor really."

"Except a murder."

She paused. "Yes, except that."

Her radio squalled her name. "Excuse me."

"Thanks for the drinks."

"Enjoy your vacation," she said and left to find a quiet place to talk.

"More beer?" said Standard. "You are too much."

"No, it's okay. I found out it's free on this card."

"You stole a card. Of course it's free for you," said Garrett.

"No. The drinks on this card are automatically credited toward public relations. It's a good thing."

"Bullshit," said Standard.

Garrett nodded.

"Seriously, guys," I said. "Seriously."

"Seriously?"

"Seriously."

"Well, okay," said Standard. "Give me another."

We drank beers and watched the tables fill up with hungry mosquito-bitten tourists until we felt obliged to leave the table or get food. We wandered down to the beach. Standard and Camila wanted to explore at their own pace, while Garrett and I fell into the nature tour. I almost turned around when I saw Allie and Dara in the line already. I tried to turn and run but drew their attention when I tripped over the bucket ice chest I was still carrying.

They looked at me and I waved. They acknowledged me but didn't say anything. It may not have been the cold shoulder but it surely wasn't the warm and fuzzies.

Also in our group, to my chagrin, was Doctor Belinda Phillips. From her I got a look of pitiful derision. She was part of the large fawning club of pyramid-scheming Nutri-Pods schmoozers who were following their master, Paul Vinalez, on his Nutri-Pods-sponsored adventure hike. Ashley stood beside him in matching green windbreakers. She'd apparently made up with her husband. Denny the bodyguard had his dark glasses on and faced into the crowd away from the trail. Sennegar was there and caught my eye. We had matching head wounds. We shared a secret concussive smile. The two bunco cops in matching black windbreakers fell in with the crowd of marketers I recognized from before. And just so everyone was accounted for, Bailey Peigne sidled into the group like a leech up a pant leg. He pretended not to notice me while Candy tried to figure out how to remove the lens cap from her camera.

The sign said the tour was meant for thirty-five people, but we had easily fifty.

"How much nature can we see in this mob?" said Garrett.

"I gotta go on this one," I said. "You can take the next one."

"Why?"

"Allie's on this tour," I said. "Plus, interesting things often happen on these. Remember the glacier and the boat trip?"

"Yes. Now that you mention it," said Garrett. "Bye." He got out of line as fast as he could. Once clear of the crowd, he broke into a run.

"Welcome to Adventure Island, where adventure lives," said our Royal Danish Cruise Line official guide. "Before we go, does anyone need any bug spray?"

Fifty hands went up.

By the time the entire crowd was sprayed down, we'd gone through five cans of repellent and the next tour was already forming. Our guide, a perky Alaskan native named David—but we could call him Davey—was a member of the crew, and I'd seen him with Sandra. He had the same radio she had but kept his in a canvas messenger bag on his shoulder. He wore a ranger's hat over a ship's officer uniform that had to piss off the real seamen, and under his satchel, on his hip, I saw a pistol holstered.

"What's with the gun?" I asked.

"Just a precaution."

"The mosquitoes get that big in the interior?" I asked, half expecting a positive reply.

"Kodiak bears are sometimes on the island. If we're lucky, maybe we'll see one."

"And if we're unlucky, we'll get eaten," I said. It was the kind of joke I make all the time, filling in the next line after a setup. I didn't expect a laugh, just some attention, maybe something to remind Allie why she liked me. What I didn't expect was the look of concern on Davey's face.

"We'll be fine," he said, a little tremor in his voice. "We should be fine."

39

WITH A WHISTLE in his mouth Davey led us down the trail. It wasn't much of a trail, more of a gravel path connecting rock shelves and poured concrete steps that led around the rocks and up a hill into the trees. A shorter paved trail offered 'scenic wonders' for the wheelchair and stroller crowd. We didn't have any of those, so we plodded down the crackly road two or three abreast.

I saw the cameras of the reality show team behind us. They were running out of conflict but did their best when the camera light went on.

"I think we should get sprayed against mosquitoes," said the first. "They can carry disease."

The other rubbed his unshaven chin and nodded. "That's the first smart thing you've said all week," he said.

"What do you mean by that?"

"You're an idiot," the other said.

"No. You're the idiot." The camera filmed it all.

We walked for a hundred yards or so when Davey stopped us and pointed out an interesting tree. Or maybe it was a rock. It could have been a frog or a root. We couldn't hear anything way in the back where I was. When the group moved again, I wiggled my way forward and tried to figure it out.

Another fifty feet and we were on a railed ledge overlooking the bay with the ship in the distance. The trail split again with the nature walk *Guided Only* continuing through the fence to the left, and a *Beach Combs* continuing down and to the right. A map carved in a wooden sign showed the three-mile guided loop and promised several more even steeper climbs than the ones we'd already gone up. Most people decided this was far enough and went down to look for sea otters or went back the way we'd come.

The thought of three miles of mosquito hiking in sandals didn't do much for me, but Allie turned left, and so I followed.

I passed the two undercover cops, and they asked me to take a picture of them together. They were a cute couple in matching outfits. I got the ship in the background.

A last sign on the fence as we passed through warned of dangerous wildlife and admonished us to keep our distance. It had a real *Jurassic Park* vibe to it, but I kept moving. If I stopped, the mosquitoes would descend looking for chinks in my chemical armor. My sandaled feet were particularly vulnerable. I should have worn socks. Since when did I care how stupid I looked? Oh, yeah. Since I lost Allie's affection.

The group had thinned considerably. The cops were gone, and most of the pod people too. Sennegar looked about as anxious to make the hike as I did, but his boss puffed up his chest, squirted black ink into his mouth with his patented ecstatic zeal and pushed on. The gesture was repeated by some of the faithful. Ashley winked at me. I blushed. Allie scowled.

Of course she had to be looking then.

The pod-fueled mob took the lead. Vinalez talked shop, telling his followers the best way to get through the door when doing door-to-door cold calls of your neighbors. Belinda Phillips was right up there, absorbing the wisdom. The guide encouraged us to stay together, but it was hard with so many people.

Fifteen minutes past the gate, Allie and Dara fell back, the knot of admirers being too thick to see anything at the front. This was my chance.

"Hey, guys," I said. "Fancy meeting you here."

"I should fucking rip your guts out, Tony," Dara said.

I relaxed. I'd been afraid she'd be mad at me. This was practically a kiss hello compared to what I thought was coming.

"I'm on it," I said.

We walked for a while. The gravel gave way to an actual trail, dirt under our feet, roots to trip over, holes to snap an ankle in half. Real outdoor charm. The trail snaked around boulders and trees and at times we lost sight of the other tourists but there was no chance of losing our way. We had only to follow the discarded Nutri-Pods bottles like Hansel and Gretel to find the tour again.

"These people," said Allie, picking up a bottle and dropping it in her bag. I collected a couple. We picked up the litter as we went, each time getting a little more angry at the arrogant pricks ahead of us.

In a clearing with a pond that was hard to see for all the stupid bald eagles, we found cigarette butts, and Dara explored the heritage of the smokers in colorful adjectives and impossible biologies.

"What the hell is this thing?" said Dara. "It stinks."

Bailey Peigne watched us pick up the litter and laughed. Candy, his girlfriend, sat on a bench rubbing her feet. How she'd made it this far in heels that high was beyond me.

"Flaner," Bailey said, walking over to us.

I didn't feel a need to answer. I think he was trying the word out, seeing what it felt like to say something intelligent.

I didn't like the way he strolled over so casually, not looking at me, glancing around to see who was watching us.

"Who's your friend, Tony?" asked Allie.

"This guy cheated on his wife several times and hid money in the Caymans," I said. "His wife gave me five thousand dollars to prove it."

"Did you ruin his life?"

"He thinks so."

"He did," said Bailey Peigne into my face. He'd walked right up to me, toe to toe. We were about the same height, but he must have had on lifts. He stared into my eyes with malice. I stared back with condescension.

"Listen, Peigne," I said, "why don't you go stick your—"

I didn't see it coming, but I should have. He went for the stomach, my soft spot. If he'd gone for the jaw, I'd have seen it coming and been able to duck. I'd have surely, instinctively, struck back with lightning reflexes, possibly killing him. As it was, I doubled over, Bailey laughed, Allie screamed, and Dara stood stunned. She wasn't used to sudden violence erupting around her that wasn't her doing.

I'd been hit harder and better, and dammit, I was a detective. I straightened up and sucked air back into my lungs. He reared back to go for my jaw, but I readied my rabbit-like reflexes and sprung away. He swung and he missed. I fell backward onto the ground and he did a one-eighty, unable to halt his momentum.

I crab-walked away from him.

He advanced.

"What'd you hit him for?" asked Candy. "He's a nice guy."

"Shut up," he barked at her.

His blow had ripped my stitches and I felt new wet sticky blood sticking my sticky shirt to my sticky side.

I rolled over and got to my feet. I turned to run, but he spun me around and went for another shot to my gut. I thought he was going for my head and made it happen by ducking into it, catching his fist on my left eye. I heard a crack and saw stars. I didn't black out, but I staggered to confuse him.

I went down in my three-point stance, ready to unleash hell when I heard a scream.

I looked up and saw Bailey Peigne holding his hands to his face. It was him screaming. The sound was picked up from farther away like a growing echo.

I stood up. Bailey screamed and staggered. The other screaming came closer. Then the clearing was full of running, screaming tourists. We watched them come from up the trail, and still screaming, run past us and back down the trail.

I noticed then a little aerosol can of pepper spray in Allie's hand, smelled the pungent odor, and understood Bailey's sudden discomfort.

More tourists screamed into the clearing. There was the guide, Dr. Phillips, Ashley, and Vinalez, all leading a big brown bear that loped after them on all fours.

When the people paused to catch their breaths to scream some more, the bear hesitated and sniffed the air. From its red-brown fur, terrifying size, and unpleasant disposition, I knew I was looking at a Kodiak bear. A male. A thousand pounds of burly animal.

Dara took out her camera and snapped a picture.

There was a moment of silence as everyone waited, then Bailey, still with his hands over his eyes, screamed again. Though the sound warmed my heart, it really pissed off the bear and it charged him. I wouldn't have minded this at all if Allie and I hadn't been standing between Bailey and the charging monster.

Without thinking, I ran at the bear as fast as I could, waving my arms above me like a drunk monkey. I sang an ad-lib version of *Sugar Magnolia* at the top of my lungs because that was the first song in my head. If that didn't confuse the bear, nothing would. He stopped his running and got up on his hind legs to prove he was bigger than McDonald's.

"...Head's all empty, but there's a bear!" I screamed as loud as I could. My lung capacity had been challenged by Bailey's punch, but I'd found new strength in protecting Allie.

The bear roared.

"Saw that killer down by the river!"

Roar.

"While I'm singing you all go elsewhere!" Arms a-waving.

Out of the corner of my eye I noticed the guide fumbling in his satchel. His gun belt, I saw, was empty. He was crying. Candy led Bailey down the trail, hushing him. The others, led by Sennegar and Ashley, edged away from the bear back toward the ship.

The wind shifted. I noticed something else. A new smell. A real stink. An ammonia scent not unlike cat piss, if a cat pissed on a cabbage with stinkbugs. Then I smelled the pepper spray again.

Paul Vinalez squirted a pod into his mouth like it was an Underdog Energy Pill and readied to make a break for it. I saw his coat was torn open.

"Paul Vinalez," I sang, *"Take off your jacket!"*

They weren't the song lyrics, but the beat was right.

Roaring and wiggling, the bear was getting into it.

"If you do as I say now, you might survive!" My voice was going. I backed away.

Allie understood or at least gave me the benefit of the doubt and was on Vinalez trying to pull his jacket off. He pushed her aside, and I turned and roared at him. The bear backed me up, and he stripped out of his jacket and ran out of the clearing followed closely by Denny, the broad-shouldered bodyguard, who'd wet himself and was about to pass his ward at a dead run.

It was just me, the guide, Allie, and the bear.

"We can discover the wonders of living," I sang. My throat unable to yell anymore. *"Ditching this bear down by the riverside."*

"What do you want me to do with it?"

"Is it not at all delightful," I sang, *"Is it covered up with pee?"*

Wiggle and head shake. Me, not the bear.

"Can you throw it into the bushes, as far as you can away from me?" I sang.

Allie waved the coat like a matador, wafting the pungent smell at us. The bear moved toward her. She threw it into the pond. It landed on a stump scattering the eagles like so many shitting pigeons on a New York street. The bear galloped toward it. Allie ran. I ran. The guide had a book open to an index. I grabbed his arm as we passed and dragged him down the path with us.

Twenty yards away, we paused to catch our breath. Dara was there, holding a tree branch like a Louisville slugger ready to get in the game. Vinalez was nowhere to be seen. Bailey was on a stump on the side of the trail with Candy. A couple of the pod people were treating his wounds with Nutri-Pods. He screamed again, fell down, rolled on the ground and rubbed dirt into his eyes.

"Strawberry?" I asked, seeing the newly spent Nutri-Pods.

"Lemon," said a pod lady.

"It's the cloves that burn," said the other one. "But the healing power of the garlic will clear his sinuses."

"What about the ginseng and aloe root?"

"That's just filler for the New Age hippies."

"Stop screaming, honey," said Candy. "You'll bring the bear back."

"Yes," said the guy. "Best you man up and hold your tongue."

"I'll handle this," I said. I lifted him into a sitting position. His nose was running like a spigot, his skin was blistered, his eyes red from the pepper and eel juice, and now scratched from the dirt. He couldn't see me.

"When I get my hands on that little—"

He didn't see it coming. Couldn't, really. I socked him in the gut as hard as I could, and he fell silent for a moment, inhaled a gasp, made a little whimper and fell over.

"Bears," I said.

"Bears," agreed Allie.

"Bears," said Dara.

I volunteered to drag Bailey back to the ship by his ankle, but he decided to try and walk instead. My eye was swelling up with a new shiner, but my side had stopped bleeding after it scabbed into my shirt. My foot was swollen with mosquito bites, and my knuckles hurt where I'd sucker-punched Bailey. I'd caught a rib. We didn't say anything, but Allie held my hand as we walked back. I felt great.

When we got to the gate in the chain-link fence, half the crew was there with automatic rifles.

"Where'd all the guns come from?"

"The ship," said Doctor Reyes. "We sail to Mexico sometimes."

Reyes had a full medical team with him. Paul Vinalez was sucking on an oxygen mask. His shirt was off, torn like his jacket had been, but his back was unscratched.

The guide, half crying and hysterical, tried to explain.

"It was Pablo," he said. "He's never been like that before. He's always so nice. He's tame. He's not even from Alaska. He's from a zoo in Tampa. I have no idea why he turned on us. I dropped my gun. The fat guy saved us. I want to go home."

"He's not fat," said Allie. "He could lose a few, but he's not fat."

I was in love again.

Bailey was brought over to the medical crew who flushed pod slime out his eyes with saline solution. The smell of peppers made me hungry and reminded me of something.

"Where's that trash you picked up?" I said to Dara.

"You put him in jail, remember?"

"That was a good one," I said. "No. You said something stank."

"Look in Allie's little trash bag."

She handed it to me. I took a whiff and my eyes watered. I dumped it out.

Among the many Nutri-Pods vials, water bottles, cigarette butts, and assorted trash, there was a single empty glass flask the size of a cigar tube. It read, *Golden Trail Panning Iditarod Adventure—Bear Musk. Guaranteed to attract bears.*

40

PABLO THE KODIAK bear was not an Alaskan native. His grandparents, named Elmer and Delilah, were a gift from Alaska to Ohio for the Cincinnati Centennial in 1919. Colorado gave them a pair of grizzlies in return. Apparently, bears were an appropriate present for a hundred–year state anniversary: paper, wood, gold, diamond, bear.

Elmer and Delilah were put in a bear habitat with the grizzlies from Colorado, where they grew up, got big, and ate the grizzlies on a slow Sunday afternoon. Colorado was incensed. Zoo visitors were traumatized, and Elmer and Delilah were quickly moved out. Boston had them for a while, long enough for them to have cubs in 1960. A male named John and a female name Jackie, in honor of the new First Couple.

John and Jackie had a pampered life and never had to hunt. Even so, they managed to hospitalize six handlers before being sold cheaply to a traveling carnival out of Wichita in 1979. In 1982, the two, having no other mates to choose from, had a single offspring, Pablo, named for the carnival's silent partner, Pablo Escobar, whose cocaine cartel helped finance the failing carnival through the 90's in a money laundering scheme Skyler White would appreciate.

Inbred Pablo, unlike his mean parents and ferocious grandparents, was a cute little cuddle-bear. When the real Pablo Escobar visited the carnival in 1997 and tried to feed a DEA agent to him, the bear supposedly loped up to him, drooled, and rolled over for his tummy to be rubbed. When the same DEA agent was covered in Bulls-Eye original tangy barbecue sauce, and the bear starved for a week, Pablo the bear loped up, licked him clean, drooled, and rolled over on his back for his tummy to be rubbed.

Escobar executed the agent himself and left him in a ditch by the fairgrounds outside of Houston, Texas, where his body lay undiscovered for two weeks because there was a BBQ cook-off, and everyone assumed the Bulls-Eye smell was just someone trying to cheat.

Pablo, the bear, was seized by the DEA in 1999 with the rest of the carnival and three hundred kilos of cocaine in Tampa, Florida. A local zoo put him in with their grizzlies, who considered him something of a fat-ass pansy and wouldn't play with him.

When the recession hit in 2007, the zoo unloaded the bear on the Royal Danish Cruise Line, which wanted a "wildlife attraction that wouldn't kill its guests" for its newly purchased island at the top of the Alaskan inside passage.

For years, Pablo stayed on the island, king of all he surveyed, sharing the little forested rock with eagles and squirrels and generous regular feedings where he grew huge and lazy. The guides were told to sell the dangerous nature of the bear if he was seen, but unless the guide shooed him away, Pablo invariably loped up to the group, drooled on them, and rolled over for his tummy to be rubbed.

Pablo had not had the company of another bear for years, let alone one in heat. It was natural for him to be interested in the musk splashed on Vinalez's coat. He's really a sweetie, we were told. There was no need to press charges or bring the law in. Nothing but a jacket was lost. Here, have a dinner voucher.

Allie had a new respect for me. I was content. I took the voucher anyway. Steak would be nice. I'd cut the fat off. I'd be a hero. Again. Most of the others were content just knowing Pablo wouldn't have hurt them and happily took the free meal, excited to have a good story to tell when they got back. Paul Vinalez was not one of these.

"Are you kidding?" he screamed into the cruise director's face. He'd left his cool confidence in his bodyguard's soiled pants. "It was a thousand-pound bear. A bear! A thousand-pound bear!"

"Yes, but he's very gentle," said Sandra. "And usually he keeps to himself."

"Did you see my jacket?"

"No. Was it nice?"

"I was attacked by a bear!"

"Well, you were told not to provoke the wildlife."

"What did I do?"

"You must have done something. Why else would he attack you?"

"It was a bear!"

Allie held my hand. I felt three inches taller.

Ola Peterson stepped into the midst. He'd been taking witness statements like a cop but must have sensed Sandra's PR campaign failing and came to her rescue.

"From what I've ascertained," said Ola, "you approached the bear for a photo."

"I didn't even have a camera."

"No, you asked to have your picture taken with the bear. For publicity."

"I hardly got close at all."

"When did you smell it?" I asked.

"What? The bear stink? I smelled it at the pond," he said.

"How much farther before you saw the bear?"

"Around the corner."

"Is the bear usually there?" I asked Sandra.

"When we see him, it's often in that clearing. He's fed there."

"Excuse me, you stupid bitch!" Vinalez yelled into Sandra's face. "You're talking to me, remember? I'll have your job for this and your company's insurance."

It was hard to like Vinalez, so I didn't.

Who knows how far Pablo's amorous advances might have gone? I might have just saved Vinalez's life, and he hadn't even thanked me.

"You signed a waiver," said Ola.

"What?"

"It was part of the cruising agreement," he said. "You must not have noticed it."

"I'll have your job too, jerk-off," he said, putting a finger in Ola's face.

Ola didn't react. He wore his bored, defeated-cop-on-a cruise ship look I'd come to love.

"Was the bear mentioned specifically in the agreement?" I asked. Ola gave me a look of betrayal. "I'm trying to figure out who knew Pablo would be there and tried to use him to kill this eel-oil-oozing conman."

"What did you say?" Vinalez turned on me, ready to unleash his silver-tongued charm. But I wasn't afraid. With Allie beside me, I was bulletproof.

"Shut up, Paul," I said. "It's not always about you."

"What!"

"Well, maybe this is," I said. "But shut up anyway. It's not just about you."

"I—"

"Shut up!" said Allie. "Let the man work."

There was a moment of silence where Vinalez moved his jaw up and down but no sound came out.

"Well?" I said.

"It's kind of a surprise," said Sandra. "We deliberately don't advertise it because we don't want to pollute the experience of a wildlife adventure. Plus Pablo is usually too lazy to come out and we don't want to disappoint people's expectations."

"The crew knows," said Ola.

"This is all very interesting," said Vinalez, "but it doesn't excuse the fact that I was nearly killed by your thousand-pound bear."

"There was no crew on the tour," I said, ignoring Vinalez.

"The guide."

I shook my head. "Someone would have been noticed."

"Wait," said Sandra. "You're not thinking this Pablo thing has anything to do with what's happening on the ship, are you? I mean, this isn't the ship."

"The cruise line owns the island," I said. "Fits the MO."

"This was targeted at me, not the stupid cruise line," said Vinalez. "Besides, didn't you already catch the guy letting rats loose on the ship?"

Ola looked at me and raised a blond eyebrow. Allie squeezed my arm.

"Yeah," I said. "We might have the wrong guy."

"Maybe not, if Mr. Vinalez is correct," Ola said, "if the attack was about him personally."

"Of course it was."

"Agents," I said to Ola. "The villain could be using agents."

"What, like hitmen?" said Ola. "With bear piss?"

"When in Alaska…"

"You're going to put that bear down right now," demanded Vinalez. "Give me the rifle. I'll do it."

"Are you good with a rifle, Mr. Vinalez?" I asked.

"Dead shot."

"Could you hit a badger at a couple hundred yards?"

"With the right optics, not a problem at all."

"Very interesting."

"We're not giving you a rifle," said Ola. "You're not shooting anything."

"We'll buy you a new jacket," said Sandra. "At a boutique on board."

"You can buy clothes on board?" I asked.

"Yes."

"Shoes?"

"Italian loafers," said Sandra. "Very nice."

"How about walking shoes?"

"Nothing that simple."

I looked down at my feet. They were brown from dirt. I kicked, and the dust flew up in a cloud of buzzing wings and then settled again on my bare feet. It wasn't dirt.

"Tony! Mosquitoes!"

"That's what it looks like," I said. "Strange, I don't feel them."

"That's not a good sign," said Reyes.

"No?"

"No."

He sprayed repellent on me. The mosquitoes quivered and buzzed and then died, stuck to my feet with bug spray.

"I'm done here," I said.

Still holding Allie's hand, I headed back to the ship.

"Oh, Flaner," called Ola after me.

"What?"

"Well done with the bear."

"They say if you want to know what a man really values, light his house on fire."

"What the hell does that mean?"

"Uhm...maybe there's more to it."

Allie kissed me on the cheek. "Thanks," she said.

We walked back to the ship at dusk. Most of the passengers were already on board. The outside buffet court was closing down. I thought to get another drink on Sandra's card, but the bar had already been packed up and taken back aboard. It was too late. It gave me an idea, though.

"Where's your room?"

"I have something below the waterline," she said. "No windows."

"Dara moved us to a nice room."

"Cabin. She told me."

"Come with me."

The security checkpoint was light but not gone. We had to show our keycard for entry. Remembering I didn't have my real one, I flashed it without letting them scan it. I moaned and screamed and showed them my swollen feet and reminded them of the impending lawsuit they had for the Taser shot and they let us by. I hurried Allie to an elevator and with Sandra's card, went to the fourteenth floor.

"Deck," said Allie. "What are you doing?"

"I'm taking liberties," I said. "With the ship now, with you later."

"What?"

"I'll show you."

The elevator door opened onto fourteen and Allie gasped.

"We don't have fountains in the hall where I am."

"Shhhh," I said. "We're stealing."

"What are we stealing?"

"Accommodations."

We heard Led Zeppelin blasting from the left side. *Immigrant Song,* the one about coming from ice and snow land. Seemed appropriate. Pity I can't quote the lyrics. Copyright and all. "Ahh-ahhhh—AH!"

"That's loud," said Allie.

"That's the crabbers," I said. "It's coming from their room."

"Cabin."

"Stop it."

"Sorry."

The sound of female giggles and male laughter poured out of the room as loud as if they were in the hall.

"You'd think these expensive rooms would have been better insulated," I said.

Ola had told me that between Vinalez's suite and Bror's, there was an empty room. I made for that. Sandra's key turned the light green and I pushed open the door.

There was a sitting room, a table for four, and a private balcony. Behind a door was a king-sized bed, bathroom with dual sinks, shower, and a tub with a window. There were no towel animals, but the room was clean and ready for guests. I slid the lock shut and wiggled my eyebrows at Allie.

"You need a shower," she said. "You smell like bug spray."

"So do you."

"So I need a shower too."

"Cool."

Our clothes fell away like fraud charges from a connected bankster. In no time we were lathering each other up. I was reminded of an ancient Chinese proverb: a woman's breasts are never so clean as when she bathes with her lover. Okay, maybe the Chinese didn't say that. I heard they don't have breast fetishes like Westerners do. Still, if they didn't say it, they should have. A missed opportunity if they didn't. Maybe it was the Jedi.

No matter.

It was a nice shower. Allie got to see all my wounds and cleaned me up as best she could. She carefully washed around my bullet hole, shampooed around the stitches in my hair, soaped the Taser bites on my shoulder blades, scrubbed the blood off my lip and kissed my blackening eyes.

My feet felt like giant itchy slippers and looked like localized smallpox. The bandage on my toe fell off and raced for the drain.

"Allie, I'm sorry."

"I know you are."

"I'm figuring it out," I said. "I'm trying to do the right thing, not just the easy thing."

"Being with me isn't easy?"

"Not if you're me and you think responsibility and commitment are four-letter words."

She leaned back and let the water wash the shampoo out of her uncannily straight hair while the streams of water accentuated it. Like me, she was approaching middle age, but she was lean, strong, and tanned from outdoor work. The sun and wind may have given her a few more lines than her contemporaries in middle-class suburbia, but she wore them like grace. She was not an ideal, not a model, not the kind of woman you could put on a pedestal. She was real and grounded, and was one of the guys, a friend first. A lover second.

"Have I been making demands?" she said, breaking me out of my reverie.

"No. Well, kinda," I said in my usual succinct way. "We're to the point where certain expectations are...well, expected. I'm not as mature as I act, believe it or not."

She laughed, and the water got warmer.

"I want to meet those expectations. It's a matter of who's in charge, you know? My subconscious is afraid of change."

"You?" she said. "Tony, you are all about change."

"Only when I'm sure I can change out again," I said. "I'm not like you, Allie. I don't like doing hard things. I change because it's usually easier to leave a project than finish it. I'm working on it. I've had some success, but this time there's another person involved. A person I'm very fond of and afraid of hurting. It's one thing if I disappoint myself. I'm used to that. But I'm not sure I can live with myself if I disappoint you."

She put her arms around my neck and looked up into my bruised eyes.

"Nothing's written in stone, Tony. We do the best we can. I can't promise you that I won't change. I'm sure I will. We take what's available to us and make it work. If it doesn't, we'll try something else."

"I know."

"So?"

"So I'm working on it," I said. "That part of me that left you in Salt Lake without a call has to come to grips with the fact that I'd fight a thousand-pound bear for you."

"You knew it was tame, though, right?"

I shook my head. "I didn't know anything. I didn't think anything. I just acted. Kind of like when I got on this stupid ship."

"Not at all like that," she said.

"No, it was a selfish act. If Pablo hadn't run at you, I'd have stayed away. I wanted to protect you, for me. See?"

"You won't cut yourself a break, will you?" she said, kissing me.

"I don't deserve one."

"Well, I'm giving you one anyway," she said.

I'd put together a plan of romantic foreplay after the shower, including slow kissing and foot massage, but it wasn't to be. Allie pulled me into the bed like a sailor hauling a ditty bag over her shoulder. I bounced once on the mattress and she was on me. She held my hands down and kissed me.

"Thanks, Allie," I whispered.

"That was quick," she said.

"No." I laughed. "Thanks."

"You're an idiot, but I love you."

There it was.

It hung in the air like a big red French balloon. Allie looked as surprised as I'm sure I did. She pulled away from me and bit her lip.

I laughed. "Allison Braise, you have no taste," I said, "but I love you too."

41

A RESPECTABLE WHILE LATER, two laters really, we rolled over and stared at the ceiling on sweaty pillows. The ship had set sail again, and we could see a clear bright night sky through the window across the cabin.

"Let's look at the stars," I said.

"Okay."

We found 'His & Hers' terry cloth robes in the closet and took the bedspread with us on the balcony. It wasn't Glacier Bay, but there were islands and moonlight, still water, and intriguing ripples suggestive of whales, otters, salmon, or Russian submarines.

"I still can't believe you flew all the way out here."

"What else do I have to do to convince you?"

"Pinch me. Ouch!"

"You said to."

"True," I said. "I am trying you know. Have you noticed I lost weight?"

"No."

"Well, I have. I've been dieting."

"You're nuts."

"I'm doing it for you."

"Why?"

"So you'll find me sexy," I said. "Ouch! Why'd you pinch me again?"

"To convince you of the obvious, stupid," she said. "If I didn't find you sexy, would I have sex with you?"

"Pity sex? Ouch!"

"Don't be an idiot."

"Well, I still want to lose weight."

"Okay."

"But I'm doing it for you too. Wait—let me finish. Ouch! I'm already hurt everywhere. You're just bruising the bruises. What I mean is that I'm doing this to prove that I can do something I should do but don't want to do."

"That's a big deal?"

"For me? Yeah. Hell yeah."

"Sounds like self-abuse, like you're trying to punish yourself. You're ruining your vacation."

"There might be something to that," I said. "I took the case for the same reason."

"Now I'm confused about this whole thing," said Allie.

"You and me both."

"You don't think it was Xavier, do you?"

"What's he to you again?"

She looked at me crossways.

"Just asking."

"He's a nice guy," she said.

"Good, good," I said. "Nice. So, how nice?"

"Tony, I just met him. Don't be so insecure."

"Oh, I'm not. It's nothing to me. I mean, we were kind of broken up. Ouch!"

She hit me that time.

"Stop it. Nothing happened."

"I never thought it did. Ouch!"

She hit me harder. My arm was bruised for sure now.

"When did you get so punchy?"

"I don't know. Just kinda felt right. Cathartic," she said. "I was pretty mad at you."

"You can hit me again if you want. Ouch! I didn't really mean it."

"Oops." She kissed it better.

There was a steady wind blowing. It was cold but not biting. A bright moon shone on the water painting the darkness bright in milky reflections.

"It doesn't make any sense, Tony," she said.

"It's poetical. 'Painting the darkness bright,' like 'Painting the roses red' from Disney."

"What are you talking about?"

"Oh, you didn't hear that, did you?"

"What?"

"Never mind. What were you saying?"

"I'm saying that your Cruise Chaos theory doesn't make sense," she said. "If I were trying to cause chaos on the ship, and I was willing to kill somebody, I'd go to the middle class, not the VIPs. I'd make it random. Terror you know. It seems to me that these attacks have been pretty targeted."

"Vinalez?"

"And you," she said. "What do you two have in common?"

"Neither of us is Chinese."

"There you go."

"I can't see any other scenario that makes sense," I said.

"But it doesn't make sense," she said. "I just told you."

"I don't want to think about it."

"Too bad. What about Peigne? He seems to be involved with both you and Vinalez."

"So?"

"I don't know. Seems like that makes more sense. Didn't you say Vinalez was attacked in Salt Lake? Peigne is from Salt Lake."

"Everybody on the ship is from Salt Lake."

"Which would suggest that it's not about the cruise line, but about Utah."

"It?"

"The mystery," she said.

"Which one?"

"I was thinking about Bror, but you're right. There are lots."

"I'm hungry," I said. "I need food."

"Me too."

I didn't relish getting into my mosquito-sprayed clothes again, but I thought walking around the ship in terry cloth robes would be too conspicuous. Led Zeppelin seeped under the door as we took a final look around the suite. Robert Plant was having some good times, and some bad times.

"Are we going to get in trouble for this?" asked Allie.

"Only if we get caught."

We stepped outside the door before we saw the maid in the hall. We froze. She waited in front of the crabbers' door with a rolling cart of food trays and buckets of beer bottles like they had on shore.

We retreated.

The music muted for a moment, then went loud again. We waited another minute and came out. The hallway was empty.

We crossed to the fountain and were just at the elevator when the door next to the crabbers opened.

"Hey, Flaner. You're just the guy I'm looking for."

It took me a minute to recognize the producer from the crabber show. Without his cameraman, I had to stare at his three-day beard stubble and uncombed greasy hair for a second to place him.

"How do you know who I am?"

"I talked to the captain," he said. "I wanted to include the murder as a subplot of the show."

"Let me guess. He wouldn't let you?"

"Threatened a lawsuit if I mentioned it and promised to leave me on an iceberg if I even talked to you," he said. "That's why I haven't been in touch."

"So now you want to be left on an ice floe? What? No longer feel you can contribute to the caribou hunt?"

"The Eskimo thing? That's a myth."

Zeppelin was rambling on when the door to the crabbers' room opened and a topless brunette in pink panties pushed a cart out the door. She gave Allie a look, waved at me, and giggled. Behind her, I saw a room like the one Allie and I had just left but in much worse shape. The mattress had been pulled out of the bedroom and lay in the hall. Food trays and empty bottles of booze lay on top of it along with a face-up, dick-down, naked crabber. His brother was outside on the balcony, also naked but with his back toward us. The brunette shut the door.

"What do you want?" I said to the producer.

"A better job."

"Looks okay to me."

"Are you kidding? This is a disaster. There's no way this show's getting picked up. Look at them. They're dimwitted fishermen, but they think they're rock stars. Tell me, what kind of woman is a fishing groupie?"

"They have a TV show," said Allie.

"Have you seen the show? They throw cages over the side of a boat. That's their big skill."

"It's dangerous, isn't it?"

"Sure. Okay," he said. "But that's hardly proof they're bright. They think drama is yelling, and conflict is argument."

"Reality TV," I said.

"I used to film for National Geographic, you know?" he said, shaking his head.

"You could have been a contender," said I.

"Exactly."

"Good luck."

"No, wait," he said. "I really did want to talk to you. Well, show you something, really."

He gestured for us to come into his cabin. Allie and I went into a cabin across the hall.

"I got upgraded to here for not including the murder," he explained and opened the door.

His cabin layout was the same suite design we'd spent the last hour in. It was an order of magnitude smaller than Bror's but still not a cheap berth on this tug.

The producer had put the extra space to work. Banks of batteries were lined up on the floor like dominoes in their chargers. Two computers and three large monitors were arranged on a table with cables snaking over the edge and across the floor like an Indiana Jones tomb. Several cameras were in different states of disassembly on the couch and microphones spilled out of a padded aluminum trunk like it had sneezed them out.

"I'm Oliver," he said. "Oliver Danks. I'm the guy whose career is going to crater for being associated with this stinker. *Most Perilous Catch on Vacation*. God, I'll never work again."

"Nice room, though," said Allie. "Big, I mean."

"Balcony," I added.

He stared at us. His unshaven face housed hopeless eyes. From the next room, Robert Plant was measuring his love in inches.

"Sit down," he said, rubbing his eyes and kicking chairs out for us from under the table. We sat.

"So I heard about the shooting on the glacier," he said. "And your friend Perry told me about the boat ride."

"And you'd like to confess?" I said hopefully. A new theory was forming: disgruntled cinematographer goes postal—film at eleven.

"First look here," he said. The monitor came to life, and a virtual control panel and a center image showed the Alaskan inlet where I'd nearly drowned. He hit play.

In the center of the scene, the two crabbing brothers were two inches apart being crabby at each other at the top of their lungs. The brewing violence centered around the perpetual question of paper versus plastic.

"Every piece of plastic is a stab in the earth's heart!" screamed one.

"And killing trees makes sense?" Loud enough to bring an avalanche down in Kamchatka.

Oliver turned the volume down and let it run for a minute before pausing it and then zooming in over one brother's shoulder.

"Okay, there on the right are all the boats you were going out with," said Oliver. "On the left is you guys."

There we were, Dara, Garrett, Perry in his survival suit, Dr. Phillips, Ashley Vinalez, and the guide. Leaving it paused, he panned over to the right behind the other crabber. He zoomed in on a fishing boat on the outside of the flotilla of whale watchers. Using his mouse, he outlined a square and zoomed in again. It was grainy, but we could clearly see two men in camouflage fatigues standing on the back deck with binoculars.

He let the video roll and zoomed out a little for context.

"They're not looking at the water," Oliver said. "Not looking for whales. They're looking at you."

The video played, and one of the men lowered his glasses, stepped back and picked up a rifle. It was grainy, but after enhancement, it was pretty plain. Allie shot a look at me. I shot one back. The man looked through the scope and then put the rifle down. The crabber's face filled the screen.

"This was on the way out, right?" I asked.

"Oh god, yeah. The brothers were too drunk to stand on the way back. Didn't get an inch of usable film after thirty minutes."

"We were attacked on the return ride," I said. "Did you hear the shots?"

"Yeah, they were loud, but our guide said it was hunters. There're always hunters out there, he said."

"Is that the best picture you have of those guys?"

"Yeah."

"Wait," I said. "You went to Mendenhall Glacier in Juneau, didn't you?"

"Yes."

"I saw those guys there. Do you have any crowd footage from then?"

"Yeah."

"Let's see it."

"Hours of it," he said.

"Order room service."

"Why not?" he said. "That's what expense budgets are for, right?"

"Right."

Allie took our order and called it in. Club sandwiches all around, the only universal metric of room service.

"Will you give me an interview when all this is done?" asked Oliver.

"What about the captain?"

"He might change his mind," he said. "It's better to have it and not use it than need it and not have it."

"I doubt the captain will change his mind."

He ran his fingers through his hair and wiped his hands on his pants. "I used to be a journalist. I'm dying here. Give me a few minutes of something interesting."

"If I get something," I said.

"Please."

Oliver set up viewing stations for Allie and me to scroll through film files and we all went to work. Led Zeppelin took us on the *Stairway to Heaven* six or seven times before our food finally arrived. It makes you wonder.

We finished our sandwiches, and I was about to give up when Allie shouted.

"There!"

She pointed to a group of tourists at the Mendenhall Glacier parking lot. Two men in camouflage outfits and rifle cases got out of a car.

"I was shooting setting," he said. "Parking lot. Worthless."

Zooming in, it was grainy, but we saw the men lock their car, a white SUV, look around the lot once and then, instead of following the tourists into the visitor center, stroll out the other way into the brush and disappear.

"I saw those guys," I said. "In Juneau, they were waiting at the boat dock in those same outfits."

"Did they see you?"

"Didn't seem interested in me," I said. "Gave Dara a look. She gave it right back."

"Disembarking in Juneau?" said Oliver.

"Yeah."

"I got some of that too."

We drank coffee as Oliver set up another file. It was taken from the deck above the exit and followed the tourists off the ship.

"Again, another setting piece," he said. "Trying to get the feel of the ship. I thought I could compare the energy of the people leaving the ship on the first stop to how they'd be on the last."

"There," I said.

There they were—two men behind a barricade watching people exit the ship.

"I got this in HD," said Oliver.

"What's that they're holding?" said Allie.

A group of pod people crossed in front of the men, and they glanced down at a blue folder. Something slid out of it onto the ground.

"It's one of those pictures from the ship," I said. "Everyone got one taken when we boarded."

"I didn't get one," said Allie.

"In Seattle," I said.

"How'd they get it?" asked Oliver. "They weren't on the ship. They were waiting in Juneau."

"Good question."

Oliver froze the frame on the men's faces and zoomed in. It was like a CSI episode.

"HD is pretty cool," I said.

"Now everyone can count your zits," he said.

"Not a fan?"

"Meh."

He saved still pictures of the two men. They were as good as any snapshot I'd ever taken.

"Now the picture," I said.

He rewound and zoomed in on the photograph after one of the men had retrieved it from the ground.

"Enhance," I said. "Make it so."

"I'm sensing the crew is confused," said Allie.

I smirked.

No enhancement was needed. The zoom feature and high-definition picture was enough.

"Do you know this gentleman?" asked Oliver, rotating the picture.

"I do," I said and sighed.

"Who is it?" said Allie.

"That is no gentleman," I said. "That's Dr. Belinda Phillips."

42

OLIVER PRINTED pictures of the men and Phillips photo and gave them to us.

"I'll show the captain the video, but you can't have it," Oliver said. "Looks like I might have gotten something worthwhile on this trip after all."

"Fair enough," I said.

It was half past one in the morning when Allie and I left Oliver. Led Zeppelin continued to play out of the crabbers' room, glowing angels of Avalon in the east.

A pile of dishes lay on the floor in front of the crabbers' door. Anyone coming in or out needed to jump over them.

"I'll go deal with this," I said, waving the printed pictures like a fan. "I'll meet you in your room."

"That's pretty forward," she said.

"I can't stay with you?"

"Oh, you can," she said. "You just can't get rid of me so easily."

"Shit," I said.

We took the service elevator down to the security office, my home away from home when I wasn't in the infirmary.

"Go wake up Ola," I told a dozing guard.

"Why?"

"Damn it, Jim. I'm a detective, not a narrator!" Not exactly true, but I was feeling a little punchy. Allie punched me.

"Ouch."

"Tony? Is that you?"

Kristen opened her unlocked cell door and looked out. It's good to be rich.

"Hey, Kristen," I said. "This is Allison Braise. I love her."

Allie blushed but didn't take her eyes off Kristen.

"Nice to meet you," said Allie.

"What happened to you?" said Kristen.

"I got laid," I said. "I didn't know it showed."

"No," she said. "Your head, your eyes. What the hell?"

"Oh, sorry. TMI," I said. "It's all in a day's work."

The guard was on the phone to Ola.

"Why is she staring at me?" asked Kristen.

"Ask her," I said.

"Why are you staring at me?"

"You're not what I expected," Allie said.

"What did you expect?"

"Something more like his wife, I think."

"Oh," Kristen said. "Allison, Tony, and I have been over with for decades."

"Yeah, I know," she said. "It's still interesting."

"What are you doing here, Tony?" Kristen asked.

"Who is it?" came a voice behind her.

"Is that Kline?"

Kristen blushed. "He fell asleep in the chair."

I smiled. "We need to talk to Ola. We got pictures of some decent suspects."

"Vincent's killer?"

I'd been pretty stoked on the way down to the security office, thinking I'd broken the case. Kristen's question took the air right out of me.

"Uhm," I stammered. "They're connected. I think."

"Oh, want to tell me about it?"

"Sure," I said. "Let's wait for Ola though. No need to say it twice."

"Why did you burn Tony?" asked Allie. "In college?"

"What?" she said. Kline peeked out of the cell, rubbing his eyes.

"Hey, Flaner," he said.

I waved.

"Tony told me that you guys were a thing and then you marked him down a grade for a class because he handed in a paper late after you said he could."

If it had been anyone other than Allie, I'd think she was checking up on my story, testing my veracity. I could have been insulted. However, since it was Allie and since I'd been honest, I figured she was doing me a favor. I hadn't had the courage then or now to ask for an explanation. I'd simply broken up with her.

Kline put his arm protectively around Kristen. She looked from Allie's face to mine and then nodded in understanding.

"Is that why you broke up with me?" she asked.

I squirmed beneath her gaze. "Well, yeah," I said. "It was pretty shitty. I slipped a grade in that class because of it."

"You blame me for that?" she asked.

I put my arm around Allie to mimic Kline. "Yes," I said. "Who else?"

"Tony, remember how you broke up with me on the phone?"

"You didn't break up with her face-to-face?" asked Kline.

"She was out of town."

"I was out of town because my grandmother had died," Kristen said. "Another TA graded your paper. I was in Vermont."

"That skinny guy with the acne?"

"Yes."

"He never liked me," I said.

"And your paper was late," she said.

"Oh."

The silence hung around us like a fart.

"I'm sorry," I said. "I didn't know that."

"It's okay. It was going to end, anyway. You lack commitment."

I slapped my forehead.

Allie gave me a half smile and kissed the tip of my nose. I figure she was looking for a place that wasn't bruised, stitched, broken, or shot. She was running out of targets.

"I'm working on it," I said.

"I know."

"Hey, Flaner! I wanna talk to you."

"Xavier?" said Allie.

"Yeah, it's me. Tell your boyfriend I want to talk to him."

Allie communicated the request by raising one eyebrow.

I followed the voice to a cell beyond Kristen's. Unlike hers, Xavier Polates' door was locked. I slid the peephole open and looked in. He was standing right up to the door, an inch from the slit. All I could see were big brown worried eyes in a dark face. They met mine, grew wide, squinted, then softened before he said, "Hi."

"Hey," I said. "How you doing?"

He squinted again.

"Sorry," I said. "This is awkward."

"Yeah," he said.

"What do you want?"

"You're wrong about me," he said. "All wrong."

"That's what I hear."

"I've been talking to Kristen Bror. I didn't kill her husband."

"Uh-huh."

"No, I have an alibi. I couldn't have done it. I was with Roxy."

"Roxy?"

"She's a Gray," he said. "I mean, an old lady. She lives on the ship. I was with her."

"I know her."

"Go ask her. I was with her all night."

"Playing cards?"

"No, don't be dense," he said. "*With* her. Sex. We were having sex."

"Why didn't you say anything before?"

"I am now," he said. "Peterson says I was a saboteur. I just found out you sayin' I killed someone."

"Well, it's kinda all the same thing."

"And I tell you I've done none of it," he said. "You know Roxy. Go ask her."

"Uhm, okay."

"Be a good Joe. Get me out of here. Allie there loves you very much. You all she talk about. I tell her to give you another chance. I'm on your side. Don't do me like this."

"She told you about me?"

"Yeah, mon. All she say."

I looked at Allie who nodded.

"I'll talk to Roxy," I said. "But I doubt I can get Ola to let you out."

"Sure you can, mon."

"It's better if you're here," I said.

"What you sayin'?" he said, his eyes flashing wild and desperate behind the peephole.

"If you're here and something else happens to the ship, you have an alibi."

"And if nothing happens?"

"Uhm, you'll be safer?"

"That's shit. Get me out of here."

"No, it's good," I said. "Something's already happened. Look at my eyes."

"You look like shit."

"See?"

"No."

"That's the magic of it."

"Flaner, this better be good," hollered Security Head Peterson from down the hall.

"I gotta go."

"Get me out of here, Tony!" Xavier said from behind the closed door.

I left the cells and returned to the office. Ola was in his chair, his feet up on the desk. He was dressed in gray sweats, white slippers, and a Royal Danish Cruise Line T-shirt. His blond hair had been combed by a blender, and he had a salty drool line in the corner of his mouth. His bloodshot eyes accurately measured his patience. He was on empty.

"About Polates," I said.

"Staying right where he is."

"But he says he has an alibi," I said.

"So check it," he said. "But he stays where he is. He's involved somehow."

"But..."

"Why'd you get me up?"

I handed over the photos Oliver had printed out and explained.

"These men were at both Skagway and Juneau," I said.

"So were you."

"They're not on the ship. They have rifles. They have this picture."

He looked at the picture of Dr. Belinda Phillips.

"They weren't after me," I said. "These guys were after Phillips. I just happened to be nearby."

"Kinda thin," he said, yawning.

"Bullshit. We'll be in Ketchikan in the morning, right? Call them and have these guys picked up. I bet they'll be there."

"Why are they trying to kill a doctor?"

"We'll ask them when we catch them."

He looked at the photos, examined the grainy one on the inlet and the clear ones on the dock. He called up a file on his computer and compared the photo of Phillips in the photo to the actual photo taken by the ship photographer. Yes, he had access to that.

"Can you get me a copy of mine?" I said.

"I'll charge your room."

"Never mind."

The picture the men had was exactly the one the ship's photographer had taken in Seattle. The green blouse looking of desperate fatigue was unmistakable.

"How does all this fit?" Ola said.

"Let's ask them," I said. "I have a theory, but I don't want to say anything until I'm sure."

"That's not good enough."

"It'll have to be," I said. "Now call the cops in Ketchikan and keep Phillips on board tomorrow."

"And if I don't?"

"And something happens?"

He pondered for a minute. "Okay," he said. I'm not sure if it was defeat or exhaustion in his voice. I wonder if he knew.

Kristen was sent back to her cell and Kline ordered back to his cabin. Ola took the pictures I gave him and faxed them to the mainland and to show the captain later. Allie and I yawned and turned to leave.

"Oh, Flaner," said Ola. "I forgot to tell you. I canvassed the entire crew.

No one is claiming to have made the 'Code Oscar' call for your friend Perry."

Allie said, "Code Oscar?"

"Calling man overboard," I said.

"An anonymous hero," said Allie.

"The hero Gotham deserves."

"We reward crew for that. Somebody missed out on a payday," Ola said. "That's suspicious."

"This whole cruise is," said I.

Something in the back of my mind switched over at that detail from Ola but was lost in the haze of a long day.

It was late but the coffee we'd had with Oliver kept Allie and me talking. I took her to the most forward place on the bow I could get to and made her stretch her arms out while I screamed, "I'm the king of the boat!"

"That's not the line," she said.

"No? What is it?"

"'King of the world.'"

"How do you get that by standing on the prow of the ship with your arms out?"

"Box office receipts."

"Ah," I said.

"We're on top of the boat!" I yelled.

"That'll work."

I kissed her neck. She turned and kissed me back. We kissed for a while, then we just hugged each other because it was freakin' cold.

"Shall we go inside?" I suggested.

We took the inside stairs down to the lobby and through the main public spaces of the ship. Roadies were setting up a Nutri-Pods banner advertising an all-ship afternoon presentation *Cooking with Nutri-Pods!* There was a signup sheet for 'limited seating.'

"We should go," I said.

"Why?" she said.

"What they're doing here is opening up one of their seminar sessions to the public."

"And?"

"And it costs a lot of money to go to a seminar."

"So it's a bargain?"

"Yeah."

"A sale is a good price on something you don't want to buy."

"You are wise," I said.

We stopped by my cabin on the way to Allie's to collect some clean clothes and other personals. Dara was there, which surprised me. She was in the big bed and ordered me to turn off the fucking light before doing physically impossible things to myself with a lampshade and a garden gnome.

"Hi, Dara," said Allie.

"Hey, Allie," she said and rolled over. "I didn't move rooms. Too big a hassle."

Allie took me to her room. It was deep in the middle of the ship. It had full spectrum lighting and enough mirrors to trip out Roger Waters if the closet doors were left open. Today's towel animal was a bear.

We stumbled inside, then out of clothes and into bed in one fluid motion. We fell asleep in each other's arms to the low thrumming of the ship's engines just a few floors below us—*decks*.

43

KETCHIKAN, Alaska, is called the Salmon Capital of the World, so it's got that going for it. It also calls itself Alaska's "first city," not because it was founded first or is the largest or most important or had a winning kayak team, but because sailing north along the Inside Passage, it is the first town in Alaska you pass. It's a stretch for fame, but what are they going to do? Like most towns on the Inside Passage, it clings to the edge of a mountain on a thin ribbon of flattish land falling away into the sea. The impression is of a town falling down the mountain into the water like a landslide. They brag that the town is ten miles long and three blocks wide, which is only half the story. It's also ten stories high with more stairs and trestles than streets. To make things more interesting, the cute touristy parts of the village were actually set up on stilts over a tidal plane. Every six hours, the water rises or falls thirteen feet. That's like a hundred and eighty meters. A lot. By city ordinance, every tourist has to hear the story of how the town fathers played baseball on the Thomas Basin when the tide was down, thus allowing a brisk sale in Ketchikan Low-Tiders baseball jerseys and refrigerator magnets sold in every single stinking kitschy shop in town.

Ketchikan Creek is a salmon-spawning river. Even so, the Tlingits didn't have a full-blown village there, only a seasonal fish camp to catch and smoke salmon before leaving it to the goats. During the gold rush, prospectors passed through Ketchikan as fast as they could to get north where the gold was. One of the rarer get-rich-slow types noticed how easy the fishing was on the river and set up a cannery that still operates today. Five different species of salmon swim past Ketchikan every year and the fishing has been so good that the government has had to step in and stop it before the entire industry collapses from species die-off. Ah, progress.

Though fishing was good, the trees were easier to catch. Before the pulp market bottomed out sometime in the post-pulp years, lumber was the primary occupation of the Ketchikaners. Now it's—wait for it…tourism. Fishing is second. I don't know what's third. Probably refrigerator magnet manufacturing.

Besides the very cute and colorful turn-of-the-century boardwalk of shops selling magnets and baseball jerseys, Ketchikan's tourist world revolves around a totem pole museum, conveniently located up a hillside too steep for stairs so they put in a sidewalk.

It was my bright idea to walk from the docks up to the museum, part of the new me, a healthy go-getter who'd walk a mile up a mountain to see old carved wood.

Allie and I slept in late, and the gang had already gone to town when we woke up. The stop in Ketchikan was only half a day, ten to four. Six hours. I guess that's a quarter day.

We left at about one thirty, skipping the shops for the museum since Allie wanted to see it, and we didn't know how long it would take. It took us forty minutes to walk there. I think it was a half a mile. I was dipped in sweat when we arrived. I know I'm not in the best shape, but it was a steep hill. Even Allie was breathing hard at the top of it. Naturally she'd stopped breathing hard by the time we got to the museum. I can't say as much.

"We should have taken the bus," she said.

"There's a bus?"

"A free one."

"It's okay," I gasped. "I needed the heart attack."

I staggered to the window on rubbery legs. "Two, please. Where is everybody?"

"The last crowd just left on the free bus. The next one will be here in a few minutes."

"Of course."

We had the place to ourselves. Outside there were a few modern examples of totem poles and inside was a great collection of nineteenth-century poles from all over Alaska—the biggest collection of totem poles in the world. So suck on that, Phoenix!

Supposedly there were fragments of older ones in some glass cases but we had to take their word for it. It could have been petrified dinosaur snot or caramelized driftwood for all we knew. What was left after rot, time, and beaver attacks wasn't easily recognized as part of the proud Tlingit heritage, but experts had sussed it out as a raven head over a salmon.

"Looks like a stump," I said.

"It's not painted."

"None of these are."

"These are the originals," Allie explained. "The paint wore off."

"They're kinda boring," I said. "The colored ones outside are more interesting."

"Those are modern reproductions."

"I like color."

"I think these are interesting."

"Oh yeah. Best totem poles in town. No doubt."

"Look," she said. "Learn something."

I bent over a plastic plaque describing one pole and had to laugh.

"What?"

"This one is a 'shame pole,'" I said. "It's about one guy taking all the credit for a group hunt. It's calling him a liar and a cheat and warns women to stay away from him."

"It's a big pole."

"That's a lot of rage," I said.

"We'd use a billboard today."

"Yeah. That's a good idea."

"Don't," she said.

"Just filing away the idea," I said. It was a good one.

I went on a hunt for more shame poles but couldn't find any, only celebratory and religious ones. I figured it didn't do for the ideal of noble Tlingit heritage to have too many examples of petty rivalry and carved libel. It made the visit for me, though. I liked the idea of the shame pole and couldn't wait to make my own. So many possibilities.

The museum wasn't very big, and we found ourselves circling the aisles several times to get our money's worth and justify the calorie expenditure to get up there. People came and went in waves. It filled up and emptied twice while we wandered around.

After forty-five minutes, we looked for the free bus. I collapsed on a carved wooden bench with a blue and white killer whale motif while Allie studied the posted schedule.

I tried to call Salt Lake to talk to my son Randy but got his voice mail. Nancy too was gone. Allie fell onto my lap and stretched out on the bench looking up at the pole above her. We fell into a comfortable silence.

A bus arrived and disgorged tourists. After they'd poured out, we climbed in. The spent Nutri-Pods on the seats told us we were on the right bus.

In five minutes, we were let out at the shopping district, a picturesque assembly of restored buildings snaking up a creek on stilts. The shops, not the creek. It was all boardwalks and bridges, souvenirs and art stores, food vendors, and tour guides.

Allie and I took in the ambiance, and listened in as a tour guide explained how this building was once a brothel and that one a brothel too, and the one next to it, and the one next to that one. A big-breasted woman in a red velvet period costume swaggered in front of a backdrop for photos to prove the point that prostitutes used to inhabit the area.

Once I tuned out all the refrigerator magnets, I noticed a surprising number of shops selling 'ulus.' An ulu is a really strange knife. It's a semi-circularly bladed stabby thing you hold like a pair of brass knuckles tipped with the business end from *The Pit and the Pendulum*. It's an Inuit device. It's best used in a concave bowl.

We'd seen them everywhere. I finally picked one up in an art store and examined it.

"How have I never seen one of these before?" I asked Allie.

"You're not an Eskimo."

There was a looped DVD showing on an old television demonstrating how to use an ulu to cut carrots and cabbage, fish heads, and elk meat. The trick seemed to be to push the blade into what you wanted to cut and let the blade do the rest.

"This has 'infomercial' written all over it," I said. "If they can sell an electrified salad spitter to insomniac sufferers at four am, they can sell this thing. 'The ancient wisdom of the native peoples.' It'll be huge."

"I can see it," said Allie. "But it won't happen. It can't be patented."

"You are wise," I said.

An alarm bell went off. We turned to see Ashley and Paul Vinalez across the store in one of those magnetic detector gates. Denny rushed back from outside and nearly knocked the couple down.

He raised his fists like a fighter and scanned the room.

"I'm here," he said as if anyone hadn't noticed.

A clerk was quick to attend to them. She was maybe eighteen, and wore a simple, stylish blue floral dress with a *My Antonia* feel to it. Her calm was in direct opposition to the panic on the couple's faces.

"You didn't pick up anything you forgot to pay for, did you?" she asked.

Allie and I moved closer. The store was relatively crowded already with cruise tourists, and the bell brought in more from outside.

"Of course not," said Paul, glancing around. His cheeks went red.

"Do you mind if I look through your purse, miss?"

Ashley went red.

"Listen, lady," said Paul, poking a finger at the clerk. "If we wanted to steal something, rest assured we could. Your Podunk security measures are crap."

"You know what I always do?" I said. "Sometimes the store forgets to neutralize those little magnetic strips. They're always in DVDs. I usually save them and slip them into someone's pocket. It's great fun."

"He does," said Allie. "It's not fun. It's like this."

"What are you saying, Flaner?"

"Maybe someone slipped one of those magnetic things into Ashley's purse."

The clerk waited. The alarm alarmed. Police arrived.

"If I could just look in your purse," said the clerk.

"I'm not dumping my purse out here for everyone to see," said Ashley.

"How about the office?" said a cop.

Ashley looked at Paul who shrugged.

With the cops in tow, they followed the clerk through a back door and disappeared.

"I hate it when you do that with magnetic strips," said Allie.

"It's hilarious," I said. "Hey, you got me last month."

"Were you embarrassed?"

"Took me a while to figure out what was going on," I said. "You'd think I'd have seen it coming."

"You'd think," she said. "Some detective."

Sennegar rushed into the store then. Vinalez's manager held a phone pressed to his ear and scanned the room. His eyes fell on me, and I pointed to the door to the office. He scrambled over to it, knocked, and was admitted.

"She did it," I said.

"How can you be so sure?"

"The way she acted. And Paul knew it the second the alarm went off. She's done it before."

"But they're rich."

"Who's ever rich enough?" I said. "Maybe it's a thrill thing. Maybe she's sick. Maybe greedy. Maybe all of the above."

"Maybe embarrassed to buy something," said Allie. "Or something she didn't want her husband to see her buying."

"Like what?"

"From what you said, condoms?"

I blushed.

I moved closer to the door. There was a display of very expensive ulus made from hundred-year-old lumber saw blades. They were etched works of art and cost plenty. They came with a complimentary copy of the looped DVD and a cooking book. The concave cutting board was extra.

"I know those things are prone to error," I heard Vinalez say from behind the door. "I used to install them, for God's sake."

"Calm down, Mr. Vinalez," said a male voice I assumed to be a cop. "I'm sure it's all a misunderstanding."

"I'll be right back," said the clerk.

I retreated to Allie who was admiring shot glasses and coffee mugs. *I heart Alaska, Ketchikan me if you can, my other glass is a moose.*

Another eighteen-year-old rang up baseball caps and jerseys.

Ten minutes went by and then Paul, Ashley, and Denny came out of the door and immediately left the store. The cops followed. Five minutes later, Sennegar came out with the clerk. The clerk went to the register and rang up a sale and put cash in the machine. Sennegar went out front for a cigarette.

I followed him. He no longer wore a bandage on his head, but the scab was visible under his hair from the rock in Juneau.

"Get it all handled?" I said, flipping a thumb back at the shop.

He rolled his eyes.

"Allie, this is Adam Sennegar. Sennegar, this is Allie."

"How do you do?"

"Fine."

"Expensive?" I said.

He nodded.

I had a sudden revelation looking at Vinalez's money man.

"Bailey Peigne is helping Paul hide his money in the Caymans, isn't he?"

Sennegar went white.

"I can't believe I didn't think of it before," I said. "Of course. Why else?"

Sennegar drew on his cigarette and looked over a wooden railing at the creek below.

I said, "You know a shoplifted trinket is nothing compared to the world of hurt you're going to be in once the bunco squad gets wise."

"There is no bunco squad," he said.

"Yes, there is. See?" I waved at the two men from the bunco squad up the boardwalk. One had an ice cream up to his face, and the other wore a T-shirt with a big splatted mosquito on it that read *Alaska state bird.* They waved back.

"Okay, they're not great cops, but they are cops," I said.

He blew his smoke out in a long steady sigh.

"So what did it cost?" I leaned on the rail too, Allie next to me, all of us in a row.

"In there?"

"Yeah."

"Six hundred," he said. "Paul didn't know when to shut up. He kept making it worse."

"What did he mean, he used to install those?" I asked.

"You heard that?" said Sennegar. "God, what a baby. Tell me the Gardeners didn't hear."

"The pod people?"

"Yeah."

"I don't think so."

"Rather than just dump out the bag and claim she took it on accident, he accused the store of entrapment."

"So he was lying?"

"No," said Sennegar. "He used to work for Uinta Security in Provo. He installed security things."

"Uinta Security? That place with all the little signs in people's yards?"

"Home security."

"What did he do for them?"

"Installation. He was a journeyman electrician for a while before he became an entrepreneur."

"A man of many careers," said Allie. "Like someone else I know."

"I resent the association. Plus, I've settled into a full-time slacker, part-time detective."

"I thought you were done slacking?"

"No. I'm going to be a more responsible slacker, open to commitment, but slacking is my life."

"How would it be?" said Sennegar.

Not liking his snarky tone, I said, "Good to know Vinalez has something to fall back on after prison. How are you fixed?"

"Ugh," groaned Sennegar, and he chain-lit another cigarette.

We left him to his thoughts staring over the rail at the water. We visited a few more stores and galleries and wandered back to the ship. We still had an hour until it sailed, but I was tired from the walk. Allie was kind and took me home.

At the security station, they x-rayed Allie's bag and demanded my card. I couldn't bluff it this time, and rather than have another dance with the Taser, I handed over the card I had—Sandra's. The computer beeped green, and I was pleasantly but firmly asked to wait beside the security station for a minute.

"I'll catch up," I said to Allie, trying to get her away.

"It's okay," she said. "I'll wait with you."

I knew she needed a restroom, and I knew I was about to be bawled out. For both of us, I shooed her away.

"I'll catch up."

She squirmed a little, kissed me, and boarded the ship.

"Washy-washy!" They were back. The ship had been re-provisioned with hand sanitizer. I took some from the grinning attendant.

The security guard was on the phone. I figured I had about five minutes before Sandra came down and I had to explain her kindness and alcohol blackout the night in Skagway. The guard glanced at me, nodded, and hung up the phone.

He walked over and put the card in my hand.

"Welcome aboard, Mr. Flaner," he said.

44

YEAH, that was weird.

They'd busted me. I caught a glimpse of the terminal when they scanned the card. It wasn't my name or picture. It was Sandra's. Even if he'd accounted for the weight difference and lack of makeup, the cheekbones were all wrong. Mine were much more attractive. Still, I'd gotten through security, been admitted to the ship, and even given back the passkey to the cruise. I added it to the stack of interesting tidbits I'd collected but not assembled properly in my brain.

I cheated. I took the elevator up to my room. When I got there, Dara and the gang were waiting.

"What's up, guys?" I said.

"We heard you and Allie got back together," said Garrett. "Good job."

"Did Polates confess?" said Perry.

"Only if they tortured him," said Dara.

"Who's they?" said Garret

"They."

"Oh, them."

"He didn't confess," I said.

"But he's the guy, right?" said Garrett.

"Of course not," said Dara. She'd opened one of my moonshine jugs and was passing out drinks.

"Give me some," I said. "I paid for it."

"Is he the guy?" Perry asked again. He passed me a glass of lighter fluid.

"Well?" said Critter. "Dara's been saying some shit about you."

"Behind my back?"

"You weren't here," she said. "Do you want me to repeat it?"

"No," I said. "I can guess."

"Well?" said Critter, holding me in his plastic stare.

"Well," I said. "No. I don't think so."

"Damn straight," said Dara.

"What changed your mind?" asked Perry.

"The bear," I said. "Plus, he says he has an alibi. I'm on my way to check it out. But he won't be getting out anytime soon."

"Why not?"

"The head of security thinks he's involved," I said. "They don't have anyone else. It makes them feel better having someone in jail."

"Who's them?"

"They," said Dara.

"The powers that be," said Perry.

"I thought they had your old girlfriend locked up," said Critter.

"They do. She makes them feel better too. Kline is spending a lot of time in the cells. More warm and fuzzies. They must be tickled pink," I said.

I took a big sip from the glass. It looked like water and numbed my tongue on contact.

"Thith ithn't very good," I said.

"Why'd you buy it?"

"I wath drunk."

"You will be again if you finish that," said Standard.

It was the first thing he'd said since I got there.

"What are you guys doing in my room, by the way?"

"Cheering up Stan," said Garrett.

"There's a whole big open ship out there to hang out in. Why are you here with my towel monkeys?"

"Getting sick of the cruise," said Standard, taking a drink.

"He's upset because Camila shined him in Ketchikan," said Perry.

"Dumped?"

He shrugged.

"Tell Uncle Tony all about it," I said.

"Nothing to tell," said Standard. "I dropped by her cabin this morning with plans to take a walk along the tide pools."

"Who doesn't love tide pools?" I said. "Did you have a flotsam and jetsam guide?"

"Know your slimes and oozes," said Critter.

"She said she wasn't getting off the ship."

"And?"

"And she didn't go with me to the tide pools."

"And?"

"And what?" he said.

"And?" I said.

"And she was dressed," he said. "I got dumped."

"Because she was dressed?"

"Up," he said. "Dressed up."

"Still don't follow."

"She had a date," he said.

"She said that?"

"No, she said we'd get together for drinks later tonight."

"Wow," I said. "That's pretty hard. I can't believe you haven't thrown yourself off the ship yet."

He glared at me.

"I was under the impression you were looking for a short-term affair. 'Shipboard romance' was the term you used."

"No one likes to get dumped." It's not a dialogue tag, but he sulked.

"I heard about somebody killing themselves over it," I said. "Just recently."

"She didn't dump you, you idiot," said Dara. "She's meeting you for drinks."

"But not dinner."

"You chew with your mouth open," said Critter. "I don't blame her. It's disgusting."

"I do not."

"Someone had to tell you," said the puppet.

"You're not helping," Standard said.

I looked at Dara, whose blank stare told me that that wasn't her first glass. Perry kept his back to the wall and his eyes on the door. Garrett looked concerned but Critter mimicked me and shook his fanged head.

Standard said, "I'm dumped."

"Maybe she didn't feel good," I said.

"Or she dumped you because you're too clingy and sensitive," said Critter.

"She told me to have a good time. She was staying on the ship."

"You poor thing," said Dara.

"I thought we'd connected."

"I hate to be the one to tell you this, Standard. Wait. No, I don't. You're being a baby," I said. "Let the woman have some space. Maybe she hates totem poles. Maybe she has an aversion to tidal pools and seventy-degree streets."

"She ruined my day," he said.

"No," I said. "If your day was ruined, you did it yourself."

"See," said Dara. "Even fucking Flaner gets it, you baby."

"Thanks."

"Don't mention it," she said.

I changed clothes in the bathroom. I pulled on my new sweatshirt I'd bought in town with a hunter, dog sled, bear, eagle, salmon, and gold nugget on it. Just the thing for a romantic dinner.

The steep hills of Ketchikan were moving outside the door when I came out. Critter was explaining how the filthiest part of the ocean is in tide pools. "The slime that made people came from there," he said. "Disgusting."

Standard stared out the window like his dog was on life support.

"Standard," I said.

He looked over. His eyes were watering.

"It could have been her ladies' time."

He shook his head.

"Whatever," said Dara.

"Go find her and pretend like none of this happened. Don't be a putz," I said. "We'll all meet for drinks later."

"You locked my date up in the brig," said Dara, turning on me. Her drunken wild eyes filled with blame and fury.

"Gotta go." I left.

I stopped by the game room but the Grays weren't there. I searched the other ignored locations—library, chapel, exercise room without a fitness coach—but all for naught. Then I tried the buffet. They were there. It was five o'clock. The buffet had turned over for dinner. They were the only ones in line.

"Washy-washy!"

In my pocket, I had a "Captain Finn's complimentary steakhouse dinner for being chased by a bear" coupon, so the buffet was just a little tortuous. Not wanting to look out of place, rude or ungrateful, and figuring I didn't want to pig out in front of Allie later, I picked up a roll and a banana. And a piece of fish. A bit of pasta salad. Three cookies, a slice of white layer cake, another of key lime cheesecake, and a piece of cherry pie with soft-serve ice cream.

"Mind if I join you?" I said to the Grays.

"You're a hungry one," said Susan. Her blue hair was done in a towering vertical design that would attract aliens to the Wyoming desert and drive Richard Dreyfuss to distraction.

"Let the man be," said Melva.

Their plates were turkey, potatoes and gravy, steamed carrots, and broccoli. All in small portions. I looked at my plate and peeled the banana.

"Did you catch the dyke?" said Melva.

"She didn't do it," I said. "She has an alibi."

"Sorry, sport," said Arnold. "Better luck next time."

"Tony, I'm crashing. Here's my other room key. I'm going to get some sleep."

"'Kay babe," I said. "Love you."

"I love you too."

Seriously, I felt like a colossus standing over a fjord just then. The love of a good woman is steel in the veins. I don't know why I wasn't tired. Maybe it was Allie's affection, but I felt like a supercharged space plane. Those exist, right?

"So? What happened?"

"One guy got arrested," I said, keeping my eye on Roxy. "Xavier Polates. The gym teacher."

"Fitness coordinator," said Roxy.

"Health officer," said Melva.

"Yoga instructor," said Susan.

"Exercise technician," said Drew.

"Yeah, that's the guy," I said. Roxy adjusted her napkin on her white slacks and dipped the corner of a roll in gravy.

"What'd he do?" said Arnold.

"Maybe he wore the same ugly blue jumpsuit every day for a week, like somebody I know," said Roxy.

Arnold was indeed wearing an ugly blue jumpsuit. I couldn't comment on how long he'd worn it, but I seemed to remember him being in one just like it the other day.

"Screw yourself," said Arnold.

"The security head thinks he's involved in everything that's happening on the ship."

"So a 'lone gunman'?" said Drew. "You're into conspiracies now?"

"Why do you say that?"

"We know about Polates being nicked," said Susan.

"And the bear on the island," said Melva.

"Yes, well done there, sport," said Arnold.

"Have you been drinking?" said Drew.

"A little in my room. That moonshine will make you blind."

"And grow hair on your palms," said Arnold. "Or is that the other thing?"

Roxy shoved him playfully.

"Polates said he has an alibi for the night Bror was killed." I waited. They ate their food in slow, deliberate bites, re-salting it every third forkful.

"Well, what I'm saying is," I said, "do any of you remember seeing Xavier Polates that night?"

I waited. They chewed.

"How about you, Arnold?" I said.

He shook his head.

"Roxy?"

"I think I saw him that night," she said.

"Do you remember where and when?"

She put her fork down and looked around the table.

"'When' would be between one and six," she said. "'Where' would be my bedroom."

"Roxy!" said Susan. "You didn't..."

"Oh, girl!" said Melva. "Back home, they'd have something to say about that."

"Because he's black or because he's young?"

"Both," said Melva.

"Why didn't you tell us?" said Susan.

"I don't kiss and tell, plus Kirby died that night."

"How was it?" asked Susan.

"Oh, please," said Melva.

Arnold smirked at her while Drew just stared.

"None of your beeswax," said Roxy.

"But it did happen?" I said. "You'd swear to it?"

"You're making a federal case out of it?" said Roxy. "You didn't strike me as a racist or an ageist."

"I'm not, but it could get to federal," I said, "depending on where the trial will be held. There's a murder here, remember?"

"Oh, right," she said. "Yes. I'll swear."

I finished my banana and looked at the week's worth of calories on my plate.

"He has a scar on his right inner thigh," Roxy said. "Crescent-shaped. I didn't ask where he got it, but I saw it."

"Got a good close look, did you?" said Drew.

Roxy blushed.

"You'll have to tell me all about it later," whispered Susan.

Melva fanned herself with her napkin. Everyone broke out laughing.

"Are you going to eat all that food?" said Susan. "It'd make me sick."

"Oh, to be young with a working digestive system," said Drew.

"No," I said. "My eyes were bigger than my stomach."

"That's not so much for a big guy like you," said Melva.

"I'm trying to be a littler guy," I said. "I gotta go. Thanks for your help, Roxy."

Her cheeks were blushed pink.

I took my plate and left. Only the banana had been touched. My stomach growled as I set the tray down on an empty table to be cleared away.

I tarried by a window, admiring the blue mountains lit up in warm sunlight. A vagrant piece of ice floated by. A pair of birds stood on it watching the ship. I thought they were pelicans and pressed against the glass to see, but they were only stupid eagles.

The buffet was filling with early diners. The Grays had company, but they had excellent seats and weren't half done with their meals yet.

I watched the ice float by and stared at the light playing on the hills when a silent streak of darkness passed down the window. A wall of rain hit the side of the ship like a snapped towel and was gone.

I paused for only a second, just long enough for it to register.

"Oscar! Oscar! Oscar!" I shouted.

"Who the hell's Oscar?" said the crowd.

"He's—it's a…ah—man overboard! Man overboard!"

45

I BOLTED THROUGH THE RESTAURANT, dodging tables and chairs filled with confused, foraging tourists, to the back of the ship. The back door opened to a deck with tables more popular on the warm Caribbean cruises than the freezing Alaskan ones. It was empty. There was rain on the deck but none falling just then. A squall was moving across the inlet like a hose in a pool.

I rushed to the rail and looked for a struggling swimmer in the immediate wake. I saw no one. Wind kicked up whitecaps and stray light from between clouds illuminated the fluorescent foam in passes, but I saw no one in it.

I ran upstairs to the upper deck for a better view. There was no one there to help me. I stared behind the ship, looking for movement until my eyes watered. Then I ran back down to the lower deck thinking to get closer to the water.

A group of ship's officers and crew were waiting when I came down.

"What's going on?" It was Marvelous Martin McGuire, majestically mustached food service officer, or handle-barred cook, depending on your rank.

"Someone fell overboard," I said.

"You saw someone fall over? Where?"

"I was in the buffet. I saw a shape pass the window. Right side. There."

Binoculars big as a briefcase appeared as if by conjuring and a Filipino officer in white and blue stripes used them to scan the water and work out his biceps.

"How long ago?" asked McGuire.

"A minute. Less. Maybe two."

"You're very helpful," he said. "Are you sure it was a person? Could it have been a bird flying by? A cloud shadow?"

"I, uhm. What?" I said. "It looked like someone falling."

"Did anyone else see anything?" McGuire asked. A crowd was forming around us then, made up mostly of the diners who'd followed me out of the buffet.

"He said it was his friend Oscar," said a woman holding a plate of oriental noodles and chicken.

"Did you see anything?"

"Only that man stepping on my purse," she said.

"Palo?"

"I don't see anything, sir," said the crewman with the eighty-pound binoculars.

"He could have sunk," I said.

"It was a he?"

"No."

"So a woman?"

"I can't be sure."

"Old? Young? Fat or thin?"

"Kinda tannish," I said.

A cold wind blew the gathering clouds in herds across the sky, throwing shadows like migrating animals on the water. One crossed the deck, then another, then a big one, and it got dark.

"We don't want to panic the passengers," said McGuire. "Are you sure you saw something?"

I thought back. I'd been sure, but now I wasn't. I looked at the other passengers, and watched noodles disappear in a puckery slurp.

I said, "No one else saw anything?"

Everyone shook their heads.

"Can you call the bridge?" I asked. "Ask about the starboard side lookout?"

"They'd have said something already," he said. "It's what they do."

I'd seen the protruding watch stations from the bridge, one on each side which gave complete vision of that half of the ship.

"They're not always manned," I said. "My friend Perry fell off the ship in Skagway."

"That was in port," he said. "But I remember that. It was manned if I recall. There was a Code Oscar called out."

I said, "Call the bridge, or I will."

The cook flashed his waxed mustache at the waiting passengers and sensed the scene I was about to create. When in doubt, begin to shout.

"All right," he said. "Come with me."

The Filipino with the glasses remained at the rail, scanning the wake, while Marvin escorted me into the kitchen.

"We have a man stationed in front of CCTV at all times while sailing," he said.

"CCTV is knocked out," I said. "Has been the whole cruise. Three different ways if I understand it correctly."

He sucked in his lower lip as if being caught in a lie.

"Yes," he said finally. "That's true. If we had it, we could always check the tape."

"This is taking too long," I said. "That water is cold."

He took me into a cramped, windowless white-walled office. The walls were covered in clipboards and charts, whiteboards with names and check marks, reminder notes to "find caviar ASAP" and to thank a vendor for the dragon fruit.

"This is Martin McGuire in the kitchen," he said into a phone. "I have a passenger here who thinks he may have seen an Oscar on starboard."

I scanned his desk as he listened and waited. There was a memo that a missing can of olive oil had been found.

"A memo for a single can of olive oil?" I said.

"A can is thirty-five gallons," he said.

"Oh."

"Yes, Captain. About six minutes ago," he said. "Starboard. Mid-aft. That is unfortunate, yes. Palo is there now. Yes. No. Yes. No, he saw nothing. Yes, he's still there. No. No. Yes. Could lose a few pounds. Yes, that's him. No. No. Yes, sir. Thanks, sir."

He hung up the phone. "Captain wants to see you," he said.

"The Oscar?"

"There was no one at the lookout," he said. "Shift change."

"How convenient."

"It's also the least populated time on the ship," he said. "Between five and six on these late days of a cruise, the ship's a ghost town. People retreat to their rooms."

"So, opportunity," I said.

"What?"

"If the killer knew that kind of thing, it would have been a good time to strike, don't you think?"

"Who said anything about murder?"

"Just talking out loud," I said. "How do I get to the captain?"

He escorted me forward to the bank of elevators that accessed the bridge. He slid his card in, pushed the button, and stepped out.

"What do you use thirty-five gallons of olive oil for?"

"That one? It's for the last dinner. It's very good olive oil. Glad we found it."

The doors shut, and I was lifted to the bridge. Ola Peterson was waiting for me when the doors opened. He led me to the captain's office, a glass-enclosed room with open blinds and the uncluttered desk of a reigning executive. He looked up from a laptop computer when Ola knocked and gestured us in.

"Mr. Flaner, take a seat," said Captain Finn Olsen. I did. Ola did not.

"I think you should do a roll call," I said. "Just in case someone did fall off the ship."

Olsen looked pained. "No," he said.

"Why?"

For an answer, he just shook his head.

"Bad PR?" I suggested.

He sighed and glanced at Ola, whose blue eyes flashed in confirmation.

"People fall off cruise ships all the time," he said. "More than you think."

"It's happened three times on this cruise."

"Twice," he said. "But even so, they're often suicides."

"You're pissing me off," I said.

"If we'd have seen anything, we'd have taken all action to retrieve them," he said.

I waited for him to continue his lame excuses, but he didn't. I guess he thought his point was made.

"Huh," I said.

"Can you at least check on Paul Vinalez and Belinda Phillips and make sure they're all right?"

"Mr. Vinalez is fine. He's teaching a seminar as we speak."

"And Phillips?"

"Won't be told what to do," Ola said.

"How do you mean?"

"She would not stay on the ship in Ketchikan," he said.

"So she's dead?"

"Mr. Flaner," said Captain Olsen. "Control your imagination."

"She returned to the ship safe and sound," said Ola. "I saw her by the kitchen after we sailed. She's fine."

"Or she was two hours ago."

"Yes."

"What about the men I told you about?"

"That's why you're here," said Captain Finn.

Ola picked up the thread. "Local police found the two men you identified and arrested them."

"What did they say?"

"They didn't confess, if that's what you're thinking. They had pictures of some of the passengers."

"Dr. Belinda Phillips?" I said.

"And others."

"Who?"

"You."

"Shit."

"The men were never passengers on the *Success*," said Ola. "They were caught waiting at the dock. They were armed and had a rented car. They had a motel room and had checked in that day. The police were able to establish that the two had been at each of our ports."

"Who are they?"

"Local hunters," said Ola. "The police told me that they have a survival cabin up north and advertise in *Soldier of Fortune* magazine. They teach survival and claim to have been trained by the military. What branch and whose military, they're unclear about. We believe they were hired as agents."

"Ya think?" I said. My American sarcasm was lost on the Danes. "So we have a couple of wannabe Rambos hired out of the want ads of a trash testosterone doomsday snuff rag. What does that tell you?"

"That Circus Line will stop at nothing," said Captain Finn. "I need to know if you suspect another mole."

"Mole?"

"Someone had to deliver the photos to the crooks," said Ola. "As you pointed out, the one of Dr. Phillips was taken when she boarded. The one of you was taken at the private island with your girlfriend. Mr. Polates was locked up when we were at the island."

"So there must be someone else?" said Ola. "Who?"

I pointed my finger dramatically at Captain Finn Olsen. His eyes grew large.

"I don't know," I said dramatically.

Olsen sighed.

"You have free rein of the ship," said Ola. "What good are you?"

"I'm working on it," I said. "Don't rush me."

"We're back in Seattle the day after tomorrow," said Finn. "At eight in the morning."

"The Alaskan cops will figure it out," I said and felt myself shrink for saying it. I was already priming myself for failure.

"I doubt it," said Ola. "Besides, I'm told those two guys are acting like POWs, giving name, rank, and serial number only. One of them tried to swallow a cyanide pill, but it was only a Tic-Tac. He mumbled something about his poor dog Spike and then refused to talk. The police can't hold them much longer."

I wanted to argue but realized he was right. No one had actually seen them shooting at anyone. There was circumstantial evidence, a film of them being nearby and armed, but not of them shooting. I'd been shot but no one else. We had no bullet for ballistics, shell casings, or fingerprints. Even if we did, they could always say they were shooting badgers in Juneau and salmon in Skagway. The Alaskan tourist bureau would back them up, I was sure.

"I'm working on it," I said.

"Work faster," said Captain Olsen.

"Yes, sir."

The captain turned back to his computer and woke it out of sleep.

"You're dismissed, Mr. Flaner," he said.

"You're not the boss of me, Finn," I said. Yeah, I was cranky.

He scowled. I left with Ola, who rode the elevator down with me.

"Hey, just out of curiosity, can you tell me what room Belinda Phillips is in?"

"Cabin."

"Et tu, Ola?"

"I can't tell you that," he said.

"Can you confirm that it's 8044?" I remembered the number from my interview at the bar with the prostitute who had alibied Phillips for the Bror killing. At least, I *thought* it was 8044.

"That might be it," he said.

"You're supposed to be helping me."

He sighed. "For a detective..." he muttered.

"Go on," I said. "I'll trade insults with you, you tin-plated, vanilla-bleached, mouth-breather."

He sighed again. "We on the ship are held to a very strict code of conduct. If we break our code of conduct, give out cabin numbers, make accusations, search people's cabins without permission and such, we are legally liable. It's in the boarding agreement you signed when you came on. It's our promise to respect privacy, and one of the things that makes Royal Danish Cruise Line the exceptional cruise line that it is."

"Like the washy-washy?"

"Exactly," Ola said.

"But nobody cares," I said. "Or notices."

"No. But the corporation does. Captain Olsen believes that part of Circus' plan to embarrass us is to have us break that trust and show us to be hypocrites. Do you understand now?"

"So that's why I'm here."

"I can watch the crew, but you have free rein over the ship's passengers in ways we do not," he said.

"Huh," I said. "On ship or on shore, PIs do the dirty work."

The doors opened. Ola gestured for me to get out.

"I believe you were at dinner," he said. "Enjoy your meal but don't take too long. The captain wants results."

46

I HAD a lot to chew on and an empty stomach. I went in search of Allie for our dinner date and found her having a drink at the bar with Standard and Camila.

"You two made up?" I said.

"Were we fighting?"

"No no no," said Standard, giving me the look.

"I'm hungry. Let's eat," I said to Allie.

"Where you been?"

"I'll tell you over dinner."

"Where are you going?" asked Camila. She was a beauty—dark damp hair, tan skin, chocolate eyes, casual, yet sophisticated in a blue floral blouse and white capris. Her accent was subtle, lyrical, and exotic. She was way out of Standard's league. I was about to point that out because I have no class whatsoever, when Allie spoke.

"We got a free dinner at the steakhouse for the bear thing on the island," she said.

"You'll have to tell me about that," said Camila.

"Maybe tonight over drinks," I said.

"You don't want to go for steaks?" asked Standard.

Camila had picked up the hints where my dense friend had not. "I think they want a private dinner. We'll do sushi."

"Laters," I said.

The experience of eating at an expensive restaurant is somewhat undermined when you present the maître d' with a coupon while waiting to be seated. I was one of the few people there not wearing a tie, the others all being women. We were shown to a corner table, but I liked the one by the window better and politely refused to sit anywhere else. Allie blushed, but she was used to me. We got the nicer table. I could stretch out my sandaled feet better there, letting my toe bandage dry out from the rain on the deck.

The menus had tassels and prices without decimal points. The coupon covered everything, so I naturally found the most expensive meal and ordered it, along with two appetizers and a bottle of wine.

"I thought you were dieting," Allie said.

"Lobster is healthy," I said.

"And twenty ounces of prime rib?"

"I'll cut the fat off."

"No, you won't."

"No. I won't."

The clouds remained from earlier and the squall I'd seen was replaced by a steady sprinkling of rain that blew onto the window, collected, and then beaded down at a leisurely pace.

I told Allie about my adventures since she'd last seen me.

"I thought I'd be posting bail for you," she said, "with that stolen card."

"They know I have it," I said.

"They said something?"

"No, but they know. They expect me to use it in plausibly deniable ways."

"So they're setting you up to take a fall?"

"I don't think it'll go that far," I said, slurping an oyster off a half shell.

"But if it does?"

"Another Oscar. A man thrown overboard," I said. "It's part of the job."

"Like getting shot and beat up?"

"Exactly."

I was being good. I kept away from the bread and savored the mercury in the oysters instead. Such is how health is measured in the western world. Our food arrived, and I sent the waiter back for more au jus and horseradish. The lobster would make do with the cup of melted butter I had. I was dieting.

"So what happens when the mercenaries get released?"

"They go back to their shack and work on their manifestos," I said.

"What if you find evidence to implicate them?"

"Then they don't go home," I said. I needn't have bothered with the horseradish. It was too hot to eat. A couple parts per million were all I'd need to turn the rare prime rib into a magma flare.

"I don't see them as the villain," I said.

"They shot at you. Twice."

"Not me," I said. "The picture they had of me was one with you in it. So after Skagway."

"But the glacier?"

"I was collateral damage. They were after Belinda Phillips."

"That makes them villains in my book."

"They were hired. They were the tool. Mercenaries don't kill people. The people who hire mercenaries kill people."

"That's the stupidest thing you've ever said."

"Not even close. But you see what I mean? Yeah, they suck and deserve to hole up in a cave drinking their own urine, but somebody sent them, and somebody gave them photos. That somebody is on this ship, and that somebody is my target."

"So you have Bror—dead. Vinalez attacked, Phillips attacked, you attacked, and the cruise line tormented. How does it all fit together?"

"Poorly."

"And you have two days."

"About that," I said. "How's your pheasant?"

"The best I've ever had."

"Have you ever had pheasant before?"

"Of course not."

I refilled Allie's wine glass and topped off mine. I scraped off all but a tiny white film of horseradish from a corner of my beef, rinsed it in au jus and ate it. My sinuses blew open like a breaching submarine and tears rolled down my cheeks before I could swallow.

"That good?" said Allie.

"Oh yeah," I rasped.

"The gang's getting together for drinks later," she said.

"When?"

"Later."

"I probably shouldn't," I said. "I'm trying to be responsible."

She swirled her wine in her glass and looked at me over the flickering candle. With the sky so dark outside, it was the primary light source.

"Let me get this straight," she said. "To show me how responsible you've become, you're going to abandon me on the second to last night of an already abridged cruise vacation?"

"And you fall madly in love with me for it," I said.

"What are you going to do?"

"Talk to people. Check things out. Use this card while I can now that I know I'm supposed to."

"Burglary?"

"A little louder. The engineer might have missed it."

"Who?"

"I got a list. Vinalez, Phillips," I said. "Maybe Polates."

"Xavier?"

"Maybe."

"Tony…"

"Maybe," I said.

I was pretty full by dessert but split a cheesecake with Allie anyway.

"You need to eat more smaller meals," she said. "You can't starve yourself all day."

"Isn't that what a diet is?"

"It doesn't have to be," she said. "If you have meals all day, you won't be hungry."

"But I like the big meal once-a-day thing," I said. "It gives me something to look forward to."

"Your body goes into starvation mode. It'll store calories instead of burn them when you eat that way. It'll have the opposite effect of dieting."

"Really?"

"Yeah."

"Well, shit," I said. "Looks to the contrary. I'm not good at this dieting thing."

She smirked and offered me a forkful of cheesecake. I ate it. I didn't want to be rude.

We left the coupons on the table and left. The dinner had been long and enjoyable. The best meal of the cruise. Actually, I think it was my only meal of the cruise. Everything else had been foraging and abstinence.

We took the stairs down to the eighth-floor—*deck*, and followed the numbers until we found 8044.

I knocked.

"I thought you didn't like this woman," Allie whispered.

"I don't like any of them," I said, listening at the door. "Vinalez is a jerk, Peigne is well-named, Bror was a bastard, and this creep here is one for the books."

I knocked again.

"Hello? Belinda?" I said, in case there were witnesses. "It's me. Can I come in? I can? Good. Coming in then."

With the help of Sandra's key, I opened the door.

The room was dark.

"Hello?"

Nothing.

I switched on the light. The room was the same configuration as mine—a single bed with a sofa by the balcony that pulled into a bed, a hideaway in the roof, a bathroom to the left. There was no one there.

It had been made up. Today's towel monkey sat happily on the turned-down bed but it was not neat. The desk and table were cluttered with NutriPods, test tubes, literature, and bottles.

"What the hell's that?"

I picked up a box of pods, assorted flavors. They were all empty.

"Look at that," I said.

"Some people will eat anything."

"They're empty. No, more than that. They're clean. Look, not even residue."

She held one up the light.

"It's a food coloring bottle."

"They got a deal in Mexico," I said. "But see? It's clean."

"Or unused."

I looked through a stack of marketing literature—brochures, scripts, binders marked *not for public distribution*, off-shore banking connections, and twenty-four-hour lawyers.

"I think she's running experiments on the pods," Allie said. She lifted a test tube out of holder and inspected it.

"Make sure you put everything back where you found it."

She put it back.

I picked up a box of actual food coloring bottles. Red, blue, yellow, and green. There were some medical saline bottles, some hypodermics, a stack of broken EpiPens like I'd seen in the infirmary and pH litmus paper.

"It's all greasy," said Allie, handling a bottle.

"It's the eel oil. The pods are based on it."

"How can it fail?"

"I think she was experimenting with less exotic oils," I said. "This looks like vegetable oil."

"This smells like olive," Allie said, sniffing a cloth.

"Here's a peanut oil bottle," I said, seeing one in the garbage can.

"Grape seed oil?"

"Is that a thing?"

"Yes."

"Who knew?"

"Everyone."

We froze and listened. We heard voices in the hall, laughter, and conversation. I nearly pissed myself. I was about to dive into the bathroom, and pull Allie in with me when the voices passed.

"Let's hurry," Allie whispered.

I nodded.

"What are we looking for exactly?"

"I'm not sure," I said.

"Will you know it when you see it?"

"I might."

"What's with all the fly strips and bug traps?"

"She had an issue with spiders."

"Don't we all?"

I opened a drawer. Cotton panties. Silk panties. A vibrator. Another vibrator. A strap-on. An old photograph.

"Anyone you know?" Allie said over my shoulder. I jumped.

"No. But that's a University of Utah sorority house," I said. "This must be her."

"Who?"

"I heard that the good doctor is holding a torch for a dead friend. Patricia Wohler."

"'Patty Patty Patty Patty, I love you like a piece of candy,'" said Allie.

"What?"

"It's written here on a notepad."

"God help us."

I studied the girl in the picture. Her hair dated it to my college days. The color was faded but not the excitement in the picture. The woman in it waved awkwardly at the camera, fingers down like she was prancing.

"Man, I'm dense," I said out loud.

"Recognizing it is half the battle," said Allie. "What is it?"

"She's showing a ring. In the picture, see?"

"I saw it the first time."

I replaced the photo in the drawer and opened the next one. Passport, cruise papers, business cards. More Nutri-Pods literature, old schedules, addresses, maps. I thumbed through them. Glossy pictures of Provo and Orem, pitch phrases in italics—*the innovative nutritional dietary supplement everyone is talking about*. It just rolls off the tongue.

Her checkbook told me she had money. The money in the drawer said she had some with her. Two grand in paper and eighty-six in the bank. A portfolio summary tucked in a book said she had nearly seven figures with a brokerage firm in New York. She was rich. If I had any doubt, the biweekly pay stub of $18,500 before deductions settled it. I did the math.

"She's making over forty million dollars a year," I said.

"What?"

"No, wait." I did the math again. "Four hundred forty-four grand per year. Salary."

"And?"

"She's rich."

"And?"

"And she made the gold club with Nutri-Pods by selling a piddly hundred fifty dollars' worth last month."

"And?"

"She makes twice that in an hour."

"And?"

"Why is she selling snake oil?"

Allie paused and pondered. "Greed?" she said. "Let's get the hell out of here."

"What's in the bathroom?"

"Bath stuff. Let's go."

I quickly shuffled through a last pile of papers on the nightstand and that's when I saw it: a single white business card with blue and gold lettering. Pieces fell into place. I put the papers back.

"You're moping?" Allie whispered. "What did you expect to find? Not everybody has a skeleton in a closet."

"Yes, they do."

"Maybe, but they don't bring them on vacation. Let's go. My nerves can't handle this."

I turned off the light and pushed my ear to the door. When I heard no one, I opened it, peeked out, and then shuffled away with Allie behind me. We didn't speak until we were in the elevator.

"I need a drink," said Allie.

"I know a seedy place with a piano," I said, "where they speak Noir."

47

THE BARS on the main deck were fine, but they were touristy. Tourists went there. The bars in the middle of the ship, in the dark recesses and corners of the hull, were where the real action was. It's where the pros hung out.

"Pros?" said Allie. "You mean professional drinkers or prostitutes?"

"Yes."

It was past ten when we walked into The Two Olives. I'd met Chris there, Belinda's alibi, but I was hoping to run into Belinda. I wanted to ask her some more questions, and press her on her association with the stupid Nutri-Pods cult. I also wanted to make sure she was alive.

The bar wasn't crowded. The lounge on the upper decks would be spilling over yet. They had acts and a view. The Two Olives wouldn't begin swinging for hours still.

We took a table too near to the piano but moved when the singer began her tribute to Jimi Hendrix.

"*So, I stand nearby to a mountain, Then I chop it down with a hedge in my hand,*" bellowed the singer. It was the same disco duo as before, the operatic big-haired woman and a boy toy. I could smell the booze on her breath from across the room. The gold tooth of the piano player caught the spots and made it look like he was eating a flashlight.

"It loses something without the sizzling guitar," Allie said, sliding into a booth.

"Something," I agreed.

"And male vocals."

"And right lyrics."

I ordered a bourbon and soda. Allie asked for a margarita but changed her mind when the waitress raised an eyebrow.

"I mean a Manhattan," she said. That got her a nod.

"You're lucky they let you in looking like you do," I said.

"What's wrong with this?"

"It's sensible, comfortable, and fits you well. You haven't slept in it, and you're showing no cleavage. They have standards here. You're lucky you're with me."

I couldn't see Belinda Phillips or Chris. I figured it was a good sign that they were both gone, for Belinda anyway. There were other single women who looked up when people came in and they always smiled at the men.

Our drinks came, and we giggled together, recounting our terror in the burgled room.

"What would you have done?" she asked.

"Had she come in? I'd have started to cry," I said.

"Really. What would you have done?"

"Cry. I mean it. It's very distressing and awkward to see a man crying. She'd have been so uncomfortable she'd have pushed us out the door, happy just to be rid of me."

"You've done this before?"

"No, but I always have it in reserve. That and peeing myself. You can get out of any socially awkward situation by pissing yourself."

She stared at me.

"'Excuse me, sir, do you have an invitation to this affair? I don't see you on the guest list.' Piss myself and start crying. Immediate exit. No cops. Perfect."

"You're sick."

"You mispronounced 'genius,'" I said.

We drank and talked, laughed and whispered about personal stuff, movies, and songs, cringing when the singer moved to the Beatles and sang about Strawberry Lanes.

We were on our third drink when the gang wandered in. Perry led them through the door with a wave to one of the working girls and a nod to the bartender. It was Garrett, Critter, Standard, and Camila. Dara stumbled in after a couple of seconds, rubbing sanitizer up her arms.

I waved them over, and we made room.

"You missed a great show," said Standard. "We did skit ad-lib."

"Was that tonight?"

"Yes," said Perry. "We could have used you."

"No, it was great," said Standard. "I brought down the house."

"With a fart joke," said Dara with the appropriate amount of disgust.

"Critter was good," said Perry.

"I don't know," said Garrett. "I think he came off looking psychotic and unhinged."

"You are," I said.

"Don't tell him," said Critter, giving me the stare. "Shhhhh."

"How was it really?" said Allie.

"Ah, it was okay. Flaner would have been welcome. We got coupons for another cruise."

"Fifty percent off," said Critter.

"If you book the suite, it could mean thousands of dollars," said Camila. "A good payday for an hour's work."

I liked how easily Camila had joined the gang. She spoke familiarly with my friends which told me I hadn't spent much time with them on this trip.

We ordered a round and began telling stories. Allie and Camila were in stitches by the second. You can't put five comedians around a table with booze and an audience and not expect silliness.

"Kiss you? I shouldn't be screwing you."

A classic punchline only Standard could ruin. We all slapped our foreheads in unison and laughed at the choreography.

The singer was butchering early Beatles with a highball glass in one hand and a microphone in the other. *"Love, love me too. You know I do glue."*

"So why did you miss the show?" said Garrett.

"Trying to figure out this shit on the ship," I said.

"Told you," said Garrett.

"Did you guys have sex?" said Dara.

"What?" said Allie.

"That was my guess. Sexy time. You had sex tonight, right?"

"None of your business," I said.

"No," said Allie and shrugged.

"Ha! Pay up," said Critter.

Dara slapped a ten on the table. Critter collected it in his mouth and handed it to Garrett, who slid it into his pocket with a smile.

"How goes the investigation?" asked Camila. "Standard told me about you. It's very exciting."

"It's a tangled nest of snakes," I said, or maybe slurred, but she seemed to understand. "I don't know what the hell is going on."

"You'll figure it out," said Allie.

"I don't know," I said. "I'm not being very productive right now."

"Cut yourself a break," cooed Allie.

I shook my head. "I only have a day or so left. My best suspect can't be made to fit the crime."

"Xavier?" said Dara.

I nodded.

"Told you." She sulked.

"What would you be doing now instead?" said Allie.

"Fighting crime. Hey, anybody see Vinalez today?"

"Which one?" said Perry.

"Either. After Ketchikan. Lately?"

"I saw him at the show," said Dara. "He and the missus look to be made up. They were playing foot sex under the table."

"'Footsies,'" I corrected her.

"Not when her foot is in his crotch," she said.

"Foot sex it is."

"They made a beeline for the elevator after the show," said Critter.

"So no more B&E tonight," said Allie. "Relax."

"But—"

"Relax with me," she said.

I smiled.

"What about Vinalez?" asked Perry. "Is he the guy?"

"No. He's a target," I said. "How about Dr. Phillips? Anyone see her lately?"

"Give it a rest, Tony," said Allie.

"I'm still here. Anyone see her?"

They all shook their heads.

"Is she the guy?"

"Target," I said.

"What's the connection?" asked Garrett.

"Hell if I know."

Camila smiled.

"What?" I said.

She shook her head.

"What?" I said again.

"Utah," she said. "It has such a reputation for religion and yet here on a ship crawling with Utah people, there's greed and murder. The man who gave you those black eyes was from Utah, was he not? It breaks the stereotype."

"Religion and violence?" I said. "Who'd have thought?"

"Still, it's funny," she said.

I pondered this and said, "It's got to be Utah. Maybe the pods."

"They'd never be allowed to market them the way they do here back home in Valparaíso. It's a pyramid scheme."

"Perfectly legal in Utah."

"But it's not staying in Utah. They're pushing out," said Dara.

"Utah law will protect them," said Perry.

"It's also bullshit," said Camila. "Diet nutritional supplement with fish oil?"

"Eel oil," I said.

"It's still untested. How you people can let such a scam go unchecked is beyond me. America is strange."

"You have the coolest accent," I said. "Where are you from?"

"Valparaíso, Chile," she said. "It's a port city on the Pacific. Very beautiful."

"How's the economy?" asked Perry.

She drained her martini and signaled for another. Her hand slid beneath the table. Standard smiled above it.

"Are you thinking of immigrating?" she said to Perry.

"With the NSA monitoring our every move, yeah, I've considered leaving the country."

She shrugged. "There's a different work ethic down there."

"What does that mean?" I asked.

"In Chile, you have to do what you're paid to do," she said.

"How revolutionary," said Allie.

Camila laughed. "I'm sorry. I'm being insulting."

"I missed it," said Dara. "What'd you say?"

More drinks came. "Americans have a reputation," she said. "Every country has stereotypes of other countries."

"Out with it," I said. "How are Americans seen in Chile?"

"They're seen as lazy," she said, grimacing.

"A gross generalization," said Standard too loudly.

"But with any generalization, there's usually some truth to it."

"Do you see that?" I asked.

"We should change the subject."

"No. We're cool," said Perry. "I'm curious."

"Well, there's a reason this ship is crewed with Filipinos."

"They work cheap?" I said.

"And hard."

"Proves nothing," I said.

"Okay," she said. "I agree, it's a generalization, but also true. I have personal experience. Americans can be lazy and ineffective." She swayed from the effects of her last drink.

"You can't judge an entire country on Taco Bell's drive-thru," I said.

"God, they're the worst," said Critter.

"I always thought they imported idiots for that position," said Dara. "You mean those are Americans back there? How can they screw up a cheese quesadilla every single fucking time?"

Camila nodded.

"If you want anything done right in America," Camila said, "you have to do it yourself. Get your hands dirty. You can't count on anybody."

Standard started necking her, and she closed her eyes and leaned back to enjoy it.

I sipped my bourbon and felt uneasy. I'm no patriot. I'm probably the worst critic of my country of anyone I know, but my hackles were up with her stereotypes.

"You know," I said. "One of the stereotypes I've encountered is that people in other countries put too much faith in stereotypes."

She wasn't listening.

I looked at Allie, who rolled her eyes.

I looked at Camila and squinted. She'd lost something of the charm she'd brought to the table, but she was still pretty. Her hair was dry now and though Standard was doing everything he could to mess it up with his teeth, it was nice and neat. She'd changed clothes from before, her blouse and capris traded for semi-formal. It was a basic black with a plunging neckline that showed her skin. I had to admire that she'd dressed up. Americans could learn something from that.

She turned and kissed Standard. We all watched them in mute voyeuristic fascination as they played drunk tongue hockey. Then the gears slid into place. The squall, the Oscar. The spider.

"Camila," I said.

She broke her lip lock on my friend and regarded me warmly. She was drunk. Drunk make-out sessions are the same all over the world over, I thought.

"Yes, Tony?"

"In Salt Lake City, we have black widows, you know?"

Her face looked puzzled and wary. My heart quickened.

"Those are the worst," said Dara. "I had one in my shoe once. Found it only after I squished it."

"Well, what I'm saying is that the black widow isn't the most dangerous spider in Utah. It's the brown recluse. A terrible little shit that can really do a number on you."

She waited. Standard slid his hand clumsily under the table.

"Well," I said, "what I was wondering is, do you have them down in Valparaíso?"

"We have them all over Chile," she said.

"Really? Are they dangerous too?"

"They make yours look like house pets," she said. "What made you think of that?"

"Drunk thinking," I said.

She turned back to Standard's mouth.

I asked, "What do you do for a living?"

"Tony," said Allie. "Can't you see she's busy?"

Camila looked at me.

"I'm in the service industry," she said. "Family company. Named after my father."

"What's that?"

"Flores Limited," she said.

Click.

"What's wrong, Tony?" said Dara. "You look like fucking hell."

"I was just thinking about the cost of these drinks," I said. "How about I go get that bottle of moonshine and meet you guys?"

"We drank it," said Dara.

"Both?"

"You have two?"

"I did."

"Yeah, go get it," said Perry. "That'll be awesome."

"Have you ever had moonshine?" asked Standard.

"No. I've heard about it, though," said Camila. The drunk was out of her voice, and her eyes were fixed on mine.

"I'll meet you guys in the game room," I said.

"Good idea," said Perry. "The Grays will be in bed by now."

"See you there." I got up quickly and left.

Allie watched me go, looking concerned. Camila watched me go, looking determined.

48

I HAD TO GET AWAY. I had to think. I had to hide my expressions while I put the pieces in order. Vincent Bror had sent Flores Limited twenty thousand dollars for unknown services. It all made sense. Well, no. That's not true. It made some. I hadn't solved the puzzle, but I had collected a few edge pieces and felt I had a corner coming together. As sure as it was dark outside and we were sailing to Canada, I knew that Camila Flores had killed Dr. Belinda Phillips that afternoon on the upper deck in the rain.

What to do about it?

I rode the elevator down to nine and headed toward my room for the jug of moonshine. It's what I said I'd do, and my body moved in obedience to the suggestion. My mind was otherwise engaged. I walked instinctively on autopilot, staring six feet through the carpet until I came to my door and slid the key in. The green light lit up, out came the card, and down went the handle.

Did I have evidence or suspicion? I thought I was sure, but convincing someone else could be trouble. And maybe I was wrong. According to, well, everybody and everything, I'd been wrong about Xavier Polates. If I accused Stan's girlfriend and was wrong, I'd be out of friends.

I turned on the light and dug the jug out of the closet. I'd hidden under my dirty clothes with sweaty underwear on top. It was better than a safe. I had to admit that the cleaning staff was pretty mellow. They'd not turned me in for the one jug I'd had out for days that my friends had drunk. They'd not done anything about Belinda's chemistry experiments either. I'm sure they saw weirder and more illegal stuff all the time. It'd probably take a wall of blood spatter and a working meth lab to get a manager involved.

I was fighting alcohol. My drinks had cut through the prime rib and lobster and formed a beachhead in my higher-functioning reasoning centers. It was hard to concentrate.

I had a problem. A clue, a hunch, and a clay jug of white liquor that would raise a blister on an aluminum can. I had to get myself together. I had to face Camila with the devious design of entrapment. I needed some proof. If she was the killer I suspected her to be, I doubt she'd break under my sarcastic wit. What I might get, however, would be her room number. With my magic passcard, I might get the proof I needed to link up the whole web into a single unified crime theory and win a Nobel Prize.

I had to get back. I'd be missed and didn't want to look any more suspicious than necessary. The look Camila had given me warned me to tread carefully. If my suspicions were correct, I was in danger. I'd ply her with my 120-proof jug of lighter fluid and knock her out tonight. It would be self-defense.

Jug in hand, I turned off the overhead and opened the door.

Camila stood in the hall.

I gracefully stumbled back, tripped over my heels, and fell on my ass.

"Camila," I said.

"Tony." She stepped in and closed the door behind her. She looked around the room but didn't turn on the light. A single reading lamp in the corner was all the light in the room.

"What are you doing here?" I said. "You scared me."

"I want to talk to you for a second," she said, peeking into the bathroom.

I slid back into the side of the bed. I didn't have far to go, the room being the size of a Cadillac's trunk. I don't mean those old ones like the guys in *Goodfellas* had, but the new crappy ones that won't hold a body for shit.

She took a step closer which put her feet against mine. I pushed myself up the side of the bed and sat on it as nonchalantly as possible.

"I appreciate your interest in me," I said. "But I have a girlfriend, and as much as I loathe Standard half the time, he's my buddy and I wouldn't do this to him."

I thought it was a good cover. One corner of her mouth pulled up in a mirthless smirk. My hands grew sweaty.

"Whatcha doing in here?" she said.

"I came for the moonshine." I held up the jug. "Weren't you listening?"

"Oh, I was listening," she said. "And talking. Talking too much, am I right?"

"I don't know what you mean." My voice was calm and flat, but the sweat running into my eyes put the lie to that. I hoped the light behind me concealed it.

"Stan says you're a smart man," she said, taking a step closer.

Her exotic accent was no longer charming in my ears. It was positively menacing. I squirmed back another inch or two and cradled the jug over my groin. Any little bit helps.

"Standard said that? And you believed him?"

Another smirk. More sweat into my eyes. It stung.

"What'd I say?" she said.

"You said Stan says I'm smart."

"At the bar," she said. Her hand slid into her pocket.

"I'm not a stenographer," I said. "I don't remember."

"You're not a good liar either."

"Sure I am."

Her hand came out of her pocket. I expected a gun, but it was a cylinder about the size of a cigar case.

"Tony."

"Yes?"

"I'm sorry about this." She flicked her wrist, and the tube telescoped into a black steel baton with a round tip. It was the kind of thing bodyguards carried and postmen used on pit bulls, a secret weapon of choice of closet kung fu artists and hired assassins.

"I screwed up," she said. "I blame myself."

"I forgive you."

She smiled and glanced over her shoulder. "Nothing personal. My fault. I'm sorry. Goodbye."

I started to cry. It was part of my socially awkward situation escape plan. She shook her head. I pushed my bladder for plan B, but I was too clenched for anything to happen. "Give me a minute," I sobbed.

She raised her baton and swung. I held up the jug to block the blow. It exploded in my hands, drenching me and half the room in clear Alaskan liquor.

She moved in for another strike. I rolled off the bed and felt it jump as the baton hit it.

I threw a pillow at her. It was all I could reach. No effect. She batted away the towel monkey too like a telegraphed change-up.

She leaped on the bed.

I dove for the corner table but was too slow. She caught me on the left shoulder. A glancing blow, but I heard a crack and felt the pain in my toes.

The empty jug from before was on the table. I lobbed it as hard as I could with one arm. She ducked it easily and came at me under it. I covered my face, which might be why she slammed her club into my knees.

I probably should have been screaming the whole time. But I was concentrating too hard on living. Only a single "ouch" escaped my mouth before she raised the baton for a backhand.

I dove to the floor, and she hit the wall, leaving a deep dent.

I kicked the chair at her, but she sidestepped it by getting back up on the bed. She was now higher than me but couldn't get the clearance she needed for an overhead smash that I knew would pop my skull like a December jack-o'-lantern.

My left arm hung limply at my side, and my knees wanted to issue an official complaint. My back to the glass balcony door, I pushed myself upright having some vague idea of a dive and tumble to the door for an escape.

She swung two-handed. I knew the baton had weight, but she moved it like a flashlight, and I barely had time to duck.

The steel ball at the end smashed the glass and like the jug, the door exploded, showering the room with glass shards. My support gone, I fell backward onto the balcony but kept my feet.

Camila kicked the chair to the door and took a heavy sigh.

Her face was firm and stern. She was impatient and irked, but not worried. This was taking too long, but the end result, we both knew, was a foregone conclusion. She used that club like she'd been born to it. If we'd been sumo wrestling, I'd have had the sure advantage, but here it was all hers. She was healthier, swifter, faster, and meaner than I ever was or ever could be. I might, however, one day have bigger boobs. That's why I was dieting.

Standing on glass, she brought the baton back like a rapier, ready to stab with it, perhaps to push me over the railing. She cast a dark menacing shadow, appearing twice the size as she was. I gave more thought to pissing myself.

She dropped her shoulders, and I squirted a little, but just a little.

I dove past her, back into the room, and caught a strike on the back of legs, managing to push her off balance and landing on the bed.

I rolled over and felt excruciating pain in my shoulder as fractured bones parted company. I grabbed the lamp, the only thing movable within reach, and threw it at her.

It was tethered to the wall and stopped short before even reaching her. She ducked anyway and I took it as a victory.

The lamp crashed to the floor in a flash of a popping light bulb. For a brief second, we were thrown into darkness.

It only lasted a second, then there was a sizzle, a spark, and the room exploded in fire.

The homemade corn alcohol was as flammable as I'd imagined. It was in the carpet, my clothes, in the air, made aerosol by the crushed jug. Every surface and person in the small room was about to do a Fantastic Four cosplay.

My eyebrows evaporated and my groin burned. Literally.

Camila screamed but strategically cut off my escape to the door.

I rolled in the glass, trying to put myself out. My crotch was a torch at the moment, soaked as it was with moonshine. My decision to pound the flames out with my hands had the obvious result, and I curled up in a ball and smothered the fire with my tears.

The air grew dark with carpet smoke and toxins.

Camila lunged, a terrifying monster rushing at me from the smoke. Her arms were on fire, her hair ablaze, singed and smoldering.

I tried to catch her momentum and use it to take her over the rail. Her eyelashes burning as they were, she'd misjudged my position, and the baton caught the edge of the door. The force of the strike spun her around and crashed her into me bodily.

Our flames mingled, and I choked on smoke.

My left shoulder finalized its request for new management. I screamed and bent over.

She kneed me in the jaw and I flipped back up. She shoved me to the railing. I gasped for breath.

Thick black smoke poured out of the room over the balcony and into the northern night like a polluted tide. There might have been breathable air at my ankles but she wouldn't let me look. Alarms went off. Hissing water jets burped and sputtered, then sprang to life.

"Code Bravo! Code Bravo!" rang in my ears.

Camila spun me around and pushed my face over the railing. That wouldn't have been so bad, but the entire upper half of my body went along with it, being attached as they were.

My left arm was in full-on rebellion and my right tried to cover my mouth from the smoke. I felt her slide down my back and wrap her arms around my legs. She lifted me.

"For fuck's sake!" I yelled. "What are you?"

She didn't answer.

I grabbed the railing to steady myself and began kicking for all I was worth. My sandals were gone. I don't remember losing them, but I was barefoot now. My feet were pincushions of glass shards.

She let go from my kicking but gave me a jab to the side as a parting gift. She'd chosen the side with the gunshot wound. I felt the stitches snap open as what little breath I had shot out of me.

I turned around to get my back to the railing. She raked my face with her nails but missed my eyes. The water was slowing the flow of smoke and I could make her out enough to slap her.

I didn't think I'd hit her that hard but she staggered.

Score one for the fat guy.

She stepped back into the flames, and when she came out, she was again ablaze. She leaped at me like a tiger. She wrapped her hands around my throat, not to strangle me but to cut me. Her nails dug into my flesh.

"Okay, I'll sleep with you!" I screamed. "But only with two condoms!" Sarcasm has always been my most effective weapon.

"Code Bravo. Code Bravo."

I couldn't pull her hands off me. I felt her fingers wriggling to get around my trachea. Summoned by executive order, conscientious objector status revoked, my left arm finally joined the fight.

I grabbed her wrists and tried to pull them apart.

She pushed forward, bending me backward over the rail. The balcony was narrow and she'd found purchase on the wall behind her and was walking up it to push me over. She was horizontal. I was thirty degrees off perpendicular and bending.

She flexed her thighs and pushed.

My spine joined the confederacy and I screamed.

The leverage was too great. She shoved. My feet came off the deck at the urgent request of my back and I felt my weight slide over.

I released Camila's wrist and grabbed the railing. She let go. I didn't. I still went over.

My diet was paying off. My right arm held onto the railing.

"Code Oscar! Oscar!" The sirens were getting loud. The voice calling the warning now a familiar friend.

My feet dangled over the black water speeding by beneath me. God, in his infinite wisdom, lubricated my hands with sweat, which was probably a good idea when hanging from branches over cliffs but not so helpful when hanging off ships with polished railings.

I flung my left arm up. I knew it was broken at the shoulder, but I needed fingers and muscles, not bones.

Camila looked down at me. The fire had taken some of her beauty away with her bangs.

"At least your mustache survived the fire," I said.

She shook her head and laughed.

"Glad you like it," I said.

I saw the arching baton coming down in the silhouetted light from the billowing fire.

My left arm shot up and grabbed her wrist before it landed. It still landed, but I grabbed it and slowed it a little. I saw stars but held onto everything as tightly as I could.

I pulled.

What fibers or muscles were there to save me, I would never know. Some sleeper cell I didn't know existed in my extremities yanked the killer forward.

I felt more than saw her come over the side.

My right arm summoned its own sleeper cell and clung on, holding hers and my weight.

I held her by the wrist. She swayed beneath me over the frothy darkness, the club still clenched in her hand.

I felt bone pain that doesn't exist outside of trauma wards and screamed as my fractured bones told me to let go.

My sweaty right hand seconded the motion and moved to drop us both.

I tried to keep hold. I really did. But I am out of shape. My hands were sweaty and burned, broken, and bruised.

I heard my fingers snap against my palm when she slipped away, but not the splash she made when she hit the water. The sound of one hand clapping is loud, and eerie, and sad, murderous, and painful. The Zen masters should stop recommending it.

I glanced down and saw no ripples or sign of passage beyond the white crests on black water from a ship speeding in the night.

I stuck my nose under the bottom of the railing and saw one of my sandals smoldering. I was right, though. There was a little breathable air at ankle level. It smelled like smoke, feet, and death.

49

THE FIRST EUROPEANS TO see Alaska weren't the English or even the Spanish. It was the Russians. They're European, right? Anyway, they noted the sea ended there on a coastline in 1732, made a log entry, and sailed back home, never putting a foot on the ground. Because, you know, why? Other Russians did that in 1741. The Spanish, hearing about a piece of dirt they didn't already have claim on, sent ships to claim it in the 1770s but gave it up at the turn of century because nobody was really taking the Spanish seriously then, and let's face it, Alaska's not exactly close to Barcelona.

The British made their big appearance in 1792 when George Vancouver on the famous Vancouver Expedition "discovered" the inside passage aboard the *Discovery*. He liked the coastline of modern-day California, Oregon, and Washington, but once past the future Vancouver Island, he soured on the place. Whereas he envisioned English manor houses and condos along the lower coastline, he didn't think much of Alaska. It shows in the names he applied to his new discoveries, *Deception Pass, Desolation Sound,* and *Oh My God I'm Sick of This Shithole Point.*

The English had beaten Spain in a war and in restitution, the Spanish offered to give them some of North America's northwest coast that they'd sailed past once. Lucky for them, they had a map to show. The ink was probably still wet, but the English took it, and the Spanish giggled themselves silly for getting off so cheap. Vancouver's job was to make a survey of the lands the Spanish were giving over to England, and if he found any Spaniards, tell them about the new landlords. Vancouver found a few in California and Oregon, but they were pretty scarce in Canada and Alaska.

Although he spent only a few months in Alaskan waters, hating every single minute of it, Vancouver's expedition circumnavigated the globe from

1791 to 1795. It was an exciting cruise, billed to follow in the wake of Captain Cook and Magellan, and the crew was pretty stoked. Some of the English gentry signed on for the adventure. It might possibly be considered the original Alaskan cruise with tourists sketching glaciers instead of aiming their cameras at them.

It wasn't a nice cruise, though. Vancouver was by all accounts a real fuckface. His expedition happened just after the mutiny on the *Bounty* so English officers were skittish. They saw what happened to fuckface Bligh. Fuckface Vancouver's solution to possible mutiny was to flog his crew as much as possible.

He flogged often and hard. He flogged the lowest menial member of his deck-washing gang to his officers. He borrowed native people and flogged them. Alone in his bunk, we can only imagine what he flogged, but we know it didn't stop there.

One man he flogged was a young officer of some note. Because he was a fuckface, Vancouver flogged him twice. Then to be different, he sent him back to England to teach him a valuable lesson.

When Vancouver returned to England, instead of being hailed a hero, he was called a fuckface. The officer he'd twice whipped and sent home in disgrace, whom he knew as Thomas Pitt, the Second Baron of Camelford, had a few connections among the movers and shakers of English society as you might imagine, plus his father had died. By the time Vancouver tied up in London again, Thomas Pitt was no longer second, but THE Baron of Camelford and his cousin, William Pitt the Younger, was Prime Minister of the whole soggy country. Thereafter, Vancouver had a bad time and died a poor fuckface at the age of forty.

The irony of course is that if you hadn't just read my little story about Camelford, you'd not know the name, and I bet you can find Vancouver on a map of the world. Fuckface George Vancouver lives on, his flogging forgotten, his hatred of the places he saw and named ignored. He stands atop the British Columbia Parliament Building in Victoria, cast in solid gold. If you look at him at the right angle, with the right light and shadows, you can just see the whip in his hand and his face twisted up in disgust from "an attack of bilious colic" as he overlooks the waters he couldn't wait to get away from.

I was the first passenger ashore in Canada. I was airlifted by helicopter before dawn from the top deck. Dr. Reyes waved my smoldering passport at the EMTs as they loaded the stretcher. I didn't think I needed so much attention, but we were close enough, and Royal Danish wanted to put its stamp of responsibility on the whole "narrowly averted tragedy at sea" thing.

I hadn't hung long from the railing. I couldn't have. Maybe thirty seconds after Camila went for her dark, cold swim, and two seconds before my grasp gave out, I was pulled up by four white-clad crew members, two pod people, and Allie, who screamed like she was on fire.

The fire was out by then. The smoke lingered and everything was wet and getting wetter from the overhead sprinklers. The water came down orange for the rust in the pipes. This was the first time the system had been used in the entire history of the ship—or any ship of the Royal Danish Cruise Line, I was later told. Gold star for me.

Down in the infirmary, Reyes diagnosed a broken collarbone, lacerations all over me, blunt trauma to my head, knees and legs, plus singed eyebrows and blackened, bruised crotch. He made it sound like the daily dinner special.

"So you found the culprit?" said Captain Finn Olsen as we waited for the helicopter.

"No, afraid not," I said.

"But you said Miss Flores attacked you," said Ola.

"I also said I think she chucked Dr. Phillips over the side, but she's still not behind all this."

"Of course she is," said the captain. "Of course."

"Okay," I said. "If you insist."

"I have some questions for you about the fire," said Ola.

"Oh, leave him alone," said Sandra. She was there holding Allie's hand on the deck doing PR damage control to the best of her ability. Ola's security detail held the other passengers back. I glimpsed my friends in the crowd. Perry looked suitably concerned, as did Garrett. Critter was harder to read. Dara and Standard were not so much concerned as mildly angry, Dara no doubt because I'd torched her cabin and Standard because I'd killed his new girlfriend. Ah, they'd get over it.

Allie looked bad, worse than me in fact. I hadn't noticed she'd put on makeup that night until it had run down her face in streaks, and I called her Allison Cooper. That made her laugh, which did as much good for me as the morphine shot Reyes had jabbed me with, both of which made the experience not at all unpleasant.

I was loaded into the helicopter, a red and white emergency thing the crabbers dread seeing on their fishing trips but always make for good ratings. I was strapped down like cargo, but I had blankets, morphine, and Allie's tears. I was okay. It lifted off into the night while I dozed. When I awoke, there was sunshine coming in the window and a very polite nurse adjusting icepacks on my forehead.

"Oh, I'm sorry," she said. "I woke you. I'm sorry."

"How long have I been here?"

"Oh, only half a day," she said. "They brought you in last night. You got a nasty break there on your clavicle, and it looks like you walked across glass."

"And somebody bashed me with a club."

"And shot you, I hear."

"Rifle and Taser," I said. "And I was punched." I pointed to my eyes.

"You're either very unlucky or a very bad man."

"Wrong places at the wrong times."

"I hear you're a detective."

"Can't you tell?"

She giggled. She was a big woman, tall and full-figured, with short brown hair and red cheeks with dimples when she smiled.

"Heard you solved it, whatever it was."

"What?"

She pointed to a huge basket of flowers. It took up half the wall behind me. I could see it if I craned my neck over my right shoulder.

"It's from the Royal Danish Cruise Line. There's some champagne here too," she said, opening a closet. "Well, there was. The card says, 'Thanks for cracking the mystery.'"

"Hallmark has a card for everything."

"Nice flowers, though," she said. "And they're paying your hospital bills."

"I thought this was Canada."

"Are you Canadian?"

"No."

"Someone has to pay then."

"True," I said. "I wish I could figure out who it was."

"But I just—"

"No. Sorry. Something else. Is there a phone I can use?"

She handed me a receiver and got me an outside line. I tapped in the number and waited.

"Hey, Nancy, it's me, Tony."

"The phone says Vancouver Mercy Hospital."

"Yeah."

She sighed. "How bad?"

"Not 'what happened?'" I said. "I'm impressed."

"What happened?"

"Detective work. Not too bad. Lots of little things."

"Enjoying your trip?"

"Oh yeah. How went the sale of the house of Peigne?"

"That's good. You just think of that?"

"I was saving it."

"It hasn't closed yet, but it will."

"I hope it's nice."

"It is," she said.

"Good."

"Yes."

There was an awkward pause, then she said, "Is that why you called?"

"No. I'm looking for Randy."

"I'll get him."

I could tell she wanted to get away. I told myself she had an open house, but I suspected a date. I've got no place to be jealous, but I am anyway, and she knows it.

I heard the phone hit the table and waited. Just then, Allie appeared in the doorway and came in. She had a pizza box, a bag of cookies, and cotton candy.

"Hey, Allie."

She came over and kissed me. "You look terrible. Worse. Your black eyes have gone green," she said.

"Two sets of stitches on my head now."

"Cool."

"How's the ship?"

"It wasn't an official announcement, but everybody is saying you dispatched the villain last night."

"The villain?"

"They're not saying 'killer.' They're not saying 'saboteur.' But they are saying it's over. They even let Kristen out."

"What?"

"I guess they didn't have much of a case to begin with. Maybe some DA will pick it up, but Washington dropped everything. She's free."

"Well, I guess that's no surprise."

"Who is it, Mom?" I heard my son scream from across the house that used to be mine. "Hey, Dad," said my son. "What's going on?"

"I have a day to figure out what's been going on the ship, and I have no idea how it all fits together. And I'm not even on the ship anymore."

"I'm sure it'll work out."

"I got flowers for solving it already."

"Are you going to have them give them back?"

"I don't know."

"Well. Bummer."

"Did you look those things up for me?"

"Still no internet, huh?"

"I don't even have my wallet."

"Bummer."

"What did you find?"

"Okay," he said. "You want to write this down?"

"Just tell me."

"THAFF," he said. "It's one guy living in his mother's basement with spotty internet. He has nothing to do with whatever you're doing in Alaska."

"How do you know that?"

"I asked him."

"Oh."

"Flores Limited," he said, and I heard paper shuffling. "They're in Chile.

A private security company but probably organized crime. Nothing's proven, but their name has appeared in some ATF, DEA, and DOD documents. They're suspected mercenaries. Sent people to Colombia once."

"That fits."

"You don't sound happy. I did a lot of work."

"You haven't told me anything I didn't already know or suspect or had blown up in my face."

"Well, you'll like this," he said. "Paul Vinalez and Vincent Bror—"

"Worked together at the University of Utah."

"Yeah." I could hear the air seeping out of him like a punctured tire.

"I'm sorry. Go on."

"So you know he challenged the patent?"

"No I didn't."

"Right after the press got hold of the story about Bror's microchip patent making him rich, Vinalez challenged. He claimed joint ownership. It didn't last long. It was withdrawn practically immediately. Probably because it was a bullshit case."

"Why was it bullshit?"

"Twenty years late," he said. "Also, the best he could do is claim 'inspirational provenance.' He said he'd given Bror the idea way back when. Try to prove that without witnesses, documents, or logic. It lasted like three days. There were other challenges. Some are ongoing, but they're being dealt with by lawyers. I'm told that isn't unusual."

"Who told you that?"

"A guy in a chatroom. Said he was a patent attorney. Actually there were five or six of them in the room. I guess patent attorneys have a lot of time on their hands."

"That rings a bell, but I don't know what to do with it. I can't see suicide."

"Bror?"

"If he hired the mercenaries."

"Mercenaries?" said Allie.

"And someone's trying to kill Vinalez besides. And me. But I might have solved that one. And there's the ship. Circus is involved."

"Sounds like it."

"Anything about Nutri-Pods?"

"You mean the innovative nutritional dietary supplement everyone is talking about?"

"Yeah."

"Pyramid scheme."

"Anything else?"

"I think your man Vinalez financed it through his divorces," said Randy.

I didn't tell him I'd already heard that too.

"He likes to get married. He's done it a lot."

Again I held my tongue.

"He publicizes it every time. Big ads in the paper announcing engagements and weddings."

"The first one killed herself," I said. "Maybe she got off easy."

"Patricia Wohler? She killed herself? That explains why there wasn't a wedding announcement after the engagement was announced."

"Relationships are tough," I said.

Allie gave me a look.

I shrugged and I scratched my head.

Patricia Wohler.

The pieces spun in my brain like cash in a tornado money booth. You know the ones like they have at fairs and on TV where you go in, they drop money and it swirls around like a cyclone? You've got twenty seconds to grab as much as you can. I had less than a day, but I had some assembly required.

"Oh, Randy. Hey, I'm sorry I forgot to ask. Isn't your dance tonight?"

"Yeah, but I'm not going through with it."

"Why?"

"Remember how I was going to ask Julie to go?"

"Chickened out, huh?"

"I asked her."

"Oh. Sorry. Turned you down, huh?"

"She was waiting to hear back from Chris, who she asked."

"She went with Chris?"

"No. Chris asked me."

"Is Chris a girl?"

"No. He's a guy," said Randy. "Can you believe that? I'm not gay. Why would he think I'm gay?"

"Same reason Julie didn't know he was," I said. "Be flattered."

"I guess, but the whole thing's a mess."

"Why don't you all go together?" I suggested. "You like her, she likes Chris, he likes you. The circle of life."

"That's just weird, Dad."

"All right," I said. "I'll be home in a couple of days. Thanks for helping me."

"Did I?"

"Yes, you did."

"Okay."

We hung up.

"You brought me food," I said to Allie.

"Not just food. Comfort food."

"You know me so well." I ate a cookie. "I'm going to be back on my diet after this."

"Don't worry about it."

"So they kicked me off the ship, huh?" I said.

"For your own good. Look at you. You can't even walk."

"So?"

"So the ship is done with you. This is where you get off."

"It wasn't my fault."

"No one said it was. We'll relax here for a couple of days and fly back home first class."

"Us?"

"They gave me a ticket too."

"That was generous," I said, trying the pizza.

"Dara got a new room." Seeing my face twist up, she said, "What?"

I put the pizza down. "No," I said. "I'm going to do it."

"Diet? Now? Really?"

"That and everything. I'm not giving up."

"You're talking about the case, aren't you?"

"Yeah. I think I'm close?"

"Because of last night or something Randy said?"

"Yes."

"So how does it all fit together?"

She took a bite of pizza. I left mine on the napkin and looked at her.

"I don't know."

She chewed.

"I need to get back on the ship," I said.

"Why?"

"I don't know."

She chewed.

I thought.

"I owe it to Kristen," I said. "I owe it to you, to me. To Captain Finn."

"Captain Finn now too, huh?"

"He hired me."

"Oh."

She chewed and stared. I tried to catch flying dollar bills in my head.

"What would Marlowe do?" she asked. "Isn't that what you always say?"

"Yeah, but it's not working. I wish there was somebody I could lean on and beat a confession out of. Dashiell Hammett never had so damn many moving parts."

"So Agatha Christie?"

I grabbed a fiver in my head. "Maybe. I just can't see it pointing at anyone. It's not like I don't have an angle, but I just can't narrow it down. And I'm out of time."

"The ship sails in an hour," she said. "Maybe you should stop worrying about it."

"What should I worry about?"

"Me."

I smiled.

"And you, getting better," she said. "But mostly me. What did you mean when you told Randy that relationships were hard? Am I hard to get along with?"

"No, of course not. You're great. Too good for me."

"Damn right."

"Randy invited a girl name Julie to the dance, but she invited a guy named Chris, who ended up asking Randy to go."

"That's the circle of life?" Allie giggled and took another slice of pizza from the box, a sloppy triangle of pepperoni, mushrooms, and jalapeños. My favorite.

"What a mess," she said.

I watched her take a bite and smiled. My eyes fell to my own untouched piece of triangular treasure. I pulled a piece of cotton candy off the stick and looked at it like it was spun gold.

"And then there's Oscar," I said.

"What?"

"Get me back on the ship," I said. "I've figured it out."

50

AS TERRIBLE AS I LOOKED, I could be released. A quick inventory of injuries produced the following list: Gunshot wound, Taser wounds (2), ripped toenail, blunt head wound requiring stitches (2), black eye (2), glass cuts on foot requiring stitches (3), broken collarbone, fingernail lacerations on throat (10), miscellaneous bruises, cuts, abrasions, and hurt feelings (incalculable).

The checkout procedure took an excruciatingly long time. I knew the ship wouldn't wait for us, and the Coast Guard helicopter service wasn't a round trip.

While I initialed paperwork and collected prescriptions, instructions, and duplicates, Allie called the ship and set things up. She then maxed out her credit card on a wheelchair for me. It was a nice one, a TXYR-564 LazerRide with 14-gauge cross braces, dual axle positioning, urethane rear tires, five-year warranty, and a five hundred American pound weight limit.

"I'll get a spoiler for it when we get home," I said.

"Don't forget the chrome mud flaps."

"Fog lights."

"Forward-mounted rocket launchers for Christmas."

I liked Allie.

The chair was required because my feet wouldn't hold my weight and my arm wouldn't hold a crutch. Allie couldn't hold her excitement.

"Who did it?"

"Not telling," I said in the cab. "You'll have to hear it with the rest."

"But it wasn't Camila?"

"I'm not saying that."

She sulked. "Remember the last time you did this?"

"Rode a cab?"

"Unmasked a villain."

"With Scooby and the gang?"

"These don't go well, Tony," she said. "Shouldn't you tell me what's going on for a backup?"

"Relax," I said. "We're on vacation. Oh, did you remember the Sharpie so everyone can sign my cast?"

"Yes, I have it."

We arrived after dusk, just as the final gangway was being withdrawn into the ship. When I started crying and threatened to piss myself if they didn't put it back down, they relented and we boarded the *Success* for the final night of the cruise.

Principal Medical Officer Reyes was there to meet us.

"'What's up, PMO?' Just doesn't have the same ring to it, does it?" I said.

He took inventory of my injuries and shook his head. "To think this wasn't all a single incident," he said.

"To think."

"You've more bandages than clothes."

"Where's Ola and Captain Finn?"

"Captain *Olsen* is on the bridge. Mr. Peterson said he'd meet you later."

"Okay."

The ship moved laterally away from the dock and the door was pulled closed and latched. Next stop Seattle and disembarkation in the morning.

"So?" I said.

"Where's the pod dinner?" Allie asked Reyes.

"I'll take you."

We boarded the elevator. Reyes steered my chair like he'd been trained to do it.

"Why's the brake on?" he said.

"There's a brake?"

The Nutri-Pods farewell "Go Grow!" dinner was by invitation only. But thanks to my close ties and cufflinks, I got the gang in. Ola met us at the door.

"I thought this was happening after dinner?" he said to me.

"A man's got to eat. Where's Marvin?"

"I'll send him to your table."

"We have a table?" said Allie.

The dinner was being held in the same huge convention space where the seminars had been. It had been dressed up with curtains hanging over walls, red and white tablecloths, extinguished overhead lights, and more candles than a blackout at the Vatican, but it still felt like a convention center. If I let my imagination slide a little, I might have compared it to my high school cafeteria on prom night. I thought of Randy.

Perry waved at us from a table near the pencil machines and Reyes wheeled me over.

"Remind me never to travel with you again, Flaner," said Dara.

"So you killed Stan's girlfriend," said Critter. "Nice one."

"Sorry, Standard."

"Tell Tony I'm not talking to him."

"He's not talking to you," said the puppet.

"Where are your eyebrows?" said Perry.

"With Stan's girlfriend," Allie said.

Standard sulked.

"You want a drink?" asked Dara. "You're going to love this." She held up her hand, and a server rolled a cart up to the table. "Dinner special."

We watched in horror as a bartender poured a measure of top-shelf gin in the shaker and then, before I could stop him, uncorked not one but two black-capped Nutri-Pods and squirted them inside like they were meant for ingestion. He shook it up and poured it out in the highball glass and handed it to me.

"You've got to be kidding."

He shrugged and made one with vodka and pink pods for Allie, green and Everclear for Standard, and white and tequila for Dara. Perry had his own water bottle.

Allie dropped a five in his tip jar and the waiter pushed the cart away.

I dipped a crust of bread in a plate of olive oil and balsamic vinegar and munched. "It's my only one," I said to Allie.

"Who's counting?"

We ordered and ate our Italian-themed fish, chicken, or beef in the corner of the room while Nutri-Pods dignitaries made speeches, handed out plastic trophies, and patted themselves on the back for an hour.

I refused to tell anyone what I was planning, but my friends were okay with that. They were showmen, after all, and understood what I was going for.

During dessert, Marvelous Marvin McGuire dropped by the table. "Hello, Mr. Flaner."

I held up the olive oil bottle on the table and shook it.

"You were right," he said.

"You get it all?"

"Yes."

"You going to come to the thing?"

"After dinner? Hell, yeah!"

He gave us a wink and sent us a free bottle of champagne.

"How's your martini?" asked Allie.

"How's your uhm…thing."

"Greasy."

"Like drinking fermented licorice tar," I said.

"It'll be good in a Red Bull," said Standard. He was on his third drink and was talking to me again. Lucky me.

After Tiramisu, Paul Vinalez took the podium. Happy, smiling, stock-photo people appeared by the projector behind him.

"And in God's name," he said, holding a defiant fist in the air à la Mussolini. "Go grow the world a better place with Nutri-Pods!"

Raucous applause, and it was over.

I expected the audience to linger, but they didn't. Most looked tired and worn out, ready to go home, for the vacation to be over, to get away from greasy little pods of eel oil and Vinalez's medicine show. Multi-level marketers aren't completely stupid. Not all of them.

The last holdouts were sent away by crew members and invited guests brought in. I took roll and knew it was time.

Vinalez's group was asked to stay. Ashley was a little tipsy and probably high. I'd watched her disappear into the bathroom half a dozen times during dinner, each time coming back with more pep. Sennegar and Denny sat together off the stage and looked bored.

Kristen and Kline were brought in and placed at a circle of tables near the stage. I'd asked for that, a theater-in-the-round thing. My friends took a table by them.

Bailey Peigne and Candy had skipped the dinner but had been rounded up by security. His face was still crimson red from Allie's pepper spray, the whites of his eyes blood-red like he'd been in a scuba accident.

"Did I do that to his eyes?" whispered Allie.

"I think it was the Nutri-Pods, with new flavor enhancements, vitamins, minerals, garlic, and cloves," I said.

"That'd do it," said Perry.

I'd invited the Grays, but only Roxy and Arnold showed. The others were already in bed at ten.

Then there was the crew. Captain Finn Olsen, Security Head Ola Peterson, Principal Medical Officer Reyes, Cruise Director Sandra, Yoga Instructor Xavier Polates—released for the event, marvelously mustached Martin McQuire from the kitchen, Peter Samson, electrician, and two washy-washy ladies who materialized in the room like the twins from *The Shining*. "Come washy-washy with us, Danny."

The filmmakers without the crabbers wandered in with cameras and equipment.

"The brothers wouldn't come," he said. "Do you need them?"

"You'll see," I said.

"Should I get them?" asked Ola.

"You were supposed to," I said. "But as long as we know where to find them after I tell this, it'll all work out."

I was playing my cards close to my chest and didn't want to give anything away, but I was anxious to get started.

"I don't know where they are."

"We'll find them," I said. "We know they're on the ship."

"Actually, I don't," said their producer.

"We can catch them. If we need to."

"I better go look for them."

"Dammit!" I said. "Forget it. I invited you here to keep my promise to you. I don't care about those arguing idiots. They didn't do it."

Sennegar tapped Denny on the shoulder. The bodyguard reluctantly handed him a twenty from his wallet.

"Balls," I said. "Okay, no more spoilers."

I rolled myself into the center of the tables and signaled the producer to start filming.

"Hi," I said. "How's everyone doing tonight?"

Nothing.

"Anyone from out of town?"

Stares.

"Tough crowd."

"He's usually pretty good," whispered Perry. "He's having an off night."

"I'm just getting started."

"Get on with it, Mr. Flaner," said the captain. "I'm sure our guests have things to do."

"Okay," I said. "We're all wondering who's responsible for all the mayhem and violence happening on the ship. Well, I figured it out."

Everyone leaned in close.

"Rats on the ship. People falling overboard. A murder in the penthouse. A missing person. Electrocuting microphones. Mercenaries on shore. Missing jugglers and caviar. People pushed down steps. A lubricated bathtub. A horny bear. Rifles and rocks. Clubs, crabs, and assholes everywhere. And a security system sabotaged three different ways."

"I done none of that," said Polates. "I'm innocent."

"You're no more innocent than I am," I said. "And I peed in the pool!"

"Everyone does," said Sandra. "Nothing to be ashamed of." The rest of the crew looked at her funny.

"What?" she said.

"Circus Cruise Line," said I.

"I knew it! Give me proof and I'll bury them!" exclaimed the captain.

"Finn, Finn, Finn, relax. I'm still setting the scene."

"We know who's behind it," he said. "We just need to know who the other operatives are."

"Other operatives?" said Xavier. "I'm innocent."

"He's talking about Stan's girlfriend," said Dara.

"You seem to have a problem with your friends having dates," said Roxy. "What do you have against them?"

"They won't shut up," I said. "Shut up. Where was I?"

"Telling everyone to shut up," said Samson, the electrician.

"Thanks."

I looked in the camera and went three-quarter profile, my good side. "Motive, means, and opportunity are the ingredients of a crime," I said all Ironside. "We've had plenty of it all. And plenty of crime." I looked hard in the camera.

"Please," said Dara. "For fuck's sake, Tony."

"From the beginning, this cruise has had issues. It sailed on a Friday, and that's not a good thing. Its schedule was a mess because Circus Line's ship was taken out due to fungus. And the Danes are getting a new ship up here because they have washy-washy ladies, and after the security cavity searches, let the passengers have their privacy. They have a good reputation. I want that on the record."

The camera panned to the captain who noticed and tried to look wise.

"The first day here," I went on, "I saw Dr. Belinda Phillips fall off the ship into Puget Sound. I'd like to point out that she isn't here now."

"Told you she did it. Pay up," said Standard to Garrett.

"She's not here because she was pushed over again yesterday. That's two Oscars."

"You are making so little sense, I can't believe it," slurred Ashley. "I mean, I think you're talking English. I get the words, but dammit—just out with it. Who's doing all this shit?"

All their faces stared back at me with the same demand.

"Okay," I said. "Here's the deal. Absit omen."

"Who's Aman?"

"Was he supposed to be here?"

"Is someone taking roll?"

"Absit omen," I said. "It's Latin for 'let this not be an omen.'"

"And?"

"And…and okay. It doesn't fit."

"So?"

"So, I saw it in a pizza," I said.

"Oh god."

"And I heard it in my son's weird dating problems. What we have here is not a single force working to screw up the ship, but several forces working to screw up all kinds of things. We don't have a single murderer, but three."

"Okay," said Kline. "And…"

"Who killed Vincent?" said Kristen. "Who?"

"Let's save that one for last," I said. "Let's first look at who Vincent killed."

"What?"

"Vincent Bror was a vindictive asshole. He got rich and got mean. He was divorcing you, Kristen. Vincent ruined people who he thought had wronged him. Kline helped him do it. It was always anonymous and always in proportion to what was done to him. He killed Dr. Belinda Phillips."

"Wait," said Sandra. "I thought it was Camila Flores."

"It was," I said. "He hired her family's mob family to kill her. Camila was the hitman. She followed Phillips on board to hit her on vacation, taking advantage of the dirty little secret that crimes committed on a cruise ship usually go unnoticed. After the failed drowning the first day when Camila pushed Oscar overboard, she decided to recruit some local talent, afraid she'd blown her cover. The local talent was a couple of amateur mercenaries who pretended to be badger hunters."

"Badger hunters?" asked Finn.

"That is what the people at the glacier called them."

"Why?"

"Tourism."

"What?"

"Anyway, they didn't work out. American work ethics and all."

"She was mad," said Perry. "'Americans are lazy,' she said."

"She had just met Tony," Dara said.

"Anyway…" I continued. "As near as I can figure, Vincent did not even know Phillips was going to be on this cruise. He was surprised to see her the first night at dinner. He was so upset to see her alive he had to leave the table."

"Why'd he want to kill her?" asked Ola.

"Many years ago, Bror's brother, David, died in a hospital under Phillip's care after a terrible car accident. He was high on drugs, drugs that Vincent Bror himself made and sold. A young couple died in the crash too. It was David's fault, maybe even Vincent's himself, but he blamed Phillips because she was easy to blame. She was a bitch."

"So Phillips killed Bror in self-defense?" said Perry.

"No. She didn't know who Bror was. She didn't come on this boat for Vincent Bror. She came on this boat to kill Paul Vinalez."

"What?" said Vinalez. "Me? Why?"

"Oh, that's easy. Patricia Wohler."

"Patty?" he said. He popped the lid off a Nutri-Pod and downed it with gusto. He couldn't help himself and gave his patented wink of "damn, that's good."

"She's been trying to kill you for a while," I said. "She cut your brakes, burned your office back in Utah, and probably got you on a few call lists. She followed you. She even joined your little multi-level marketing cult to get closer to you."

"She's one of my best."

"Was," I said. "I'm convinced Flores threw her off the ship yesterday."

The captain squirmed a little. The camera picked it up.

"Phillips loved Patty Wohler and blamed you when she committed suicide."

"A lot of people did," said Ashley. "It was a really shitty thing to do."

"Oh, yeah," said Sennegar.

"If it'd been my sister—" began Denny.

"Shut up," Vinalez said.

"So far, here's what we have. The rock dropped on Sennegar in Juneau. That was Phillips. The electrical shock at the presentation, also Phillips, as was the bear stink squirted on you. She wasn't much for planning. She seemed to use what she found. I think she's the one who pushed me down the stairs the first day, hoping I'd hit you and all that. The exception came tonight," I said.

"Tonight?"

"I saved your life tonight," I said to Vinalez.

"You did?"

"She replaced the olive oil meant for tonight's dinner with peanut oil."

"That's right," said Marvin. "She was in the kitchen a lot. I thought she was just a health freak, but it makes sense now. She was trying to poison you."

"Oh my God," he said. "Well, thanks, Mr. Flaner, for saving me."

"Hold that for later," I said.

"When did Patty kill herself?" asked Captain Finn.

"Years and years ago. She kept the torch burning because, well, I don't know why. The irony, of course, is that Patty didn't even know Belinda was a lesbian, let alone interested in her. It became some kind of romantic poem of unrequited love when Belinda never even talked to her. She blamed the wrong person, see?"

"What about Vincent?" said Kline.

"The clusterfuck is unclustering. We have crimes aplenty, but not the same ones. Vincent had Phillips killed. Phillips was here to kill Vinalez, and Paul Vinalez, well, he killed Vincent Bror."

"The hell you say!" he said, standing up.

Ola flexed, showing that his muscular Nordic arms could take a snake-oil salesman apart without breaking a sweat.

"The hell I will," I said. "Opportunity. You were on deck fourteen when it happened."

"With Ashley," he said.

"Who was passed out. You killed him and hid in the room while Kristen called for help. Then you snuck back to your cabin. Anyone who didn't have a room on fourteen would have been seen."

"The door was locked. Mine was never opened then. Peterson said so."

"Samson," I said. "You're an electrician. Could a journeyman electrician defeat the lock and cover his tracks getting out of one door and into the next?"

"Maybe," he said.

"What if he used to work for a security company who installed them?"

"Then without a doubt," he said.

"Uinta Security in Provo," I said. "One of your many jobs. That gives you means. You messed up the elevator to make it look like an amateur did it, but it was you."

"Why would I do that?"

"Everyone in this little triangle is an asshole," I said. "You told me yourself that you always get even when you're wronged. You made a claim on Bror's billion-dollar patent, claiming you inspired it and wanted your share. When that didn't pan out, you planned this little trip."

"I planned it?"

"Kristen announced on Twitter that she and Vincent were going on this cruise. Again taking advantage of the lax law enforcement on cruise ships, you arranged to have your pod thing here."

"You can't prove any of this," he said, tearing open another box of pods. "It's your word against mine."

I looked at the others.

"I'm out of time," I said. "This is what happened. This is how it all fits together. Once I realized there were several crimes happening, it all made sense. I don't know if I can actually prove it, but this is what happened."

"You breathe a word of this again, Flaner, I'll have you for slander."

"What if I write it?"

"Libel?" said Perry.

"You're not helping."

"Wait," said Captain Finn. "So, who let the rats out?"

"Who greased your tub?" asked Garrett.

"Oh, yeah," I said. "The cotton candy."

"You're doing it again, Flaner," said Roxy.

"Who called the Code Oscar when I was hanging off the balcony yesterday?"

"One of my midshipmen," said the captain.

"That was Alpha," I said. "The voice changed."

"Sandra took over while we mobilized for the fire," said Captain Finn.

"I thought so," I said. "Sandra's your mole, Captain. She's the one who screwed with your computers on the bridge. I recognized her voice when she called Oscar for Perry. She didn't claim her prize for calling it because she couldn't have you know she was on the bridge at the time putting magnets on your navigation computer."

"So she cut the security feeds?" said Ola.

"She did one of them," I said. "Vinalez, the electrician, did another, and I bet Camila Flores did the third cut. I don't think Dr. Phillips did any. She wasn't that organized."

Sandra broke down and cried.

"Why, Sandra? Why?" said Captain Olsen.

"She doesn't feel appreciated, Captain. It's a tough job. You think aiming a ship is hard, try keeping two thousand tourists happy. Circus Line, via Mr. Toover, arranged it all."

She nodded and bawled. "I'm sorry about the tub, Tony. It was meant to be a joke."

"Least of my worries," I said.

"You can't prove any of this, Flaner," said Vinalez, smugly leaning back in his chair and sucking down another pod with the patented twitch.

"Maybe not the murder, but I'm going to burn you with the bunco squad I met on the ship earlier. You and Bailey Peigne there. Laundering money in the Caymans is so last century but might get you twenty."

"What!" screamed Bailey. "You've got no…you can't…there's a bunco squad on the ship?"

Vinalez stood up. His face twisted in rage. It went red. His eyes bulged, his hand went up to his throat. He collapsed to his knees.

"Just say it and get it out of your system before the Oompa Loompas juice you," I said.

The camera zoomed in on his furious face.

"What's he doing?"

"I think he's choking," said Roxy. "Maybe on his tongue."

Vinalez's mouth hung open as if midscream, but there was no sound.

"No. There it is. I see it wagging away."

"He looks terrible."

"He's having a conniption over Tony," said Dara. "We've seen it before."

"Oh my god!" yelled Sennegar.

"What?"

"It's his peanut allergy."

As if fueled by chemical enhancers, Ashley dumped her purse on the table and scattered its contents. "My EpiPen is gone," she said.

Reyes stepped up. "Get him to the infirmary. I've got some there."

In a mass, we all followed in the elevator as Denny picked up his employer and rushed down the stairs.

When we got there, Vinalez was blue and shaking and Reyes was rifling through his cabinets in a panic. He dug behind bottles and boxes, chucking them to the floor before running into another room and tossing those cabinets in the same way.

"My EpiPens are all gone!" he yelled. "But I have an idea."

We never found out what it was. Paul Vinalez, plumb-colored purple, hand to his throat, smelling of snake oil, was already dead.

51

WHEN THE *RMS Titanic* sunk in 1912, there was a lot of blame thrown around. Even before the bodies were counted, there were accusations, spin, and responsibility dodging that would make a modern political campaign adviser blush. With the help of the media, money, and maniacs, the White Star Line, who owned the sunken ship, ducked its rightly deserved blame by adding insult to injury in the grandest terms.

Let's gloss over for a second the fact that the *RMS Titanic* was on fire when it left port—actually burning—and remained that way below decks for the entirety of the voyage until twelve thousand five hundred feet of Atlantic ice water finally put it out. We can gloss over that because that little nugget didn't come up in the inquest. It was brought to light only later and confirmed as fact. Keep that in mind for the rest here, just in case you think everything was kosher in the investigation.

Titanic's captain, Edward Smith, had a history of wrecking ships but that was glossed over during the investigations at the time. They were hellbent for a speed record, but that didn't matter either. There weren't enough lifeboats, not enough training, never enough imagination, and too much gross loss of life, among the lower classes especially, but bullocks to all that.

What ended up happening in both the American and British investigations into the disaster was a preoccupation with the movements of the *SS Californian* which quickly became the scapegoated villain of the tragedy and a handy distraction from the culpability of the actual culprits.

Here's what happened.

The *SS Californian* was a British ship owned by JP Morgan, who owned most everything in those days. It was the biggest ship ever built in Dundee which I mention only to establish that it was not a small boat. It was four hundred forty-six feet long, fifty-three wide, and displaced 6,300 tons of something, probably American jobs and savings, knowing JP Morgan. Its primary mission was to transport cotton and cargo.

In 1912 the *Californian* was going to Boston from England, more or less paralleling the *Titanic* across the Atlantic Ocean but a little ahead. It was commanded by a fellow with the uncannily English name of Captain Stanley Lord, who'd run the ship since 1911.

Sunday, April 14, 1912, was a dark, moonless night, as we all know from the movie. Leonardo DiCaprio was king of the world and sketching Kate Winslet's boobs in the hold of the ship, a big-ass diamond around her neck.

The *Californian* steamed happily west and hit ice. Yes, that ice. It nearly hit an iceberg, in fact. Thanks to the evasive maneuver Picard Gamma Six, Captain Lord managed to go into full reverse and stop the 6,300-ton ship from preceding the *Titanic* to the ocean floor by half a day.

The ice was so nasty in fact, that Lord actually stopped his ship flat in the middle of the ocean. He just turned it off and parked it in the middle of the ice field for the night rather than risk the danger of navigating it in the dark.

Meanwhile, aboard the humongous *Titanic*, Captain Edward Smith steamed speedily on.

Here comes my favorite part. Aboard the *Californian* was a wireless operator called Cyril Evans. He radioed the *Titanic* specifically to report the icebergs lying in their path. The *Titanic's* wireless operator, Jack Phillips—no relation to Belinda, now deceased—was in the middle of sending and receiving personal messages for the rich stuck-up snob dick passengers. It being the early days of wireless, and them so close, Evan's message came in loud and clear and across every frequency. Phillips told Evans to, "Shut up, shut up! I am busy!"

What are you going to do?

It was dark, cold, and eleven-thirty pm. The message was sent and received if not appreciated. The *Californian* wasn't moving. Everyone was asleep. Feeling wholly unappreciated, Evans turned off his wireless and hit the sack. Ten minutes later, the *Titanic* hit an iceberg. Two hours and forty minutes after that, it decorated the floor of the Atlantic Ocean.

Titanic fired rockets and the lookout aboard the *Californian* saw them, but their meaning was unclear. The captain was told but thought they were normal "company messages—colored flares used between ships of the same line," which is how they were usually used back then. At best, the rockets were interpreted to mean "stand by." What they really meant though, was, "Oh my fucking God, are we stupid or what?"

By the time the radio was turned back on in the *Californian* the next morning, *Titanic* was gone and 1,514 of the 2,224 souls were fish food. Captain Lord carefully maneuvered his ship through the ice, and only after he was clear of the danger, turned to the wreck site. But he was too late to help. A ship called the *Carpathia* had already rescued those able to be rescued.

Captain Lord observed empty lifeboats, deck chairs, violins, a strange floating wooded door big enough to hold two people very easily, and then he sailed to America.

So who came out of the investigations with the most shit on him? Captain Edward Smith? Phillips? Billy Zane? Bill Paxton? Of course not. Yeah, it was Captain Stanley Lord.

True, his story changed and he was defensive, but he was pilloried with a bunch of "if you had onlys," and "imagine what ifs." If he hadn't turned off the wireless, for example, think of the lives that could have been saved. Never mind that it was normal practice among all ships to turn it off like that. It was only after the *Titanic* and because of it, that a twenty-four-hour watch was required to stay on the radio. If he'd correctly guessed the rockets' meaning, if he'd turned south first instead of west, yadda, yadda, yadda. You the baddie. You gotta pay.

With all the "if only Captain Lord had been psychic" chatter, the White Star Line could whitewash the "if only Phillips had listened to the warning the *Californian* had sent them" and the host of other very accurate accusations that could depress their stock price if anyone paid attention to them.

Captain Lord was demonized. The drunk ship-crashing Captain Smith has a statue. The below-deck fire never even mentioned.

What always gets me in this story is that there was reason to believe that the sea around the *Titanic* and *Californian* might have been perilous, maybe even bad enough to sink a ship, a big ship. A state-of-the-art ship. Whereas the hero captain steamed forward in the best ship the world had ever seen and sunk it, the villain captain stopped, went slow, was careful and brought his ship safely into port with all hands accounted for. Maybe Captain Lord recognized the danger of trying to maneuver a big-ass ship through icebergs in the pitch-black night and was cautious, not wanting to die or kill anyone. This is just speculation of course.

Things haven't changed much. Nobody likes to take the blame. Among sociopathic corporations and psychotic assholes, it's always easier to assign blame on innocents than to take responsibility for their own incompetence and wrongdoing.

The issue of the *Californian's* responsibility was readdressed recently. There's still blame to be had there, but anybody who claims that Captain Lord could have saved everyone is full of shit. The British Admiralty said that, at most, in the best-case, no-way-in-the-world-could-this-ever-really-have-happened scenario, the *Californian* might have been able to rescue maybe three hundred more people. That still puts twelve hundred plus under the water. Look at the papers from 1912 and you'd think Lord had sent a heat-seeking ice block at the side of *Titanic* out of malicious meanness. Lord had his faults; he was no hero. He probably cheated at Pinochle. He might have been a coward, but he doesn't deserve the blame assigned to him for that famous disaster.

On my ship, misplaced blame was again at the heart of things, at least in my pizza metaphor, where Vinalez, Phillips, and Bror had each wrongly blamed the other, killed them, and been killed in turn. It was a neat trick. The cotton candy suggested an exception and told me that Sandra's ship sabotage may not have had the same direct motivation. Plus, since I improperly blamed Polates, it all fit neatly under the same heading: blame misbestowed.

I'd underestimated Phillips. I thought I had worked out her MO—*modus operandi* for you novices. How she worked. I'd seen all her attacks as spontaneous reactions to situational opportunities. The push on the stairs, the rock on the cliff. I should have seen the planning of the bear scent attack and put it together. I figured out the peanut/olive oil switch, but I'd neglected to recognize the poisoned pods. I'd even seen the doctor give Sennegar two boxes of samples in the buffet line, specifically telling him to return them to Paul.

I told Reyes about all the broken EpiPens in Phillips' cabin. Phillips had destroyed everything on the ship that could have treated anaphylactic shock, even breaking into first aid cabinets in the kitchen and dining rooms. As a doctor, she knew what to look for.

"How'd she know about the peanut allergy?" asked Allie.

"I don't think it was a secret. They told me. Plus, Phillips would have access to medical records. If not recently, then from the old days at the university."

Allie wheeled me down the gangway off the ship into Seattle. I didn't have any luggage left. My wallet and phone were whale bait, my clothes smoke-scented ballast.

Kristen was satisfied with my findings. The captain took a report for the company and thanked me. Vinalez's death was not announced. No need to upset the pod people. Sennegar sought out the bunco squad and Bailey Peigne was the first off the ship. The filmmaker said he'd be in touch.

The Grays stayed on board, as did Perry. He still had two months on his contract and a gently used survival suit. He probably wasn't going to sign on again.

"What's going to happen to Sandra?"

"Not sure," I said. "Maybe she can wiggle out of it."

"And keep her job?"

"Oh no. That's over. But maybe she won't go to jail. Royal Danish Line is allergic to bad publicity. A trial would be the last thing they want."

"Xavier?"

"You heard Finn apologize to him. He'll be fine. He's an attraction."

"Like the prostitutes in the martini bar?"

"Just like."

We passed through immigration. I got singled out for a cavity search because I didn't have a passport or any luggage, which made me suspicious. When I got out, Allie was waiting with Standard, Garrett, and Dara. Critter was in the carry-on.

"Hey, dipshit," said Dara.

"Hey."

"We're going straight to the airport," said Garrett. "SeaTac is bullshit. Give yourself three hours and prepare to miss your plane."

Standard nodded. "You look stupid without eyebrows," he said.

"You look stupid with them."

We all hugged. I hopped on one foot and promised to see them all back in Salt Lake.

"You're not flying back today?"

"Kline arranged a charter for us to get back to Moab," I said. "And he put some money in my pocket."

"I gotta get back to work. I have responsibilities," said Allie.

"And I'm going to help," I said.

"You?" said Dara.

"I'm doing better," I said. "I can be responsible if I want to be."

"In short spurts," said Standard.

"Leave him alone," said Allie.

"I meant, look at you," said Dara. "You're an invalid. You don't have any eyebrows."

"I'll draw some on him," said Allie. "I'll find something for him to do. I'll make him useful."

"Good luck," said Standard.

"I have my moments," I said.

"Yes, you do," said Allie.

ACKNOWLEDGMENTS

Let me recognize first my family who suffered with me on an Alaskan Cruise for my research. Yep, that's them. Second, thanks to Tony for babbling. Third, thanks to the fans who encouraged him to babble. And Fourth, much gratitude to Patience Bramlett, Tony's new editor and fan. Welcome aboard.

A LOOK AT BOOK FOUR:
THE COUNTERFEIT CONNECTION

In an avalanche of lies, one real slacker stands against the wave of pretenders.

After months of chasing shadows, Tony Flaner, the insecure sleuth, is about to have his life turned upside down. In the blink of an eye, four cases land on Tony's plate, igniting a fire within him. But these cases are no ordinary mysteries—they come with a price.

But Tony's journey is far from ordinary. As he dives into a realm of international intrigue, fading fame, and ferocious canines, he's confronted by the one case he dreads the most—a domestic situation that threatens to shatter his carefully constructed world.

From actors and agents to hippies and obscure obsessions, every step uncovers new layers of deceit and danger. Even a Burmese coup and the most abominable song from Rogers and Hammerstein put Tony's luck, skill, and patience to the ultimate test.

Art and artifice intertwine, creating a world of fakes and facades where nothing is as it seems.

AVAILABLE OCTOBER 2023

ABOUT THE AUTHOR

Johnny Worthen is an award-winning and best-selling author of books and stories. Trained in stand-up comedy, modern literary criticism and cultural studies, he writes upmarket multi-genre fiction, symbolized by his love of tie-dye and good words.

"I wear tie-dye for my friends, but I write what I like to read," he says. "This guarantees me at least one fan and easy dressing in the morning."

Johnny teaches writing at the University of Utah and lives in a house with his wife, sons and assorted cats. There's also a lawn.

www.ingramcontent.com/pod-product-compliance
Lightning Source LLC
Chambersburg PA
CBHW010815250626
47156CB00011B/3077

* 9 7 8 1 6 8 5 4 9 3 2 3 3 *